Gothic Fiction and the Invention
of Terrorism

Also Available from Bloomsbury

Milton, Evil and Literary History, Claire Colebrook
Evil: A History in Modern French Literature and Thought, Damian Catani
Coleridge and Kantian Ideas in England, 1796–1817, Monika Class

Gothic Fiction and the Invention of Terrorism

The Politics and Aesthetics of Fear in the Age of the Reign of Terror

Joseph Crawford

Bloomsbury Academic:
An imprint of Bloomsbury Publishing Plc

B L O O M S B U R Y
LONDON · NEW DELHI · NEW YORK · SYDNEY

Bloomsbury Academic
An imprint of Bloomsbury Publishing Plc

50 Bedford Square	1385 Broadway
London	New York
WC1B 3DP	NY 10018
UK	USA

www.bloomsbury.com

BLOOMSBURY and the Diana logo are trademarks of Bloomsbury Publishing Plc

First published 2013
Paperback edition first published 2015

British Library Cataloguing-in-Publication Data
A catalogue record for this book is available from the British Library.

ISBN: HB: 978-1-4725-0528-6
PB: 978-1-4742-2778-0
ePDF: 978-1-4725-0995-6
ePUB: 978-1-4725-0912-3

Library of Congress Cataloging-in-Publication Data
A catalog record for this book is available from the Library of Congress.

Typeset by Integra Software Services Pvt. Ltd.

Contents

Acknowledgements   vi

Introduction   vii

1   Terror Before Terrorism   1

2   The Reign of Terror   37

3   The Secret Masters Walk Among Us   93

4   Popular Gothic   131

5   The Gothic Legacy   153

Epilogue: The Wars on Terror   189

Bibliography   199

Index   211

Acknowledgements

This book was researched and written over the course of a research fellowship at Murray Edwards College, Cambridge. Without the support provided by this fellowship, the writing of this book would never have been possible; and I wish to extend my most sincere thanks to the college and its fellows for the extraordinary hospitality and generosity which they extended to me throughout my two-and-a-quarter years at Murray Edwards. In particular, I wish to thank my colleagues in English Literature, Heather Glen, Raphael Lyne, Leo Mellor, and Oliver Wort, for the invaluable support, advice, and encouragement which they unstintingly offered me during my time in Cambridge. Thanks are also due, as ever, to my wife and family – Filipa, Richard, Elaine, Rosa, Oliver, and Sophia – for tolerating my long immersion in the esoteric and often gruesome material which forms the subject matter of this book. Finally, I wish to thank my students at Cambridge, whose energy, enthusiasm, and intelligence made my teaching work there a genuine pleasure. Shine on. Fear nothing.

Introduction

As a graduate student, I once sat in upon an undergraduate lecture in which the lecturer asked the students a question: judging from the Gothic fictions they left behind, what was it that frightened the Victorians? The group was silent at first, but, gradually, responses began to trickle in. They were scared of the old aristocracy: witness Count Dracula. But they were also scared of the poor: thus the panic over the Ripper murders in Whitechapel. They were scared of modern science: *Frankenstein*. But they were also scared of ancient religions: *The Beetle*. They feared the city: *Bleak House*. They feared the countryside: *The Hound of the Baskervilles*. They feared the very old: *She*. They feared the very young: *The Turn of the Screw*. The past: *Ghost Stories of an Antiquary*. The future: *The Time Machine*. Foreign invasion: *The War of the Worlds*. Inner corruption: *Dr Jekyll and Mr Hyde*. Revolution. Despotism. Sex. Women. Industry. Art. Evolution. Degeneration. Victorian Gothic, it seemed, demonstrated that the Victorians had been afraid of virtually everything.

But had they been? Walking home past some of Oxford's exuberantly Gothic Victorian architecture, I found it hard to believe: the emotion I associated most with the nineteenth century was a slightly manic sense of self-confidence. Had the Victorians built their world-girdling empire, uprooting and exterminating entire peoples in the process, because they were *afraid*? That hardly fitted with my own reading of Victorian texts, fiction and non-fiction alike; and yet it was undeniably true that this blustering empire had produced a literature of fear unparalleled in any earlier epoch of English letters. But if Victorian Gothic was not an index of actual Victorian anxieties, then what was it? If it was not the expression of the unprecedented fearfulness of its readers and writers, then where *had* it come from? As I thought the matter over, it seemed to me that the question was being asked backwards. It was not that Gothic fiction was generated by the fears of its authors; it was that Gothic, as a form, provided a methodology for writing about a subject – *any* subject – in such a way as to make it seem fearful and threatening. Gothic was a network of tropes which, collectively, served to either literally or metaphorically demonise its subject matter, whether that subject was a person, a house, a social group, or an entire civilisation, by describing it as though it was an object of numinous dread. The proliferation of Gothic fictions did not necessarily demonstrate that the Victorians had felt more fear than their predecessors, any more than the proliferation of Petrarchan sonnets in the early modern period demonstrated that the men and women of the Renaissance had felt more love than those before them; only that fear had become a topic of literary interest to their writers, just as love had been three centuries before.

As I studied the matter further, I became increasingly struck by the speed with which this Gothic rhetoric – whose hallmarks I took to be the description of human wickedness and suffering in supernatural terms, an insistence upon the numinous, incommunicable, incomprehensible quality of true evil, and an emphasis on the power and significance of evildoers, often articulated in terms of the Burkean sublime of terror, and their ability to fill their victims with feelings of helplessness and dread – seemed to have become assimilated into English in the years on either side of 1800. When eighteenth-century authors wrote about evil, violence, or fear – which they often did – they generally did so in strikingly non-Gothic terms: the preferred idiom of the British Enlightenment seemed to have been one of practical, matter-of-fact moral realism, tempered with satirical scorn for the wicked and, later in the century, with sentimental pity for the sufferings of the innocent. It was only at the very end of the century that this Gothic rhetoric of evil appeared, but, once it did, it took hold rapidly and thoroughly; a few decades later, it seemed to have become virtually the default idiom for writing about evil in English. It has remained so ever since; even today, when tabloid journalists or authors of popular fiction wish to write about the evil that men do, they almost always use a recognisably Gothic rhetorical vocabulary to do so.

There is an extensive and flourishing critical literature on Gothic, which has generally placed the genre's origins a few decades earlier – in the mid-eighteenth century, rather than at its end – with Burke's *Philosophical Enquiry* (1757) and Walpole's *The Castle of Otranto* (1764) as its founding documents. One popular explanation for its rise, found in Punter and Hogle, among others, attributes the existence of Gothic fiction to the anxieties of the newly dominant British middle classes.[1] The middle classes, the account goes, were surrounded by reminders of the old aristocratic and ecclesiastical social order they had displaced, in the form of ruined monasteries and castles; these locations thus became sites of anxiety for them, reminders both that their social dominance was historically recent and that it had been born out of the violent seizure of wealth and power from their previous possessors. The Gothic narrative, with its evil monks, wicked barons, and falling castles, enacts the foundational myth of the middle classes, first demonstrating the moral bankruptcy of the old order – and thus the necessity of its destruction – and then representing its fall into oblivion, and its replacement by a new and virtuous generation whose values are in closer accord with those of the contemporary bourgeoisie.[2] It is a persuasive account, and it maps fairly neatly onto the handful of Gothic texts which have tended to be most studied by literary scholars: Walpole's *Otranto*, Radcliffe's *The Mysteries of Udolpho*, Lewis's *The Monk*, and Stoker's *Dracula*. But it has two chief problems: its chronology, and its range of reference.

The account is chronologically problematic insofar as it does not appear to actually map onto the social history it purports to describe. The British gentry in Walpole's day *had* benefited enormously from the dissolution of the monasteries, and the subsequent transfer of monastic estates into private hands; but these events had taken place in the 1530s, over two centuries before the birth of Gothic fiction.[3] Likewise, the growing importance of the House of Commons had increased the political power wielded by the land-owning gentry of the period, while the political significance of the British monarchy and aristocracy had waned since the days of the Tudors; but the major battles in this long political struggle had been fought in the seventeenth century, crucially in the War of Three Kingdoms and the Glorious Revolution of 1688. If Walpole's contemporaries passed a ruined abbey, it was likely to have been ruined by Henry VIII; if they visited a ruined castle, it was likely to have been ruined by Oliver Cromwell. Why should the middle classes of the 1760s, heirs to three generations of relatively untroubled political and economic success, have felt so much more anxious about their historical origins than their ancestors, who had actually seized their wealth and power at the expense of the church and king in the first place? And if they *were* so troubled by their origins, and so keen to establish their own legitimacy, then why was the mainstream political writing of the mid-eighteenth century characterised by respect and deference for the church and aristocracy, rather than the defiance which such an account would lead us to expect?[4]

The second problem with this explanation is its range of reference: simply stated, the more Gothic fiction one examines, the less persuasive it appears. As James Watt has pointed out, most early Gothic fiction actually defends monarchy and aristocracy rather than critiquing them; for every work which, like Walpole's *Otranto* or Sophia Lee's *The Recess*, presents the old order as both doomed and not worth saving, there is another, such as Clara Reeve's *The Old English Baron* or William Hutchinson's *The Hermitage*, which endorses and celebrates the value of the old aristocracy.[5] Furthermore, studying the Gothic fiction of the 1760s, 1770s, and 1780s rapidly indicates that most of it does not express such cultural anxieties, less because it was not concerned with class or history than because it was not really a literature of anxiety at all. The idea of a single Gothic literature of terror, stretching continuously from the 1760s to the present day, imposes a false unity on these early works, which were referred to as 'Gothic stories' only because they were set in the 'Gothic ages' (i.e. the medieval or early modern period) rather than the present day, and were more likely to be sentimental romances than tales of terror; the preoccupation with evil, fear, and violence, which is the defining characteristic of later Gothic literature, did not become a prominent part of the genre until the success of Radcliffe's later novels in the 1790s. I thus became increasingly convinced that, although works referring to themselves as 'Gothic' had existed since the 1760s, the true roots of the Gothicised rhetoric I had observed in the nineteenth century were to be found not in the anxieties of the mid-eighteenth-century middle classes, but a generation later; in the fearful decade at the century's end.

It was in the 1790s that Gothic fiction and rhetoric first became truly popular in Britain; it was also in these years that Britain, like the rest of Europe, was struggling with the consequences of the French Revolution. Correlation does not equal causation; but it did not seem accidental that this new literary fascination with fear and violence should have arisen in the same decade that witnessed the Reign of Terror, and the consequent adoption of the words 'terrorist' and 'terrorism' into English. Several critics, such as Ronald Paulson, Robert Miles, and Leslie Fiedler, have already written on the relationship between the French Revolution and the rise of Gothic fiction, but they have tended to articulate this relationship in terms of an already-existing genre of Gothic terror fiction gaining new relevance and popularity due to its resonances with the events of the Revolution.[6] It is my contention, however, that the relationship between Gothic fiction and the Revolution, 'terrorist novel writing' and 'terrorist' politics, is more fundamental than that described by Paulson and Fiedler. Gothic fiction did exist in the decades before the Revolution, but its character changed markedly over the course of the 1790s, with the Reign of Terror itself constituting a major watershed in the development of 'terror fiction'; and I take seriously Kilgour's suggestion that Gothic fiction could easily have remained a minor and little-read sub-genre of English literature, or even have dwindled away entirely, had it not been seized upon by writers eager to find new vocabularies of evil in the years following the revolutionary Terror.[7]

In a very real sense, the Revolution *created* Gothic, transforming a marginal form of historical fiction chiefly concerned with aristocratic legitimacy into a major cultural discourse devoted to the exploration of violence and fear. But I have come to believe that this was a two-way process, and that if the Revolution created Gothic, then, at least for the British, Gothic played a major role in creating the Revolution, or at least in creating that body of Gothicised historical mythology which, since the 1790s, the phrase 'the French Revolution' has chiefly signified. Obviously, it was not Gothic fiction which brought out the Parisian crowds on 14 July 1789, or 10 August and 2 September 1792; but it was the tropes of Gothic fiction which allowed many British writers to articulate what they believed those crowds to have done, and what their actions might mean, so that when they wrote their accounts of the unfolding events in France, they often did so in markedly Gothic terms. As Mary Favret has shown, one crucial fact about the British experience of the Revolution and the wars which followed it was that the British, unlike the inhabitants of most other European countries, experienced them *at a distance*, and that most Britons thus understood them – to the extent that they *did* understand them – not through the direct experience of battle or invasion, but in various mediated forms, through stories, letters, newspapers, fictions, and so on; and I would argue that Gothic fiction, and the Gothic rhetorical idioms which it gave rise to, was one of the forms through which this mediation took place.[8] As the 1790s progressed, the rise of quasi-fictional genres such as conspiracy theory and anti-revolutionary propaganda further blurred the line between factual revolutionary reportage and Gothic fiction, so the revolutionary decade bequeathed to the nineteenth century a body of mixed mythology in which the historical figure of the revolutionary 'terrorist' increasingly merged into the fictional figure of the Gothic villain. This was the cultural matrix in which the discourse of 'terrorism' was born; for, as I shall argue, the very conceptual category of 'terrorism' arose as a result of the application of Gothic rhetorical tropes to real acts of historical violence. The earlier eighteenth century, despite being an age of colossal violence and insecurity, possessed neither a word for 'terrorism' nor a literature of terror; the two were born together, interdependent from the start, in what one contemporary conspiracy theorist called the 'season of anxiety' which followed the Reign of Terror.[9]

I am by no means the first person to note that the vocabulary of terrorism originated with the French Revolution; but academic writers on terrorism, while often mentioning this fact, tend to do curiously little with it. Perhaps the most common account of the history of terrorism, found in the works of Barnett and Reynolds, Spencer, O'Hair,

Rosenfeld, and Rapoport, among others, describes it as being ancient in origin – with the Zealots of antiquity and the *hashishin* of the Middle Ages often cited as terrorists *avant la lettre* – but only attaining its current form in the 1870s, after the invention of dynamite.[10] Within such historical accounts, in which the French Revolution tends to play an extremely minor role, the fact that the discourse of 'terrorism' arose neither in the ancient world nor in the later nineteenth century tends to be presented as a mere curiosity, an accident of linguistic history: it is, for example, telling that David Wright-Neville's recent *Dictionary of Terrorism* includes no entries on Robespierre, the Jacobins, or the French Revolution.[11] In modern usage, the word 'terrorism' has come to be associated almost exclusively with ideologically motivated acts of violence carried out by irregular guerilla armies, clandestine conspiratorial organisations, and similar non-state actors; and while historians still write of the 'Stalinist terror' in Soviet Russia or the 'Nazi terror' in occupied Europe, neither Stalin's Russia nor Hitler's Germany is generally described as a 'terrorist' state, despite the heavy reliance of both regimes upon campaigns of violent mass intimidation.[12] The state-sponsored violence of the French revolutionaries, carried out under the highly organised and bureaucratic Jacobin government, hardly fits this modern paradigm of terrorist activity, which is probably why contemporary writers on terrorism generally have so little to say about it; but it is my belief that if we are to understand the cultural role that the concept of 'terrorism' has played over the last two centuries, then the origins of the term in the revolutionary struggles of the 1790s are a matter of considerable significance.

'Terrorist' is not a word like 'aviator', coined to describe a new form of human activity: campaigns of assassination, intimidation, and political violence have occurred throughout history, but before 1795 such campaigns were apparently adequately described in terms of criminality or war. Instead, the terrorist, like the Gothic villain, is essentially a rhetorical construct, marking the rise not of a new form of political violence, but of a new way of writing and thinking about a very old one. The notorious difficulty which scholars have encountered in agreeing on a workable definition of 'terrorism' is surely a result of this, for terrorism is not and never has been the name of a specific activity, but only a figure of speech which can be applied to certain forms of political action in order to achieve certain rhetorical goals.[13] As such, its literary and linguistic origins are of central importance, and I concur with Marc Redfield in seeing our cultural haunting by the ghostly figure of the terrorist as beginning neither in antiquity, nor in the anarchist bombing campaigns of the 1870s, but in the political rhetoric developed during the 1790s in response to the growing violence of the French Revolution. Crucially, I also see this haunting as having been interdependent, from its earliest beginnings, with the mythology of Gothic fiction, which arose alongside it and has enjoyed concurrent popularity ever since. As Redfield puts it, 'since the Enlightenment, we have lived increasingly in a world of ghosts'.[14]

It is in these events that I believe the roots of Victorian Gothic, and its fascination with states of extreme fear and figures of superhuman evil, are to be found. It is my belief that this shift from Enlightenment to Gothic modes of thinking and writing about human evil has been a matter of substantial historical significance, for this Gothicised rhetoric, which casts evildoers as sublime, incomprehensible demons rather than as the regrettable but understandable results of malfunctioning psychology or social structures, played an important role in much Victorian non-fiction writing, on subjects ranging from war and imperialism to eugenics and crime. The much-remarked-upon medievalism of Victorian Britain, whereby a nation whose strength rested on coal mines, steam trains, ironclads, and Enfield rifles articulated its geopolitical ambitions in terms of Chivalric crusades against the demonic evils which were asserted to lurk in the dark places of the world, owed much to the permeation of such Gothic rhetoric into British political discourse.

It is the aim of this book to trace the development of Gothic as a cultural phenomenon, from its earliest beginnings in the mid-eighteenth century to its flourishing in the 1790s and 1800s. My methodology has been historicist, insofar as I have assumed throughout that no hard barriers exist between 'literary' and 'non-literary' writing, or between fiction and non-fiction; that rhetorical tropes can and do slide back and forth between, say, journalism and theatre, and that literary works are thus best understood in a broad cultural context, rather than in isolation. At heart, however, this book remains a study of words, forms, genres, and fictions, less concerned with historical events themselves than with how those events were written about and understood. I do not believe that 'poetry makes nothing happen': indeed, it is my contention that the rhetorical shifts with which I am concerned have helped to make a great many things happen, some of them very serious and very destructive indeed. But poetry (or fiction, or drama) makes very little happen on its own; and the extent to which our responses to events are caused or altered by the rhetorical structures through which we articulate and understand those events is seldom clear. Eighteenth-century cultural critics often confidently ascribed large-scale cultural change to the effects of literature; but, lacking their certainty, I have tried to avoid making any such grand causal claims, preferring instead to offer more cautious suggestions regarding the ways in which forms of rhetoric, originating in literature, may contribute to the conceptualisation of historical situations, and may thus shape the decisions made in response to them. I do not believe that Gothic rhetoric 'caused' the French revolutionary wars, the violent suppressions of the Wexford Rebellion of 1798 and the Indian Rebellion of 1857, or the contemporary 'War on Terror'; but I do believe that the fact that the French, Irish, and Indian rebels, like the Islamist terrorists of our own day, were persistently figured in Gothic terms must have made it easier for them to be conceptualised as unfathomable evils requiring extermination, and harder to think of them as rational political actors with whom some form of reasoned compromise might potentially be reached, with what I fear have been very real political and historical consequences.

This book is divided into five chapters. Chapter 1, 'Terror Before Terrorism', explores the pre-Gothic ways of writing about evil, violence, and fear which dominated discussions of those topics during the British Enlightenment, and the origins of Gothic fiction during the mid-eighteenth century. Chapters 2 and 3 are devoted to the 1790s: Chapter 2, 'The Reign of Terror', investigates the flourishing of popular Gothic 'terror fiction' and the simultaneous emergence of the discourse of revolutionary 'terrorism' in the context of British responses to the French Revolution, while Chapter 3, 'The Secret Masters Walk Among Us', discusses the impact of German *sturm und drang* literature in 1790s Britain, and its influence upon the rise of the new and interlinked genres of supernatural Gothic fiction and revolutionary conspiracy theory. Chapter 4, 'Popular Gothic', investigates the extent to which Gothic art and fiction were able to find an audience beyond the British cultural elite, exploring the popularity of Gothic chapbooks, prints, and melodramas from 1790 to 1820. Chapter 5, 'The Gothic Legacy', considers some of the nineteenth-century consequences of the Gothic cultural forms investigated in Chapters 2–4, mapping out the rapid naturalisation of Gothic rhetoric in works by early-nineteenth-century authors such as Scott, Ainsworth, Dickens, De Quincey, and Carlyle. Finally, an epilogue – 'The Wars on Terror' – considers some of the ways in which this Gothicised understanding of evil, and especially the mythology of 'terrorism' to which it has given rise, has continued to strongly influence not just our art and literature, but also our political culture, with results which are still very much with us today.

This book was written in 2010 and 2011, years in which the politics of terror have seldom been far from the news. The death of Osama bin Laden, the withdrawal of American troops from Iraq, and the tenth anniversary of the 9/11 terrorist attacks have collectively seemed to mark the end of an era, one defined by what has come to be known as the 'War on Terror'. These occurrences have prompted much reflection on the events of the last decade; this book, in its own way, is part of that. I was eighteen years old when I watched the Twin Towers fall on live TV; the War on Terror has dominated my entire adult life. For ten years, the news media has been full of Gothic stories about a breed of murderous monsters called 'terrorists', informing us that while some of them live in caves in far-away countries, others lurk among us, passing for human, meeting in secret, forming dark conspiracies, and plotting our destruction. In writing this book, I have tried to investigate the origins of this rhetorical and conceptual vocabulary, and of that terror of the evil that men do which such rhetoric appears to imply. I believe that the research I have carried out will contribute to the existing scholarship on early Gothic fiction in English, and on British literary responses to the French Revolution. But I also believe, like the Enlightenment thinkers who are in many ways the heroes and heroines of this book, that understanding something a little more usually helps us to fear it a little less; and my main hope for this book is that, by helping to uncover the historical roots of our fascination with terror and 'terrorism', it may give some grounds for us to be a little less afraid.

Notes

1   Jerrold Hogle, 'Introduction', in Hogle, ed., *Cambridge Companion to Gothic Fiction* (Cambridge: Cambridge UP, 2002), pp. 4, 8, 16; David Punter, *The Literature of Terror* (London: Longman, 1980), p. 53.
2   This argument can be found in, for example, Diane Hoeveler, *Gothic Riffs* (Columbus, OH: Ohio State UP, 2010), pp. 10–27.
3   G.R. Elton, ed., *The Reformation*, 2nd edition (Cambridge: Cambridge UP, 1990), pp. 272–3.
4   On political deference to aristocracy in eighteenth-century Britain, see Gerald Newman, *The Rise of English Nationalism* (London: Weidenfeld and Nicholson, 1987), chapter 2.
5   James Watt, *Contesting the Gothic* (Cambridge: Cambridge UP, 1999), chapter 2.

6   See Ronald Paulson, *Representations of Revolution* (New Haven: Yale UP, 1983), chapter 7; Robert Miles, 'The 1790s: The effulgence of the Gothic', in Hogle, ed., *Companion*, and Leslie Fiedler, *Love and Death in the American Novel*, revised edition (Harmondsworth: Penguin, 1984), pp. 126–32.

7   Maggie Kilgour, *The Rise of the Gothic Novel* (London: Routledge, 1995), p. 23.

8   Mary Favret, *War at a Distance* (Princeton, NJ: Princeton UP, 2010), pp. 9–15.

9   John Robison, *Proofs of a Conspiracy Against all the Religions and Governments of Europe, Carried on in the Secret Meetings of Free Masons, Illuminati, and Reading Societies*, 5th edition (Dublin, 1798), p. 493.

10 Brooke Barnett and Amy Reynolds, *Terrorism and the Press* (New York: Peter Lang, 2009), pp. 13, 25–9; Alexander Spencer, *The Tabloid Terrorist* (Basingstoke: Palgrave Macmillan, 2010), p. 9; Dan O'Hair *et al.*, *Terrorism: Communication and Rhetorical Perspectives* (Cresskill, NJ: Hampton Press, 2008), p. 44; Jean Rosenfeld, ed., *Terrorism, Identity, and Legitimacy* (London: Routledge, 2011), pp. 6, 138.

11 David Wright-Neville, *Dictionary of Terrorism* (Cambridge: Polity Press, 2010).

12 See, for example, Eric Johnson, *Nazi Terror* (New York: Basic Books, 2000), and Barry McLoughlin and Kevin McDermott, eds., *Stalin's Terror* (Basingstoke: Palgrave Macmillan, 2003).

13 On the difficulty of defining terrorism, and its construction through metaphor, see Spencer, pp. 11, 78–91, and Carol Winkler, *In the Name of Terrorism* (Albany, NY: State University of New York Press, 2006), p. 13.

14 Marc Redfield, *The Rhetoric of Terror* (New York: Fordham UP, 2009), pp. 6–10, 72–3, 86–91.

1

Terror Before Terrorism

I

It is a commonplace of literary histories that the genre of the Gothic novel arose one night in 1764, when Horace Walpole had the nightmare which inspired him to write *The Castle of Otranto*.[1] Walpole gave his own account of its genesis in a letter to William Cole:

> I waked one morning [. . .] from a dream, of which all I could recover was, that I had thought myself in an ancient castle (a very natural dream for a head like mine filled with Gothic story) and that on the uppermost bannister of a great staircase I saw a gigantic hand in armour. In the evening I sat down and began to write, without knowing in the least what I intended to say or relate.[2]

And so, the story goes, was Gothic born, changeling-fashion, into the very heart of the Age of Reason, out of the nightmares of the son of England's first Prime Minister, ready to take its place as the dark shadow of the Enlightenment and to articulate all those things that the Enlightened were unwilling or unable to say. But such an account raises more questions than it answers. If this night of unquiet sleep in 1764 is truly the origin of the literature of terror, then how did people write and think about terror before then? In his 1814 *History of Fiction*, John Dunlop expressed his surprise that 'emotions so powerful and universal' as fear 'should not have been excited by fiction at an earlier period'.[3] Few subsequent writers on the topic seem to have shared Dunlop's surprise, but he was right, all the same: it *should* surprise us. If 'English Literature' began somewhere around Chaucer, why did it take almost four hundred years to generate a literature of terror? Why did Gothic take so long to come into existence? And what was used before it when authors wished to write about horror and fear?

Obviously, Walpole was not the first person to write fiction in English containing fearful scenes. With their battles, murders, and martyrdoms, their ghosts and demons and headless knights, the literatures of Old and Middle English contained their share of terrifying events: indeed, in *The Castle of Otranto* Walpole drew heavily and self-consciously upon such medieval horrors, as he indicated in his letter to Cole through his description of his head being 'filled with Gothic [i.e. medieval] story'. Nor was early modern literature in English lacking in dark and fearful tales, or deeds of blood; the gory brutality of English tragedies, in particular, was famous across Europe in the early seventeenth century.[4] What was new in 1764 was thus not the specific material that Walpole employed, which he freely owned, having drawn from older sources, but the association of a particular constellation of fictional tropes – gloomy castles, secret passages, terrified damsels, evil and domineering aristocrats, ghosts, storms, ancestral curses, inherited sins, and mysterious and unnatural happenings – with a name, 'Gothic'.[5] When he originally termed his work 'a Gothic story', Walpole was alluding to its fictional provenance as the translation of a medieval Italian story he had recently discovered 'in the library of an ancient Catholic family in the North of *England*' – a story, in other words, that dated from the medieval or 'Gothic' ages.[6] Yet the title page of the second and subsequent editions, in which Walpole confessed the hoax and admitted the novel to be of his own invention rather than a translated medieval tale, still bore the words 'a Gothic story'; words which were now presumably meant to imply not that *The Castle of Otranto* was actually written during the Gothic ages, but merely that this was the historical period in which its action took place.[7] Other 'Gothic stories' and 'Gothic romances' were to follow, gradually etching the pattern of tropes established by Walpole deeper and deeper into the collective imagination of the English-reading public, until by the early nineteenth century aristocratic villains, ruinous Gothic castles, sinister monks, and storm-wracked mountains had become their default mode for imagining what 'evil' and 'fear' might look like, and how they might be written about. They established themselves so successfully that today, almost two-and-a-half centuries after *The Castle of Otranto*, they are *still* our basic symbolic shorthand for evoking such concepts: if the director of a modern TV advert or music video, for example, needs to establish a sense of danger or dread with just a few seconds of footage, they will probably do so with a shot of some Gothic tableau that could easily have come from a novel of the 1790s. As Punter writes, 'it is remarkable that such a literature should be able, as Gothic has been, to dominate a culture's imagery of fear for a century and a half after its ostensible supersession'.[8] But how did it come to pass that, in 1764, the literature of fear was such open cultural territory? Why did such a form not already exist? In this chapter I aim to consider some of the answers to this question; first by discussing the process by which these earlier literatures of fear were dismantled in the early eighteenth century, then by exploring how the rise of patriotic antiquarianism and the aesthetics of terror in mid-century helped prepare the way for the birth of Gothic literature, and finally by investigating some of the forms taken by very early Gothic fiction in the decades following the publication of *Otranto*.

One might not unreasonably expect a literature of terror to arise in a society that had, itself, been terrorised, born out of some immense collective trauma. Yet, for Walpole's England, this hardly seems to be the case; and if the historical traumas of the 1760s, such as they were, were sufficient to give rise to such a literature, it is by no means apparent why earlier epochs should not also have generated equivalent forms. The early eighteenth century, the age of Locke and Addison, Pope and Swift, Richardson and Defoe, was an epoch of great violence, and if its wars are today remembered by few except students of history, they were no less ferocious for all that: the exact figures will never be known, but historians estimate that the War of the Spanish Succession (1701–14), the Great Northern War (1700–21), the War of the Austrian Succession (1740–8), and the Seven Years War (1755–63) each claimed hundreds of thousands of lives, with their greatest set-piece battles such as Blenheim witnessing anything up to 30,000 casualties in a single day, all at a time when the overall population of Europe was less than a third of what it would be in the twentieth century.[9] The same decades witnessed the enslavement and death of millions of Africans, victims of the burgeoning Trans-Atlantic slave trade; while, closer to these authors' homes, the Jacobite Risings of 1715 and 1745 saw the last armed uprisings and full-scale military engagements to take place on the soil of mainland Britain. It was an age of widespread and often violent criminality, the age of Jonathan Wild, Dick Turpin, Blackbeard, and Jack Hall; the murder rate in London was six times as high in 1700 as it would be in 1800, and the pirates, smugglers, and highwaymen who haunted the roads and seas were still concrete and dangerous, rather than the mere romantic legends they would later become.[10] And yet, for all this, the writers of the period regarded their age – which to most modern Westerners would probably seem almost unbearably cruel, unjust, violent, and insecure – as one of relative peace, knowing full well that in the seventeenth century their grandparents and great-grandparents had suffered through wars and persecutions more cataclysmic still. It thus seems highly unlikely that, as is sometimes suggested, the early eighteenth century had no need of a literature of terror because it was a quiet and decorous age, whose writers had not yet been forced to confront the realities of human evil: Defoe, Addison, Johnson, and their contemporaries were extremely familiar with violence, disorder, atrocity, and criminality, as a glance at Hogarth's *Stages of Cruelty* prints should amply confirm.

What differentiated their era from the period which followed it was not the actual extent to which its inhabitants were exposed to violence and disorder – which was at least comparable to that of subsequent generations – but the attitude of its intellectual culture towards such phenomena, and indeed towards human evil in general. In *Forms of Evil in the Gothic Novel*, Reddin writes that '[t]he earlier eighteenth century novelists, Defoe, Richardson, Fielding, and Smollett, expressed an aggressively secular, outward-looking view of evil', and that '[t]he vision of evil expressed by these writers tends to be outward-looking and confined to a distinct time and space – the high and low roads of eighteenth century social life', while 'the Gothicists, on the other hand, are obsessed with chaos' and 'express an intensely inward psychological and metaphysical view of evil'.[11] While I would query her description of Richardson's view of evil as 'aggressively secular', Reddin does highlight a crucial difference between the pre- and post-Gothic attitudes to evil. To the contemporaries of Addison and Johnson, human evil was primarily a social problem, requiring a social solution; it was rooted in specific situations, what Reddin refers to as 'a distinct time and space', and by improving those situations – by reforming political and religious institutions, for example, or by reducing levels of poverty and ignorance – it could hopefully be done away with, or at least reduced to more manageable levels. It is an attitude that Phillip Hallie articulates in *Cruelty*:

> Hogarth knew the sick orphans and the gin-soaked people of London, and Fielding was justice of the peace for the counties of Middlesex and Westminster. Like so

many other Englishmen, they saw the horrible waste of life that was commonplace around them, and they saw it not in terms of an evil that iron tradition and the innate sinfulness of the passions made fixed and unchangeable; they saw everything around them as *malleable*. They believed that once the facts are clearly seen in their powerful particularity, their here-and-nowness, they can be changed, if they are destroying life; and once we know they can be changed, they *will* be changed.[12]

Evildoers abound in pre-Gothic literature. In fact, many of them are precisely the sort of characters who would subsequently appear as archetypal Gothic villains: wilful aristocrats who believe their social status places them above the law, and who use force and fraud to obtain their desires. *Pamela, Clarissa*, and *Tom Jones* all feature a scenario that would go on to become a staple of Gothic fiction: virtuous maidens who are imprisoned by powerful men with designs upon their virginities. Dangerous criminals abound in the novels of Defoe, and also appear as the protagonists of other works of the period, such as Gay's *The Mohocks*, Fielding's *Jonathan Wild*, and Smollett's *Ferdinand Count Fathom*. Collectively, the literature of this era features innumerable acts of murder, seduction, deception, fraud, theft, oppression, exploitation, and the occasional rape; nor does it shy away from sometimes exploring to the fullest and most horrible extent the ways in which such acts can destroy their victims (and occasionally also their perpetrators) physically, mentally, and socially, especially in a world with as few social safety nets as that of early-eighteenth-century England.[13] But all these works differ crucially from those of the later Gothic writers in their depictions of evil. In the literature of this era, acts of evil are never *impressive*, never grand: they demonstrate only the failings and weaknesses of those who perform them. (Indeed, Fielding's *Jonathan Wild* is chiefly concerned with satirising and rebutting the idea that one might attain any kind of 'greatness' simply by increasing the number and heinousness of one's crimes.) In Gothic novels, characters confronted with scenes of human evil often find their faith in God, humanity, or the very order of the universe itself profoundly shaken, but in the novels of the early eighteenth century this almost never happens; some unfortunate characters are driven mad, as a sort of mechanical reaction to the extremity of their distress, but those who are not never seem to regard the evil by which they are victimised as anything particularly mysterious, or even confusing. They know that individuals with free wills and vicious dispositions will often choose to do evil rather than good, and that acts of evil will often ruin the lives of those upon whom they are inflicted; these facts may be regrettable, but they are hardly baffling. As Reddin says, the vision of evil presented by these writers is 'confined' to the time and space in which it actually occurs, and in which its wretched consequences are played out. Most of them held that evildoers would ultimately have to answer to God for their sins; but, unlike Reddin's 'Gothicists', they did not attribute to their acts of evil any grander, more 'metaphysical' dimension. Fielding's dismissal of the follies of vice in his Dedication to *Tom Jones* is typical:

I have shown that no acquisitions of guilt can compensate the loss of that solid inward comfort of mind, which is the sure companion of innocence and virtue; nor can in the least balance the evil of that horror and anxiety which, in their room, guilt introduces into our bosoms. And again, that as these acquisitions are in themselves generally worthless, so are the means to attain them not only base and infamous, but at best uncertain, and always full of danger.[14]

In these lines, which are saturated with the language of accounting and commerce, human evil shrinks to a bad business proposal: a matter of acquisition, compensation, balance, uncertainty, and loss, in which no 'metaphysical' reference points are required. Evil is to be avoided simply because it is a bad investment, 'uncertain', 'full of danger', and 'generally worthless'. Men should seek virtue, Fielding writes, because 'their true interest directs them to a pursuit of her'; in contrast, the potential rewards of evil are simply not worth the practical risks and psychological costs needed to acquire them.[15]

This carefully limited depiction of evil was entirely deliberate, for behind the era of Hogarth and Fielding loomed the awful memory of the seventeenth century: an age in which men really had believed in unlimited, 'metaphysical' evil, and had consequently denounced their ideological enemies as the literal agents of Satan. The exterminatory viciousness of many seventeenth-century conflicts – the Thirty Years War in Germany, the Wars of Religion in France, the War of Three Kingdoms in Britain and Ireland, and the massacre of the Waldensians of Piedmont, for example, as well as the witch-hunts which flared up across Europe on an unprecedented scale in the wake of these political and religious conflicts – had, in the view of these writers, been stoked by just such beliefs, which had encouraged men to view their enemies not just as evildoers whose misdeeds needed to be prevented in the name of social order and justice, but as incarnate fiends whose spiritual stain needed to be blotted out of the universe entirely.[16] The continent was wracked with wars more destructive than anything it had seen for centuries, and for some nations perhaps worse than anything they have suffered since: the War of Three Kingdoms is estimated to have led to the deaths of 800,000 people, perhaps 10 per cent of the population of the British Isles, while the population of Germany fell by somewhere between 15 per cent and 20 per cent over the course of the Thirty Years War.[17] The European order which emerged from these bloody decades was consequently extremely wary of unleashing such forces, which had proved all too capable of engulfing lords and kings as easily as their subjects. Eighteenth-century European states still went to war with one another as a matter of course, but by 1700 they were likely to do so in the name of preferential trading rights, or in defence of 'the balance of power in Europe', rather than in order to strike a blow against the heretic followers of Antichrist. Mercenary though such motives were, the very concreteness of their objectives – the capture of *this* province, the destruction of *these* fortifications – helped to contain the scale of these *Kabinettskriege*, preventing the kind of completely unrestrained, unlimited violence which had devastated Europe in the century before.[18]

Accordingly, the intellectual elites of the early British Enlightenment were extremely keen to avoid anything that savoured of their favourite cultural bugbears, 'fanaticism' and 'superstition', as for them it was axiomatic that where these flourished, ignorance, violence, and intolerance would inevitably follow: as Addison remarked, 'as it is the chief Concern of Wise-Men, to retrench the Evils of Life by the Reasonings of Philosophy; it is the Employment of Fools, to multiply them by the Sentiments of Superstition'.[19] Following Locke, these writers and thinkers favoured 'rational' interpretations of Christianity, rooted in their interpretations of the actual text of the Bible rather than the mass of popular beliefs which had grown up around it.[20] They continued to believe, for the most part, in the old cosmic structure of heaven and hell, but heavily de-emphasised the role of Satan and his human and spiritual minions; demonology and witchcraft, which in the seventeenth century had been believed in even by men so superlatively intelligent and well educated as Thomas Browne, found no place in their metaphysics, and, after 1736, no place in their legal system, either.[21] They certainly did not deny that men often performed acts of evil, and that such acts merited punishment at the hands of both God and man; but evil, for them, was born out of personal and comprehensible failures of reason, education, empathy, or self-control, rather than from some numinous communion with the powers of darkness: as Dryden wrote of the villains of tragedy, 'To produce a villain, without other reason than a natural inclination to villainy is, in poetry, to produce an effect without a cause'.[22] The proper cure for such evil was thus the removal of such causes in the here and now, through the improvement of education and social organisation and the implementation of a suitably weighted system of rewards and punishments, rather than through exorcism and extermination. 'Whatever their differences', Hunter writes of the thinkers of the British Enlightenment, 'they united in their desire to leave behind the rural culture of primitivism, paganism, and superstition, a past associated with narrowness, darkness, and terror. No one could imagine the rolling back of the darkness without the aid of better education...'[23]

One crucial element of an education system which would work to discourage evil behaviour was, naturally enough, that it would have to refrain from glorifying evildoers, or over-estimating their power. No longer, insisted a whole succession of Enlightenment writers on education, must small children be encouraged to emulate glamorous villains, taught to fear churchyards and dark places, or terrified with stories of supernaturally powerful witches and demons lurking in every shadow.[24] Here is Locke, offering advice on the education of a child:

> Be sure to preserve his tender Mind from all Impressions and Notions of *Sprites* and *Goblins*, or any fearful Apprehensions in the dark. It being the usual Method of *Servants* to awe Children, and keep them in subjection, by telling them of *Raw-Head* and *Bloody Bones*, and such other Names, as carry with them the Idea's of some hurtful, terrible Things, inhabiting darkness.... Such *Bug-bear* Thoughts once got into the tender Minds of Children, sink deep there, and fasten themselves so, as not easily, if ever, to be got out again, and while they are there, frequently haunt them with strange Visions, making Children dastards when alone, and afraid of their Shadows and Darkness all their Lives after.[25]

Here is Addison, walking at night through the ruins of an old abbey reputed to be haunted, and invoking the authority of 'Mr. *Lock*' in order to dismiss the fears of the weak-minded and ignorant:

> These Objects naturally raise Seriousness and Attention; and when Night heightens the Awfulness of the Place, and pours out her supernumerary Horrours upon

every thing in it, I do not at all wonder that weak Minds fill it with Spectres and Apparitions. [. . .] As I was walking in this Solitude, where the Dusk of the Evening conspired with so many other Occasions of Terrour, I observed a Cow grazing not far from me, which an Imagination that was apt to *startle* might easily have construed into a black Horse without an Head: and I dare say the poor Footman lost his Wits upon some such trivial Occasion.[26]

Here is Addison again, demonstrating his Enlightened fearlessness in that great Gothic monument, Westminster Abbey:

Upon my going into the Church, I entertain'd my self with the digging of a Grave; and saw in every Shovel-full of it that was thrown up, the Fragment of a Bone or Skull intermixt with a kind of fresh mouldering Earth that some time or other had a Place in the Composition of an humane Body. [. . .] I know that Entertainments of this Nature, are apt to raise dark and dismal Thoughts in timorous Minds and gloomy Imaginations; but for my own Part, though I am always serious, I do not know what it is to be melancholy; and can therefore take a View of Nature in her deep and solemn Scenes, with the same Pleasure as in her most gay and delightful ones. By this Means I can improve my self with those Objects, which others consider with Terrour.[27]

Here is Johnson, objecting to the depiction of superhuman forces of 'terrour' in poetry:

Pleasure and terror are indeed the genuine sources of poetry; but poetical pleasure must be such as human imagination can at least conceive, and poetical terrour such as human strength and fortitude may combat. The good and evil of Eternity are too ponderous for the wings of wit; the mind sinks under them in passive helplessness . . . [28]

And here is Johnson's judgement on the depiction of evil in literature aimed at the young and impressionable:

There have been men indeed splendidly wicked, whose endowments threw a brightness on their crimes, and whom scarce any villainy made perfectly detestable, because they never could be wholly divested of their excellencies; but such have been in all ages the great corruptors of the world, and their resemblance ought no more to be preserved, than the art of murdering without pain.[29]

These men did not deny the potential power of evil, or the possible existence of supernatural beings. They knew only too well that human evil, especially when spurred on by 'fanaticism' or 'superstition', could cause suffering on the most monumental scale: Britain's recent history was proof enough of that. Addison and Johnson both believed in spirits; Defoe probably believed in supernatural apparitions; Johnson was quite willing to believe that the famous Cock Lane Ghost might be genuine, and was disappointed to discover it a hoax.[30] But they did not believe that the proper reaction to ghosts, or spirits, or bones and corpses, or human villains – the great recurring props of Gothic fiction – was *awe* or *fear*. An entire literary genre of 'dialogues of the dead' grew up in this period, most of them satirical, and all of them resolutely non-Gothic in their attitudes to the afterlife, depicting the spirits of the departed as a mere resource to be drawn upon for information; an attitude also visible in the Cock Lane Ghost affair, in which it never seems to have occurred to any of the ghost's investigators that they should feel fear, rather than curiosity, when confronted with apparent manifestations of supernatural forces.[31] No intelligent Christian, Addison argued, should fear the activities of spirits: they might be powerful, but God was good, and He would surely not have granted such beings the ability to transgress their proper, divinely ordained places in the world.[32]

Perhaps the most damning Enlightenment critique of the pernicious effects of fear was that of the era's greatest political theorist, Montesquieu, who viewed it as the inevitable ally of despotism:

> As virtue is necessary in a republic, and in a monarchy honour, so fear is necessary in a despotic government: with regard to virtue, there is no occasion for it, and honour would be extremely dangerous. [. . .] Persons capable of setting a value upon themselves would be likely to create disturbances. Fear must therefore depress their spirits, and extinguish even the least sense of ambition.[33]

What emerges from all of these passages is the idea that fear, fear itself, was seen by the writers of the Enlightenment as one of the major problems that would have to be overcome if they were ever to bring about any amelioration of the situation of mankind. Fear was the ally of fanaticism in religion, and the foundation of despotic tyranny in politics; as Johnson remarked, 'the Roman tyrant was content to be hated, if he was but feared'.[34] Fear fostered ignorance, intolerance, and persecution, and encouraged the emulation of vice, by granting to despots and criminals a spurious aura of greatness and awe. If history had been bloody and chaotic, it was because men and women had been too much afraid: they had been taught to live in fear of kings and priests, ghosts and witches and devils, and that fear had made them cruel and cowardly when they should have been generous and brave.[35] It is thus unsurprising that their writings, and the writings of those contemporary novelists (such as Fielding and Richardson) who broadly shared their ideological position, generally avoided depicting scenes of supernatural terror, or investing evildoers with the kind of fearful grandeur that would later become the Gothic villain's stock-in-trade. This is not to say that the perpetrators of evil deeds appear in such literature merely as pitiable moral imbeciles, without any positive characteristics; Jonathan Wild and Ferdinand Count Fathom are, at the very least, men possessed of courage, ambition, and quick wits, while Lovelace – liar, kidnapper, and rapist though he is – is articulate, inventive, intelligent, charming, and not without generous impulses.[36] But the demonic charisma with which the villains of later Gothic fiction would be invested – the manic energy, the overwhelming force of personality that inspires terror and obedience, the blazing eye before which all rivals must give way – was entirely foreign to them, and would probably have seemed to these writers to be profoundly morally suspect. Such 'splendidly wicked' men, as

Johnson said, 'have been in all ages the great corruptors of the world'. What could be gained from granting such glamorous attributes to characters whom the reader should surely not be encouraged to emulate or admire? Who but a friend of despotism would encourage their readers to look upon the wicked and powerful with awe and fear?

For similar reasons, these novelists were keen to avoid encouraging 'superstition'; they remembered how recently the Witchcraft Act had been repealed, and were uncomfortably aware how fragile their progress might still be. Thus, on the rare occasions when these novelists mention supernatural forces other than divine providence, they do so only to dismiss them, like Locke and Addison, as things not to be heeded or feared.[37] In *Tom Jones*, Fielding famously declared:

> I think it may very reasonably be required of every writer that he keeps within the bounds of possibility; and still remembers that what it is not possible for man to perform, it is scarce possible for man to believe he did perform... Nor is possibility alone sufficient to justify us; we must keep likewise within the rules of probability.[38]

On these grounds, Fielding goes on to lament the extravagant supernaturalism of Homer's epics, and to argue that modern authors should make as little use of the supernatural as possible:

> The only supernatural agents which can in any manner be allowed to us moderns are ghosts; but of these I would advise an author to be extremely sparing. These are, indeed, like arsenic, and other dangerous drugs in physic, to be used with the utmost caution; nor would I advise the introduction of them at all in those works, or by those authors, to which, or to whom, a horse-laugh in the reader would be any great prejudice or mortification.
>
> As for elves and fairies, and other such mummery, I purposely omit the mention of them, as I should be very unwilling to confine within any bounds those surprising imaginations, for whose vast capacity the limits of human nature are too narrow...[39]

Fielding's rhetoric of rules and boundaries serves to implicitly divide writers into two groups, legitimate writers and literary outlaws. The legitimate are those who obey the 'rules of probability', and remain within 'the bounds of possibility'; they are just and reasonable men, willing to do that which 'may very reasonably be required of every writer' and whatever is 'sufficient to justify' their works. Those who transgress these boundaries and break the rules are, implicitly, unjustified and unreasonable, and they are thus aligned with a whole suite of semi-criminal outsiders; quack doctors who poison their patients (and perhaps themselves) with overdoses of 'arsenic, and other dangerous drugs', fools whose works are so ridiculous that they prompt 'a horse-laugh in the reader', charlatans and low performers who traffic in 'fairies, and other such mummery', and lunatics whose 'surprising imaginations' are so fantastical that even 'the limits of human nature are too narrow' for them. The supernatural thus becomes the domain of the fraudulent, the ignorant, and the criminal: precisely the social stratum which the novel, in Fielding's day, was attempting to raise itself out of, shaking off its old associations with criminality, pornography, and low culture. The author who, like Fielding or Richardson, wishes himself and his works to be regarded as reasonable and respectable must obey the 'rules of probability', and forswear the use of the supernatural. A novel, Johnson declared, should 'exhibit life in its true state', and 'it is therefore precluded from the machines and expedients of the heroic romance'.[40]

Thus, even at those moments when their narratives seem to come closest to the haunted world of the previous century, these writers are careful to make clear their disdain for popular superstition. When Lovelace finally succeeds in carrying Clarissa away from her family home, he does so in exemplary Gothic surroundings; through the back door of the gardens, which opens onto what Clarissa calls 'a place so pathless and lonesome':

> A piece of ruins upon it, the remains of an old chapel, now standing in the midst of the coppice; here and there an overgrown oak, surrounded with ivy and mistletoe, starting up, to sanctify, as it were, the awful solemness of the place. A spot, too, where a man having been found hanging some years ago, it was used to be thought of by us when children, and by the maidservants, with a degree of terror; as the habitation of owls, ravens, and other ominous birds; and as haunted by ghosts, goblins, spectres. The genuine result of country loneliness and ignorance; notions which, early propagated, are apt to leave impressions even upon minds grown strong enough, at the same time, to despise the like credulous follies in others.[41]

These fearful attributes serve to mark the spot as an unlucky one, a place of ill omen – as indeed, for Clarissa, it proves to be. Yet neither she, nor anyone else, actually shows the slightest belief in such supernatural phenomena, and in the letter in which she describes her departure from her family home with Lovelace, she makes no reference whatsoever to this ruined chapel or its supposed ghosts. For Richardson and Fielding, following Addison and Locke, such fears were simply 'credulous follies', the result of 'ignorance', capable of touching the strong-minded only if they were unwisely exposed to them in early childhood. Clarissa's friends and relatives, surprised by her refusal to marry Solmes, accuse her of 'witchcraft', call her a 'fallen angel', and say she has a 'demon' within her.[42] But for them – and for Richardson – these have dwindled into mere figures of speech; they do not actually fear, as they might have done just a few generations earlier, that she has been possessed by evil spirits, or that she may be secretly using black magic against them.

The primary fictional form employed in this period to write about scenes of terror was the tragedy, for the neoclassical critics of the early eighteenth century held fast to Aristotle's dictum that the purpose of tragedy was to cathartically purge its audience of pity and fear. But in tragedy, as in so much else, the writers of the eighteenth century were eager to distance themselves from what they saw as the barbarism of the past: from the amoral violence of the Jacobean stage, whose monstrous villains had murdered and mutilated one another in self-perpetuating cycles of pointless atrocity, amidst a ceaseless welter of blood and thunder. They did not banish violence from their drama – although they increasingly preferred to report it through dialogue, like their classical Greek models, rather than show it onstage – and the tragedies which were popular in the theatres of early-eighteenth-century England could sometimes be extremely bloody affairs: Dryden's adaptation of *Oedipus* infamously ended with the deaths of five of its six major characters, and Dr Johnson's weary remark on Dodsley's *Cleone* – 'Come let's have some more, let's go into the slaughter-house again' – could serve just as well for a number of other contemporary works.[43] But it was of the highest importance to these tragedians that their dramas should be *moral* – this was, after all, the age which refused to perform *King Lear* without a happy ending – and, like the contemporary novelists, they consequently took care to avoid glorifying their villains, shunning the ambiguous hero-villains of Jacobean tragedy who threatened to throw all around them into moral chaos.[44] 'Every Tragedy ought to be a very solemn Lecture', asserted John Dennis, 'inculcating a particular Providence, and showing it plainly protecting the good, and chastising the bad, or at least the violent': and while many of Dennis' contemporaries felt that such a model of tragic drama was too schematic, they were in broad agreement that tragedy, and especially scenes of tragic suffering, should always have a clear moral purpose.[45] Thus, despite its calamitous death toll, Dryden's *Oedipus* – unlike its much more unsettling Greek original – presents a perfectly clear and comprehensible moral universe, in which Oedipus is good and admirable, Creon is evil and contemptible, and the other characters line up on one side or the other according to their allegiances. The British neoclassical interpretation of the role of fear in tragedy – based on their interpretation of Aristotle – was that it should be summoned up only to be put down; terrifying scenes were permissible only on the condition that the audience left the theatre less afraid, and more morally certain, than they were when they entered it, having witnessed the edifying spectacle of good men struggling with adversity, and evildoers punished for their wickedness. Anything else would have been socially irresponsible.

The literary culture of early-eighteenth-century Britain, then, was one which to a great extent had been deliberately stripped of its traditional demonology. The old vocabulary of demons, witches, sorcery, and Satanic pacts, which had been used for centuries to write about and understand the nature of human evil – the language that had allowed Lady Macbeth, for example, to articulate what she was doing and feeling as she planned the murder of her king – had fallen out of favour, dismissed as a remnant of superstition with no place in any rational man's religion. The amoral avengers and destroyers who had stalked the Elizabethan and Jacobean stage – Barabas, Aaron, Tamburlaine, Vindice, and their ilk – had been banished as barbaric aberrations, not befitting the drama of a civilised society. Aiming to create a literature which would help to free society from prejudice, fanaticism, despotism, and superstition, which they saw as having been the besetting sins of the previous era, writers from Locke to Fielding set a literary agenda in which such incarnations of radical, 'metaphysical' evil had no place. When Walpole and his followers began to write the first Gothic novels, they found the field empty of any existing literature of terror, because the previous one – what we might call the literature of 'theological evil', which for centuries had served as the default way to articulate the extremes of human wickedness – had been deliberately and systematically dismantled two generations before.

To see how thoroughly this new mood of fearless moral seriousness inflected the literature of the early- and mid-eighteenth century, and how impossible it rendered the creation of any sort of literature of terror, one need look no further than the school of 'graveyard poetry', which was immensely popular in the years leading up to the publication of *Otranto*. These poems, with their ghosts and graves and corpses, now often seem Gothic or proto-Gothic in their trappings, and certainly demonstrate that no amount of Enlightened optimism was able to quell the public appetite to read about ghostly and ghastly material: what Patricia Meyer Spacks referred to as the 'insistence of horror'. But they also serve to demonstrate how very differently these tropes were approached by the generation of writers who preceded the invention of the Gothic. In these works, poet after poet – Parnell, Gray, Young, Blair – sits down to meditate among the tombs; but their reflections are always characterised by pious melancholy, rather than horror or dread, even when they are confronted with legions of ghosts or by King Death himself.[46] In his 1722 'Night-Piece on Death', Parnell sets the tone for most of his successors by attributing to Death these words, 'speaking from among the Bones':

> When men my Scythe and Darts supply,
> How great a *King of Fears* am I!
> They view me like the last of Things:
> They make, and then they dread, my Stings.
> Fools! if you less provok'd your Fears,
> No more my Spectre-Form appears.
> Death's but a Path that must be trod,
> If man would ever pass to God ...[47]

Mindful of their Christian duties, the graveyard poets explicitly reject the idea that death, or the trappings of death, should inspire fear in those who witness them: like Addison contemplating the bones and graves in Westminster Abbey, 'this great Magazine of Mortality', they endeavour to improve themselves 'with those Objects which others consider with Terrour'.[48] In Blair's *Grave* (1743), even the walking dead seem more a source of amusement than a cause for serious concern:

> Strange things, the neighbours say, have happen'd here.
> Wild shrieks have issu'd from the hollow tombs;
> Dead men have come again, and walk'd about;
> And the great bell has toll'd, unrung, untouch'd!
> Such tales their cheer, at wake or gossiping,
> When it draws near the witching-time of night.[49]

The scene Blair describes is nightmarish, as horrific as anything in the works of Lewis, Maturin, or Poe: bells ringing of their own accord, screams emerging from sealed tombs, and walking corpses hauling themselves out of their own graves. But in the poem, this fearful scene is doubly undercut; we are first assured that it is not the poet but 'the neighbours' who claim these events have taken place (a pattern also visible in the passages from Locke, Addison, and Richardson already cited, all of which attribute the fear of ghosts and goblins to ill-educated members of the lower classes), and then once we have been told about them we are once again reminded that this is not an account of something that has actually happened, but merely a story told among those who live nearby. This framing device discourages the reader from taking the story seriously, as the 'neighbours' are evidently simple, superstitious folk, the kind of people who engage not in discourse but in 'gossiping', and entertain each other with ghost stories at midnight; indeed, by associating the story with such people, the net effect is to encourage the reader to actively *disbelieve* such tales, both in the poem and in real life, thereby demonstrating how different they are from the foolish, credulous gossips who tell such tales.[50] Even the 'neighbours' clearly don't take the 'tales' very seriously, as they tell them for 'cheer'; not as serious warnings of the horrible danger this haunted graveyard may pose, but merely as entertaining stories to pass the time at night. The horrific is raised from its grave only so that it may be more firmly reburied.

II

The theory behind Gothic was penned some years before Gothic literature itself came to exist. It was written in the years 1746–7: years that witnessed the last pitched battle fought on the soil of mainland Britain, the last execution by axe for High Treason on Tower Hill, and some of the fiercest fighting of the War of the Austrian Succession. Its writers were young, as it is the prerogative of the young to be at the forefront of change: one, William Collins, was a poet of twenty-six, while the other, Edmund Burke, was a precocious student of just eighteen. Their works did not win immediate recognition; but, over the decades which followed, they would help to create the cultural climate which would make possible the rise of Gothic fiction in Britain.

In 1747 Collins published his major poetic work, the *Odes*, among which appeared his 'Ode to Fear'. In the same year, Burke – then a student at Trinity College, Dublin – wrote much of the text of what would later become the *Philosophical Enquiry into the Origins of Our Ideas of the Sublime and Beautiful*, although it was not published until ten years later, in 1757.[51] Between them, the 'Ode' and the *Enquiry* helped lay the groundwork for the subsequent construction of Gothic literature, by introducing into English letters the idea that the deliberate inspiration of fear in one's readers could be a legitimate artistic aim in and of itself, rather than only when, as in contemporary tragedy, it was yoked to some appropriate moral or religious lesson. In the 'Ode', Collins writes:

> Ah *Fear*! Ah frantic *Fear*!
> I see, I see Thee near.
> I know thy hurried Step, thy haggard Eye!
> Like Thee I start, like Thee disorder'd fly,
> For lo what *Monsters* in thy Train appear![52]

Beholding Fear and her terrible retinue, Collins reacts as none of the graveyard poets react when faced with tombs, or ghosts, or Death: *he is himself afraid*. Nor, he makes clear, is this merely a sign of his own personal failings, as the fear of death is in the works of the graveyard poets. After enumerating the '*Monsters*' in fear's 'Train' – Danger, Vengeance, and the 'thousand Phantoms' who 'prompt to Deeds accurs'd the Mind', Collins writes: 'Who, *Fear*, this ghastly Train can see,/And look not madly wild, like Thee?' The reader, who has just seen this 'ghastly Train' in the immediately preceding lines of the poem, is thus *invited to feel fear*, and reassured that such a reaction is natural, even inevitable. In the work of Collins' poetic contemporaries, fear is only raised up in order to be put down: King Death and his armies of walking corpses are allowed to look fearful for only a dozen lines or so before the graveyard poet sternly reminds his readers that the fear of death is a thoroughly un-Christian sentiment, while the tragedy villain stalks the stage for the five acts allotted to him, but incurs his inevitable punishment before the final curtain falls. Yet in Collins' 'Ode' this dauntless perspective, able to gaze coolly and levelly at the worst the world has to offer, is dismissed as improbable. As he writes of Danger: 'What mortal Eye can fix'd behold?'

As was conventional in the 1740s, Collins associates Fear primarily with the genre of tragedy, and thus depicts the literature of fear as having been born in Ancient Greece. In the Epode of his 'Ode', he describes the earliest origins of the form:

> In earliest *Greece* to thee with partial Choice,
> The Grief-full Muse addrest her infant Tongue;
> The Maids and Matrons, on her awful Voice,
> Silent and pale in wild Amazement hung.
> Yet He the Bard who first invok'd thy Name,
> Disdain'd in *Marathon* its power to feel:
> For not alone he nurs'd the Poet's flame,
> But reach'd from Virtue's Hand the Patriot's Steel.
> But who is he whom later Garlands grace,
> Who left a-while o'er *Hybla*'s Dews to rove,
> With trembling Eyes thy dreary Steps to trace,
> Where Thou and *Furies* shar'd the baleful Grove?[53]

In these lines the two earliest major Greek tragedians, Aeschylus and Sophocles, are juxtaposed. Aeschylus, the first 'Bard' to invoke Fear, is himself fearless; the tragedian famously fought in the Athenian phalanx against the Persians at the Battle of Marathon, where he presumably saw Danger's 'Limbs of Giant Mold' and the rest of Fear's 'ghastly Train' up close, but Collins imagines him facing them and yet remaining unafraid. It is thus evidently not *impossible* for a 'mortal Eye' to see Fear without looking 'madly wild', or to remain 'fix'd' when looking upon Danger: but to do so is not, it seems, the prerogative of the poet *qua* poet. Aeschylus is able to do so because he is not just a poet, but also a heroic patriot, able to 'reach from Virtue's Hand the Patriot's Steel'; and thus armed, he is able to stand his ground at Marathon and confront the armies of Persia while remaining unafraid. But his successor, Sophocles, is only a poet; and consequently Collins imagines that when *he* invokes Fear, it is not with 'fix'd' but 'trembling' eyes. Fear herself is terrified; Collins, who beholds Fear, is terrified; Sophocles, who invokes Fear, is terrified; the Greek 'Maids and Matrons' who watch the tragedies of Aeschylus with 'wild Amazement' – Collins is probably thinking of the story that the appearance of the Furies in Aeschylus' play *The Eumenides* inspired such fear in some of the women in the audience that they miscarried – are certainly terrified. In his ability to invoke Fear without being himself afraid, Aeschylus is not representative but exceptional, and the reader of the 'Ode' is not expected to be able to emulate him when they are confronted with her 'ghastly Train'.

Finally, in the Antistrophe, Collins lays out what is, effectively, a blueprint for the Gothic genre:

> Thou who such weary Lengths hast past,
> Where wilt thou rest, mad Nymph, at last?
> Say, wilt thou shroud in haunted Cell,
> Where gloomy *Rape* and *Murder* dwell?
> Or in some hollow'd Seat,
> 'Gainst which the big Waves beat,
> Hear drowning Sea-men's Cries in Tempests brought!
> Dark pow'r, with shudd'ring meek submitted Thought
> Be mine, to read the Visions old,
> Which thy awak'ning Bards have told:
> And lest thou meet my blasted View,
> Hold each strange Tale devoutly true;
> Ne'er be I found, by Thee o'eraw'd,
> In that thrice-hallow'd Eve abroad,
> When Ghosts, as Cottage-Maids believe,
> Their pebbled Beds permitted leave,
> And *Gobblins* haunt from Fire, or Fen,
> Or Mine, or Flood, the Walks of Men![54]

In sharp contrast to earlier writers, Collins deliberately opens himself to precisely the kind of superstitious beliefs that Locke, Addison, and the rest had attempted to discredit. He *wills* himself to believe that ghosts and goblins may haunt the darkness; he *chooses* to be afraid to go out after dark on Hallowe'en. He dwells deliberately on such locales as the 'haunted Cell/Where gloomy *Rape* and *Murder* dwell', and coasts from which one may 'hear drowning Sea-men's Cries in Tempests brought' – both subsequently to become stock scenes in Gothic novels – not as part of a religious or moral meditation to steel his mind against fear, but *in order to make himself afraid*. And why would anyone want to deliberately suffer such fears? In the poem's closing lines, Collins explains:

> O Thou whose Spirit most possesst
> The sacred seat of *Shakespear's* Breast!
> By all that from thy Prophet broke,
> In thy Divine Emotions spoke:
> Hither again thy Fury deal,
> Teach me but once like Him to feel:
> His *Cypress Wreath* my Meed decree,
> And I, O *Fear*, will dwell with *Thee*![55]

By invoking Fear, Collins hopes, in other words, to gain access to the same level of emotional intensity that Shakespeare and Sophocles were able to realise in their tragedies. Notably, he does not ask Fear to enable him to *write* as well as they did, only to be able to *feel* as deeply: to experience the same 'Divine Emotions' that he imagines they must have felt. The idea that a tragedian must himself experience the extremes of fear in order to write successful tragedies is quite foreign to most eighteenth-century dramatic criticism, which generally viewed the main problem of tragedy-writing as being not how to summon up enough fear, but how properly to balance it with pity in order to have a suitably morally uplifting effect upon the audience. In 1747, the eighteenth-century re-evaluation of Shakespeare was just starting to begin in earnest; but, while Shakespeare's ability to write fearful scenes was widely noted and admired, probably few of his contemporary admirers would have recognised the 'god of their idolatry' in Collins' depiction of him as the 'Prophet' of Fear, his 'breast' dominated more by the spirit of terror than by any other. Garrick was famous for his depictions of extreme fear onstage in his tragic roles, but in Fielding's *Tom Jones* – published two years after the *Odes* – it is a sign of poor Partridge's hopeless lack of sophistication that he, as well as Garrick's Hamlet, is scared by the appearance of Old Hamlet's ghost; a scene which suggests that Fielding hardly viewed Shakespeare's ability to inspire terror in his audiences as his defining excellence.[56] Yet Collins systematically links Shakespeare with fear, and indeed his catalogue of horrors seems to aspire to literary legitimacy through its use of Shakespearean allusions: 'gloomy *Rape* and *Murder*' are the alter-egos adopted by Tamora's monstrous sons, Chiron and Demetrius, in *Titus Andronicus*, the 'drowning Sea-men's Cries in Tempests' recall *The Tempest* and various other Shakespearean shipwrecks (such as those in *Pericles* and *A Winter's Tale*), and the '*Gobblins*' who are sometimes permitted to 'haunt from Fire, or Fen,/Or Mine, or Flood' presumably allude to Horatio's famous speech in the first scene of *Hamlet*:

> The cock, that is the trumpet of the morn,
> Doth with his lofty and shrill-sounding throat
> Awake the god of day, and, at his warning,
> Whether in sea or fire, in earth or air,
> Th'extravagant and erring spirit hies
> To his confine...[57]

Shakespeare was a shrewd ally for Collins to invoke, as in 1747 his defenders were engaged in arguing that his use of such supernatural and violent scenes did not mark him out as an irredeemable literary barbarian – a 'drunken savage' still mired in 'Gothicism', as Voltaire would accuse him of being in 1765 – but as an original genius of great creative power, even if no contemporary tragedian would then have written a play as heinously violent as *Titus Andronicus*, or as overtly supernatural as *The Tempest* or *Macbeth*.[58] When David Garrick re-opened the Drury Lane Theatre in April 1747, he unveiled a statue of Shakespeare, and read out a Prologue written by Johnson for the occasion:

> When Learning's triumph o'er her barbarous foes
> First reared the stage, immortal SHAKESPEAR rose;
> Each change of many-coloured life he drew,
> Exhausted worlds, and then imagined new:

Existence saw him spurn her bounded reign,
And panting Time toiled after him in vain:
His pow'rful Strokes presiding Truth impressed,
And unresisted Passion stormed the breast.[59]

In these lines, the standard criticisms of Shakespeare's works – that they were too wild and too violent, and made too much use of obsolete superstitions – are pre-empted and turned into grounds for praise, as Johnson and Garrick praise Shakespeare for having 'imagin'd new [worlds]' and 'storm'd the Breast' with 'unresisted Passion'. The implicit defence employed by Collins in his 'Ode' is that, if Shakespeare could imagine and write such scenes, there is no reason why he, Collins, should not write or imagine them, too; but Collins' fear-filled, cypress-wreathed Shakespeare is hardly the figure that Garrick and Johnson were then promoting, and if they defended his use of ghosts and murders in his tragedies, they did not claim that what made them most worth defending was their ability to make their viewers very much afraid. The attitude to fear described in Collins' 'Ode' stood out as an oddity at the time, and it was poems such as this – along with his well-known interest in obscure and ghastly folklore, which would culminate in his unfinished poem, *Superstitions of the Scottish Highlands* – which contributed to the contemporary rumours that Collins was a man of unbalanced mind, whose spells of insanity were attributed the unhealthy nature of the subjects which he had chosen to study.[60] Editing Collins' poems after his early death, John Langhorne remarked that the unfortunate poet had been 'wholly carried away' by his love of 'gothic *diableries*'.[61]

While Collins was writing his invocation to Fear in England, Burke was penning a more philosophical approach to the same topic in Dublin. His *Enquiry* was a contribution to the already well-established genre of eighteenth-century aesthetic theory dealing with the sublime: that quality of greatness or grandeur in art and nature which serves to uplift and overwhelm the mind of the observer. Before Burke, the sublime had been primarily associated with the qualities of magnitude, infinitude, divinity, and moral excellence. But Burke, while building on these accepted definitions, gave the sublime a new and distinctive interpretation of his own:

Whatever is fitted in any sort to excite the ideas of pain and danger, that is to say, whatever is in any sort terrible, or is conversant about terrible objects, or operates in a manner analogous to terror, is a source of the *sublime;* that is, it is productive of the strongest emotion which the mind is capable of feeling. I say the strongest emotion, because I am satisfied the ideas of pain are much more powerful than those which enter on the part of pleasure.[62]

Here, Burke makes two claims which would go on to be of crucial importance to Gothic literature; first, that 'whatever is in any sort terrible…is a source of the *sublime*', and second, that the effect of sublimity generated by terrifying phenomena is 'the strongest emotion which the mind is capable of feeling'. No prior writer on the sublime – and by the 1740s there had been several – had linked sublimity to terror so specifically. Burke may well have been aware of the works of John Dennis, who had written in his *Grounds of Criticism* (1704) that 'We Name those things wonderful, which we Admire with fear', and that 'Enthusiastick Terror contributes extreamely to the Sublime': but although Dennis had proclaimed the sublimity of whatever was most grand and passionate in man and nature, including such terrifying spectacles as rages and storms, Burke was the first to argue that terror was the basic and necessary foundation of the sublime, rather than one of many possible triggers capable of evoking feelings of sublimity.[63] For Burke, the sublime flows directly from fear; it is the name of that aesthetic response called forth by witnessing awesome displays of force, whether they happen to be unleashed by nature, man, or God, and it stems from our knowledge of how easily such forces could obliterate us if they happened to be turned in our direction. Prior to Burke, accounts of why terrifying spectacles might be aesthetically pleasing generally hinged on something other than their fearsomeness: a storm might be pleasing because of its magnitude, the horrible fate of a tragedy's villain might be pleasing because of its justice, and so on.[64] But in Burke's account, a fearsome scene can be aesthetically pleasing *simply because it is fearsome;* indeed, a sufficiently terrifying scene can, simply by being superlatively scary, be 'productive of the strongest emotion which the mind is capable of feeling'.

Living two-and-a-half centuries on from the invention of Gothic fiction, the idea that one might gain aesthetic pleasure from watching or reading about horrific or terrifying scenes has become so familiar that it takes something of an imaginative effort to recognise how counter-intuitive the existence of such a pleasure truly is. We generally try hard to avoid actual exposure to violence, disasters, and other terrifying events; so why should we enjoy them if we happen to be spectators rather than actual participants? As already mentioned, the writers of the British Enlightenment had generally argued that most people *don't* enjoy watching such things, and that people who do *shouldn't*: that an appetite for horror as horror, unconnected to any spiritual or moral purpose, was a barbarous taste unfit for a civilised age, laden with dangerous consequences for society. In his *Theory of Moral Sentiments*, published in 1759 (two years after Burke's *Enquiry*), Adam Smith would argue that our capacity to imagine and share in the feelings of those around us forms the very foundation of morality; in a properly constituted mind, witnessing a scene of violence or suffering should make us suffer, too.[65] But Burke argued that to take pleasure in terrifying scenes was not monstrous but natural, indeed healthy; that the shock to the senses provided by such sublime events served to exercise the nerves, preventing them from falling into a 'relaxed state' that could lead one to take a 'gloomy view of things', culminating ultimately in 'melancholy, dejection, despair, and often self-murder'.[66] In Burke's account, it is not the man who exposes himself, like Collins, to the representation of ghastly scenes who is in danger of 'self-murder', but the man who does not; by shunning the manly aesthetic of the sublime for the merely beautiful, such a person allows themselves to become weak and enfeebled, and ultimately risks subsiding into suicidal depression as their energies prove unequal to the strains of life. Addressing the apparent paradox of how a scene can be delightful to observe if it would be hellish to experience, Burke writes:

> When danger or pain press too nearly, they are incapable of giving any delight, and are simply terrible; but at certain distances, and with certain modifications, they may be, and they are, delightful, as we every day experience.[67]

Burke's central literary examples for his sublime, the Bible and the infernal books of *Paradise Lost*, serve to illustrate this point. It is obviously not 'delightful' to actually be damned to hell; there would be little point in damning people if it was. But it *can* be 'delightful' to *read* about such damnations, if they are presented with 'certain distances, and with certain modifications'. Placed at a sufficient remove, terror becomes sublime: viewed from far enough away, terrible events cease to cause deranging horror, and become instead a source of healthy, invigorating exercise for the nervous system. Hell is horrific: but on a stage, or in a book, or at a distance, it can also be sublime.

In the 1740s, Burke and Collins were cultural outliers. The Hanoverian British state was still fighting for its life, battling foreign empires abroad and armed rebellions at home, and its highest arbiters of taste did not view scenes of gratuitous terror as suitable forms of entertainment; instead, they favoured works which would display and promote the good, the beautiful, and the true, so that society might be improved and all this fear and bloodshed consigned to the past. In 1746–7 it was still possible for a man of property such as William Boyd to rise in arms against the state in favour of a rival claimant to the throne, lead his followers into battle, fight against the King's armies in a full-scale engagement on British soil, be defeated, captured, tried for high treason, and ultimately beheaded on Tower Hill, at the very spot where identical dramas had been played out centuries before.[68] It had been a Stuart king, James I, who had written the *Daemonologie*, and it had been during and between the reigns of Stuart monarchs that the worst of the witch-hunts had taken place; so in 1746, with the repeal of James' Witchcraft Act only eleven years old and the Crown of England still violently contested by the armies of a Stuart king, it can hardly have seemed self-evident that such Gothic darkness now belonged only to the past. But, as Favret points out, such scenes were rapidly being consigned to history:

> After the defeat of Stuart loyalists at Culloden in 1745, distance – either geophysical or temporal – was increasingly built into the British nation's understanding of war. War on home turf happened back then; it was history. If it occurred now, it occurred beyond the reach of eyes and ears, somewhere else, over there.[69]

Both Burke and Collins seem to have sensed this shift; Burke with his concern that the major psychological threat facing his contemporaries was not too much but too little exposure to fear and hardship, and Collins with his assumption that the patriotic fearlessness he attributed to Aeschylus was something exceptional and heroic, rather than part of the ordinary moral and civic duty that every man might expect to be called upon to demonstrate. But it was precisely this sort of distance from the fearful realities of violence which, according to Burke, formed a necessary precondition for the aesthetic contemplation of 'danger and pain'; and it was only once Britain had become the sort of place in which wars could be relied upon to happen 'over there' rather than here and now, it proved fertile ground for the growth of a literature of terror.

One marker of this cultural change was the career of Thomas Warton. A decade younger than Mason, Walpole, and Gray, Warton had been an early adopter of the new antiquarianism they heralded; in 1745, at the age of just seventeen, he had written a lengthy poem on 'The Pleasures of Melancholy', praising the then-unfashionable romances of Spenser. This poem, like Collin's 'Ode' – which was published in the same year – dwelt at some length on scenes of horror and the supernatural, without immediately shutting them down as the graveyard poets so invariably did. Here is Warton imagining himself, like Addison, visiting the reputedly haunted ruin of an abbey:

But when the world
Is clad in Midnight's raven-colour'd robe,
'Mid hollow charnel let me watch the flame
Of taper dim, shedding a livid glare
O'er the wan heaps; while airy voices talk
Along the glimm'ring walls; or ghostly shape
At distance seen, invites with beck'ning hand
My lonesome steps, thro' the far-winding vaults.[70]

Like Collins, the adolescent Warton *wills* himself to believe in the ghosts that may haunt the abbey's vaults. These ghosts, like the spirits in whom Addison and Johnson were willing to believe, at least do nothing worse than talking or beckoning, but Warton's poem soon leads him to more ghastly scenes:

Hail, sacred Night! thou too shalt share my song!
Sister of ebon-sceptr'd Hecat, hail!
Whether in congregated clouds thou wrapp'st
Thy viewless chariot, or with silver crown
Thy beaming head encirclest, ever hail!
What though beneath thy gloom the sorceress-train,
Far in obscured haunt of Lapland moors,
With rhymes uncouth the bloody cauldron bless;
Though Murder wan beneath thy shrouding shade
Summons her slow-eyed vot'ries to devise
Of secret slaughter, while by one blue lamp
In hideous conf'rence sits the list'ning band,
And start at each low wind...[71]

Like Collins, Warton's use of these scenes of horror is implicitly justified by the examples of Shakespeare and Milton, both of whom are explicitly singled out for praise elsewhere in the poem, and both of whom are alluded to here: Warton's 'Hail, sacred Night!' is an obvious echo of Milton's famous 'Hail holy Light' from book three of *Paradise Lost*, while the Lapland sorceresses blessing their cauldron 'with rhymes uncouth' are derived both from Milton's 'Lapland witches', who summon the 'night-hag' with 'the smell of infant blood' in *Paradise Lost* book two, and the chanting, cauldron-blessing witches in *Macbeth*.[72] There is nothing here to imply that Warton believes that the witches of Lapland actually possess any supernatural powers, but the relish with which he imagines them chanting around their 'bloody cauldron', and the 'slow-eyed' murderers gathering to plot 'secret slaughter' around their 'one blue lamp', is unmistakable. Warton's enthusiasms for such material never left him, and although his mature work never again returned to the kind of horrors that he clearly enjoyed so much as an adolescent, he would go on to champion the old traditions of Gothic chivalric romance in both prose and verse; as well as writing critical works on Spenser and the history of English poetry from the eleventh century onwards, he wrote poems in honour of Stonehenge ('Thou noblest monument of Albion's isle!'), the Round Table, and King Arthur's grave. In his late poem 'Verses on Sir Joshua Reynold's Painted Window at New College, Oxford' (1782), he described himself as 'enamour'd of a barbarous age', one who loved to 'With Gothic manners Gothic arts explore/And muse on the magnificence of yore', and he praised Reynolds for having been able to 'reconcile/The willing Graces to the Gothic pile', working with the college's Gothic architectural heritage rather than against it. In his *History of English Poetry*, Warton even argued that superstitious beliefs could be artistically beneficial: 'Ignorance and superstition, so opposite to the real interest of human society, are the parents of imagination.'[73] Yet far from being marginalised by his Gothic enthusiasms, Warton enjoyed a highly successful academic and literary career, becoming Professor of Poetry at Oxford in 1757 and ultimately Poet Laureate in 1785.[74]

After 1746, as decade after decade elapsed in relative domestic peace, the idea that an art of deliberate terror might have a place in a civilised society began to gain ground. In his ode *Melpomene* – published in 1757, within a year of the publication of Burke's *Enquiry*, John Home's immensely popular medieval Scottish tragedy *Douglas*, and Thomas Gray's gory and fantastical ode, 'The Bard' – Robert Dodsley enumerated 'the *types* of every *theme* that suits the TRAGIC STRAIN', among which were, naturally, plenty of scenes of terror: ghosts, murderers, ruthless avengers, dead bodies, and so on. In Dodsley's account, the creation of terror is by no means the whole duty of tragedy, and indeed he considers it a rare achievement to be able to make unpleasant subject matter anything other than unpleasant to watch: the gift offered by Melpomene, the Muse of Tragedy, to her favoured poets is the revelation of 'the source/*To few reveal'd*, where human sorrows charm' (my italics), implying that in the hands of most writers, human sorrows are not at all charming, merely sorrowful. In accordance with standard eighteenth-century drama criticism, Dodsley considers the secret of accomplishing this feat to lie in staying true to 'nature', maintaining a proper balance between '*Terror*' and '*Compassion*', and ultimately producing a work with a clear moral purpose, which will teach its audience 'to feel for others woe, or nobly bear their own'.[75] But Dodsley clearly does consider that the ability to evoke intense terror in an audience is at least one of the qualifications a great tragedian requires, and he himself writes of those terrors in language strongly reminiscent of Collins' 'Ode to Fear':

> Ah! whither Goddess! whither am I bourne?
> To what wild region's necromantic shore?
> These pannicks whence? and why my bosom torne
> With sudden terrors never felt before?
> Darkness inwraps me round,
> While from the vast profound
> Emerging spectres dreadful shapes assume,
> And gleaming on my sight, add horror to the gloom.[76]

Yet Dodsley, despite all his enthusing about the 'necromantic shore', 'sudden terrors', and 'spectres dreadful', was not, like Collins, a man on the fringes of the literary culture of his day. On the contrary, he was a well-established and eminently respectable writer and bookseller, then in his mid-fifties; he had known Pope, he had published works by Johnson, Gray, Walpole, and Young, and within a year he would hire the still youthful Edmund Burke as the editor of his new periodical, *The Annual Register*.

This growing interest in scenes of literary terror arose alongside another, connected, phenomenon: the burgeoning interest in patriotic antiquarianism, heralded by the historically themed works of Mason, Walpole, Gray, and Home, which would go on to produce Percy's *Reliques of Ancient English Poetry* (1765), Macpherson's *Ossian* (1760–5), and Chatterton's 'Rowley' poems (written 1769–70).[77] When, in 1737, Elizabeth Cooper had compiled her *Muses Library* of poems from the fourteenth, fifteenth, and sixteenth centuries, she had taken a strictly teleological view of the development of English poetry, in which medieval poetic practices were primitive and absurd, modern poetic practices were correct and refined, and medieval poets such as Chaucer were praised, not as exemplars of their own (barbaric) culture, but as stepping-stones on the way to modernity: as she wrote in her preface, 'so many and variously-accomplish'd Minds were necessary to remove the *Gothique* Rudeness that was handed down to us by our unpolished Fore-Fathers'.[78] But by the 1760s this automatic contempt for '*Gothique* Rudeness' was starting to change, as patriotic writers, eager to establish their own culture as a worthy rival to Greece and Rome, had started to extol the value of Britain's ancient 'Gothic' inheritance: in his 1762 *Letters on Chivalry and Romance* Bishop Hurd even praised the 'Gothic' culture and mythology of ancient northern Europe for being more sublime and terrifying than that of the Greeks, a superiority he attributed to its origins in the dark and frozen lands of Scandinavia.[79] Walpole himself was a leading member of the simultaneous (and similarly patriotically motivated) Gothic revival in architecture, steadily turning his house at Strawberry Hill into 'a little Gothic castle' from 1749 to 1776, and thereby establishing a model that would become increasingly popular with architects over the following decades.[80] This new spirit of patriotic antiquarian revivalism ensured that by the time Walpole published *Otranto* in 1764, bloody old stories about wars and ghosts and murders long ago were no longer regarded as inherently barbarous and unsuitable for civilised readers, as they might have been just a few decades before.[81] It was in this post-Augustan (or pre-Romantic) cultural climate, building on the literary and architectural foundations established by Walpole, informed by the new patriotic antiquarianism of mid-century scholarship and by the aesthetics of sublime terror described by Burke, that Gothic began to emerge as a recognisable literary genre.

III

The history of eighteenth-century Gothic fiction is often presented as a smooth progression from Walpole to the major Gothic novelists of the 1790s, with the Gothic literature of the 1770s and 1780s simply an intermediary step between the two; yet such a narrative overlooks the major discontinuities between the Gothic literature written in the years following the publication of *The Castle of Otranto*, and that which arose in the years immediately after the French Revolution. In the 1790s, Gothic would become a major and popular literary genre in Britain; numerous Gothic novels would be published every year, the most successful of them attaining colossal popularity and international fame. But in the 1770s and 1780s Gothic was a much more minor form, attracting fewer readers and far less critical attention; and so it might well have remained, had the events of the French Revolution not given the genre a new relevance to the last years of the eighteenth century.

The familiar claim that the Gothic novel begins with Walpole gives the misleading impression that, from 1764 onwards, a self-conscious literature of terror existed in English: a literature that, like the Gothic fiction of the nineteenth and twentieth centuries, aimed to shock, frighten, disturb, and horrify its readers. Yet even a brief exploration of the 'Gothic' literature of the 1770s and 1780s suffices to show that this is not the case; these works form part of a literature of terror only insofar as they have subsequently been assimilated to a later and larger genre of Gothic fiction. It is true that Walpole emphasised the importance of terror in *The Castle of Otranto*, and in the preface to its first edition he described its effects in terms of the familiar Aristotelian theory of tragedy:

> Terror, the author's principle engine, prevents the story from ever languishing; and it is so often contrasted by pity, that the mind is kept up in a constant vicissitude of interesting passions.[82]

According to contemporary interpretations of Aristotle, the tragic scene should serve to purge its audience through pity and fear. Yet Walpole – still at this point pretending that he is merely its translator rather than its author – freely acknowledges that *Otranto* is deficient in tragic moral seriousness: terror is its 'principle engine', but the moral purpose that supposedly justifies all these terrifying events is slight:

> I am not blind to my author's defects. I could wish he had grounded his plan on a more useful moral than this; that *the sins of fathers are visited upon their children to the third and fourth generation*. I doubt whether in his time, any more than at present, ambition curbed its appetite of dominion from dread of so remote a punishment. And yet this moral is weakened by that less direct insinuation, that even such anathema may be diverted by devotion to saint Nicholas. Here the interest of the monk plainly gets the better of the judgement of the author.[83]

Walpole goes on to express his hope that 'the lessons of virtue that are inculcated' in *Otranto* will 'exempt this work from the censure to which romances are but too liable'; but, unlike contemporary authors of tragedy, he is clearly sceptical of the idea that the terrors of his story can serve any very useful moral purpose. If *Otranto* is to be useful at all, it is not because it teaches moral lessons, but because it keeps the reader's mind 'in a constant vicissitude of interesting passions': the sort of mental and emotional exercise that Burke had recommended to the inhabitants of over-peaceful nations such as Britain. Yet *Otranto* was unusual in thus prioritising terror over moral instruction, and few of the 'Gothic' novels that came after it followed its lead.

In *Contesting the Gothic*, James Watt argues convincingly that literary critics have tended to impose a false unity on the genre, linking together modes of fiction which at the time were regarded as largely unconnected.[84] Walpole's *Otranto*, like William

Beckford's later *Vathek* (1786) – which is often regarded today as a 'Gothic novel', despite being set in mythic Arabia rather than medieval Europe – was seen by its original readers as a 'wonder tale', the work of an eccentric antiquarian immersed in the legend-lore of a defunct civilisation. It was not coincidental that both Walpole and Beckford initially claimed that their works were translations of genuinely ancient material, from Italy and Arabia respectively: with their scenes of grotesque violence and blatant supernaturalism, both works stood well outside the main tradition of eighteenth-century British fiction. Such 'wonder tales' were very few and far between in these decades, and far from being the progenitor of a genre, *Otranto* was very nearly a literary dead end; for almost three decades it was regarded primarily as a mere curiosity, an essay in a fictional form generally regarded as obsolete. Even its sales seem to have rapidly declined: after running through three editions in the 1760s, no new edition of *The Castle of Otranto* was printed until 1782.[85] As Clery notes, 'The concept of a modern mode of "Gothic story" was seemingly immobilised by the reputation of Otranto as a one-off novelty or caprice.'[86]

The patriotic antiquarian vogue for all things medieval, however, continued to gather strength. Having begun to stir in the mid-1740s, in the years in which the defeat of the Jacobites and the end of executions on Tower Hill seemed to mark the steady disentanglement of Hanoverian Britain from its medieval past, it blossomed in popularity in the early 1770s, when the fall of the very last weather-beaten human skull from its spike atop Temple Bar appeared to confirm that the nation was in no danger of lapsing back into Gothic barbarism, and that the bloody chaos of the past had been truly left behind.[87] As the political threat of the past receded, its aesthetic appeal grew, leading to the slow growth of the fictional genre that Watt calls 'loyalist Gothic': historical 'romances' with medieval or Renaissance settings, capitalising on the contemporary taste for romantic antiquarianism, whose plots usually revolved around an aristocratic heir struggling to reclaim their birthright from a corrupt usurper. Perhaps the first example of this form was *The Hermitage*, by the topographer and antiquary William Hutchinson.[88] Published anonymously in York in 1772, this 'British story' told the story of a medieval lord who was driven from his estates by the schemes of a wicked monk, became a hermit, and ultimately returned to reclaim his title with the aid of a magical amulet blessed by one of his saintly ancestors. Like *Otranto* it was extravagantly supernatural, and the critical response was one of bewilderment at its peculiarity; it seems, like Walpole's novel, to have enjoyed only a brief popularity, being reprinted (still anonymously) under different titles in 1773 and 1775 before lapsing into complete obscurity, never to be subsequently republished.[89] Much more enduring popularity was enjoyed by Clara Reeve's *The Champion of Virtue* (1777, renamed *The Old English Baron* in its second and subsequent editions), which was described by its author as a deliberate re-writing of *Otranto*, one which aimed to strip away all Walpole's marvels and mayhem in order to reduce his story to a more acceptable form:

> This Story is the literary offspring of The Castle of Otranto, written upon the same plan...it is distinguished by the appellation of a Gothic Story, being a picture of Gothic times and manners.[90]

[Walpole's] machinery is so violent, that it destroys the effect it is intended to excite. Had the story been kept within the utmost *verge* of probability, the effect had been preserved, without losing the least circumstance that excites or detains the attention.[91]

Judging by the number of similar historical romances published over the next twenty years, Reeve's formulation of the 'Gothic Story' proved a great deal more popular and influential than Walpole's with the British reading public. Written against the backdrop of the American War of Independence and its aftermath, these romances generally asserted the moral validity of the monarchical order against which the Americans had rebelled: their historical settings were often idealised, and emphasised the legitimacy of the feudal social order they depicted, with evil and corruption resulting from usurpation, and social regeneration occurring once the true heir is returned to their rightful place. These works eschewed the kind of spectacular supernatural events that appeared in Walpole, Hutchinson, and Beckford's tales, and which, by appearing in them, had sentenced those authors to positions on the margins of contemporary literary culture; lucky coincidences, prophetic dreams, and the occasional discreet and benevolent ghost were generally as far as they were willing to go in this direction. Unlike Walpole's 'Gothic story' and Beckford's 'Oriental tale', these romances kept closely to the conventions of mainstream eighteenth-century fiction, and enjoyed an according popularity with the reading public: when William Lane, future founder of the Minerva Press, began to branch out into popular fiction publishing in the 1780s, such romances – easily identifiable by their titles, which usually included the words 'Castle', 'Abbey', or 'Baron' – already made up a substantial part of his list, and Robert Miles estimates that by 1788 they may have accounted for up to 30 per cent of new novels published in Britain.[92] But this popular genre of historical romance fiction did not constitute a literature of terror; these novels did not aim to frighten or disturb their readers, and the techniques of shock and suspense that would be popularised by Radcliffe in the 1790s are almost wholly absent from their pages. Terror may have been the 'principle engine' of *Otranto*, but *The Old English Baron* and its successors – which collectively represented the vast majority of Gothic fiction actually being written and read in Britain between 1777 and 1790 – drew upon more conventional sources of narrative power.

Together with the eccentric and largely ignored 'wonder tales' of Walpole, Hutchinson, and Beckford, and the popular but resolutely un-terrifying 'loyalist Gothic' of Reeve and her followers, modern historians of Gothic sometimes include under the heading of 'early Gothic novels' works from a much larger body of writing: sentimental fiction, which by the 1780s had become the dominant form of popular novel writing in English.[93] Derived ultimately from the works of Richardson and Prévost, which had enjoyed immense popularity in both France and Britain from the 1740s onwards, the sentimental novel generally centred on the story of a sensitive, virtuous hero or heroine forced to make their way through a treacherous world of hardship, sorrow, and deceit; the grand originals of the genre, Prévost's *Cleveland* (1739) and Richardson's *Clarissa* (1748), had been filled with tragedy, but in its popular form the sentimental novel of the later eighteenth century usually ended with the restoration of the protagonist to their rightful place in the world and their marriage to a partner as sensitive and virtuous as themselves. On the long and difficult road to happiness, however, the sentimental hero or heroine was often tempted and persecuted by the vicious and corrupt, who attempted to force them into bad marriages, seduce them into improper relationships, or cheat them of what is rightfully theirs. In those novels where this persecution is most persistent and most pronounced, the protagonist can come to seem besieged in a world of corruption, and for this reason modern critics sometimes describe sentimental novels such as Charlotte Smith's *Emmeline* (1788) or *The Old Manor-House* (1793) as Gothic or proto-Gothic; Hoeveler even writes that *Emmeline*, part of which actually takes place in a Gothic castle, 'is a sentimental novel with a gothic novel buried within it, struggling to emerge as a full-blown genre in its own right'.[94] But it would be highly misleading to class, say, *Emmeline*, *Vathek*, and *The Old English Baron* together as 'early Gothic novels'. It is true that all three fed into the genre of Gothic terror fiction which emerged in the 1790s; but readers in the 1780s regarded them as quite distinct. The sentimental novel had a modern setting, and a domestic plot hinging on marriage; the historical romance had an idealised historical setting, and a plot that hinged on murder or forgery; and the 'wonder tale' had a geographically and historically remote setting, and a fantastical plot that hinged on supernatural and impossible events. The sentimental novel and the historical romance were mainstream genres, largely written by women, which enjoyed wide popularity; the wonder tale was marginal, written by eccentric men (whose writings were taken as further proof of their eccentricity), and little read. Of the three, only the wonder tale could really be described as forming part of a self-conscious literature of terror, which aimed to scare and disorientate its readers; the rest, like almost all mainstream eighteenth-century fiction, aimed to instruct rather than to terrify, just as Johnson and Addison had recommended decades before. It is true that all three shared a preoccupation with matters of inheritance, often centred on grand old buildings and aristocratic estates, and with young women pursued by predatory men eager to seize their property, their persons, or both: but these two concerns run through virtually all eighteenth-century fiction, from Fielding and Richardson onwards, and their presence can hardly qualify a work for inclusion in the genre of Gothic fiction.

As I have discussed, Gothic motifs continued to enjoy substantial success in British culture more broadly during this period; Gothic revival architecture continued to flourish, while the enthusiasm for all things medieval even extending extended even to the staging of mock-tournaments, such as the Mischianza tournament famously held by British officers in Philadelphia in 1778 during the American War of Independence.[95] In the visual arts a growing taste for dark, 'picturesque', and fantastical compositions culminated in works such as Fuseli's *The Nightmare* (first exhibited in London in 1782) and Boydell's 'Shakespeare Gallery', which opened in 1789 and featured images of ghosts, witches, faeries, and murders painted by many of the leading artists of the day. The Gothic past had come to seem sufficiently remote that the cultural achievements of medieval Britain, such as Gothic architecture and customs, could start to be safely re-appropriated as proof of the nation's glorious history, or put to use as pro-government propaganda with which to combat the claims of the American rebels, and the artistic re-appropriation of Gothic 'superstition' followed a similar pattern. Addison and Locke, born into a world where it was still possible for people to be put to death for consorting with demonic spirits, had viewed the belief in such entities to be dangerous, destructive, and worthy of suppression. But for Walpole and his successors, living in an age when witchcraft was believed in only by the credulous and ignorant and such ghosts as still appeared seemed to have lost almost all their old violence, such beliefs were no more than quaint relics of a bygone age, a fit subject for amusement and scholarly curiosity rather than an active threat to all that was rational and just.[96]

However, it was a very heavily mediated 'medievalism' which was communicated to the readers of Walpole's *The Castle of Otranto*, and of the 'loyalist Gothic' romances which followed it. By the 1760s, the old demonological darkness of the past was no longer regarded as a threat to the present social order, but it was not thereby rendered appealing; to be admirable, or even acceptable, it had to be presented in a suitably modified form. Gothic revival architecture was not a genuine attempt to recreate the military and ecclesiastical architecture of the Middle Ages, murder holes and all; rather, it was an attempt to apply medieval stylings to the architecture of the mid-eighteenth century. The most important and successful literary product of eighteenth-century antiquarianism, Macpherson's *Ossian*, had a similar relationship to the legendary past upon which it drew; it was inspired by Scottish folklore, and heavily based on Homer's *Iliad*, but contained much less of the kind of extreme violence and overt supernaturalism which eighteenth-century readers found so problematic in both Homer's epics and medieval folklore, and was accordingly praised by its admirers as resembling a much less barbaric, and thus superior, version of its Ancient Greek original.[97] (Home's *Douglas* was praised as being superior to Shakespeare's tragedies on similar grounds: as Hume wrote, it possessed Shakespeare's 'true theatric genius' without his 'unhappy barbarism'.[98]) Walpole, enthusiast for Gothic revival architecture that he was, took a similar tack with *Otranto*; like *Ossian*, his novel *claimed* to be a genuine relic of the past, but in practice it presented its readers with a very modern version of the medieval, and thereby rendered itself more acceptable to them than its romance originals would have been. As the novel's initially marginal position in the genre it notionally founded demonstrates, there were still plenty of readers who found the supernatural grotesquery and arbitrary violence of *Otranto* to be objectionable; but even at its most bizarre, it remains very much a mid-eighteenth-century text. Aside from its fantastically outsized ghost, its characters are drawn on the human scale of eighteenth-century novels rather than the sublime scale of the old tragedy and romance heroes, of whom Walpole complains in his preface to the second edition:

> The actions, sentiments, conversations, of the heroes and heroines of ancient days were as unnatural as the machines employed to put them in motion [...] Desirous of leaving the powers of fancy at liberty to expatiate through the boundless realms of invention, and thence of creating more interesting situations, he [i.e. the author] wished to conduct the mortal agents in his drama according to the rules of probability; in short, to make them think, speak, and act, as it might be supposed mere men and women would do in extraordinary positions.[99]

As Patey points out, Walpole's assumptions in this passage are very much those of the contemporary critical orthodoxy, which regarded literary adherence to 'the rules of probability' as desirable, and 'unnatural' actions and conversations in fiction as inherently bad.[100] Walpole obviously deviated from that orthodoxy by including supernatural forces – the 'unnatural…machines' of 'ancient days' – in his novel, but the supernatural events in *Otranto* resemble the farrago of nonsense that the supernatural beliefs of the Middle Ages appeared to be when viewed from an educated eighteenth-century perspective, rather than actual medieval magical thinking: they are contrived and arbitrary, rather than being rooted in any coherent folkloric, occult, or theological system.[101] As Briggs writes:

> Fascinated by the world of medieval romance and determined to create a pastiche of it, as he had created a pastiche of Gothic architecture in his house at Strawberry Hill, [Walpole] recognised that such romance lacked the scientific logic of his own day, and therefore assumed that it lacked a logic of any kind.[102]

It is telling that the characters in *Otranto* are essentially terrorised by an assortment of medieval *props*, such as helmets, gauntlets, paintings, and swords, rather than by an actual spirit or monster as in most genuine medieval romances: its medieval setting is that of the antiquarian collector, who views the past primarily as a collection of fascinatingly strange objects – what Hogle calls 'signs only of older signs' – rather than as a living world that makes sense on its own terms.[103] In his writing, as in his house-building, Walpole presented his audience with the trappings of medievalism without requiring them to actually leave the comfort of their own century and engage with the medieval world itself.

As I have discussed above, until the later seventeenth century a well-established set of literary conventions existed for writing about evil and fear in English, which I have called the literature of 'theological evil'. In this literature, the extremes of human evil were referred, ultimately, to Satan and his demonic minions; those who performed evil acts were understood to be servants, consciously or otherwise, of the Evil One, and the proper response to them and to the fear they inevitably engendered in their victims was the faith and courage befitting of a Christian solider – and, if necessary, a Christian martyr. Both evil and the opposition to evil were thus grounded in transcendental, metaphysical structures of significance, in a continuous literary tradition running all the way from medieval romances, morality plays, and martyrologies to the works of Shakespeare, Bunyan, and Milton. This literature contained much that was terrible, but it was not a literature of terror in the way that the Gothic would later become, aiming to arouse pleasurable terror in its audience by depicting extremes of horror and fear. The scenes that would come to define Gothic art, in which the reader or viewer is invited to contemplate the awesome and baffling magnitude of the powers of evil and the utter helplessness of their victims, almost never occurred in this literature, for the entire point of this theology was that the victims of evil are *not* helpless, and in their deepest suffering have spiritual resources upon which they can draw which suffice to dwarf the power of their tormentors, as Christian discovers when he walks through the Valley of the Shadow of Death and escapes the Castle of Giant Despair in Bunyan's *Pilgrim's Progress*.[104] The villains of this literature may inspire fear, contempt, or defiance, but never the kind of terrified awe with which Gothic hero-villains are habitually regarded by those around them, in the hope of arousing a corresponding shudder in the audience. It was a commonplace of early modern demonology that witches and demoniacs, however wicked and mighty they might be, lost all their powers when apprehended by the legitimate representatives of divine authority, such as magistrates and kings; and accordingly, though Macbeth, Apollyon, and Satan all channel the powers of hell itself, they can be (and are) defied by those who remain faithful and pure of heart, and all three are ultimately cast down by righteous warriors who fight in the name of God.[105]

This literature was very largely dismantled in the early eighteenth century, as the advocates of a new, rational Christianity sought to de-emphasise the importance of holy warfare against the followers of Antichrist, in the hope of encouraging forms of religion whose followers did not butcher one another with quite as much alacrity as they had displayed during the mid-seventeenth century. Evil was attributed to social forces, or failures of education and personal development, rather than demonic influence or simple, inexplicable innate wickedness; religion was still sincerely commended to those in adversity, but proper Christian behaviour was now likely to be seen as consisting of taking a rational and balanced view of the situation and working to alleviate it, rather than taking up the cross and marching to martyrdom or victory against the legions of Hell. Samuel Richardson, second only to Defoe as the most popular novelist of the early eighteenth century, gave the age both its archetypal hero and its archetypal villain in the forms of Grandison and Lovelace, respectively, and the contrast between both and their sixteenth- or seventeenth-century counterparts is striking. Compared to Satan, Macbeth, Barabas, or Diabolus, Lovelace is positively timid in his acts of evil, wavering, uncertain, torn between his better nature and his over-mastering desires; it is part of Richardson's point that a better education, a little more empathy and self-control, would have sufficed to make Lovelace a good man, whereas it is hard to imagine anything short of a Damascene conversion sufficing to redeem these earlier villains from their careers of Satanic atrocity. Compared to Christian, Macduff, or Milton's loyal angels, Grandison is a vastly more restrained, polite figure, for whom true Christian speech takes the form of reasoned argument rather than battle-hymns; when challenged to a duel by the sinful kidnapper Pollexfen, he counters not by invoking Christ and running the miscreant through the body, but by laying out for his would-be adversary a point-by-point explanation of why he believes the practice of duelling to be irrational, un-Christian, and injurious to society, complete with references to history and scripture. (It is a mark of Richardson's commitment to the power of rational Christianity that this argument actually has the effect of winning Pollexfen over, rather than merely provoking him to stab Grandison to death at the next opportunity.)[106] Prior to the rise of Gothic fiction, the period thus had no literature of radical evil and fear at all, and tended to view terror as an entirely illegitimate (and irrational) response to any situation whatsoever.

The Gothic literature of terror, which Walpole pioneered, harked back in some ways to the old literature of theological evil, which over the course of the previous three generations had been largely swept away. But it did not truly represent a return to the old ways, and would probably never have won even the limited acceptance it found among mid-eighteenth-century readers if it had; the cultural world which had produced that literature had, by then, grown much too remote, and very few of Walpole's first readers were likely to have felt (as, say, most of Milton's first readers probably did) that the world was a battleground between the armies of Christ and Antichrist, stalked by powerful and dangerous supernatural beings, in which it was the duty of every Christian to play a soldier's part in the cosmic war that raged around them. Walpole's ghosts, heroes, and villains are not tethered to any overarching metaphysical structure, and the assumptions in which they are rooted are those of the eighteenth rather than the sixteenth century; and for this very reason, just as *Ossian* and *Douglas* were able to provide versions of epic and tragedy acceptable to the times, so *Otranto* was able to provide a new model for a literature of evil and fear. Yet, unlike *Ossian, Otranto* was by no means an immediate success, and the very idea of such a literature of fear remained marginal for some decades after its publication.

When we now read *The Castle of Otranto*, or *Vathek*, or *The Old English Baron*, our readings of them are inevitably coloured by our knowledge of what happened later, and our awareness that they stand at the fountainhead of a genre which would go on to have major significance for Western culture as a whole. But it is unlikely that any observer in the 1780s, however perceptive, would have expected so relatively insignificant a literary form as the Gothic novel – insofar as such a form was even recognisable within the literary landscape of that period – to have any future worth considering. As late as 1789 these novels, set in the barbarous past and sometimes awash with blatantly supernatural events, probably still seemed to be nothing more than a minor side effect of the recent craze for all things primitive, medieval, and uncouth; and the form could easily have died out altogether, had not a series of cataclysmic historical events brought horror, violence, fear, and the unnatural squarely back into the centre of every reader's concerns.

The events in question were, of course, those of the French Revolution.

Notes

1 On Walpole's dream, see Timothy Mowl, *Horace Walpole: The Great Outsider* (London: John Murray, 1996), pp. 127, 182–3.
2 Horace Walpole, letter to William Cole, 9 March 1765, in W.S. Lewis and A. Dayle Wallace eds., *Correspondence* (London: Oxford UP, 1937), vol. 1, p. 88.
3 John Dunlop, *The History of Fiction* (Edinburgh, 1814), vol. 3, p. 380.
4 On the European reputation of seventeenth-century British tragedy, see Clarence Green, *Neo-Classic Theory of Tragedy in England* (Cambridge, MA: Harvard UP, 1934), pp. 37–8.
5 In the preface to the second edition of *Otranto*, Walpole identified his sources as, first, 'old Romances', and, second, the tragedies of Shakespeare. See Horace Walpole, *The Castle of Otranto*, ed. W.S. Lewis (Oxford: Oxford UP, 1996), pp. 9–12.
6 Walpole, *Castle*, p. 5.
7 On Walpole's hoax, see Emma Clery, 'Against Gothic' in Alan Lloyd Smith and Victor Sage, eds., *Gothick Origins* (Amsterdam: Rodopi, 1994), pp. 36–43.
8 David Punter, 'Social relations of Gothic fiction', in David Aers, ed., *Romanticism and Ideology* (London: Routledge and Kegan Paul, 1981), p. 103.

9   On the population of Europe in the eighteenth century, see Jeremy Black, *Eighteenth-Century Europe* (Basingstoke: Macmillan, 1999), p. 1. On the bloodiness of eighteenth-century battles, see Jeremy Black, *European Warfare, 1660–1815* (London: UCL Press, 1994), pp. 111–12, 134–6.

10 On the dramatic decline in murder rates in London over the course of the eighteenth century, see Robert Shoemaker, *The London Mob* (London: Hambledon and London, 2004), pp. 170–1. On the massive, continent-wide decline in public violence during this period, see Manuel Eisner, 'Long-term historical trends in violent crime', *Crime and Justice: A Review of Research*, vol. 30 (2003), pp. 83–142.

11 Chitra Reddin, *Forms of Evil in the Gothic Novel* (New York: Ayer, 1980), pp. 12–13.

12 Phillip Hallie, *Cruelty*, revised edition (Middletown, CT: Wesleyan UP, 1982), p. 15.

13 See, for example, Tobias Smollett, *The Adventures of Ferdinand Count Fathom*, ed. Paul-Gabriel Boucé (London: Penguin, 1990), chapters 49 and 67.

14 Henry Fielding, *Tom Jones*, ed. John Bender and Simon Stern (Oxford: Oxford UP, 1996), Dedication, p. 5.

15 Fielding, *Tom Jones*, p. 5.

16 On early modern political demonology, see Stuart Clark, *Thinking with Demons* (Oxford: Clarendon, 1997), pp. 358–62, 384–8, 560.

17 Diane Purkiss, *The English Civil War* (London: Harper Perennial, 2006), p. 3, Geoffrey Parker, *The Thirty Years War* (London: Routledge and Kegan Paul, 1984), pp. 210–11.

18 On the limited nature of eighteenth-century wars, see J.O. Lindsay, ed., *The Old Regime* (Cambridge: Cambridge UP, 1957), pp. 164–6, and Mary Favret, *War at a Distance* (Princeton, NJ: Princeton UP, 2010), p. 16.

19 Joseph Addison, 'Spectator 7', in Donald Bond, ed., *The Spectator* (Oxford: Clarendon, 1965), vol. 1, p. 41.

20 Frank Manuel, *The Eighteenth Century Confronts the Gods* (Cambridge, MA: Harvard UP, 1959), p. 125; Margaret Jacob, *The Radical Enlightenment* (London: Allen and Unwin, 1981), p. 101. On the general turning away of Enlightenment thinkers from the versions of Christianity they had inherited from the seventeenth century, see Peter Gay, *The Enlightenment* (London: Wildwood House, 1973), vol. 1.

21 James I's Witchcraft Act, which had sent so many to their deaths in the 1640s, was repealed in 1735 by a new law which forbade anyone from being prosecuted for 'Witchcraft, Sorcery, Inchantment, or Conjuration'; the use of supernatural powers was no longer illegal, because it was no longer believed to be possible. The same law made it illegal to defraud 'ignorant Persons' by pretending to possess such abilities, transforming witchcraft from a problem of spiritual corruption to a problem of public education; the practice of black magic was viewed as socially harmful not because witches and demons were real, but because people were too ill-educated and credulous to know that they were not. See 9 George II, Chapter 5, in *The Statutes*, 3rd revised edition, vol. 1, p. 547 (London: HMSO, 1950). On changing beliefs regarding the afterlife in this period, see Philip Almond, *Heaven and Hell in Enlightenment England* (Cambridge: Cambridge UP, 1994). On the de-mystifying, anti-Gothic project of Addison and his contemporaries, see Robert Geary, 'From providence to terror', in Donald Morse ed., *The Fantastic in World Literature* (Westport: Greenwood, 1987), pp. 11–13.

22 'The grounds of criticism in tragedy', in John Dryden, *Of Dramatic Poesy and Other Critical Essays*, ed. George Watson (London: Dent, 1962), p. 248.

23 J. Paul Hunter, *Before Novels* (New York: W.W. Norton and Co., 1990), pp. 84–5.

24   On the attack on traditional ghost stories and fairy tales in Enlightenment educational writings, see Hunter, pp. 144–8.

25   John Locke, *Some Thoughts Concerning Education* (London, 1693), pp. 159–60.

26   Addison, 'Spectator 110', in *The Spectator*, vol. 1, p. 454.

27   Addison, 'Spectator 26', in *The Spectator*, vol. 1, pp. 109–11.

28   Samuel Johnson, *Life of Milton*, in Donald Greene, ed., *Major Works* (Oxford: Oxford UP, 2000), p. 710.

29   Johnson, *The Rambler*, number 4, in *Major Works*, p. 177. On eighteenth-century discomfort with heroic villains, see Marlies Danziger, 'Heroic villains', *Comparative Literature*, vol. 11 (1959), pp. 35–46.

30   On Addison's willingness to believe in spirits, see 'Spectator 7', 12 and 110', on Johnson's, see James Boswell, *Life of Johnson*, ed. R.W. Chapman (London: Oxford UP, 1970), pp. 900, 951. It is hard to be sure of Defoe's true beliefs on any subject, but his *History of the Devil*, *Essay on the History and Reality of Apparitions*, and *Relation of the Apparition of Mrs Veal* suggest some such beliefs: see Riccardo Capoferro, *Empirical Wonder* (Bern: Peter Lang, 2010), pp. 129–30. On belief in the supernatural in this period more generally, and the declining belief in the reality of witchcraft and demonic possession among the educated elite, see Patricia Spacks, *The Insistence of Horror* (Cambridge, MA: Harvard UP, 1962), pp. 3, 9, 11–27, 133, and Sasha Handley, *Visions of an Unseen World* (London: Pickering and Chatto, 2007), chapter 4.

31   On the dialogues, see Frederick Keener, *English Dialogues of the Dead* (New York: Columbia UP, 1973). On the Cock Lane ghost affair, and Johnson's role in it, see Douglas Grant, *The Cock Lane Ghost* (New York: St Martin's Press, 1965).

32   Addison, 'Spectator 12'. In a similar vein, Richard Baxter had asserted in 1691 that 'we may know (what must suffice us,) 1. That no Spirits can do any thing, but by God's Will or Permission. 2. And that God will never permit them eventually to frustrate his Love and Mercy to his People, nor to break any one of his Promises to them.' See Owen Davies, ed., *Ghosts: A Social History* (London: Pickering and Chatto, 2010), vol. 1, p. 56.

33   Baron de Montesquieu, *The Spirit of the Laws*, trans. Thomas Nugent (New York: Hafner, 1949), book three: 9, p. 26.

34   Johnson, *The Rambler*, number 4, p. 178.

35   It was commonly asserted at the time that, before the Reformation, the Catholic clergy had deliberately encouraged the belief in 'Lying Stories of Apparitions' – and even staged apparently ghostly manifestations – in order to strengthen belief in purgatory, and to encourage people to donate money to the Church in the hope that they could thereby ease the torments of their dead loved ones. See Davies, vol. 1, pp. x, 129–30.

36   On Lovelace, see Susan Weisser, *A 'Craving Vacancy'* (New York: New York UP, 1997), pp. 44–5.

37   On the deliberate, anti-supernatural realism of the early eighteenth-century novel, see Ian Watt, *The Rise of the Novel* (London: Chatto and Windus, 1957), chapter 1, and Hunter, pp. 23–4.

38   Fielding, *Tom Jones*, pp. 346, 348.

39   Fielding, pp. 348–9.

40   Johnson, *The Rambler*, number 4, p. 175.

41   Samuel Richardson, *Clarissa*, ed. Angus Ross (London: Penguin, 1985), p. 352.

42   Richardson, pp. 63, 70, 161.

43   Boswell, p. 1079; Green, pp. 187–193.

44 On eighteenth-century discomfort with the hero-villains of early modern tragedy, see Frans De Bruyn, 'Hooking the Leviathan', *The Eighteenth Century*, vol. 28, number 3 (1987), pp. 195–215.

45 John Dennis, *The Advancement and Reformation of Modern Poetry;* quoted in Green, p. 139.

46 Spacks points out that although these poems made copious use of ghosts, they almost always deployed them as props or scenery rather than actors, and usually described them in stock poetic language that changed very little from poem to poem. See Spacks, pp. 83–4.

47 Thomas Parnell, 'A night-piece on death', in Claude Rawson and F.P. Lock, eds., *Collected Poems* (Newark: University of Delaware Press, 1989), p. 170.

48 Addison, '*Spectator* 26', in *The Spectator*, vol. 1, pp. 109–11.

49 Robert Blair, *The Grave* (London: Methuen, 1903), p. 3.

50 On the persistent attribution of supernatural beliefs to rustic characters in this period, see Spacks, pp. 31–2, 52–6.

51 Edmund Burke, *A Philosophical Enquiry into the Origins of our Ideas of the Sublime and Beautiful*, ed. James Boulton (Notre Dame, IN: University of Notre Dame Press, 1968), pp. xv–xix.

52 William Collins, 'Ode to Fear', in Richard Wendorf and Charles Ryskamp, eds., *Works* (Oxford: Clarendon, 1979), p. 27.

53 Collins, *Works*, p. 28.

54 Collins, *Works*, pp. 28–9.

55 Collins, *Works*, p. 29.

56 Fielding, *Tom Jones*, p. 752.

57 William Shakespeare, *Hamlet*, ed. Harold Jenkins (London: Methuen, 1982), p. 176. Collins may also be thinking here of Milton's 'Il Penseroso', with its 'daemons that are found/In fire, air, flood, or under ground': see John Milton, *Complete Poems*, ed. John Leonard (London: Penguin, 1998), p. 28. Milton may have been thinking, in turn, of *Hamlet*, but this need not be assumed; in his day, as in Shakespeare's, the old Hermetic lore that associated different spirits with different elements was still a living intellectual tradition, whereas by the time Collins wrote his 'Ode' it was primarily known only from old poems, and from Pope's satires on such pneumatology in *The Rape of the Lock*.

58 On Voltaire's critique of Shakespeare, see Voltaire, *Commentaires sur Corneille*, ed. David Williams, in *Complete Works* (Oxford: Voltaire Foundation, 1974), vol. 53, pp. 275–95. On the eighteenth-century cult of Shakespeare, and its significance for the development of Gothic, see Diane Hoeveler, *Gothic Riffs* (Columbus, OH: Ohio State UP, 2010), Chapter 1.

59 Johnson, p. 10.

60 E.J. Clery, 'The genesis of "Gothic" fiction', in J. Hogle, ed., *Cambridge Companion to Gothic Fiction* (Cambridge: Cambridge UP, 2002), p. 28.

61 Quoted in Spacks, p. 80.

62 Edmund Burke, *Writings and Speeches*, ed. Paul Langford (Oxford: Clarendon, 1981–2000), vol. 1, pp. 216–17.

63 John Dennis, *The Grounds of Criticism in Poetry* (London, 1704), pp. 44, 85.

64 On eighteenth-century accounts of the pleasure to be gained from witnessing justice done in tragedies, see Green, p. 234.

65 Adam Smith, *The Theory of Moral Sentiments* (London, 1759), Part 1:1, pp. 1–2.

66 Burke, *Writings*, vol. 1, p. 288.

67   Burke, *Writings*, vol. 1, p. 217.
68   As if to prove that Britain in 1746–7 could hardly be said to have definitively freed itself of the superstitious darkness of the past, the clergyman who accompanied Boyd in his final hours subsequently claimed to have been visited by Boyd's repentant ghost on the day after his execution. See Handley, p. 154.
69   Favret, p. 10.
70   Thomas Warton, 'Pleasures of Melancholy', in *Poetical Works* (Farnborough: Gregg International Publishers, 1969), vol. 1, pp. 72–3.
71   Warton, *Poetical Works*, vol. 1, pp. 78–80.
72   Milton, *Complete Poems*, pp. 159, 171.
73   Thomas Warton, *The History of English Poetry* (London, 1774), vol. 2, p. 462.
74   H.C.G. Matthew and Brian Harrison, eds., *Oxford Dictionary of National Biography* (Oxford: Oxford UP, 2004), vol. 57, pp. 518–21.
75   Robert Dodsley, *Melpomene* (London, 1757), pp. 4, 14.
76   Dodsley, p. 5.
77   On patriotic antiquarianism, see Gerald Newman, *The Rise of English Nationalism* (London: Weidenfeld and Nicholson, 1987), pp. 109–118.
78   Elizabeth Cooper, *The Muses Library* (London, 1741), p. xii.
79   Richard Hurd, *Letters on Chivalry and Romance*, ed. Edith Morley (London: Henry Frowde, 1911), p. 110.
80   Mowl, p. 127.
81   Spacks points out, however, that eighteenth-century collections of traditional ballads often softened and sentimentalised the more horrific elements of their source material. See Spacks, p. 89.
82   Walpole, *Castle*, p. 6.
83   Walpole, *Castle*, p. 7.
84   James Watt, *Contesting the Gothic* (Cambridge: Cambridge UP, 1999). Chapter 2.
85   The first edition of *The Castle of Otranto* was printed for Thomas Lownds in 1764; the second for Lownds and William Bathoe in 1765, and the third for Bathoe alone in 1766. An edition 'printed for John Murray' in 1769 still identifies itself as 'the third edition', and is physically identical to Bathoe's 1766 edition. There were also four Dublin editions, all in 1765. After this, there were no new editions until Dodsley had the novel reprinted in 1782. This pattern of republication suggests that the vast majority of *Otranto*'s sales were made in the first two years after its publication; it was a brief literary 'event', rather than a much-read standard novel. In contrast, Clara Reeve's *Old English Baron* was steadily reprinted every few years, achieving six editions in fifteen years to compare with Walpole's four editions in eighteen. Tompkins states that Reeve's novel was reprinted thirteen times between 1778 and 1786: see J.M.S. Tompkins, *The Popular Novel in England, 1770–1800* (London: Methuen, 1962), p. 231.
86   E.J. Clery, *The Rise of Supernatural Fiction* (Cambridge: Cambridge UP, 1999), pp. 83–4.
87   On the last heads on Temple Bar, see Philip Connell, 'Death and the author', *Eighteenth Century Studies*, vol. 38, number 4 (2005), p. 558.
88   Hutchinson was also a Masonic author, and it is possible that the supernatural events depicted in *The Hermitage* – which keeps much more closely to the actual magical lore of the Middle Ages than *Otranto* – may have reflected the author's own occult beliefs: in his *Spirit of Masonry*, Hutchinson praised the legendary founder of Freemasonry, King Solomon, for being 'possessed of all the mystical knowledge of

the eastern nations'. See William Hutchinson, *The Spirit of Masonry* (London, 1775), p. 146. The extreme unfashionability of such magical beliefs in the 1770s may suggest one reason for *The Hermitage* being published anonymously.

89   On the reception of *The Hermitage*, see Anne Stevens, *British Historical Fiction Before Scott* (Basingstoke: Palgrave Macmillan, 2010), pp. 36–7.

90   Clara Reeve, *The Old English Baron* (London, 1788), p. iii.

91   Reeve, p. vi.

92   Dorothy Blakey, *The Minerva Press* (London: Oxford UP, 1939), pp. 273–80; Robert Miles, 'The 1790s: The effulgence of the Gothic', in Hogle, ed., *Companion*, and Leslie Fiedler, *Love and Death in the American Novel*, revised edition (Harmondsworth: Penguin, 1984), p. 42.

93   On the derivation of Gothic from sentimental fiction, see Peter De Voogd's 'Sentimental horrors', in Valeria Tinkler-Villani, ed., *Exhibited by Candlelight* (Amsterdam: Rodopi, 1995), pp. 76–88.

94   Diane Hoeveler, *Gothic Feminism* (Liverpool: Liverpool UP, 1998), p. 38. Charlotte Smith also helped to set the stage for the Gothic fiction of the 1790s through the wide success of her poetry, with its recurring backdrops of dark woods, night scenes, storms, graveyards, and shipwrecks. See, for example, Charlotte Smith, *Elegiac Sonnets*, ed. Jonathan Wordsworth (Oxford, 1992), pp. 12, 39, 43, 44, 47, and 54.

95   On the tournament, see Linda Colley, *Britons*, new edition (London: Pimlico, 2003), pp. 147–8.

96   On the declining violence of English ghosts, see Davies, vols 1 and 2. The seventeenth-century accounts of hauntings cited by Davies describe ghosts and spirits throwing people across rooms or high into the air, levitating objects, hurling stones, breaking windows, and inflicting paralysis or sickness on their victims; in the eighteenth century, they mostly contented themselves with knocking, murmuring, appearing and vanishing, or passing on supernatural messages. Their appearance also became much less alarming, with eighteenth-century ghosts tending to appear as ordinary humans, rather than, say, immense fire-breathing hell-hounds: compare, for example, Davies, vol. 1, pp. 45, 170–1. Stories of stranger and more dangerous apparitions – headless men, talking dogs, ghostly armies, and violently aggressive spirits – clearly did continue to circulate, however, especially among the provincial rural poor. See Handley, pp. 127, 129, 136, 157.

97   See Hugh Blair, 'A critical dissertation on the poems of Ossian', in James MacPherson, *The Poems of Ossian*, ed. Howard Gaskill (Edinburgh: Edinburgh UP, 1996), pp. 351–8, Herbert Tucker, *Epic* (Oxford: Oxford UP, 2008), pp. 40–1, and Elizabeth MacAndrew, *The Gothic Tradition in Fiction* (New York: Columbia UP, 1979), pp. 46–7.

98   David Hume, *Four Dissertations* (London, 1757), pp. v–vi.

99   Walpole, *Castle*, pp. 9–10.

100   Douglas Patey, *Probability and Literary Form* (Cambridge: Cambridge UP, 1984), pp. 159–60.

101   On the integration of the natural and supernatural worlds in pre-modern epic and romance, see Capoferro, pp. 38–52. On the eighteenth-century view of supernatural forces as basically arbitrary, 'suitable expressions of the unpredictable and unknowable', see Anne McWhir, 'The Gothic transgression of disbelief', in Kenneth Graham, ed., *Gothic Fictions* (New York: AMS Press, 1989), p. 31.

102   Julia Briggs, *Night Visitors* (London: Faber, 1977), p. 31. See also Geary, 'From providence to terror', p. 16: 'Walpole resorts to procedures that no longer contain

the numinous within a providential hierarchy, yet do not supply a coherent new pattern. Appearing in the form of bizarre omens and prodigies, in which neither author nor readers believe, the numinous [. . .] veers incongruously towards primitive religious terror'.

103   Hogle, 'Introduction', p. 15.

104   On early modern conceptions of spiritual evil as a flawed reflection of the divine, see Clark, Part I, and especially pp. 61–8.

105   On the belief that witches were powerless once apprehended by legitimate authority, and the early modern trope of the demonic sorcerer discovering himself to be powerless when confronted by a legitimate Christian king, see Clark, pp. 571–81 and chapter 42.

106   Samuel Richardson, *Sir Charles Grandison*, ed. Jocelyn Harris (Oxford: Oxford UP, 1986), Part I, pp. 247–71.

2

The Reign of Terror

I

When the French Revolution began and the Bastille fell in 1789, the general response in Britain was one of approbation; as Charles James Fox famously exclaimed, 'How much the greatest event it is that ever happened in the world! And how much the best!'[1] *The Times*, though deploring the violent scenes in Paris in July 1789, concurred that the Revolution had been impressively swift and bloodless: 'That a Revolution in France should be accomplished with so little bloodshed, and that the arbitrary power of one of the first despotic Governments of Europe should be destroyed so easily, will be a matter of surprise to posterity, as it is of admiration to the present age.'[2] For a time, it seemed as though France had miraculously thrown off its centuries of despotism, transforming itself at a stroke into a modern constitutional monarchy, a move which many in Britain thought would benefit both the French and the rest of the world; a free France, they hoped, would be less likely to start aggressive wars, and more willing to engage in free trade, to the mutual benefit of all nations that interacted with her.[3] But as events moved forward in Paris – as the political storm clouds gathered, the people rioted, and the governments and ministers fell – the dominant political mood in Britain ceased to be one of celebration and became, increasingly, one of fear instead.

In France, the summer of 1789 witnessed the spontaneous wave of mass panic which came to be known as 'The Great Fear', in which rumours of advancing armies of bandits or invaders swept the French countryside; convinced that their enemies were only hours away, entire villages took up arms to defend themselves, or fled their homes in search of safety from these imaginary enemies.[4] The Great Fear was only the most obvious manifestation of that sense of heightened anxiety and dread which was so widespread in the years that followed the fall of the Bastille, in Britain as well as France; yet the moment at which the Revolution itself started to be seen as something fearful came at different points for different individuals. For some, such as Burke, the breaking point came as early as 5 October 1789, when the Parisian market-women and their allies marched on Versailles, murdered several guards, and compelled the royal family to return with them to Paris, proving to unsympathetic eyes that France was not a true constitutional monarchy governed by the rule of law, but a fallen state in which true power now lay in the hands of an anarchic mob. For others it came after the Flight to Varennes on 20 June 1791, following which Louis XVI was held under guard and the illusion of concord between the royalty and people of France was shattered forever, or else during the chaotic months of mid-1792, when France declared war on Prussia and Austria, imprisoned the royal family, and ultimately abolished the monarchy entirely and declared itself a republic on 21 September 1792. British popular opinion swung heavily against the Revolution after the massacres of September 1792, the execution of Louis XVI on 21 January 1793, and the subsequent French declaration of war with Britain. But even then, the bloodiest chapter of the Revolution was yet to come; it unfolded between July 1793 and July 1794, when for thirteen months Paris was governed by the Committee of Public Safety, who responded to the foreign invasions and civil insurrections they faced with a regime of mass executions and political purges which would became known as 'the Reign of Terror'; and it was in the years between the Great Fear and the Reign of Terror that Gothic fiction began to come into its own.

I would not wish to give the impression that these were years of fear for *everyone* in Britain, or even for everyone in France. Poor rural communities in both nations, especially, may often have had only the vaguest awareness of the current political and military situations; in such places, the 1790s would have been years of acute economic hardship, but hardly years of terror.[5] Even among the more literate and politically conscious classes, the men and women who bought novels, read newspapers, and were presumably aware of at least the broad outline of current affairs, not everyone was preoccupied with, or afraid of, the Revolution; many seem, in fact, not to have been very interested in it at all, or at least not to have shown much interest in reading about it. As Cook has pointed out, much French fiction of the revolutionary period deals with political matters only briefly and indirectly.[6] The same was true in Britain; striking though the simultaneous rise of Gothic fiction and political writing was in these years, other forms of literature remained just as popular, and not all of the fiction or non-fiction written about the French Revolution in Britain presented it as something to be feared. Many people evidently made their way through these years without ever lapsing into the kind of fearful political hysteria I shall describe in this chapter, and without acquiring any kind of taste for Gothic horrors in their fiction and art. But they were years in which both the climate of political fear and the taste for Gothic horror *did* grow, and grow together; and it is the network of connections between them that I wish to investigate here.

In this chapter, I aim to explore the relationship between the rise of Gothic fiction and the developing historical mythology of the French Revolution. First, I shall discuss the state of Gothic and proto-Gothic literature in the years leading up to the Terror, 1788–93, thus mapping out the literary and rhetorical resources they made available to British writers responding to the Reign of Terror itself. Secondly, I shall explore the process through which this period of revolutionary violence came to be known as 'the Terror', discussing both the rhetoric of political terror used by the Jacobins themselves, and the subsequent invention of the word 'terrorist' by their enemies in order to describe them. A third section deals with the actual events of the Terror, and the highly Gothicised ways in which they were represented in the contemporary British press, giving rise to a body of gory legends about the Revolution which, for subsequent generations, would serve as the original site of 'terrorism'. Finally, I shall return to literature, discussing the rise of Gothic terror-fiction proper in the mid-1790s and its close relationship with contemporary writing on the Terror itself. My aim, throughout, is to demonstrate the *interdependence* of these two bodies of writing; the ways in which rhetorical tropes slid back and forth between them as they helped to create one another over the course of the 1790s.

By the time the Bastille fell, all the props that would go on to constitute the genre of Gothic terror fiction lay readily at hand. The antiquarian revival of the mid-eighteenth century had popularised medieval settings in both poetry and prose, and served to at least partially legitimate literary depictions of the sort of violence and superstitious terror which eighteenth-century readers regarded as essential and inevitable components of the medieval world. In 1789 the first of Ann Radcliffe's Gothic novels, *The Castles of Athlin and Dunbayne*, was published in London, swiftly followed by *A Sicilian Romance* (1790) and *The Romance of the Forest* (1791): building on the patterns established by Reeve and the authors who had followed her, these 'romances' dealt with disputed inheritances and looming, Otranto-esque castles shadowed by inherited guilt, all set against vague historical backdrops of the kind the loyalist Gothic romance had made so popular. Like most of the Gothic romance authors of the 1780s, Radcliffe made no use of the supernatural beyond the occasional prophetic dream, and ensured that her works taught suitable moral lessons to their readers. Her innovation was the highly effective combination of this tradition of historical romance with the sentimental novel tradition exemplified by the then-popular works of Charlotte Smith, and her stories of sentimental heroines navigating their way through picturesque Mediterranean landscapes in perilous historical settings enjoyed increasing success among the British reading public, with *The Romance of the Forest* reaching its fourth edition just three years after its initial publication – a milestone which *The Castle of Otranto* had taken almost two decades to reach. The growing dominance of Gothic fiction can be seen in the shifting relationship between Radcliffe and Smith. In 1789, Smith – fifteen years Radcliffe's senior – was an established poet and novelist, and Radcliffe drew upon her works; *The Romance of the Forest* appears to have been based upon a story in Smith's *Romance of Real Life*, and many of the most characteristic features of Radcliffe's fiction, including people being mistaken for ghosts, persecuted sentimental heroines in Gothic buildings, and detailed descriptions of picturesque landscapes, first appeared in the novels of Charlotte Smith. Within a few years, however, Radcliffe's popularity had grown so great that their situations were reversed; it was now Smith who imitated Radcliffe, with looming Gothic buildings and apparently supernatural incidents playing an increasingly prominent role in novels such as *The Old Manor House* (1793).[7]

The growing popularity of the Gothic romance may well have been connected to contemporary events. In eighteenth-century Britain, the general assumption had been that novels – which still regularly masqueraded as collections of real letters, memoirs, or eyewitness accounts of recent true events – should be set in much the same time and place as that in which they were written and read, so that their readers might benefit more directly from their lessons and observations regarding contemporary society; the fantastical settings and improbable events of Gothic romances served to divorce them from such concerns, and while such stories could clearly be used to teach general moral lessons (such as the generic Christian righteousness emphasised by Reeve in *The Old English Baron*), they were not seen as having the same immediate applicability to the present as more mainstream novel writing.[8] Burke's argument for the value of the terrible sublime in literature had, in fact, specifically hinged around the contrast between such material and the peaceful effeminacy he assumed to be characteristic of his own day; a literature of terror was useful, he claimed, precisely because it could deliver the kind of sharp shocks to the nervous system that were so lacking in modern life. What direct relevance could tales of falling castles doomed by ancestral sins have to the lives of readers in eighteenth-century Britain? The debates over the legitimacy of aristocratic and monarchical government triggered by the events of the American Revolution doubtless provided some of the impetus behind the production of loyalist Gothic romances in the 1770s and 1780s, but only in 1789 did it became apparent that, in writing *Otranto*, Walpole had not been writing about the past at all, but the future; that in penning his story of an aristocratic fortress toppling beneath the weight of its accumulated unrighteousness, he had written the plot of Bastille Day a quarter-century before it actually took place.

It has long been a commonplace of scholarship on Gothic fiction to state that it became popular as a response to the events of the French Revolution. Such discussions almost always take as their starting point De Sade's remarks on Gothic fiction in his *Reflections on the Novel* (1800):

> This genre was the inevitable product of the revolutionary shocks with which the whole of Europe resounded. For those who were acquainted with all the ills that are brought upon men by the wicked, the romantic novel was becoming somewhat difficult to write, and merely monotonous to read: there was nobody left who had not experienced more misfortunes in four or five years than could be depicted in a century by literature's most famous novelists: it was necessary to call upon hell for aid in order to arouse interest, and to find in the land of fantasies what was common knowledge from historical observations of man in this iron age.[9]

Shocked by the events of the Revolution, the argument runs, the British reading public turned to a literature which would at once reflect and soothe their own fearful state of mind. In one of the very first major critical studies of Gothic literature, *The Gothic Quest*, Montague Summers wrote:

> Both at home and abroad dark shadows were lowering; the times were difficult, full of anxiety and unrest; there was a sense of dissatisfaction today and of apprehension for the morrow; there were wars and rumours of wars. Readers sought some counter-excitement, and to many the novel became a precious anodyne.[10]

Devendra Varma, the next major authority on Gothic literature after Summers, concurred with his predecessor's views on this subject, however much he disagreed with him on others:

> There is an unconscious indefinable relationship between the Terrors of the French Revolution and the Novel of Terror in England. The excitement and insecurity engendered by the French Revolution did quicken the nerves of literature, and

the Gothic novelists were not immune from these tremors. Montague Summers shrewdly notes: 'Readers, it is presumed, delighted in imaginary terrors while the horrors of the French Revolution were being enacted all about them.'[11]

Most subsequent critics and literary historians have followed Summers and Varma in seeing the growth of Gothic fiction in Britain as a reflection of (and/or a reaction to) the anxieties aroused by the French Revolution.[12] That some such relationship did exist between the Terror and the rise of 'terror fiction' is unquestionable; however, it is my view that it would be misleading to see the efflorescence of Gothic fiction in the years following the French Revolution as simply a case of art imitating life. The relationship between history and literature was more complex than that; and while it is true that the events of the French Revolution served to bring new relevance to a whole host of Gothic tropes, it is also the case that the developing genre of Gothic fiction provided a crucial conceptual vocabulary through which the often confusing events of the Revolution could be understood. What took place in the 1790s was not a straightforward case of literary fiction reacting to historical fact, but a process in which fiction and non-fiction drew upon one another in an evolutionary symbiosis, until by about 1800 two powerful new bodies of mythology had been codified. The first was the genre of Gothic fiction, and with it the very idea of a literature of terror; the second was the historical mythology of the French Revolution, and with it the concept of 'terrorism' as a category of political action. Each of these two mythologies drew so heavily upon the other that it should not surprise us if histories of the Revolution sometimes read like Gothic novels, or if Gothic narratives often remind us of stories from the Revolution. The two categories have been interdependent from the very start.

In his study of representations of the French Revolution in the visual arts, *The Shadow of the Guillotine*, Bindman writes:

> The result of all these images, popular and more elevated, was to establish in British consciousness, in place of the myriad complexities of the real French Revolution, a series of simple pictures and stereotypes which have proved virtually indestructible. If we still think of the French Revolution in terms of the guillotine, innocent aristocrats and brutish sans-culottes, then this represents the triumph of visual images which have a virtually unbroken history from the propaganda campaigns of the 1790s through the Victorian period to the present day.[13]

The process of simplification and mythologisation that Bindman identifies here did not just occur in the visual arts. The French Revolution is one of the most heavily mythologised historical events of recent centuries, and the legend-lore which has accumulated around it is formidable.[14] The Bastille looms up in the popular historical imagination as a monstrous house of horrors, in which luckless prisoners lay in torment; yet it is now known to have been comfortably appointed, and almost entirely empty by the time it was captured in 1789.[15] The September Massacres, usually imagined as a carnival of bloodletting by a furious and uncontrollable rabble, appear to have been a fairly methodical campaign of popular executions carried out by the working folk of Paris, in the belief that they were trying and convicting traitors who had plotted to surrender their city to the enemy; the makeshift tribunals they assembled issued pardons and executions in roughly equal numbers, and their most infamous victim, Princess Lamballe, was almost certainly subjected to a straightforward beheading rather than the grotesque dismemberment and sexual violation of historical legend.[16] As for the Terror, Donald Greer remarked in his groundbreaking work on the subject that 'the impression of the Reign of Terror as a Reign of Blood almost unique in history is ineffaceable'; yet his research, and most subsequent scholarship, demonstrates that the rate of execution among those imprisoned during the Terror was in fact fairly low, and that the famous executions by guillotine in Paris actually comprised a very small proportion of the Revolution's total body count, dwarfed by the contemporary carnage in the Vendée.[17] Revolutionary executions by guillotine are habitually imagined as acts of spectacular violence, *grand guignol* spectacles for a bloodthirsty crowd: yet both Arasse and Outram have pointed out that most spectators at a revolutionary guillotining would have been able to see almost nothing of the execution itself; just the downward flash of a falling blade. (This contrasts strongly not only with the extended execution rituals of the French *ancien régime*, but also with contemporary executions by hanging in Britain, where the often protracted and agonising death of the victim as they twisted and kicked in mid-air was played out in full view of the watching crowds: Foucault notes that, when the guillotine was first employed in France, 'people complained that they could not see anything and chanted, "Give us back our gallows" '.)[18] And generations have thrilled at the story of the *Bals des Victimes* held after Thermidor, when those lucky enough to have survived the Terror attended balls dressed as though for execution, greeting one another with an abrupt jerking of the head meant to imitate the moment of decapitation: but Schechter has demonstrated that these Gothic celebrations were almost certainly an invention of later writers, and no evidence exists of such events actually taking place in the aftermath of the Terror.[19] That the Revolution led to an enormous amount of violence being unleashed upon the people of France is unquestionable; but, as Bindman suggests, popular conceptions of the nature, circumstances, perpetrators, and victims of this violence are very largely inaccurate, owing more to subsequent historical mythology than actual historical fact.

The traditional history of the French Revolution, in other words, is less a record of actual events than a mass of *fictions about (the) Terror*, written during the same years in which terror fiction emerged for the first time as a recognisable and popular literary genre, and very largely written using the same rhetorical tools that those authors devised. Gothic writing, then, did not so much reflect the events of the Terror as invent them, distilling the confusing facts of history into what Grenby calls 'a series of powerful and only loosely historically accurate motifs', in which 'events became emblems'.[20] As Cox writes of the Gothic drama of the 1790s:

> The Gothic predates the grand and terrible days of the revolutionary era, and in a sense it provided in advance images and narratives that could be used to understand revolutionary events, while the revolution itself provided a new ideological charge to Gothic devices. If Gothic drama re-presents the events and issues of the French Revolution, the popular construction of the Revolution

itself seemed at times to move to Gothic rhythms. When one reads accounts of the liberation of the Bastille, for example, one enters a Gothic world of dungeons, torture, and miraculous liberation [. . .] The Gothic villain/hero, the charismatic yet terrifying figure at the heart of these plays, seems both to presage and to reflect the titanic figures of the revolutionary era, both the aristocrats of the *ancien regime* and such powerfully controversial revolutionary figures as Danton, Robespierre, and Napoleon. Images of sacked chateaus and liberated convents, of imprisoned aristocrats and the guillotine, and of old oppression, Terror and counter-terror both fed and were fed by the Gothic imagination.[21]

The stage was set for the construction of these co-dependent literary and historical mythologies by the development of two literary forms: the horror-poem, and what Ian Haywood calls the 'bloody vignette'. In *Gothic Documents*, Miles and Clery write:

> By the 1790s, the idea that terror, and specifically superstitious terror, could form the basis for a work of literature or art was familiar, if not universally accepted. The tentative arguments put forward in the odes of Joseph Warton and Collins were made superfluous by the overwhelming strength of public demand.[22]

Fearful or horrific scenes had appeared as components of longer poems for decades; but, increasingly, they now came to be used in the way that Collins had used them, as the basis for the poem itself, and this nascent literature of terror was unsurprisingly popular with the young. In 1788 the sixteen-year-old William Wordsworth wrote a fragmentary poem 'The Vale of Esthwaite', in which he imagined his Lakeland home as a domain of ghosts, ruins, and horrible hidden secrets; like the young Warton thirty-three years earlier, he described these scenes of unnatural terror not in order to make any moral point, but simply because such things were exciting, and thus enjoyable to read and write. Wordsworth's juvenile verses, which draw heavily upon the works of Gray, Collins, and Warton, demonstrate the extent to which their poetry had established a standard poetic vocabulary for writing about scenes of supernatural dread. Here, for example, Wordsworth has clearly been reading Gray:

> At noon I hied to gloomy glades,
> Religious woods and midnight shades,
> Where brooding Superstition frowned
> A cold and awful horror round,
> While with black arm and bending head
> She wove a stole of sable thread.
> And hark! the ringing harp I hear
> And lo! Her druid sons appear.
> Why roll on me your glaring eyes?
> Why fix on me for sacrifice?[23]

The weaving, the harp, and the sable are all drawn from Gray's 'The Bard', although the druids may have entered by way of Mason's *Caractacus*. Later, Wordsworth draws upon

Warton's 'Pleasures of Melancholy' to describe how a ghost with a 'taper blue' leads the speaker into a 'dungeon deep':

> [it] showed
> An iron coffer marked with blood.
> The taper turned from blue to red
> Flashed out – and with a shriek she fled.
> With arms in horror spread around
> I moved – a form unseen I found
> Twist round my hand an icy chain
> And drag me to the spot again.[24]

In a third passage, Gray and Warton are combined when another ghost – this time an ancient bard, like Gray's – leads the speaker into yet another hidden cavern, and a few lines later Wordsworth draws upon Collins' 'Ode to Fear', as his luckless speaker – who has already encountered bloodthirsty druids, multiple dungeon-haunting spectres, 'the ghosts of Murderers', 'the Demons of the storm', and Satan – witnesses the appearance of a series of threatening personifications, including 'Hell-born Murder', 'moody Madness', and 'Suicide with savage glance'.[25] All of these are mere effects, deployed not as part of an overarching poetic argument, or even as scenes in a coherent narrative, but simply as exercises in Warton-esque supernatural poetry; but it is the very derivativeness and indiscriminateness of 'The Vale of Esthwaite' which makes it historically significant, for it demonstrates with some exactness the creative resources which were available, on the eve of the French Revolution, to a young writer with an interest in Gothic horrors.[26] Some of these – the bards, the druids, and the personifications, all deeply rooted in the poetic practices and Ossianic imaginative world of the mid-eighteenth century – would fall by the wayside over the decade to come; but others, such as the ghosts, the caves and dungeons, the horrible hidden secrets, and the sublime mountain scenery, would go on to become mainstays of the emerging genre of terror fiction.

In a similar vein, the first work cited by Miles and Clery as an example of the growing acceptability of terror in literature is 'To Horror', written by Robert Southey in 1791. Southey was then just seventeen, and like Wordsworth and Warton at the same age – and many an adolescent boy since – he was evidently much enamoured of horrific scenes; his poem starts on the very familiar imaginative terrain of ruined abbeys, sinking ships in storms, plague-struck cities, and battlefields, before moving on to two instances of horror more indicative of his youthful political radicalism, the deathbed of a warmongering tyrant and the slave plantations of America.[27] Only when he writes of the tortured slaves does he do so with any obvious moral purpose, as part of a curse called down upon their tormentors and a prayer for the success of a future slave rebellion:

> HORROR! I call thee yet once more!
> Bear me to that accursed shore,
> Where on the stake the Negro writhes.

Assume thy sacred terrors then! dispense
The gales of Pestilence!
Arouse the opprest; teach them to know their power;
Lead them to vengeance! and in that dread hour
When ruin ranges wide,
I will behold and smile by MERCY'S side.[28]

One might question how committed to 'MERCY' anyone can really be if they choose to invoke it only once 'ruin' already 'ranges wide', and it is not clear if the people Southey imagines himself smiling mercifully upon after the vengeful uprising has run its course are the rebellious slaves, the slave-owners who survive their rebellion, or both. But, more to the point, this final verse comes only after six previous horror-filled stanzas, for which Southey offers no apologies or justifications whatsoever. Presumably 'HORROR' needs to show us the suffering of the slaves, so that we can understand why they need to rise up against their masters; and, as Bainbridge suggests, we should perhaps understand Southey's lines on the horrors of the battlefield as a criticism of war itself.[29] But why does 'HORROR' have to show us sailors drowning, ravens feeding on pestilential corpses, mothers and children freezing to death in the snow, and the rest of Southey's gallery of horrors? Why would anyone want to imagine such things? Southey's lack of any explanation implies that, as Miles and Clery indicate, he expects his readers to understand that such scenes, like Wordsworth's scenes of gratuitous supernatural terror, can be delightful in and of themselves, and that when we read poetry we might desire to 'hear at times the deep heart-groan/Of some poor sufferer left to die alone' for the sheer imaginative pleasure of doing so.

Southey's choice of 'that accursed shore/Where on the stake the Negro writhes' as the final destination in his tour of horrors is a significant one, as it points to one of the major sources from which scenes of extreme brutality and violence were reaching the British reading public. In 1790 very few novelists, poets, playwrights, or writers of non-fiction would include graphic scenes of torture or dismemberment in their work unless they happened to be writing about one specific subject: the slave trade. From its beginnings in 1783, and especially after the foundation of the Committee for the Abolition of the Slave Trade in 1787, the abolitionist movement had been industriously circulating stories of the nightmarish tortures and executions inflicted upon African slaves in the plantations, and even accounts of slavery written by authors not opposed to the institution of slavery itself, such as John Gabriel Stedman, often made mention of the extreme cruelty employed by some planters and overseers. In the context of the 1780s, the literature of abolitionism thus formed a literature of horror unmatched by any comparable body of contemporary writing, establishing the form that Ian Haywood calls the 'bloody vignette'; a style of reporting and describing scenes of extreme violence, characterised by an obsessive itemising of individual injuries, victims, and acts of cruelty, which Haywood describes as 'hyperbolic realism'. As Haywood notes, such 'bloody vignettes' would go on to be used in many other contexts from the 1790s onwards, especially in relation to the events of the French Revolution.[30] As Marcus Wood has pointed out, the specific vocabulary of horrors that appeared in early Gothic literature – with its endless scenes of abduction, captivity, and imprisonment, and its occasional forays into horrific torture, mutilation, rape, and execution – shares much common ground with that used in the abolitionist literature of the 1780s, which, perhaps more than any other body of late-eighteenth-century texts, taught contemporary readers what violent horror might look like and how it might potentially be written about. Wood goes on to suggest that the entire sado-masochistic/Gothic cultural complex which has been so strong a feature of Western culture since the late eighteenth century is, very largely, a response to the (often displaced) memory of the Middle Passage and the system of plantation slavery which it fed.[31] I would agree that much of what came later had its roots in this abolitionist literature of horror, but I feel that the dates do not support so straightforward an attribution; abolitionism was an important cultural force throughout most of the 1780s, and yet it was only after 1794, in the wake of another set of 'bloody vignettes' which rendered all forms of political reform – including abolitionism – deeply suspect, that the literature of violence and terror began to take on a major role in British cultural life.

The three years between the fall of the Bastille in 1789 and the summer of 1792 thus form a transitional moment in the development of the Gothic. In these years, Radcliffe's novels were growing popular, but were not yet the bestsellers they would become; Gothic poems such as Wordsworth's 'The Vale of Esthwaite' and Southey's 'Ode to Horror' were being written, but mostly by minor, marginal, and often very young authors; and the news from France was confusing and sometimes worrying, but was generally described even by hostile British newspapers as more worthy of mockery and disapproval than fear. Until the repulse of the Prussian and Austrian armies in the autumn of 1792, the Revolution was frequently viewed by its foreign enemies as a kind of grotesque and bloody joke, which would be swept from the stage of history as soon as the allied armies reached Paris; and even in 1793, after the execution of Louis XVI and the beginning of hostilities between Britain and France, there does not seem to have been any immediate shift towards viewing the Revolution with terror rather than guarded concern. Horrible though it was, many believed that the Jacobin Republic could not endure long; that it was an abortive historical aberration, to be deplored rather than feared, posing no threat to anyone except its own unfortunate subjects, and soon to be crushed by the allied arms of its many enemies. But in France, events were moving faster than ever: civil war erupted in the Vendée in March 1793, and June saw the Girondin faction purged from the National Convention, with political power now passing into the hands of the Jacobin-run Committee of Public Safety. Men who would have been considered radical fringe extremists a year or two before were now ruling France, and raising and directing armies against a multitude of foes: for the revolutionary state was now at war with almost the whole of Europe, as well as a sizeable fraction of its own population. Faced with such a sea of troubles, and concluding from the murder of Marat by Charlotte Corday on 13 July 1793 that any number of unseen enemies, conspirators, and assassins stalked secretly among them, the Committee of Public Safety decided that only the most extreme measures could now save the Revolution from destruction. 'Let the traitors breathe their last', Robespierre demanded on 31 August, sounding even more Gothic than usual: 'let us appease the ghosts of the murdered patriots…'.[32] Five days later, on 5 September

1793, the National Convention declared that Terror was now to be the order of the day.

The next day was marked by a total eclipse of the sun. The Reign of Terror had begun.[33]

II

The Terror, if it is to be understood as beginning in September 1793 and ending with Thermidor, lasted less than eleven months, but the shadow it cast across Western history was a great deal longer. Both French and English historical dictionaries concur in seeing it as the point of origin for such new words as 'terrorist', 'terrorise' and 'terrorism', on which Marcel Hénaff writes:

> After 1795, 'terror' becomes the noun that designates not only a moment of the Revolution, but also any kind of political behaviour founded on systematic, unlimited violence relative to the opposition, or those believed to be part of the opposition. After that, terror was a new idea in Europe. A new adjective from the same noun joined the old one: 'terrorised' joined 'terrified'. According to the *Dictionnaire Historique de la Langue Française* (Rey 2108), the word terrorism appeared starting in 1794 and the verb 'terrorize' starting in 1796.[34]

The *Oxford English Dictionary* (OED) gives 1795 as the date of the first usages of 'terrorist' and 'terrorism' in English, both in connection with contemporary accounts of the French Revolution, although its earliest citation of 'terrorise' is from 1823. Hénaff continues:

> What is extraordinary is not so much that the Revolution slid towards terror and towards the establishment of extreme measures of imprisonment and executions, it is that *the term 'terror' was officially chosen* and that under this name, the organisation of repression was proclaimed *as such*, by the sovereign authority, that is to say by the body of the representatives of the nation, exactly like the enactment of a law [italics in original].[35]

The term 'terror' was associated with the revolutionary policies of 1793–4, not by their opponents, but by their instigators. On 5 September 1793, the National Convention voted that 'terror is the order of the day', and over the next two months its machinery of repression accordingly swung into action, with the infamous Revolutionary Tribunals established across France to try those accused of crimes against the Revolution. But 'terror' was not understood by the National Convention as an *activity* that a government might undertake, in the way that it might undertake to wage a war, or negotiate a peace, or impose price controls; the Committee of Public Safety did not, like so many eighteenth-century Bin Ladens, sit in their Green Room in Paris deciding how many acts of terror to order in any given month. Rather, 'terror' was a methodology, according to which certain actions – the quashing of domestic treason, the uncovering

of foreign plots and conspiracies, the waging of war against provinces in rebellion –
could be carried out. A clear statement of what 'terror' meant to the original 'terrorists'
in the Committee of Public Safety can be found in a famous and much-quoted speech
delivered by Robespierre in the National Convention on 5 February 1794:

> If the driving force of popular government in peacetime is virtue, that of popular
> government during a revolution is both *virtue and terror*: virtue, without which
> terror is destructive; terror, without which virtue is impotent. Terror is only justice
> that is prompt, severe, and inflexible; it is thus an emanation of virtue; it is less
> a distinct principle than a consequence of the general principle of democracy
> applied to the most pressing needs of the *patrie*.[36]

'Terror', then, is not an action, any more than 'virtue' is an action; rather, it is a 'principle'
according to which actions can be carried out. And what is the principle of terror?
Robespierre tells us: it is 'justice that is prompt, severe and inflexible'. By its speed, severity,
and inflexibility, the justice of the republic was to strike terror into the enemies of the
Revolution, who would be taught by witnessing it that they too could expect immediate
and overwhelming retaliation should they dare to act against the republic. The desire
to instil this terror within its enemies was to be made an organising principle of the
Revolution; it was to be made, in fact, the 'order of the day', for how else, save by inspiring
such terror in its foes, could the democratic government of France hope to survive, beset
as it was within and without by the whole combined power of monarchical Europe?

As a reader of Montesquieu, Robespierre would have known that the obvious
objection to such a policy of terror was that it was 'despotic'. In a passage from *The
Spirit of the Laws* which many members of the National Convention must have known
by heart, Montesquieu had argued that despotisms, monarchies, and republics were
each founded on a different basis: despotisms on fear, monarchies on honour, and
republics on virtue. Roland may have had this in mind when he wrote to the National
Convention on 3 September 1792 that the royalists had been planning to 'display
over Paris the standard of death, and to reign there by terror'; his emphasis on their
reliance on terror as a means of government was surely meant to draw attention to
the despotic character of the regime he claimed the royalists planned to establish.[37] In
a republic, such as France was supposed to be in 1794, the foundation of government
should be virtue, not terror; its citizens should do what was right willingly, out of
love for their country, rather than needing to be terrorised into line. So why should
Robespierre, spokesman for a supposedly free and virtuous republic, need to resort
to terror, the characteristic weapon of the despot? His answer was that France could
get by with virtue alone 'in peacetime', but that now, in 1794, terror was needed
because the republic was in crisis, and without terror, 'virtue is impotent'. Even so,
he insisted that this republican terror would be entirely different from the arbitrary
terror of despots, because it was guided not by the caprice of a tyrant, but by the
virtue of the people: 'virtue, without which terror is destructive'. He continued:

> It has been said that terror is the spring of despotic government. Does yours,
> then, resemble despotism? Yes, as the swords that flash in the hands of the heroes

of liberty resemble those with which the satellites of tyranny are armed. Let the despot govern his debased subjects by terror; he is right as a despot: conquer by terror the enemies of liberty and you will be right as founders of the republic. The government of the revolution is the despotism of liberty against tyranny. Is force only intended to protect crime? And is it not the destiny of lightning to strike prideful heads?[38]

Robespierre's language betrays the slippery conceptual ground he stands on in such paradoxical phrases as 'the despotism of liberty', but his underlying claim is clear and coherent enough; the ends justify the means, and terror deployed against tyranny rather than in its service is thereby rendered praiseworthy rather than execrable. As Jordan explains:

> Amending one of Montesquieu's political axioms [. . .] Robespierre created a new (and dangerous) synthesis. [. . .] It was now the purpose of terror that determined its morality. He had distinguished between a 'good' and a 'bad' terror, depending upon its goal and the government resorting to terror.[39]

The good people of France would act out of virtue, but 'the enemies of liberty' and 'the satellites of tyranny' would have to be compelled into obedience by fear. Ideally, the republic would function entirely on virtue, but, under the circumstances, virtue would have to arm itself with terror if the Revolution was to survive. (Robespierre's announcement of 7 May 1794, that virtue was now to be the order of the day, was thus intended to complement rather than replace the policy of terror.)[40] Thus Saint-Just's famous question: 'What could anyone possibly want who wanted neither virtue nor terror?'[41] If the Revolution was to be saved, what possible third option could there be?

The initial British reaction to the National Convention's announcement that terror was to be the order of the day seems to have been muted; certainly no-one at the time appears to have regarded it at once as heralding an even more ominous phase in the progress of the Revolution. This was probably because, to late-eighteenth-century ears, there was nothing particularly shocking about a government embarking upon a policy of terror; it was a commonplace of contemporary political and moral thought that, while only despotisms were founded entirely on terror, some degree of fear was always going to be necessary if either individuals or societies were to function at all. An effective church would teach its followers to fear the Lord and dread the fires of Hell; an efficient army would spread terror among its enemies; and the workings of justice were intended to inspire in the people a salutary terror of the law. In his 1757 *Enquiry*, Burke described the important role that terror had to play in a well-ordered state:

> The power which arises from institution in kings and commanders, has the same connexion with terror. Sovereigns are frequently addressed with the title of *dread majesty*. And it may be observed, that young persons, little acquainted with the world, and who have not been used to approach men in power, are commonly struck with an awe which takes away the free use of their faculties. *When I prepared my seat in the street*, (says Job,) *the young men saw me, and hid themselves.* Indeed,

so natural is this timidity with regard to power, and so strongly does it inhere in our constitution, that very few are able to conquer it, but by mixing much in the business of the great world, or by using no small violence to their natural dispositions.[42]

A lifelong believer in monarchy himself, despite his sympathy with the American revolutionaries, Burke saw nothing objectionable about this state of affairs, which provided an earthly reflection of that pious and laudable fear of God about which he wrote at some length elsewhere in the *Enquiry*. In his 1791 *Letter to a Member of the National Assembly*, Burke would criticise the French revolutionaries for discouraging the fear of God in their subjects: such fear, he wrote, was 'that only sort of fear which generates true courage', because 'he who fears God fears nothing else'.[43]

Thinking along similar lines, eighteenth-century generals and magistrates saw nothing wrong with reporting proudly how much terror they had managed to spread among the malefactors they were charged with combating. The urbane scholar William Adams, friend of Dr Johnson and Master of Pembroke College, was as far from being a bloody-handed terrorist as could reasonably be imagined; yet he remarked in his *Sermons* that 'conscience is given us to impress the mind with fear and terror', and that 'the civil power' should be 'a terror to evil doers'.[44] As Foucault has pointed out, writers on capital punishment generally emphasised that the whole point of public executions was to terrify the spectators into shunning criminal behaviour; Boswell wrote in 1783 that, at a well-staged public execution, 'the spectators are struck with prodigeous terrour [sic]', while in his 1785 *Principles of Moral and Political Philosophy* Paley asserted that such executions were necessary because no other punishment evoked 'a sufficient degree of terror' in the public.[45] (On much the same principle, Johnson recommended that, among schoolchildren, the rod should be 'the general terrour to all'.[46]) The same principles applied to military operations: reporting on the slaughter of a force of Native Americans in the state of New York on 5 July 1792, the *General Evening Post* explained approvingly that 'the carnage was general among the Indians, and no quarter given, as it might operate as a terror in future to those savage freebooters', and when Sir John Moore was sent to Ireland to suppress the Wexford rebellion in 1798 he explained that 'My wish was to excite terror, and by that means to obtain our end speedily'.[47] Less than two months before his death in the September Massacres, the Royalist ex-minister Montmorin speculated on the means that would be needed to quell the Revolution: 'I think we will have to strike the Parisians with Terror'.[48] When the Princes of the Blood made their Declaration against the Revolution in September 1792, they accused the revolutionaries of using 'the terror of power over weakness' to maintain their unjust authority; but, far from viewing the use of terror as unique to their enemies, the Princes declared that they themselves would 'strike with salutary terror' against them.[49] On 23 August 1793, two weeks before the National Convention made its famous pronouncement, an editorial in *The Times* opined that 'the FRENCH REVOLUTION, which originated from *fear*, must be terminated by *terror*' – meaning not that the Revolution would inevitably degenerate into terror, but that terror would have to be used by its enemies to put an end to it.[50] Another article, published four days later, made the same point, alluding to 'the wild fury of the

Regicides, whom nothing but terror can subdue'.[51] Clearly, the authors of these articles did not believe that by proposing the necessity of inflicting terror upon the French, they were suggesting outrageous or despotic measures; only that they were facing up to the realities of the situation, and pragmatically assessing the severity of the actions which would be necessary if the Revolution's opponents were to be triumphant.

When the National Convention voted to make terror the order of the day, this is presumably what they were understood to have meant: to strengthen the still-young revolutionary state by making it capable of striking terror into its enemies, both foreign and domestic. Not anarchy, but firm government; not lawlessness, but the power to enforce the law; that, for the National Convention, was what was meant by 'terror'. They believed that the Revolution was being undermined by criminals and conspirators, who had been able to flourish because of the undue leniency with which they had been treated; if liberty was to survive in France, such men must now be terrified into submission. Just as Dr Adams had recommended, the civil power in France had to become a terror to evildoers. As Dan Edelstein has pointed out, there was abundant precedent for this mode of thinking: Montesquieu aside, the classical republican tradition had always emphasised the importance of fear as well as virtue, and the value of instilling in citizens an appropriate fear of the gods and the law.[52] Robespierre's understanding of the role of state terror was thus thoroughly conventional: he saw it as serving to awaken and supplement that fear which should already be inspired in the malefactor by the voice of his own conscience, and by the knowledge that the Supreme Being was watching his every misdeed, a position effectively identical to that articulated in the *Sermons* of Dr Adams.[53] It was this, rather than any hitherto-unheard-of principle of gratuitous atrocity, which the National Convention voted to make the order of the day.

In 1794, word spread across Europe of the massacres carried out by the revolutionaries in Lyons, Nantes, and the Vendée, and of the increasingly murderous activities of the Revolutionary Tribunals in Paris and elsewhere; yet no-one at the time seems to have identified *terror*, rather than mass violence, as being the distinguishing feature of this phase of the Revolution. Rather than being seen as a summary of what was most distinctive in the policy of the revolutionary regime, the phrase 'terror is the order of the day' seems to have been used by both sides as a snappy summary of the kind of firmness that any government might desire to use against its enemies. In November 1794, one of the Representatives of the People was reported to have written from Strassburg that 'terror is the order of the day on this frontier'.[54] Writing home from the front on 18 April 1794, one British officer related that 'with a view to making terror the order of the day, we have fired thirty villages'; while three months later, reporting on the capture of Ostend by the revolutionary armies, Barère announced that within the defeated armies of their enemies, 'terror and flight are now the order of the day'.[55] The phrase could be deployed in this way because Robespierre's concept of 'terror', as a legitimate tool for governments to use in the maintenance and defence of the state, was still essentially much the same as that of Burke, Adams, and the mainstream of eighteenth-century political thought of which they were a part. Every government in Europe agreed that states had a right and a duty to employ coercive force against those of their subjects who broke their laws, and those enemies that threatened their borders, thereby terrifying them – and others who might otherwise imitate them – into submission. Where they parted company from Robespierre and his comrades was in what constituted desirable civic Virtue and permissible civic Terror. The Committee of Public Safety inspired horror in counter-revolutionaries not because it tried to enforce virtue through terror – all governments did that – but because the virtue it wished to uphold was that of resistance to the clerical and monarchical authorities which the rest of Europe viewed as entirely legitimate, and because its idea of the kind of salutary terror which would encourage such virtue apparently included the kind of mass executions then occurring in Lyons, in Nantes, and – after the passage of the law of 22 Prairal on 10 June 1794 – in Paris. Yet the wording of this infamous law, which by forbidding the use of lawyers, witnesses, or speeches for the defence by those accused of counter-revolutionary crimes became the very corner-stone of the judicial terror carried out by the Revolutionary Tribunals, did not use the word 'terror' once.[56] In June 1794, it was clear to everyone that France was passing through a period of extreme revolutionary violence, one that would later be referred to as '*le Grande Terreur*'; but no-one on any side yet seems to have thought of, or referred to, the events of the time as 'the Terror'.

Even in the aftermath of Thermidor, the word and its derivatives did not spring immediately to prominence. The events which France had just passed through had clearly been extremely terrifying, and British journalists in the later part of 1794 sometimes wrote about them as a time in which the Jacobins ruled 'by means of terror', or through 'the terror of the guillotine'; but no-one actually wrote about 'the Terror'.[57] After the death of Robespierre on 27 July 1794, the men responsible for the violence of 1793–4 were frequently referred to as 'tyrants', 'blood-drinkers', and 'cannibals', but the word 'terrorist' had evidently not yet entered the general political vocabulary.[58] There was a pressing need for new factional labels, to allow the supporters of the Thermidorian coup to distinguish themselves both from the anti-revolutionary forces with which they were still struggling, and from the Robespierrean die-hards of the Jacobin Club who now needed to be thoroughly purged; but this was a delicate issue, since the National Convention immediately before and after Thermidor consisted largely of the same men, who continued to pursue the same policies of support for the Revolution, maintenance of the Republic, and continuation of the war in Europe against the allied powers that they had carried out under Robespierre. What was it, after all, that made this government so different from its immediate predecessor, and ensured that under it France would enjoy a progressive future entirely different from its calamitous recent past?

The answer the Thermidorians came to was that, while they still supported the Revolution, they rejected the policy of revolutionary terror. This policy was described by Barère as a 'system of terror' as early as 29 July 1794 – the day after Robespierre's execution – and within a month of the Thermidorian coup, British newspaper readers learned that speeches were being made in the National Convention denouncing 'the system of terror and blood under which [the French] have so long groaned', and arguing that Robespierre had been quite wrong to imagine that terror could be compatible with liberty.[59] On

28 August 1794, one such speaker declared that 'a government, to inspire this terror, must unceasingly menace all the world with capital punishment', and thus that:

> Terror was not compatible with a free government, but with a tyrannical one [. . .]
> Terror must either be every where, or no where [. . .] that terror is the most powerful
> weapon of tyranny; and that justice alone ought to be the order of the day.[60]

What such a position amounted to was a repudiation of the Robespierrean doctrine of limited terror, which could be directed only at the enemies of the people. In this account, either a state possessed an infrastructure of terror, or it did not; and as such an infrastructure required 'stretches of authority incessantly renewed and augmented', no state in which such a system existed could possibly remain a free republic for any length of time. Montesquieu had argued that despotism was founded on terror; now it was claimed that a policy of terror must lead inevitably to despotism, as only in a despotic state could such a policy be maintained. Robespierre had, perfectly conventionally, claimed terror and justice as allies; but now that the excesses of the previous year were associated with a time when terror had been the order of the day, the new masters of France argued that terror and justice, far from being allies, were in fact opposites, unable to coexist within the same state for any length of time.

Once these arguments had been made, it was easy to see how the defeated Jacobin extremists could be characterised in a way that would allow them to be clearly distinguished from their successors: they were the men who had supported a policy of terror, instead of a policy of justice. The Jacobins began to be referred to as the 'partizans of terror', supporters of 'a Government of terror'; and by 1795 the word *terroriste* began to appear in official proclamations, clearly intended to denominate those who had been responsible for making terror 'the order of the day'.[61] (On 27 October 1795, the British newspaper *The Oracle* explained to its readers that '*Terrorists* [. . .] is now the name substituted for that of *Jacobins*'.[62]) On 18 February 1795, a 'cart of terrorism' was dragged through Lyons, containing an effigy of Robespierre for the mockery of the populace.[63] A decree of 23 February 1795, issued by the Directory, condemned Robespierrean 'terroristes' as enemies of the Revolution; another, issued on 10 April 1795, gave orders for 'terroristes' to be disarmed.[64] Due to its convenience as a faction designation, this word – and its derivative, 'terrorism' – swiftly passed into English. Unsurprisingly, some of the first English-speakers to adopt were those who were then living among the French; in a letter to the Secretary of State, dated 14 June 1795, James Monroe – then American Minister to France – used the phrases 'system of terror' and 'terrorism' interchangeably to describe the actions of the revolutionary government under Robespierre, and in a speech to the French Convention on 7 July 1795, Thomas Paine referred to himself as having been imprisoned 'during the reign of terrorism'.[65] But the word was swift to cross the channel, and in his 1795 *Letter on a Regicide Peace* Burke mentioned the release of 'Thousands of those Hell-hounds called Terrorists'; one of the first citations listed for the word in the *OED*.[66] 'Terrorist', at this stage, was strictly a faction designation, denoting a person who had supported the set of policies which Robespierre and St Just had called 'virtue and terror', and which their successors now called 'the system of terror', or simply 'terrorism'. The distinguishing feature of 'terrorism', according to those who now hastened to distance themselves from it, was its willingness to disregard all normal laws and limits in its desire to inspire fear in its enemies; as a result, the 'terrorist' found himself committed to a programme of ever-escalating atrocity, as each new horror could only serve to terrorise the increasingly jaded populace if it was even worse than the last. It is important to note that, even at the very beginning, no-one called *themselves* a 'terrorist': it was only ever a word used to describe *other people*, in this case the supporters of a displaced and discredited extremist regime. Robespierre had claimed that he supported virtue, and desired terror only insofar as it was necessary for the protection of virtue; but, now that he was dead, his enemies implied that he and his faction – whom they now labelled the 'terroristes', as though their policy had been one of terror alone – had believed in the infliction of terrifying acts of violence for their own sake. Unsurprisingly, the term was widely criticised as unhelpful, and open to misuse; Marie-Joseph Chénier, for example, complained on 24 June 1795 that the anti-revolutionary vigilantes who called themselves the Society of Jesus were not only killing 'the true terrorists', but also, 'under the name of terrorists', murdering anyone else they wanted dead.[67] Louis Gustave le Doulcet complained in June 1795 that '[m]any abuses had originated from the use of the word Terrorist', and among the accusations levelled against Jean-Lambert Tallien on 12 April 1796 was that he had 'invented the term *terrorist*' as part of his efforts to distance himself from his Jacobin colleagues after Thermidor.[68]

At the same time, people began to seek for phrases to describe the bloody year through which France had just passed. Initially, it was simply 'the reign of Robespierre': it suited the purposes of all sides to paint Robespierre as responsible for all the excesses of the year 1793–4, as the counter-revolutionaries wanted to have a revolutionary monster to demonise, and the men at the head of the post-Thermidorian revolutionary government wished to minimise the extent to which they, too, were implicated.[69] By January 1795, the first references to 'the Reign of Terror' were starting to appear, becoming more frequent as the year went on, and by 1796 it was everywhere.[70] In his *Considerations Upon the State of Public Affairs at the Beginning of the Year 1796*, Thomas Bentley referred to the possibility that the 'reign of terror' could be restored in France; *The Bloody Buoy*, a compendium of 'bloody anecdotes' concerning revolutionary atrocities published by William Cobbett in 1796, explained that 'this murdering time…had justly assumed the name of the *reign of terror*', while in his *Examination of the Principles of the French Revolution*, Jean Baptise Duvoisin asserted that the National Convention 'vaunts itself on having destroyed the reign of terror'.[71]

In his *Secret History of the French Revolution*, published in English in 1797, François Xavier Pagès looked back on the confusion of factional names that had arisen in France after Thermidor:

> After the fall of Robespierre, the Thermidorians called their enemies, or those whom they regarded as such, Robespierrists, Terrorists, Jacobins, Blood-Drinkers, and Anarchists. The Thermidorian re-actors were in their turn called Hecatombists, or makers of Hecatombs, new Terrorists, or Furorists.[72]

As this passage implies, while the word 'terrorist' was clearly used initially to refer only to members of the party of Robespierre, it was re-deployed almost immediately for use against other targets; the description of the Thermidorians as 'new Terrorists' implies both a recognition that they were distinct from the original terrorists (i.e. the followers of Robespierre), and an accusation that their methods were essentially the same. Pagès himself uses 'terrorist' as a general term for anyone attempting to further their political aims through violence and fear, including the anti-revolutionary Royalist extremists who called themselves the Society of the Sun, of whose excesses he writes: 'Thus terror had only changed hands.'[73] 'It was natural that the terrorists, Jacobins, Cromwellists, and Robespierrists should be succeeded by other terrorists and other men of blood,' he writes, 'because in morals as well as in physics, action and re-action are proportionate to each other....'[74] (Pagès makes no effort to explain what distinguishes 'terrorists', 'Jacobins', 'Cromwellists', and 'Robespierrists' from one another; evidently all were fairly interchangeable post-Thermidorian terms for the faction which had held power in 1793–4.) Indeed, so many different groups of 'terrorists' appear in Pagès' narrative that he is forced to use a special term, 'ancient terrorists', to make clear when he is using the word to refer specifically to the party responsible for the blood-letting of 1793–4, rather than to any of the many other terror-using groups active in France during the 1790s. In a similar vein, the authors of the *New Annual Register for the Year 1799* use the word 'terrorist' five times to refer to the Jacobins, but also refer to 'the extremes of both parties, the terrorist jacobins and the terrorist royalists', demonstrating that while the word was still heavily associated with the political faction responsible for the revolutionary Reign of Terror, it could also be applied, by analogy, to violent extremists of other political persuasions.[75]

All these words and phrases were no sooner coined than they were put to more general use. When Major Cartwright, in his 1795 *Letter to the High Sheriff*, called Pitt and his colleagues 'the terrorists of England', he was still primarily using the word as a faction designation, implying only that Pitt's methods were comparable to Robespierre's. But when Peter Pindar referred to killjoy preachers as 'pulpit terrorists' in his 1796 poem 'The Sorrows of Sunday', he was clearly using the word in a more general sense, to mean anyone who accomplished their ends by inspiring fear in others; and when Charles Burney, in his 1796 *Memoirs of the Life and Writing of the Abate Metastasio*, objected to 'tragical terrorism' and argued that, judging from Metastasio's objections to Aristotle's *Poetics*, 'it is manifest that Metastasio was no *terrorist*', he evidently had a similarly broad meaning in mind. The *True Briton* newspaper for 30 July 1796 even informed its readers of 'a dog, so fierce as to have bitten several persons, and to be the *terrorist* of that town and neighbourhood'.[76] The moralistic edge implied by Robespierre's original formulation, 'virtue and terror', is still present in all but the last of these usages; Pitt, the preachers, and the tragedians are all, like Robespierre, presumably terrorising people for ideological ends, to promote their versions of 'virtue'. (Perhaps the dog was, too: in its view, the people it bit were probably guilty of trespass or *lèse majesté*.) As I have discussed, the importance of fear in maintaining social order was very widely taken for granted in this period, so what distinguished the 'terrorist' was not that he tried to enforce virtue through fear – everyone from kings to schoolteachers did that – but that the fear he aimed to inspire was extreme and excessive, going far beyond that which the circumstances required. The primary meaning of the word 'terrorism' was, for several years, evidently something like 'a policy intended to enforce virtue through the dissemination of an extreme and unnecessary degree of fear', and in the later 1790s it was accordingly applied to ideological extremists of all stripes, no matter how remote from revolutionary France: the ancient Athenian lawgiver Draco, for example, or the Unionists in Ireland, or the infamous sixteenth-century Spanish general, the Duke of Alva, whose tactics in the Netherlands were described by one historian in 1800 as a 'Robespierrean system of terrorism'.[77] Gradually, the word took on the broader meaning, so that it could be used to denote anyone who spreads terror for any reason: the *OED's* first citation for this usage is from 1803, although the example of the 'terrorist' dog mentioned above shows it was in occasional use at least seven years earlier, and by the time Mary Shelley wrote her novel *The Last Man* in 1826 she could describe those people responsible for spreading fear of a plague as 'terrorists', even though they had no moral or ideological agenda for doing so.[78]

But what was it that had made the Terror so terrifying? With their tens of thousands of direct and indirect victims, the Revolutionary Tribunals were murderous enough; but compared to the hundreds of thousands killed in the wars of the eighteenth century, or in the contemporary civil war in the Vendée – let alone the millions who were to perish in the Napoleonic Wars – the scale of their bloodshed was relatively limited. France after Thermidor remained wracked with political violence: the purge of Jacobin loyalists after the execution of Robespierre required an entire additional round of murders, massacres, and executions, with the single largest batch of people executed by guillotine in Paris during the Revolution being composed not of the enemies of the Jacobins, but of the leading Jacobins themselves, sent *en masse* to the guillotine on 11th Thermidor.[79] France was still at war with most of Europe, and the Vendée remained in a state of siege until 1796; while areas which had been hit hard by revolutionary violence during the Terror, such as Lyons, witnessed waves of lynchings and assassinations in the years which followed it, as the vengeful relatives of the Revolution's victims took justice into their own hands.[80] Howard Brown has drawn attention to the waves of famine, crime, and general social breakdown that plagued France under the Directory government: in *Ending the French Revolution*, he writes that 'it is almost impossible to grasp the extent of social collapse and criminal turpitude in the mid-1790s'.[81] Pointing out that, in 1795, much of France was starving, freezing, and desperately poor, Hampson has even suggested that 'in terms of human misery [. . .] the year that followed 9th Thermidor may well have been worse than the one before'; while Cobb notes that rates of suicide and violent crime in France peaked not during the Terror, but in the chaos of what he calls 'the great murder year' of 1795, when hunger riots took place across France in the spring and summer, ceasing in the winter only because 'the situation was by then so fearful that the potential rioter was either dead or dying, busy pawning his remaining possessions, including his bedding, queuing for bourgeois charity, roaming the countryside in search of food, or enlisting in the *bandes* of *chauffeurs*'.[82] Given that instability and violence on an enormous scale continued to grip France both before and after the events of 1793–4, how did the events of this one year come to engrave themselves so deeply upon the historical imagination of Europe? How, in other words, did this particular bout of revolutionary violence become transfigured into 'the Terror'? If the statistical facts themselves will not supply an answer, we must look elsewhere: not to the literal violence caused by the Terror, but to the symbolic and emotional violence it inflicted. We must turn from facts to stories; the implicit and explicit stories that the Terror communicated to its victims and to the world at large, and the stories that others subsequently built out of the confusing events of what they had come to call 'the Terror', constructing a historical mythology of the French Revolution which remains with us to the present day. We must examine the fictions of the Terror; and we may thereby learn something of importance about the origins of the literary genre of terror fiction.

III

Let us start with historical facts: what actually happened in France during the eleven months when Terror was the order of the day? In September 1793, much of France was a war-zone: British, Spanish, Prussian, and Austrian armies had invaded the north, east, and south of the nation, while revolts against the Jacobin government had broken out in several parts of the country, including Lyons, Toulon, Marseilles, and the Vendée. Pressed in on all sides by hostile armies, the embattled revolutionary government in Paris also feared the enemy within, the spies and conspirators it believed were working secretly to turn the people against the Revolution and encourage them to rise up against it as they had in Lyons and elsewhere. It thus began a campaign of mass imprisonment, incarcerating anyone whose loyalty to the new regime might be suspect: priests, aristocrats, foreigners, royalists, moderates, Girondins, and anyone else believed to have a questionable political record. Anyone so unpatriotic as to attempt to hoard food, commit crimes, or avoid conscription into the national army was obviously also a risk; it was an article of faith for Robespierre that public and private virtue inevitably went together, and how could individuals so lacking in virtue be expected to resist corruption by the foes of the Revolution?[83] Greer estimates that half a million people were imprisoned during the Terror; an enormous number, given that the total population of France was less than thirty million. (To put this figure in context, the strength of the French army under the *levée en masse* was about three quarters of a million.)[84] The primary purpose of this mass incarceration was to neutralise the threat that such people were believed to pose to the fragile revolutionary state, rather than to enable their physical destruction; only about 3.5 per cent of those imprisoned during the Terror were actually executed, with another 2 per cent or so dying in prison.[85] Indeed, as Sutherland has shown, part of the point of this system of imprisonment and trial was to give the Committee of Public Safety options other than indiscriminate massacre with which to deal with those groups it suspected of wishing it harm; the Revolutionary Tribunals provided the Committee with a source of coercive power independent of the Jacobin clubs and *sans-culottes*, whose chaotic revolutionary enthusiasm had led to the massacres of August and September 1792, and ultimately paved the way for Hébert and the *enragés* to be checkmated by Robespierre in March 1794.[86] The Tribunals were instituted in order to limit mass bloodshed, not to facilitate it; they only really became the judicial murder machines as which they are remembered after the passage of the law of 22 Prairal, following which the number of death sentences issued by the Paris Tribunal jumped from an average of three per day (during its first thirteen months) to twenty-eight (during its last forty-nine days).[87]

If the physical violence inflicted by the Tribunals was relatively limited, however, the psychological violence they meted out was immense. For every individual actually executed, there were dozens who spent months in imprisonment, knowing that at any time they could be dragged before a hurried and hostile court and sentenced to death on the flimsiest of grounds. For every person actually in prison, there were dozens more who were compelled to live for months in a state of fear, knowing that any hint that they lacked sufficient revolutionary enthusiasm, or any accusation – however unfounded – of sympathising with the enemies of the state could be grounds enough for their arrest, imprisonment, and possible execution. The number of people executed by the revolutionary government during this period may have numbered in the tens of thousands, but the number of people who were – to use one of the new words which emerged from the event – *terrorised* by it must have been in the millions. The Law of Suspects passed on 17 September 1793, right at the beginning of the Terror, criminalised, under penalty of death, all 'conduct, associations, talk, or writings' which implied support for 'tyranny, federalism, or enemies of liberty', a category so wide as to be virtually meaningless: under such laws, almost anything could potentially mark one out as a 'suspect', and many were indeed arrested on the flimsiest of pretences.[88] The atmosphere of corrosive suspicion and dread in which people were thus compelled to exist, knowing that it was possible to be arrested – and potentially executed – simply for being 'suspect of suspicion', clearly left deep psychological scars upon many of those who lived through it, and Thibaudeau must have spoken for many when he wrote, many years later: 'I was a witness [to the Terror] and when I think back on it, I am terrified by my own memories, my soul remains burdened, and my pen refuses, as it were, to describe them.'[89]

As the Great Fear of 1789 demonstrates, however, the fearfulness of the Revolution was not something invented by Robespierre and his allies in the autumn of 1793. Indeed, the Terror can only be understood if it is realised that the men who oversaw it and carried it out were, themselves, terrified; suspicious, anxious, even paranoid in their belief that shadowy, hostile forces lurked all around them, plotting their downfall and the destruction of all they had achieved. As Palmer remarks, 'the Terror was born of fear; from the terror in which men lived, from the appalling disorder produced by five years of Revolution and the lawless habits of the old regime'.[90] This omnipresent fear was most persistently embodied in the recurrent fear that some sinister army was gathering in secret, preparing to strike at the people of France. David Andress writes:

> Throughout the intervening years [i.e. 1789–1792], Paris had rung to the repeated alarms that the city was filling with shadowy figures, flitting over the frontiers or rising up from an unknown netherworld. There were always thirty thousand of them, for some reason – this seemed almost a talismanic figure, and no matter how many times in 1790 or 1791 the brigands of Paris failed to launch their dastardly blow, at the next alarm the same fears were trotted out...[91]

Conspiracy theories proliferated between 1789 and 1794, with every failure of the Revolution to keep to its predicted course attributed to the plotting of hidden enemies.[92] The diamond necklace affair of 1785 had convinced many in France that the royal court was a nest of secrecy and deceit, and the impression that the royalists could not be trusted was underlined by the royal family's secret flight to Varennes in June 1791; for if they were capable of conspiring to defraud jewellers, or to spirit away the king and deliver him to the enemies of the Revolution, then what else might they be plotting behind closed doors? On the Day of Daggers (28 February 1791), Lafayette arrested four hundred aristocrats on the suspicion that they were members of an anti-revolutionary conspiracy. When the fortress of Longwy fell more rapidly than expected to the Austrian and Prussian armies on 23 August 1792, it was immediately assumed that its defenders had betrayed it to the enemy – a suspicion that would be repeated each time the armies of the Republic suffered military reverses in the years to come.[93] Explaining why the September Massacres had been necessary, the journalist Gorsas – then an ally of the Jacobins – wrote that 'there were many in the metropolis, in Austrian pay' who had been secretly planning to release the prisoners and arm them against the Republic, and that just before the massacre 'the suspicious persons who swarmed in the metropolis were observed to be very busy, and to communicate with each other by signs', which sounds very much like an ordinary Parisian street scene observed through the eyes of a deeply paranoid individual.[94] The Girondins with whom Helen Maria Williams associated assured her that the Massacres had been the work of a conspiracy of *agent provocateurs;* later, the Jacobins were to insist that the murders of Lepelletier and Marat must have been carried out at the bidding of sinister anti-revolutionary forces. Rumour, propaganda, and disinformation proliferated, feeding off one another in the overheated journalistic print culture which arose following the abolition of censorship in 1789, and by 1793 the mood of anxiety had reached a feverish pitch: in February 1793, one Englishwoman then resident in France begged a British correspondent to 'make no allusion to any political matter whatever' in subsequent letters to her, explaining that 'no-one in England can form an idea of the suspicion that pervades every part of the French government'.[95] By the time the Terror began, the Jacobins had started to see treason and conspiracy everywhere: military defeats, strikes by workmen, food shortages, political dissension, popular unrest, and the display of too much or too little relish for revolutionary violence were all seen as so many signs of a vast anti-revolutionary conspiracy, set afoot either by the allied kings of Europe, or by factions within the Revolution who aimed to achieve despotic power for themselves.[96] The armies invading France were formidable, but at least they could be located and fought. But how could the spies, the assassins, the conspirators, the hidden enemies within be combated? How could the revolutionary government even know where to look?

Robespierre's paranoia was particularly acute: as Jordan writes, 'Robespierre's world, during the final year of his life, was a fearful and fatal place, inhabited by the enemy without and within.'[97] His response to this multitude of hidden threats was simple, and audacious in its totalitarian logic: if the enemies of the republic were plotting its downfall in private, then the republic must ensure that there were no private spaces for them to plot in. As Sagan puts it, 'the French Revolution represents the first attempt to annihilate the private to serve a *political* purpose', and Singer concurs: 'society [was to] form a single, smooth surface, where everyone will be visible to everyone else and where conformity to the law will result from continuous mutual surveillance'.[98] Robespierre, who had no private life, saw no reason why anyone but a traitor should object to being watched at all times by the state: as he remarked, 'innocence never fears public surveillance'.[99] But as even the most vigilant state could not keep watch on all its citizens all the time, it was also necessary to strike such fear into these secretive plotters that they would not dare attempt to put their plans in motion. Partly, this fear would be induced by the machinery of surveillance itself, and the knowledge that they might be watched or questioned at any time; but some of it, inevitably, would have to come from old-fashioned spectacular violence. As one Jacobin representative wrote, 'it is terror alone, and the most terrible punishments, that can contain men who are royalist in their hearts'; or, as Collot D'Herbois infamously stated when ordering the mass execution of rebels at Lyons: 'The explosion of mines, etc, the devouring activity of flame can alone express the omnipotence of the people; its will cannot be checked like that of tyrants; it must have the effect of thunder.'[100]

This combination of pervasive surveillance and occasional spectacular violence took a heavy toll on those who suffered through it. Constant horrors rapidly numb the mind; but, as psychological studies have shown, living in a state of constant uncertainty and insecurity tends to fray the psyche to the point of disintegration.[101] So it should not surprise us if those who lived through the Terror were, very frequently, terrified by it; left traumatised, physically and psychically damaged, and not infrequently somewhat unhinged. It is entirely fitting that the first fully documented case of paranoid schizophrenia, that of the British merchant James Tilley Matthews, should have resulted from the Revolution: imprisoned in France during the Terror, Matthews became convinced after his return to England that a group of French spies were secretly targeting him with a fantastical machine he called an 'Air Loom', with which they were able to inflict physical or psychological torment upon him at will.[102] This imaginary machine, capable of invisibly broadcasting terror and trauma through the air into the minds of its victims, could serve well as an emblem for the Terror itself, during which, for eleven months, the stuff of persecutory fantasy became reality for many inhabitants of revolutionary France.

But why should these events have so terrified those who were not directly subjected to them – the British, for example? As I have discussed, the idea that a state might need to strategically deploy spectacular violence in order to maintain social order was taken for granted in the eighteenth century: a belief that was most obviously manifested in the spectacle of public execution, which Foucault calls a 'theatre of terror'.[103] The old rituals of public judicial torture were on the wane, and the grotesque four-hour execution of the French attempted regicide Damiens – who, according to Revolution-era rumours, had secretly been Robespierre's uncle – by horse, pincer, fire, oil, and blade in 1757 had scandalised enlightened individuals across Europe.[104] But in France men were still broken on the wheel and burnt at the stake until the Revolution; in Italy men continued to be publicly executed by hammer, knife, and axe, 'like an ox in the shambles', while in Britain the bodies of criminals were still publicly dismembered or desecrated after death: the corpses of traitors were disembowelled until 1781, and beheaded as late as 1820, while the bodies of women executed for 'petty treason' (usually coining or murdering their husbands) were burned at the stake until 1790, and when John Williams committed suicide after being arrested for the Ratcliffe Highway murders in 1811, his corpse was carried in a ritual procession to the site of the murders before being buried in an unmarked grave with a wooden stake hammered through its heart.[105] The spectacle of the mangled body of the criminal, thus publicly burned, beheaded, gutted, or defiled before the gaze of the crowd, was felt to have a salutary effect on those who witnessed it, by teaching them to fear the dreadful consequences of committing such criminal acts themselves.[106] In the slave plantations of America and the Caribbean, where it was understood to be essential for the slave population to be kept obedient through fear, even more extreme forms of punishment and execution were sometimes employed, such as the scenes of torture and mutilation witnessed by Steadman in Surinam.[107]

What was so shocking about the spectacular violence meted out by D'Herbois and his colleagues in order to terrify the enemies of the republic was not that it happened at all, but that it broke the symbolic codes were supposed to govern the infliction of such violence; it happened to the wrong people, in the wrong places. As Cobb writes:

> Both contemporaries and several generations of liberal or reactionary historians were shocked by the spectacle of popular violence during the French Revolution. Contemporaries feared that these new, unexpected, and unpredictable forms of violence might be used against property-holders and respectable people, rather than against poachers and lawbreakers. In fact, what seems to have shocked contemporaries and historians alike is that the violence should have been popular (and, by implication, lawless, brutish, chaotic, undirected).[108]

Its primary targets were not mutinous slaves or rebellious subjects rising up against the social order embodied by the clergy, aristocracy, and monarchy, but the priests, aristocrats, and royalty themselves, as well as those of all ranks who supported or sympathised with them. It did not take place in physically or socially distant locations, but reached right into those spaces which were supposed to be most insulated from such violence: domestic interiors, consecrated churches, and royal palaces. For the elite reading public in Britain, these stories could not help being much more immediate than any 'bloody vignette' about plantation horrors or scaffold scenes; they described the spectacular physical destruction, not of social and racial others (whom popular contemporary theories of sensibility dismissed as being, in any case, incapable of truly suffering in the same way as the cultivated and well-bred), but of people like themselves, dragged from homes like theirs, in a country very close to, and until the Revolution not very different from, their own.[109] What such people found so terrifying about the Terror was that it appeared to have no limits: no-one and nowhere seemed safe from it, and no rules or laws that they could make sense of seemed to constrain its operation. It was characterised, as Hénaff puts it, by 'systematic, *unlimited* violence' (my italics); for, as Saint-Just remarked in a speech on 26 February 1794, 'That which constitutes a Republic is the total destruction of that which opposes it.'[110] The limited violence of eighteenth-century executions and *Kabinettskriege*, in which the destruction of human bodies was carried out within the boundaries prescribed by the laws of nations and the 'rules of war', had been containable within their mental picture of how the world did and should function; but the unlimited violence of the Terror, which rejected all such boundaries, was not so easily contained. As Ankersmit argues, it was the psychologically and culturally unassimilable nature of this revolutionary violence, rather than its actual extent, which made it so traumatic an episode in the historical memory of Europe.[111]

Due to the wealth of foreign reporting in British newspapers of the 1790s, which brought British readers daily updates on the latest events in France, it is possible to track their changing attitudes to the developing events in France with some precision. In 1789 and 1790 the tone of coverage was generally positive, except in the more conservative sectors of the British press. By late 1791 the note of concern and disapproval at the continued confusion and disorder generated by the Revolution was more widespread; many deplored such episodes of violence as the massacre of La Glacière at Avignon in October, and on 7 November 1791 *The Times* reported that 'tumults, assassinations, and conflagrations are now so frequent, the report of them scarcely makes an impression upon the callous hearts of Frenchmen, become ferocious like tygers in the forest'.[112] The storming of the Tuileries on 10 August 1792 provoked fierce debates in the British press over whether the Swiss Guard or the people of Paris had been responsible for the opening of hostilities, but was generally reported in the relatively neutral terms of a military engagement. Anti-revolutionary papers such as the *St James's Chronicle* and *The World* reported the day's events as a catalogue of horrors, printing lurid stories of up to twelve thousand dead in the streets of Paris, corpses torn open and their hearts eaten by the mob, the blood of Swiss Guards drunk from bottles by their murderers, and the women of Paris dancing amidst the bloodshed: as *The World* breathlessly claimed, 'the most atrocious crimes are daily and hourly committed with impunity'.[113] But the rest of the press initially paid little heed to these stories; *The Star* even warned its readers on 18 August that all manner of wild rumours were now arriving from France, and they should be wary of believing any of them to be true.[114]

As early as August 1792, then, the view had taken hold in some quarters that the French revolutionaries had moved beyond all normal bounds of behaviour, and into the domain of what, three years later, would start to be called 'terrorist' violence. For the readers of the *St James's Chronicle*, this illegitimate, revolutionary violence was entirely distinct from that used by, say, the Prussian and Austrian armies then in the process of invading France; the political and moral principles by which the revolutionaries decided whom they should target, and how much they should suffer, were not recognised by the *Chronicle* as legitimate, reasonable, or even sane, and the violence that resulted from them was thus persistently characterised as being both essentially arbitrary in its choice of victims, and needlessly, inhumanly extreme in its treatment of them. Thus the insistence of the anti-revolutionary press that, on 10 August 1792, the victims of the Parisian 'mob' were not just killed but torn to pieces, their hearts eaten, their blood drunk, their corpses stripped naked, their heads paraded through the streets, the innocent and guilty mown down alike in an outburst of indiscriminate violence in which no-one could be secure: the extremity of the reported violence and the randomness of its infliction served to rhetorically mirror the combination of ideological extremism and lack of rational foundations which, for these writers, characterised the Revolution itself. The *Diary or Woodfall's Register* for 1 September 1792 reported that no-one in Paris was now safe, and the *Public Advertiser* for the same day concurred: 'What necessity has the Duke of Brunswick for leading his combined armies against Paris? – The inhabitants of that *blessed city* are cutting one another's throats so rapidly that a few months more, at the rate they are going on, will leave their enemies very little havoc to make among them.' The *World* claimed that not just Paris, but all 'the Inland Towns in *France*' were now 'one continued scene of plunder and depredation'; in its view, the man chiefly to blame for this was the mayor of Paris, Pétion, of whom it declared: 'There is a degree of ferocity and barbarity in the character of this man, that cannot be paralleled in human nature.'[115] The *Evening Mail* even claimed that '[i]n no page of ancient or modern history – in sacred or prophane writings, is there to be found any account of insurrection, mutiny, or rebellion, fraught with such traits of barbarism – such inhuman butcheries', and asserted that the French had become 'the most savage and cruel race of people now known on the face of the earth'.[116] That, historically, almost none of this was true – that the death toll of 10 August was vastly less than twelve thousand, that the inland towns of France were in fact relatively tranquil, that Paris was in no danger whatsoever of depopulating itself through civil strife, and that Jérôme Pétion, though clearly guilty of encouraging a bloody urban insurrection, was hardly the most monstrous human being who had ever lived – is almost besides the point. The purpose of this kind of reportage was less to transmit true facts about the world than to communicate to its readership the extent of the writer's outrage and anxiety about what was taking place, and their sense of the complete social and moral breakdown that they regarded the French Revolution as having brought about.

In August 1792 this viewpoint was limited to certain sectors of the British press; but, as word of the September Massacres began to reach Britain, it became much more widespread. Many newspapers were initially fairly restrained in their reporting on the massacres, but as more and more horror stories arrived over the ensuing days, only the most committed pro-revolutionary newspapers, such as the *Morning Chronicle*, made any attempt to maintain such a stance. Newspapers such as the *Times* and *Diary, or Woodfall's Register*, previously relatively sympathetic to the Revolution, now carried stories of clergymen forced by the mob to murder one another, Princess Lamballe tortured, mutilated, and murdered in the street, gangs of *sans-culotte* children roaming Paris and beheading the children of the well-born with their pen-knives, people roasted alive on bonfires and others forced to eat cooked human flesh, mobs specifically targeting 'the virtuous, the innocent, the moral, and the religious', and much, much more in the same vein. The already anti-revolutionary papers lapsed even further into the domain of nightmarish fantasy, with the *St James's Chronicle* asserting that the massacres had claimed the lives of about 25,000 people – roughly twenty times the estimate of modern historians – and that they had been led by a sinister Jew who travelled around Paris with seventy bodyguards, each carrying a bleeding human head on the end of their pike, slaughtering the enemies of the Jacobins everywhere he went.[117] As with the reporting on the events of 10 August, the fact that almost none of these enormities actually took place in September 1792 is perhaps of secondary importance to these stories: what these reports primarily communicate is not what had or hadn't happened on the streets of Paris, the facts of which could not avoid being confused and uncertain, but the sense of these writers that events in France had moved into uncharted moral territory, that the revolutionaries had departed entirely from the social conventions governing the legitimate infliction of violence, and that consequently absolutely anything could be believed of them. If they were capable of killing one thousand people, then why not five thousand, or ten, or twenty? If they were capable of murdering a princess in the street, then why hesitate to believe that they might have tortured, raped, mutilated, or dismembered her, as well? Why not believe that they were monsters, animals, demons, that they sang and danced as they murdered, that they drank human blood, that they ate the hearts and livers of their victims? If they did not stop at the normal limits of violence, what grounds were there for believing they would stop at anything?

The sense of disorientated horror that characterises these reports is reflected in the vocabulary and register of their prose. Most eighteenth-century writers did not habitually report on violent events in terms like these; inhabitants of a world where large-scale human suffering was taken more or less for granted, the tone they adopted when reporting its infliction was generally much more matter of fact. Even the word 'massacre' was very little used before the Revolution, so that one must go back some decades to find a suitable point of comparison. Here, for example, is a report of a massacre in America from the *Morning Penny Post* in September 1751:

> A few days since the Indians in the French interest perpetrated a most horrible Massacre at the Town of Dartmouth, on the opposite Shore to us, where they killed, scalped, and frightfully mangled, several of the Soldiery and Inhabitants of the Town: They have not spared even the Women and Children. A little Baby was found lying by its Father and Mother, and all three scalped. The whole town was a Scene of Butchery, some having their Hands cut off, some their Bellies ripped open, and others their Brains dashed out. In short never was more inhumane Barbarity beheld.[118]

This, generally, was the way in which extreme violence was written about in the eighteenth century, even in cheap and popular newspapers such as the *Morning Penny Post*. The moral judgement that the writer passes on the scene is clear – the massacre is 'most horrible', an 'inhumane Barbarity' – but the tone is factual and impersonal, and the emphasis is on communicating an accurate picture of events: who the victims were, what kind of injuries they suffered, in what ways their bodies were damaged and destroyed. The word 'butchery' is well chosen, for the overall idea conveyed is of human bodies treated like meat in a butcher's shop, and these facts alone are assumed to be sufficient for the reader to understand how terrible an event is being described. The writer does not consider it necessary to provide all possible details, giving the reader a body-by-body description of the carnage; once a representative sample has been given, the rest can be summarised 'in short'. Even the final judgement is relatively restrained: 'never was more inhumane Barbarity beheld' implies that the inhumanity of the massacre is as bad as anything before it, but not that it surpasses all previous acts of barbarity. Yet compare this with a few extracts from a string of anecdotes from the September Massacres in Paris, published in the *St James's Chronicle*:

> The following atrocious actions lately practised at Paris, it would be *criminal* to conceal: they are given on the credit of an immediate eye-witness:
>
> The Countess du Chevre, with her five children, the oldest not eleven years of age, were massacred at her house [...] The children were first assassinated before the eyes of their parent. She bore this infernal sight with a fortitude supernatural – she embraced the bleeding head of the youngest, and met her fate with heroick contempt. The wretches first cut off the arms that sustained her last sad comfort, and then severed her head from her body.
>
> In the same street, an old Swiss Gentleman, M. d'Aubert, about 70 [...] was thrown alive into a fire [...] Thrice he ran from the flames, and as often was driven back: at last, with their pikes, the sanguinary monsters pinned him there, and, insultingly demanding him to sing *ça ira*, danced around the fire singing themselves, in the true spirit of North American savages [...]
>
> The poor murthered children were four and six years old, and no one of the accursed little fiends who despatched them, I am confident, was above twelve. Not the slightest expression of concern, much more horrour, appeared in the faces of the populace, at these unaccountable villainies; and the women even encouraged these infant furies.
>
> Many, with courage, surely pitiable, almost justifiable, gave themselves a death, that approached more terrible in the garb of these assassins. Hundreds placed themselves upon the three bridges, and, when the mob appeared, threw themselves into the Seine [...] [119]

In these stories, we have moved from the scene-painting of the *Morning Penny Post* into a kind of monstrous operatic drama. The factual record of events, of who was killed, and how, and by whom, is no longer assumed to speak for itself, even though one might presume most readers would understand that anyone who murders small children in front of their mothers and burns old men alive in the streets probably did not deserve their sympathy or support; instead the reader is made the spectator of a series of ghastly one-act horror-plays, in which every action is heightened and aggravated as far as possible. The *Post* had been content to inform its readers that the massacre it reported was carried out by 'Indians in the French interest'; the *Chronicle* makes sure we understand that the killers are 'wretches', 'assassins', 'sanguinary monsters', 'savages', 'fiends', and 'furies', that their crimes are 'infernal', 'accursed', 'terrible', 'unaccountable villainies', and that their victims are exemplary innocents: 'five children, the oldest not eleven' and their 'heroick' mother, 'an old Swiss Gentleman ... about 70', two 'poor murthered children ... four and six years old'. The events are 'atrocious', but far from meaning that their details should be decently summarised, it turns out that it would be '*criminal*' for us not to be told all about them: we apparently *need* to know, as a matter of moral or legal duty, not just that the Paris mob has been murdering innocent people, but that they cut off the arms of the Countess du Chevre to prevent her from holding the 'bleeding head' of her youngest child before she died. The frantic, hysterical edge audible in these stories, with their breathless piling up of adjectives, anecdotes, and execrations, is entirely absent from the older article.

To some extent, these differences are doubtless due to the wider changes which had taken place in British culture as a whole during the forty years that separated these two massacres; in articles such as these, the *Chronicle* was delivering to its readers the kind of overt emotionality which the cult of sensibility insisted upon as a marker of sincerity, a demand which would have been relatively foreign to the writers of the *Post* in 1751. The impact of the sentimental novel is also visible in the novelistic element at work in these stories, with their rapid sketches of place and character; all three of these anecdotes read like sentimental scenes of suffering innocence taken to lunatic extremes, in a manner reminiscent of de Sade's contemporary usage of the sentimental novel form as a vehicle for sadistic pornography. Such sentimental and novelistic traits are also prominent in the 'bloody vignettes' which appeared in the abolitionist literature of the 1780s. But, even taking these broader cultural currents into account, the fact remains that in 1792 people did not normally write like this, even about the most horrible events: late eighteenth-century writers on crime, war, and violence were usually much more matter of fact.[120] Even the infamous *Newgate Calendar*, which at the time was a byword for sensationalism, generally reported acts of violence in a much more level and factual tone. Here, for example, is its account of the teacher Thomas Hunter's murder of his two young pupils for informing their parents of his affair with a servant, a crime which it describes as 'singular and horrid' and 'most diabolical':

His knife being sharpened, he called the lads to him, and having reprimanded them for acquainting their father and mother of the scene to which they had been witnesses, he said that he would immediately put them to death. Terrified by this threat the children ran from him; but he immediately followed, and brought them back. He then placed his knee on the body of the one, while he cut the throat of the other with his pen-knife; and then treated the second in the same inhuman manner that he had done the first.

It was within half a mile of the castle of Edinburgh that these horrid murders were committed...[121]

The events described here are not dissimilar to those in the *St James's Chronicle*: a 'horrid', 'diabolical', and 'inhuman' murder of innocent children. (Hunter even murdered his victims with a pen-knife, the same weapon apparently used by the 'infant furies' to kill children during the September Massacres.) But the tone, like that of the 1751 account of the Dartmouth massacre – and of late-eighteenth-century writing about violence more generally – is level and even, emphasising factual reportage rather than overdetermined moral judgement; there is no suggestion here that there might be any difficulty in narrating, understanding, or morally evaluating such events, and adjectives and adverbs are few and far between. When the narrative does reach something it cannot adequately describe – the grief of the parents upon hearing of the murder of their sons – it simply acknowledges as much:

It is not in the power of language to describe the effects resulting from the communication of this dreadful news: the astonishment of the afflicted father, the agony of the mother's grief, may possibly be conceived, though it cannot be painted.[122]

The *Newgate Calendar* divides such acts of violence into the speakable (who did what to who), which it straightforwardly narrates, and the unspeakable (the emotional suffering such acts can cause), which it acknowledges but makes no attempt to represent; and, as a result, neither extreme violence nor the incommunicable pain it causes disrupts the smooth surface of its prose. In the rhetoric of the *St James's Chronicle*, by contrast, the two categories seem to have collapsed; here, neither the violence itself nor its emotional effects on those seem to be properly communicable, and yet the narrative attempts to represent them both. This is language under pressure, struggling to keep up with the demands placed upon it, and seemingly aware of its own inadequacies as it gestures into moral and emotional spaces it attempts to describe without knowing how to represent them, able to say only that the fortitude of the Countess is 'supernatural', the people's lack of horror 'unaccountable', the mass suicide neither right nor wrong but 'surely pitiable, almost justifiable', and so on. Its frantic tone and rhetorical excesses reflect its pervasive sense that the normal order of things had broken down, and that ordinary language was no longer sufficient or appropriate to describe what was now believed to be taking place in revolutionary France.

Faced with such events, contemporary writers reached back to older rhetorical resources, disused for generations, to articulate what they felt to be happening in France. One common device was to compare the crimes of the revolutionaries to the historical religious persecutions carried out by the Catholic Church, which for Protestant British writers remained the epitome of foreign villainy: thus the revolutionaries were described in *The World* as possessing 'all that terrible inhuman and inquisitorial persecuting rancour' of Catholicism, the readers of *The Oracle* were warned that 'the spirit of infernal persecution is abroad', and the revolutionary massacres were routinely compared to the St Bartholomew's Day Massacre of 1572.[123] Another, related tactic was to employ the old language of supernatural terror, and describe the revolutionaries as monsters, demons, or Satanists: the *Evening Mail* asserted that the Revolution seemed to be directed by Satan, as 'every act and deed of course wears the infernal stamp of his advice', the *World* declared that the revolutionaries were an 'infernal gang of Assassins', and called them 'monsters in human form' who, like Satan, 'went about … seeking whom they may devour', and *The Oracle* described a Jacobin spokesman as 'an APOSTLE of Assassination'.[124] Even when they were notionally writing about real events, the scenes they described often sounded less like historical facts than episodes from some ghastly folk-tale; the gang of murderous children who were supposed to have roamed Paris during the September Massacres sound like goblins or malevolent faeries, while the monstrous Jew reported by the *St James's Chronicle*, travelling Paris with his mobile forest of severed heads, is a straightforward folk-devil who seems to have stepped directly out of traditional anti-Semitic mythology: he would not have been out of place in Marlowe's *Jew of Malta*. One anti-revolutionary pamphlet of 1793, *An Account of a Most Horrid, Bloody and Terrible Apparition*, took the trope of the revolutionary-as-Satanist to its logical conclusion by asserting that a gathering of revolutionary conspirators in Scotland had been interrupted by the appearance of a bloody ghost from hell, which had delivered a divine warning against their seditious crimes.[125] As I have discussed, in his 1693 *Thoughts Concerning Education* John Locke had warned against the propagation of stories about '*Raw-Head* and *Bloody Bones*, and such other Names, as carry with them the Idea's of some hurtful, terrible Things, inhabiting darkness'; in his view, such stories encouraged feelings of helplessness and radical insecurity in their listeners, thus spreading the kind of unnecessary, irrational fear of arbitrary power which led to despotism, fanaticism, and superstition.[126] It was on these grounds that the writers of the early eighteenth century had dismantled the old literature of theological evil; but now, a century later, faced with an enemy which seemed to combine all the worst traits of historical despotism and fanaticism, these writers reached for just such supernatural and diabolic imagery to articulate how radically insecure the events of the French Revolution had made them feel.

Horrified and aghast though these various commentators doubtless were at the events unfolding in France, it would be misleading to describe them as being terrified. The Duke of Brunswick was marching on Paris, and these reports usually ended with the comforting reflection that the Revolution would soon be over, with order restored by Prussian and Austrian arms and the revolutionaries fled or dead, their powers of mischief spent. But on the battlefield, as in politics, the Revolution did not follow the expected script; Brunswick was repulsed one hundred miles from Paris at the pivotal battle of Valmy, and the further year of international and civil war leading up to the start of the Terror in September 1793 left the revolutionary government battered and bloodied, but still very much in power. As well as murderous capacity for violence, the Revolution appeared to possess an uncanny vitality, its imminent demise endlessly predicted but never actually taking place. The more these writers convinced themselves that the revolutionary state was a mere anarchy, a chaotic 'mobocracy' presided over by blood-crazed cannibal murderers and cynical, power-hungry villains, the more inexplicable its continued survival became; the state they described should have collapsed of its own accord within weeks, able to command the loyalty only of a lunatic rabble, and yet it continued to resist the combined powers of Europe for year after year. It was an aberration, a category error, defying all conventional political wisdom, and as such it was an object of fear; for who could tell what impossibility the 'republick of Regicide', as Burke called it after the execution of Louis XVI in January 1793, might accomplish next?[127]

From the September Massacres onwards, then, there was a growing sense in Britain that the French Revolution represented something new in modern history, something wild, fearful, and extremely dangerous. 'It is impossible not to notice the sort of communal psychosis which permeated British society in the 1790s and beyond', writes Grenby, 'fed by propaganda of various sorts which encouraged the British public to comprehend the wholly unprecedented events in France as a catastrophe of quasi-Biblical proportions, not as a series of political incidents but as a great moral offence against virtue, nature and God'.[128] As the *Evening Mail* had put it as early as August 1792, neither 'ancient or modern history' nor 'sacred or prophane writings' seemed to contain any parallel or precedent for what was now happening in France, leaving those who attempted to describe or explain it radically adrift, forced to fall back upon the language of the monstrous, the unaccountable, the infernal, and the superhuman.[129] All through 1793 and 1794, as the Terror ground on, the horror stories continued to accumulate, carried by traumatised refugees psychologically brutalised by Robespierre's regime; massacre after massacre was reported, although the events of September 1792 remained the gold standard of revolutionary atrocity, and in the last months before Thermidor the newspaper reports from Paris became almost entirely dominated by interminable lists of those executed by the Revolutionary Tribunal, giving the impression that virtually nothing now happened in the city except the infliction of death. But just as it was only in retrospect that the events of 1793–4 came to be viewed as a historical unit called 'the Terror', so it was that the historical mythology of the Terror only really came to be compiled after Robespierre's fall – a period which, in Britain, was one of anti-revolutionary political reaction, marked by the Treason Trials of 1794 and the Two Acts of 1795. Bindman has pointed out that, in the visual arts, depictions of the Terror were most frequent between 1794 and 1799, the years immediately following its conclusion; the same years saw the publication of eyewitness accounts of France during the Terror, such as Helen Maria Williams' *Letters from France* (1795) and *A Residence in France* (1797) by 'An English Lady', and of compilations of revolutionary horror-stories, such as *The Bloody Buoy* (1796, reprinted as *Annals of Blood* in 1797), by William Cobbett, and *The Cannibal's Progress* (1798), translated by Anthony Aufrer. As Bindman writes:

> The cumulative effect of the avalanche of counter-revolutionary propaganda published in England during the 1790s was to convince many English men and women that perpetual chaos prevailed across the Channel. There was little sense of the fluctuating state of revolutionary politics, even less idea of the ebb and flow of revolutionary violence [. . .] Thus, when a peace mission led by the Earl of Malmesbury went to France in 1796, its members were astonished to find an orderly and peaceful nation. They had expected to see a landscape depicted by James Gillray...[130]

IV

It was in the same years in which this historical mythology was starting to be codified that Gothic fiction first became a truly popular, mass-market genre. In his statistical analysis of the publication of Gothic fiction, Robert Miles observes:

> There is a sharp increase in Gothic 'product' starting in 1788, followed by a further upward deflection point in 1793. From 1788 until 1807 the Gothic maintains a market share of around 30 per cent of novel production, reaching a high point of 38 per cent in 1795, then dipping to around 20 per cent in 1808.[131]

Gothic fiction did not just increase in quantity after 1793; its character also changed, shifting with the tenor of the times. If one peruses the list of titles published by the popular Minerva Press, a keen producer of Gothic romance fiction from the 1780s onwards, the change becomes obvious. Initially the sure mark of a Gothic romance had been a title including the word 'baron' or 'castle', such as *The Solitary Castle* (1789), *The Baron of Manstow* (1790), or *Sidney Castle* (1792), but from 1794 onwards a new ghastliness rapidly takes hold: the barons, abbeys, and castles continue to appear, but alongside new watchwords such as 'mystery' and 'horror', giving rise to titles such as *The Haunted Castle* (1794), *The Necromancer* (1794), *Mystery of the Black Tower* (1796), *The Horrors of Oakendale Abbey* (1797), *The Animated Skeleton* (1798), and *The Madman of the Mountain* (1799).[132] Popular authors whose works spanned the period both before and after 1794 often altered their writing practices as a response to the shift in demand. Anna Maria Mackenzie, for example, began her career as a writer of historical romances such as *Monmouth* (1790), but from the mid-1790s she switched instead to more obviously Gothic novels such as *Mysteries Elucidated* (1795) and *The Fratricide; or the Mysteries of Dusseldorf* (1798), which she wrote under the pen-name 'Ellen of Exeter'; similarly, Charlotte Smith's popular *Elegiac Sonnets* had always been gloomy, but it was only from 1794 onwards that she began to add sonnets with titles such as 'On passing over a dreary tract of country, and near the ruins of a deserted chapel, during a tempest', or 'On being cautioned against walking on a headland overlooking the sea, because it was frequented by a lunatic'.[133] These changing titles point not only to the growing popularity of Gothic as a genre, but also to a shift in the genre itself; hitherto essentially a sub-genre of the sentimental novel, around 1794 the Gothic romance began to re-invent itself as a literature of terror.

The crucial figure in this process was Ann Radcliffe, whose early novels had combined the sentimental novel tradition of Charlotte Smith with the Gothic romance tradition of Clara Reeve; her novels were set in the Catholic Europe of the sixteenth and seventeenth centuries, with all the cruelty and instability that readers of her generation considered to be inevitable in such settings, but her protagonists were men and women of feeling straight out of eighteenth-century sentimental novels, whose exquisite sensibilities responded to the barbarous worlds in which they found themselves with emotions of sorrow, pity, and – above all – fear.[134] The idea that the protagonist of a Gothic romance should spend a substantial portion of the story being *terrified* was a new one in the early 1790s, one that neither Smith nor Reeve would have taken for granted; Smith because her sentimental heroes and heroines only had to deal with the everyday cruelties and injustices of their domestic, contemporary settings, and Reeve because her historical protagonists were made of sterner stuff, as befitted the inhabitants of a wild and warlike age. But in Radcliffe's Gothic romances, there is a mismatch between the protagonists and the world they live in; they are generous, sensitive, loving, and artistic, but their world is cruel, hard, and savage, constantly menacing them with its violent and arbitrary power. As Evans writes:

> Radcliffe's Adeline, Emily, and Ellena were no more born to the medieval scene than were Pamela and Evelina. Enlightened, virtuous, and 'sensible', they had been uprooted from their proper society and, with contemporary intellectual and emotional patterns intact, thrust into that era which was 'barbarous'. Subjected to the various menaces of the Dark Ages, they served as projections of the nervous

system of their own time, as sensitive registers of emotional reaction to horrors, and clearly, as transmitters of the thrill of their exposure.[135]

Persecuted by forces to which they know themselves to be unequal, these sensitive souls consequently feel *terror*; and it was for her psychological depictions of scenes of terror that Radcliffe swiftly became famous. Already strongly visible in early novels such as *The Romance of the Forest*, whose aesthetics of fear are implicitly underwritten by the examples of Shakespeare, Collins, and Warton (epigraphs from whose works appear at the heads of many of its chapters), and in which the words 'terror', 'horror', 'fright', 'fear', and their derivations appear an astonishing 343 times, Radcliffe's terror fiction technique was brought to its most developed form in her two most famous works, *The Mysteries of Udolpho* (1794) and *The Italian* (1797); and it is the former of these, which was also Radcliffe's greatest commercial success, which seems to have sparked the change in the character of Gothic romance which is visible in the Minerva catalogue and elsewhere after 1794.[136] Before *Udolpho*, Gothic romance was primarily a vehicle for sentimental stories with romanticised historical settings; works such as Sophia Lee's *The Recess* (1783), which presented history as an essentially unjust and nightmarish realm through which the innocent suffered in vain, were rare, and works which aimed to scare their readers, such as Walpole's *Otranto*, were rarer still.[137] This sentimental Gothic romance tradition certainly lived on after *Udolpho*; but from 1794 onwards, there grew up a body of Gothic literature whose chief stock-in-trade was the depiction of scenes of terror.

It is important to stress this discontinuity, as it is one that is often elided by modern histories of Gothic fiction, which frequently present Gothic as a single 'literature of terror' stretching from Walpole to Radcliffe to Shelley. Thus Alan Lloyd-Smith, for example, writes of 'the craze for Gothic fiction begun by Walpole and developed by Matthew Gregory Lewis, William Godwin, and Ann Radcliffe', as though the Gothic tale of terror had been popular as far back as the 1760s.[138] As I have attempted to make clear, this was not at all the case; Gothic fiction was hardly read at all until the late 1770s, and both its nature and popularity changed markedly from around 1793 onwards, transforming it from a moderately widely read genre of historical romance into an immensely popular literature of terror. There was nothing inevitable about the rise of Gothic fiction; as late as 1788 it probably seemed no more than a passing fad, and so it might very well have remained had the events of the French Revolution not given a new relevance to the genre. Leslie Fiedler writes that '[a]ll the major themes and symbols of the gothic were present in Walpole's book, but it did not prove capable of starting a new fashion in fiction; the European imagination was not yet ready for it, would not be ready until that imagination had been modified by the Revolution and the Terror', and Kilgour concurs: '[*Otranto*] might have been an aesthetic dead end, a one-shot eccentric mutation on the literary evolutionary line, if the terrifying events of the 1790s had not made it an appropriate vehicle for embodying relevant political and aesthetic questions'.[139] That the appearance, and growing popularity, of this new literature of terror coincided with the increasing intensity of revolutionary violence in France was not lost on contemporary observers; as Miles notes, 'Equating the Gothic with the French Revolution was a contemporary, rather than a retrospective phenomenon.'[140] In a letter of 11 September 1794, Hester Piozzi wrote that '[l]ove seems banished from the novels, where *terror* (as in the Convention) becomes the *order of the day*. Miss Radcliffe however plays the game best which all are striving to play well...'[141]

Doubtless some of this was a relatively straightforward process of cause and effect, with readers turning to Radcliffe's tales of terror because they were themselves afraid; the fears of her modern-minded, sentimental heroines confronted with the barbaric violence of the past may have mirrored the fears they felt regarding the French Revolution, in which they saw a resurgence of the kind of persecutory violence that they considered to have been characteristic of the sixteenth and seventeenth centuries. (From 1794 onwards, some of them may also have been increasingly afraid of their own government, which had responded to the revolutionary threat with repressive measures so sweeping that some radicals began to write of a 'Pittite terror' in Britain.[142]) But the chronology of events suggests another side to the story. Radcliffe's first forays into terror fiction were published between 1789 and 1791, before the French Revolution turned violent; her sentimental protagonists were quivering with terror years before the National Convention made it the order of the day, and her fiction was thus already available as an imaginative resource for writers responding to the September Massacres and the Terror. *The Mysteries of Udolpho* was written while the Terror was ongoing, and published as it approached its end; but it and its many imitators were being widely read in the years during which writers such as Cobbett were compiling the historical mythology of the French Revolution. This counter-revolutionary mythology was, in turn, being used by the supporters of Pitt's government to justify the repressive legislation and surveillance culture which was then being imposed upon Britain; measures whose purpose was, in theory, to prevent the outbreak of French-style revolutionary terror, but which in practice also served to stoke the mood of anxiety in Britain, a mood which was expressed in works of paranoid radical Gothic such as William Godwin's *Things As They Are, or, The Adventures of Caleb Williams* (1794).[143] Rather than a one-way causal chain running from history to literature, whereby the growth of Gothic fiction was simply a reaction to the news arriving from France, I would suggest that what actually took place between about 1789 and 1798 was closer to a feedback loop between the two. Gothic romances such as *The Romance of the Forest* provided journalists writing about the September Massacres and the Terror with an imaginative vocabulary with which to describe what they believed to be happening in France; their frantic reportage contributed to the mood of national anxiety and fascination with scenes of terror upon which the success of *Udolpho* and its imitators were built, and these novels in turn provided an idiom in which the historical mythology of the Revolution could be written in the years following the Terror's end, their plots functioning as a model through which the confusing and traumatic events of the Revolution could be understood.[144]

As I have stressed, if one considers the whole history of political violence in France during the 1790s, it is not immediately obvious why the operations of the Revolutionary Tribunals during eleven months now referred to as 'the Terror' should be singled out as uniquely horrific. Civil strife on a catastrophic scale continued both before and after this period, and, as I have indicated, the Committee of Public Safety was as much concerned with limiting mass bloodshed as facilitating it; the executions carried out by the Tribunals were intended to replace the chaotic mob violence of 1792, not to supplement it, and some of the most enthusiastically murderous early revolutionaries, such as Jacques Hébert and Mathieu Jourdan (better known by his nickname, 'Jourdan Coup-Tête'), were among the Tribunal's victims, executed for bringing the Revolution into disrepute through their excesses.[145] That this period came in retrospect to be seen as 'the Reign of Terror', the birthplace of 'terrorism', may partly be due to simple political contingency; as I have discussed, it was important for the Thermidorians to stress the difference between themselves and their predecessors, by characterising themselves as moderates and the men they had replaced (and executed) as 'terrorists'. The extremely wide-ranging psychological violence inflicted by the Jacobin regime of surveillance and mass imprisonment doubtless also played an important part, especially as it disproportionately targeted foreigners and the upper ranks of French society: precisely those groups who, unlike their illiterate and anonymous victims of other bouts of revolutionary violence, were best placed to communicate their stories of terror and suffering across Europe and beyond. But it must surely also owe something to the horrible theatricality of the state violence inflicted under Robespierre; its props of prisons and tribunals, tumbrils and guillotines, so much more imaginatively resonant than the squalid mass murders carried out by the *colonnes infernales* in the fields of La Vendée.[146] The vast majority of the Revolution's victims, before, during, and after the Terror, were ordinary men and women, of those humble classes who seldom appeared in eighteenth-century plays or novels except in minor or comic parts, and in whose suffering the eighteenth-century reading public generally did not appear to be particularly interested. But the Terror also claimed the lives of gentry, clergy, aristocrats, and even royalty, men and women whose rank and education made them suitable protagonists in the grandest of tragedies; Camille Desmoulins described how those who frequented executions during the Terror looked down upon the audiences of mere plays and operas, whose feigned tragic spectacles could never compete with that of the guillotine.[147] The extreme, declamatory, blood-and-thunder rhetoric favoured by Robespierre, Danton, Saint-Just, and the other leading Jacobins, with all their talk of virtue and terror, tyranny and tyrannicide, liberty and death, made them easy to cast as either heroes or monsters; indeed, they wilfully invited such comparisons.[148] In short, the Terror made for better *fiction;* more specifically, it proved very easy to adapt to the model of the Radcliffean Gothic romance, in which aristocratic innocents are imprisoned and terrorised by monstrous usurpers.

There is no indication that Radcliffe herself was particularly interested in the progress of the Revolution. In the summer of 1794, while the Terror was still ongoing, she and her husband travelled through the Netherlands and Germany visiting historical monuments, and in the process passed through the very areas which had been fought over by the revolutionary and counter-revolutionary armies in 1792 and 1793. In The Hague, she heard of a Dutch princess who had never recovered from the shock of thinking that her husband had been killed fighting the French the previous September; in Metz she toured the buildings destroyed by Prussian bombardment in the siege the year before, noting that five thousand people had perished in the fighting; in Frankfurt she visited a monument to those who had died driving the French army from the city in December 1792, and on the way to Cologne she witnessed the reunion of two Frenchmen, old friends who had both been driven from France by the Revolution.[149] Yet these scenes, any one of which might have roused a faithful reader of the *St James's Chronicle* to raptures of anti-revolutionary fury, are described by Radcliffe as mere curiosities; she is much more moved and interested by scenes and monuments relating to her favourite historical periods, the sixteenth and seventeenth centuries, and is more incensed by seeing the bullet holes left by the assassination of William the Silent in 1584 – which Radcliffe calls a 'detestable action' – than by any of the fresher wreckage left in the wake of the revolutionary wars.[150] Radcliffe did not link such historical acts of violence to those of the French Revolution; but, as I have discussed, contemporary commentators on the Revolution frequently did make such comparisons, reaching for older vocabularies of evil in order to communicate the violence and terror of the revolutionary regime. The Jacobins were described as monsters, Satanists, and demons, and their evil was compared to that of the four stock villains of eighteenth-century British culture: the arbitrary tyrant, the crazed religious fanatic, the persecuting Catholic Inquisitor, and Milton's Satan. (There was also a flourishing rhetorical sideline which cast them as freethinking libertine seducers, the stock villains of eighteenth-century novels, but this tended to be evoked when discussing their philosophical and religious views rather than their latest massacres.)[151] For readers in the 1790s, all four of these figures were strongly associated with the unenlightened past; and especially with the sixteenth and seventeenth centuries, which were generally depicted in the late eighteenth century as a period when kings and aristocrats had been arbitrary despots, inquisitors had enforced ideological conformity through torture and massacre, fanatical religious enthusiasts had killed their kings and plunged nations into chaos, and superstitious belief in the activity of evil supernatural powers had been universal. These were the cultural resources drawn upon by Radcliffe and her successors, most of whose 'romances' were set in this period, and whose villains were usually domineering aristocrats or inquisitors who enforced their desires through violence and fear.

   Radcliffe's early villains, such as Baron Malcolm and the Marquis de Montalt, were mere stock types, motivated by avarice and lust, but her later villains, Montoni and Schedoni, were the characters for whom she became justly famous; drawing heavily upon Milton's depiction of Satan's sublime evil in *Paradise Lost*, Radcliffe cast her later villains as prodigies of energy, cruelty, rage, ambition, and pride, increasingly overshadowing the other characters in the novels in which they appeared.[152] Montoni towers over *The Mysteries of Udolpho* like the mountains which are his namesake, while Schedoni's inner conflicts make him by far the most engaging and psychologically complex character in *The Italian*. It was a shift which was noted by Walter Scott, who singled it out in his biographical essay on Radcliffe as a mark of her literary development:

> Everything in *The Mysteries of Udolpho* is on a larger and more sublime scale than in *The Romance of the Forest*. [. . .] Montoni, a lofty-souled desperado, and Captain of Condottieri, stands beside La Motte and his Marquis, like one of Milton's fiends beside a witch's familiar.[153]

The development of Radcliffe's villains from corrupt libertinism to Satanic sublimity – 'full of plot, and horror, and magnificent wickedness', as Cherubina describes them in Barrett's mock-Gothic novel *The Heroine* – can be demonstrated by a comparison of her initial description of the Marquis de Montalt with her famous description, five years later, of Schedoni.[154] Here is Montalt, attending to the heroine, Adeline, who has fainted:

> [Montalt] wore the star of one of the first orders in France, and had an air of dignity, which declared him to be of superior rank. He appeared to be about forty, but, perhaps, the spirit and fire of his countenance made the impression of time upon his features less perceptible. His softened aspect and insinuating manners, while, regardless of himself, he seemed attentive only to the condition of Adeline, gradually dissipated the apprehensions of Madame La Motte [. . .][155]

Montalt, as the original readers must have understood at once, is that stock villain of eighteenth-century fiction, the aristocratic seducer; a middle-aged Lovelace transposed back into the Middle Ages. His 'insinuating' manners warn the reader that he is not to be trusted; his 'spirit and fire' suggest ill-regulated passions, and render suspicious his apparently selfless attentiveness to Adeline's condition. After such an introduction, it can come as little surprise that he attempts first to seduce Adeline, and then to abduct her; what else is to be expected from a spirited and insinuating member of 'one of the first orders in France'? But Schedoni is a villain of quite another kind:

> There lived in the Dominican convent of the Spirito Santo, at Naples, a man called father Schedoni; an Italian, as his name imported, but whose family was unknown, and from some circumstances, it appeared, that he wished to throw an impenetrable veil over his origin [. . .] There were circumstances, however, which appeared to indicate him to be a man of birth, and of fallen fortune; his spirit, as it had sometimes looked forth from under the disguise of his manners, seemed lofty; it shewed not, however, the aspirings of a generous mind, but rather the gloomy pride of a disappointed one. Some few persons in the convent, who had been interested by his appearance, believed that the peculiarities of his manners, his severe reserve and unconquerable silence, his solitary habits and frequent penances, were the effect of misfortunes preying upon a haughty and disordered spirit; while others conjectured them the consequence of some hideous crime gnawing upon an awakened conscience.
>
> He would sometimes abstract himself from the society for whole days together, or when with such a disposition he was compelled to mingle with it, he seemed unconscious where he was, and continued shrouded in meditation and silence till he was again alone. There were times when it was unknown whither he had retired, notwithstanding that his steps had been watched, and his customary haunts examined. [. . .] Among his associates no one loved him, many disliked him, and more feared him. His figure was striking, but not so from grace; it was tall, and, though extremely thin, his limbs were large and uncouth, and as he stalked along, wrapt in the black garments of his order, there was something terrible in

its air; something almost superhuman. His cowl, too, as it threw a shade over the livid paleness of his face, encreased its severe character, and gave an effect to his large melancholy eye, which approached to horror [. . .] There was something in his physiognomy extremely singular, and that can not easily be defined. It bore the traces of many passions, which seemed to have fixed the features they no longer animated. An habitual gloom and severity prevailed over the deep lines of his countenance; and his eyes were so piercing that they seemed to penetrate, at a single glance into the hearts of men, and to read their most secret thoughts; few persons could support their scrutiny, or even endure to meet them twice.[156]

Schedoni may live at the convent of the Holy Spirit, but he himself sounds more like an unholy spirit or Miltonic fallen angel than a man. Like a ghost, he is chiefly to be found in 'his customary haunts'. His unknown origins and his uncanny abilities to vanish in plain sight and see 'at a single glance into the hearts of men' hint at a supernatural nature, a hint reinforced by the 'something almost superhuman' in the air of terror that he projects, and the suggestion of ineffable otherness implied by the illegible but unmistakable 'something . . . extremely singular . . . that can not easily be defined' which is written on the features of his face. Like that other 'haughty and disordered spirit', Milton's Satan, he seems to have suffered some terrible 'fallen fortune' and to be guilty of 'some hideous crime', which has deprived him of (physical, but surely also spiritual) 'grace' and left him with nothing but his 'gloomy pride' to sustain him; and, like Milton's Death, he resembles a gigantic skeleton wrapped in darkness, 'tall', 'extremely thin', and 'wrapt in the black garments of his order' which contrast with the 'livid paleness' of his skin. No wonder the gaze of this unearthly figure inspires 'horror' in those who meet it, and that few can bring themselves to do so twice. Montalt is a traditional villain, comprehensible as the product of a malfunctioning society, but Schedoni is something new, something radically incommensurate with the rest of the world he inhabits: for, in fact, he ultimately proves not to be a demon or evil spirit, just a man in whom are collected such colossal evil energies that he appears to be superhuman. In him, and other contemporary villains like him, can be seen the origins of the literary villain as terrorist. 'Many disliked him, and more feared him.'

　　Both McIntyre and Varma have speculated that Radcliffe's villains may have been based upon the villains of seventeenth-century tragedies, several of which were reprinted and staged during the 1770s and 1780s.[157] The influence of early modern tragedies, especially those of Shakespeare, on Radcliffe's works is clear; but certain crucial differences distinguish her villains from theirs. In the older literature upon which Radcliffe and her imitators drew, such as *Macbeth*, *Paradise Lost*, and, further back, the chivalric romances of the medieval period, the main emphasis had been placed on the external struggle between righteous hero and demonic villain; but in Radcliffe's works the hero always loses, and the emphasis shifts instead to the internal struggle of the imprisoned and persecuted heroine with the terror that the victorious and apparently invincible villain inspires within her. As her villains grew into demons, Radcliffe's sentimental heroes – Theodore, Valancourt, Vincentio – increasingly dwindled into virtual nonentities; they tended, as Behr notes, to be 'passive' and 'self-reflective' characters, chronically ineffectual at rescuing her heroines from the clutches of the villains who pursue them, and often requiring rescue themselves.[158] Radcliffe's works constitute a literature of terror precisely because, unlike virtually all earlier literature, they presuppose a catastrophic mismatch between the powers of good and the powers of evil; the hero and heroine always get their happy endings in the last few chapters, but for about three-quarters of each novel they must suffer through a world in which evil seems to be unstoppable, and in which the only viable responses to it are fear and flight. For Radcliffe's more politically active contemporaries, this made her brand of Gothic terror fiction a useful idiom through which to articulate the experiences of those who suffered the physical or emotional violence of revolutionary 'terrorism'; individuals who, like her heroines, possessed the mindsets of late-eighteenth-century men and women of sentiment and yet were forced to encounter the kind of extreme, arbitrary, and seemingly demonic violence which Europe was supposed to have left behind a century before.

It has frequently been noted that, from his 1790 *Reflections* onwards, Edmund Burke persistently described the French Revolution in Gothicised terms.[159] In the *Reflections* he famously described Marie Antoinette as a 'persecuted woman' who had to run, like many a Gothic heroine, from her bedchamber in the middle of the night, fleeing 'almost naked' through the suddenly unsafe castle of Versailles in order to escape an invading 'band of cruel ruffians and assassins' intent on physical or sexual violence.[160] As his anti-revolutionary rhetoric escalated over the following years he increasingly described the revolutionaries in demonic terms, as 'furies', 'demoniacks', or 'infernal spirits' who sacrificed their victims at 'the shrine of the grim Moloch of liberty', and by the time he wrote his *First Letter on a Regicide Peace* (1796) he even depicted the Revolution itself as an immense Gothic phantom:

> Out of the tomb of the murdered Monarchy in France has arisen a vast, tremendous, unformed spectre, in a far more terrific guise than any which ever yet have overpowered the imagination, and subdued the fortitude of man.[161]

This monstrous 'spectre', like the amoral Gothic villain that it so clearly was, pressed 'straight forward to its end, unappaled by peril, unchecked by remorse'. In 1790 Burke's level of opposition to the Revolution was still unusual, but as more writers came to share his views, so too did they increasingly adopt his Gothicised anti-revolutionary rhetoric; as Clery remarks, 'The 1790s saw a process whereby, as Gothic fiction moved towards the political, politics moved towards a Gothic aesthetic.'[162] Helen Maria Williams, for example, wrote of her experiences during the Terror in strongly Gothicised terms: as Haywood notes, 'Williams' narrative of the Terror reads like a real-life Gothic melodrama.'[163] In her *Letters from France*, she had initially praised the French for having broken away from their Gothic past:

> When we look back on the ignorance, the superstition, the barbarous persecution of Gothic times, is it not something to be thankful for, that we exist at this enlightened period, when such evils are no more; when particular tenets of religious belief are no longer imputed as crimes; when the human mind has made as many important discoveries in morality as in science, and liberality of sentiment is cultivated with

as much success as arts and learning; when, in short (and *you* are not one of those who will suspect all the while that I am not all the while a good Englishwoman) when one can witness an event so sublime as the French revolution?[164]

During the Terror, however, she witnessed the Revolution sliding into the same kind of 'barbarous persecution' which she had, at first, congratulated it for bringing to an end. Employing increasingly Gothic language, she described Robespierre as a 'foul fiend' and his house as 'the monster's den'; she wrote of seeing the 'spectres of my murdered friends' in the streets of Paris, and virtually instructed her readers to understand the Terror in terms of a Gothic romance, in which the monstrous evil of the Jacobins is counterbalanced by the exemplary virtue of the innocents who suffer under them:

> The last excesses of ferocious crimes were contrasted by the sublime enthusiasm of the virtuous affections, shedding their sweetness like solitary flowers over the wilderness where serpents hiss, and beasts of the forest howl; and by the noblest efforts of heroical philanthropy bidding us cease to despair of humanity, and converting the throb of indignant horror into the glow of sympathetic admiration; –bidding us turn from the tribunal of blood, from Robespierre and his jury of assassins, to Louiserolles dying for his child; to madame Berenger, led in the bloom of life to execution with her parents, and, altogether forgetful of herself, seeking only to support the sinking spirits of her mother…[165]

Louiserolles and Berenger, here, play a more unfortunate Theodore and Adeline to Robespierre's Montalt, or Valancourt and Emily to his Montoni, their 'virtuous affections' contrasting with his 'ferocious crimes' so that the reader of their story, like the reader of a Radcliffean Gothic novel, alternates between feeling 'the throb of indignant horror' and 'the glow of sympathetic admiration'. Describing the victims of the Terror, Williams employed similarly Gothic rhetoric:

> Sometimes even when tyranny spared the life of its victim, its cruel persecutions bereaved the sufferer of reason. Of this mademoiselle ------ was a melancholy instance. This unfortunate young lady saw her father, her mother, and several of her relations dragged to the scaffold: she alone was spared, and remained a prisoner at the Conciergerie. Along the gloomy vaults of that terrific prison, by the dim light of sickly lamps, she fancied she saw the mangled spectres of her murdered parents, and in a short time became entirely bereft of reason. She obstinately refused all sustenance, and remained motionless as a statue…[166]

Multiply 'bereaved' by the Terror, which has swallowed her family, her sanity, and seemingly even her name, this unidentified woman is finally absorbed completely into the haunted 'gloomy vaults' which imprison her, becoming 'a statue', part of the Gothic architecture of her 'terrific prison'. (The Conciergerie, then as now, was famous for its medieval Gothic architecture; visiting it after the Terror, Williams described it as an 'abode of horror', and compared it to Dante's Hell.[167]) Almost a decade earlier, Williams had used similar imagery in one of her poems: 'Part of an Irregular Fragment Found in a Dark Passage in the Tower', a Warton-esque horror-poem whose speaker passes through a long-sealed door in the Tower of London, and in a succession of visions sees the ghosts of the various unfortunate members of royal families whom they imagine to have been murdered there in ages past:

Ye visions that before me roll
That freeze my blood, that shake my soul!
Are ye the phantoms of a dream?
Pale spectres! are ye what ye seem?
They glide more near ... [168]

This poem, published in 1786, demonstrates why Williams was one of the favourite poets of the young William Wordsworth, whose first published poem was addressed to her; its kinship with his own ghost-filled horror-poem of 1788, 'The Vale of Esthwaite', is strongly apparent. In the 1780s, such material had been mere historical fantasy, and Williams had been able to congratulate herself on living in 'this enlightened period, when such evils are no more'; but when, swept up in the revolutionary tumult of the 1790s, she discovered that the imprisonment and murder of kings and innocents were still all too possible in the present, she reached for the same rhetoric she had used in her 'Irregular Fragment' in order to describe the scenes she witnessed and heard about during the Terror. The sufferings of 'mademoiselle ------', so psychologically shattered by her exposure to revolutionary terrorism that she refused to eat, move, or speak, could easily have been simply unwriteable; but the Gothic terms in which Williams had described the 'pale spectres' her imaginary speaker saw in the Tower provided her, seven years later, with a language in which she could articulate the 'mangled spectres' which drove the unfortunate 'mademoiselle ------' insane during her imprisonment in the 'gloomy vaults' of the Conciergerie.

Such Gothic rhetoric, which cast the Jacobin terrorists as demonic monsters presiding over terrible (and largely motiveless) deeds of cruelty and blood, could be found everywhere in the 1790s. It was, naturally, employed as a matter of course by anti-revolutionary writers such as Cobbett, and by anti-Jacobin novelists such as Helen Craik; but it could also be found in the works of writers much more sympathetic to the Revolution, such as the then ultra-radical Coleridge and Southey, whose dramatic poem *The Fall of Robespierre* (1794) described Robespierre as 'a man, whose great bad actions have cast a disastrous lustre round his name...on a vast stage of horrors'.[169] The poem's first speech makes clear Robespierre's kinship to the villains of Radcliffean Gothic:

I fear the Tyrant's *soul* –
Sudden in action, fertile in resource,
And rising awful 'mid impending ruins;
In splendour gloomy, as the midnight meteor,
That fearless thwarts the elemental war.
When last in secret conference we met,
He scowl'd upon me with suspicious rage,

Making his eye the inmate of my bosom.
I know he scorns me – and I feel, I hate him –
Yet there is in him that which makes me tremble![170]

Like Radcliffe's villains, Coleridge and Southey's Robespierre is 'awful', 'gloomy', and has a spiritual kinship with (no doubt Gothic) 'ruins'; and, like them, he has terrible eyes which seem to see into men's hearts. As befits a master of (the) Terror, he is himself 'fearless' while filling all those around him with fear, upon which note this speech both begins and ends: 'I fear the Tyrant's *soul*… there is in him that which makes me tremble!' We go on to learn that Robespierre, like all Radcliffean villains, 'plans in darkness', and keeps his victims 'chain'd/In dark deep dungeons by his lawless rage'; and when his younger brother pleads with him to bring an end to the Terror – 'I am sick with blood' – he rebukes him angrily, declaring that his heart will soon be 'cleans'd by wholesome massacre!'[171] In Act II he ascends the Tribune of the National Convention, and makes clear that he rules France through fear:

I – Robespierre!
I – at whose name the dastard despot brood
Look pale with fear, and call on saints to help them!
Who dares accuse me? Who shall dare belie
My spotless name?[172]

Robespierre's name is spotless, we understand, because everyone is too terrified of him to accuse him of anything; and when his enemies do accuse him of tyranny he defies them furiously, harangue for harangue, until he is dragged from the stage. Faced with death, he first hacks at his attackers with a knife, then attempts suicide:

The self-will'd dictator
Plung'd often the keen knife in his dark breast,
Yet impotent to die. He lives all mangled
By his own tremulous hand![173]

Such is the demonic life-force which sustains Coleridge and Southey's Robespierre that even multiple knife-wounds to the chest are apparently not enough to kill him. Instead, he and his companions are taken to the guillotine, where they have one last opportunity to display their fearless natures and their Gothic scowls:

I saw them while the black blood roll'd adown
Each stern face, even then with dauntless eye
Scowl round contemptuous, dying as they lived,
Fearless of fate![174]

Needless to say, all these sublime and terrible goings-on bear only the most tenuous resemblance to the confused reality of the events on the 9th and 10th Thermidor. Robespierre was not dragged, ranting, from the Convention; he did not engage in knife-fights with the men who arrested him, and he did not attempt to stab himself (although he may have tried to shoot himself; exactly how he sustained the gunshot wound to his jaw on the night of 9th Thermidor has always been unclear).[175] His political rhetoric was extreme, but, unlike Marat's, it was not sanguinary; the historical Robespierre argued for the necessity of the executions carried out by the Revolutionary Tribunals, but he would never have openly boasted of the day when 'through the streaming streets/Of Paris red-eyed Massacre o'er wearied/Reel'd heavily, intoxicate with blood'.[176] Coleridge and Southey's Robespierre, like William's 'tyrant' Robespierre with his 'jury of assassins', is a political figure who has been transfigured into a Gothic demon; a man who, like Radcliffe's Schedoni three years later, contains such baleful power that he seems barely human.

I have emphasised the sense of bewildered shock that characterised much British reporting on the French Revolution in the 1790s, and its insistence that events such as the September Massacres and the Terror stood outside the normal flow of history. The kind of state violence which, for such writers, constituted historical business as usual – executions at Tyburn, pitched battles in Europe or at sea – could be articulated and understood by them as the actions of rational men performed for rational (although possibly deplorable) ends, but these episodes of revolutionary violence seemed to resist such interpretations; they made no sense in the terms these writers were used to thinking in, because they were directed against the very social and ideological structures which underwrote such assumptions in the first place. They were thus articulated in terms of madness, or magic, or historical slippage; such violence might make sense in a madhouse, or in hell, or in the barbarous past, but not in Paris in September 1792. As Punter writes:

> Terrorism is in fact defined by its own exclusions and negations – it is that which exceeds or combats the existence of a normative space within which society lives, moves, and has its being [. . .] The terrorist is, in a sense, the summation of those agencies which are already, and incomprehensibly, beyond the law; and thus their manifestation in text will always be the site of problems which cannot be expunged.[177]

This sense of the basic illegibility and incomprehensibility of revolutionary 'terrorist' violence fitted neatly with the conventions of Radcliffean Gothic, in which evil and violence were almost always mystified, Radcliffe having taken to heart Burke's lesson that sublime terror in literature is heightened by the deliberate use of obscurity.[178] Thus, in *The Romance of the Forest*, large portions of the manuscript which record the sufferings of Henry Marquis de Montalt are illegible; in both *Udolpho* and *The Italian* characters glimpse instruments of torture whose exact use is obscure to them; in *The Italian* Vincentio is brought blindfolded before the Inquisition, able to hear but not see the horrors around him; and for hundreds of pages of *Udolpho* the reader knows that Emily has seen *something horrible* behind the Black Veil, but has no idea exactly what it is. This technique of suggestion, basic to virtually all subsequent Gothic fiction, echoes the frequent insistence of contemporary writers on the Revolution that its violence was so horrible and so extreme that it might not be appropriate, or even possible, to write it at all. In *The Bloody Buoy*, Cobbett explains that he has grouped his account of several of the worst revolutionary atrocities together on one page, so that once it has been read the reader can tear it out and burn it; the reader is thus invited to create their own mutilated text, like that found by Adeline in *The Romance of the Forest*, whose missing leaf bears witness to knowledge too horrible to be permitted to survive.[179]

What writers on the Revolution drew from Radcliffe's works, and those of her many imitators, was a way of writing about those acts of violence and evil which disrupted ordinary conventions of representation. The wickedness of a Lovelace, a Jonathan Wild, or a Ferdinand Count Fathom had been explicable, a regrettable but unsurprising consequence of letting men with more energy and ability than sound morality loose upon the world. But the wickedness of a Montoni, a Schedoni, or a Robespierre is something quite different; a horrible wonder apart, seeming to belong to some other world or order of being, and thus persistently described in terms of the Satanic and the Burkean sublime. Wild's murders and robberies are criminal, but comprehensible; Robespierre's massacres, like the dark deeds hinted at in the corners of Radcliffe's novels, are so horrible as to be almost incommunicable, totally incommensurate with the rest of human experience. Cobbett remarks in *The Bloody Buoy* that 'the greatest part of the facts related here, are so much more shocking and terrific than any thing we have ever before had an idea of, that common murders appear as trifling': the horrors of the Revolution transcend not just everything that 'we' have ever heard of, but everything that has ever been imagined, and consequently they evoke not just concern or condemnation, but *terror*.[180] As Burke had explained decades before, we feel terror when we are confronted with those powers which seem to belong to a different order of magnitude to our own, and before which we are as nothing: a large, angry dog may evoke fear in us, but a flood or earthquake – or a revolution – evokes terror, especially if we sense the hand of God or Satan behind it. Wild is a criminal, and his actions are crimes, but from 1795 onwards Robespierre and his colleagues increasingly came to be understood as something different: they were *terrorists*, and their actions were acts of *terrorism*.

There were, of course, always writers such as Mary Wollstonecraft who insisted that the French Revolution was not so incomprehensible as all that; it was violent and chaotic, admittedly, but history usually was, and if one could only gain some perspective on events then most of it became perfectly understandable and explicable. But in the mid-1790s, such views were rare; much more common was the belief that the Revolution represented a bizarre and monstrous historical aberration, leading Wollstonecraft – with Locke in mind – to complain of the 'childish prejudices that have the *insignia* of raw-head and bloody-bones' which plagued discussions on the subject.[181] In Radcliffean Gothic fiction, evil generally occurs not as part of a process of historical or psychological cause and effect, but because some people are simply, inexplicably, monstrously wicked, and the violence they initiate is represented not as an act like any other, but as a traumatic, terrifying, and ultimately unspeakable rupture in the ordinary fabric of experience. This essentially mystificatory attitude towards evil and violence held obvious appeal for those writers – and there were many – who wished to insist upon a radical distinction between the violence of the Revolution and that of the rest of recent European history. However, Radcliffe's own apparent lack of interest in contemporary politics meant that she continued to draw her villains from the traditional pre-Revolutionary stock types of evil aristocrats and wicked Catholics, and while, as I have pointed out, early commentators on the Revolution sometimes compared the revolutionaries to such figures, these comparisons became increasingly uncomfortable as the decade wore on: after all, the Catholic clergy and the old aristocracy were the chief enemies and targets of the Revolution, and thus the de facto allies of the Revolution's enemies. The equation of radical evil with these representatives of the old order was rendered even more problematic by the fact that anti-revolutionary writers did not have a monopoly on the novel form, and 'Jacobin' novelists such as William Godwin and Mary Wollstonecraft were swift to make use of Gothic conventions in order to critique British institutions, showing in novels such as *Caleb Williams* (1794) and *Maria, or the Wrongs of Women* (1798) how the survival of feudal customs such as aristocratic honour and female subservience within marriage continued to facilitate the exercise of despotic power against the innocent.

The collision of these two models of evil was dramatically played out at the trial of Jean-Baptiste Carrier, which entranced and horrified all Europe in the latter part of 1794. As Jacobin representative to the city of Nantes in the winter of 1793-4, Carrier had presided over some of the worst massacres of the Terror, including the infamous mass drowning of suspected counter-revolutionaries by packing them into boats, nailing down the hatches, and then deliberately sinking the vessels in the River Loire. Robespierre had him recalled in February 1794, and he could, like Mathieu Jourdan, easily have fallen victim to the Revolutionary Tribunal of Paris, had Thermidor not cut short its operations; instead he was tried by the Thermidorian government, which was intent on using his excesses to demonstrate the extent of the difference between them and their bloodthirsty predecessors. Rather than an extremist whom Robespierre had been trying to get rid of, Carrier was now depicted as an embodiment of Jacobin ferocity, an exemplary part of 'the system of terror' which the Thermidorian coup had brought to an end. The witnesses against Carrier accused him of presiding over all manner of atrocities, including massacres of women and children, the mutilation of corpses, mass rape, and the sacramental drinking of human blood from chalices stolen from churches. Carrier admitted only to the mass executions, and insisted that these had been carried out under orders from the same National Convention that was now putting him on trial. By his account, it was the Royalist counter-revolutionaries who were guilty of all the worst atrocities: they were the ones who had tortured men to death, buried them alive, or mutilated their bodies, spurred on by a fanatical 'cannibal priest' who celebrated Mass surrounded by the blood and corpses of slaughtered patriots. The shootings and drownings he had authorised, Carrier asserted, had not been gratuitous atrocities, but the just and necessary executions of the murderous counter-revolutionary insurgents he had been sent out to deal with.[182] The 'cannibal priest' drinking Eucharist wine in the midst of a massacre and the revolutionary terrorist drinking human blood from a stolen Eucharistic chalice are obviously mirror images of one another, revolutionary and counter-revolutionary alike imagined as Satanic figures willing to transgress all religious and moral laws in their pursuit of illegitimate power. 'Concerning the realities of the Terror at Nantes,' Baczko writes, 'the trials do more than provide overwhelming evidence; they add a completely phantasmagoric imagery which emanates from the Terror.'[183] This 'phantasmagoric imagery' would rapidly become an element in both Gothic fiction and the historical mythology of the French Revolution. But it points to the difficulty in assimilating Radcliffean Gothic to anti-revolutionary purposes: resolutely traditional in her choice of villains, the embodiments of evil Radcliffe described were much closer to the monstrous priests and aristocrats Carrier insisted he had been fighting against than to the monstrous revolutionary tyrant he himself was accused of having been.

Fortunately for Revolution's enemies, from 1794 onwards the translation of new novels from Germany soon provided a new archetype of villainy, one which exercised such power over the British imagination that by the decade's end many had come to believe their existence and power to be a matter of actual historical fact. The archetype in question was that of the Illuminist conspirator, and, like the terrorist, it is still very much with us today, an essential component of our modern demonology. For, as well as being the conceptual birthplace of terrorism, the 1790s also saw the invention of what has come to be called conspiracy theory; and, with it, the belief that sinister cabals of Gothic terrorists did not just preside over the occasional scene of atrocity, like Carrier at Nantes, but actually turned the wheels of all human history. It is these conspiracy theories, which in the later 1790s rendered the distinction between revolutionary history and Gothic fiction more blurred and confused than ever before, which are the subject of my next chapter.

Notes

1   Letter to Richard Fitzpatrick, 30 July 1789. Quoted in Chris Evans, *Debating the Revolution: Britain in the 1790s* (London: I.B. Tauris, 2006), p. 12.
2   *The Times*, 8 August 1789, p. 2.
3   On these hopes, see Robert Dozier, *For King, Constitution, and Country* (Lexington, KY: UP of Kentucky, 1983), p. 4.
4   On the Great Fear, see Georges Lefebvre, *The Great Fear of 1789* (London: NLB, 1973).
5   For the minimal direct impact of the Revolution on the lives of many ordinary Frenchmen and women, see Richard Cobb, *The French and Their Revolution*, ed. David Gilmour (London: John Murray, 1998), chapters 9 and 10.
6   Malcolm Cook, 'Politics in the Fiction of the French Revolution, 1789–1794', *Studies on Voltaire and the Eighteenth Century*, vol. 201 (Oxford: Voltaire Foundation, 1982), pp. 233–335.
7   On Radcliffe's use of *The Romance of Real Life*, see Ann Radcliffe, *The Romance of the Forest*, ed. Chloe Chard (Oxford: Oxford UP, 1986), p. 367. On Smith's grudging use of the Radcliffean Gothic in order to appeal to changing public tastes, see M.O. Grenby, *The Anti-Jacobin Novel* (Cambridge: Cambridge UP, 2001), p. 181. On both, see Carol Fry, *Charlotte Smith* (New York: Arno Press, 1980), pp. 115–37. Smith's distaste for such material may not be unconnected to her resolutely un-fearful and un-Gothic depiction of the French Revolution in her most political novel, *Desmond* (1792).
8   On the contemporary and educational character of mainstream eighteenth-century fiction, see J. Paul Hunter, *Before Novels* (New York: W.W. Norton and Co., 1990), pp. 23, 54–7.

9   De Sade, *Idee sur les romans* (Paris, 1800), cited in E.J. Clery, *The Rise of Supernatural Fiction* (Cambridge: Cambridge UP, 1999), p. 156. For three representative examples of the use of this passage in modern Gothic criticism – which all, bizarrely, appear on the thirteenth page of their respective books, demonstrating how early in such arguments De Sade tends to be cited – see Jerrold Hogle, 'Introduction', in Hogle, ed., *Cambridge Companion to Gothic Fiction* (Cambridge: Cambridge UP, 2002), pp. 12–13, Dale Townshend, *Orders of Gothic* (New York: AMS Press, 2007), p. 13, and Diane Hoeveler, *Gothic Riffs* (Columbus, OH: Ohio State UP, 2010), p. 13.

10 Montague Summers, *The Gothic Quest* (London: Fortune, 1938), p. 13.

11 Devendra Varma, *The Gothic Flame* (New York: Russell and Russell, 1966), p. 257.

12 See, for example, Robert Miles, 'The 1790s: The effulgence of the Gothic', in Hogle, ed., *Companion*, and Leslie Fiedler, *Love and Death in the American Novel*, revised edition (Harmondsworth: Penguin, 1984), p. 42: 'In some deep way the Gothic novel was an expression of the historical circumstances that made the French Revolution possible, and even necessary.'

13 David Bindman, *The Shadow of the Guillotine* (London: British Museum Publications, 1989), p. 78.

14 See, for example, Stanley Loomis, *Paris in the Terror* (Harmondsworth: Penguin, 1970). Notionally a work of non-fiction, Loomis' book presents the leading Jacobin revolutionaries as a collection of crazed monsters straight out of Gothic fiction; yet it was reprinted, as history, as recently as 1990. On popular perceptions of the Revolution, see Colin Haydon and William Doyle, 'Robespierre: After two hundred years', in Haydon and Doyle, eds., *Robespierre* (Cambridge: Cambridge UP, 1999), p. 15.

15 Bindman, pp. 37–40.

16 On the difference between the actual events of the September Massacres and the subsequent legend-lore concerning them, see David Andress, *The Terror* (London: Little, Brown, 2005), chapter 4, George Rudé, *The Crowd in the French Revolution* (Oxford: Clarendon, 1959), pp. 110–11, and Brian Singer, 'Violence in the French Revolution', in Ference Fehér, ed., *The French Revolution and the Birth of Modernity* (Berkeley, CA: University of California Press, 1990), p. 157.

17 See Donald Greer, *Incidence of the Terror During the French Revolution* (Cambridge, MA: Harvard UP, 1935), pp. 27–37. More recent historians have generally accepted Greer's figures for the Terror itself, whilst radically revising upwards his estimations of the level of bloodletting in the Vendée: Greer compares 17,000 formal executions and between 7,000 and 12,000 deaths in prison during the Terror with 100,000 deaths in the Vendée revolt, but some modern estimates place the true figure for the latter as closer to 250,000. See Donald Sutherland, *The French Revolution and Empire* (Oxford: Blackwell, 2003), p. 217.

18 Michel Foucault, *Discipline and Punish*, trans. Alan Sheridan (Harmondsworth: Penguin, 1991), p. 58. On execution by guillotine, see Daniel Arasse, *The Guillotine and the Terror*, trans. Christopher Miller (London: Lane, 1989), pp. 35–6, and Dorinda Outram, *The Body and the French Revolution* (London: Yale UP, 1989), pp. 113–16. On contemporary British hangings, see V.A.C. Gatrell, *The Hanging Tree* (Oxford: Oxford UP, 1994), p. 7.

19 On the development of the myth of the *Bals des Victimes*, and its almost certain falsehood, see Ronald Schechter, 'Gothic Thermidor', *Representations*, number 61 (1998), pp. 81–2.

20 Grenby, p. 38.

21 Jeffrey Cox, 'English Gothic theatre', in Hogle, ed., *Companion*, p. 129.

22 E.J. Clery and Robert Miles, eds., *Gothic Documents* (Manchester: Manchester UP, 2000), p. 136.

23 William Wordsworth, 'The Vale of Esthwaite', in John Hayden, ed., *Poems* (Harmondsworth: Penguin, 1977), p. 51.

24 Wordsworth, *Poems*, p. 57.

25 Wordsworth, *Poems*, pp. 58–61.

26 For other examples of Wordsworth's Gothic jottings in this period, see William Wordsworth, *Early Poems and Fragments*, ed. Carol Landon and Jared Curtis (Ithaca, NY: Cornell UP, 1997), pp. 551, 560–1.

27 On 'To Horror' as a political, anti-war poem, see Simon Bainbridge, *British Poetry and the Revolutionary and Napoleonic Wars* (Oxford: Oxford UP, 2003), p. 24.

28 Clery and Miles, p. 137.

29 Bainbridge, p. 24.

30 On the 'bloody vignette', and its use by abolitionists, see Ian Haywood, *Bloody Romanticism* (Basingstoke: Palgrave Macmillan, 2006), pp. 4, 11, 22–5.

31 Marcus Wood, *Slavery, Empathy, and Pornography* (Oxford: Oxford UP, 2002), chapters 1 and 2 (see especially p. 91).

32 Quoted in Donald Sutherland, *Murder in Aubagne* (Cambridge: Cambridge UP, 2009), p. 172.

33 Robert Palmer, *Twelve Who Ruled* (Princeton, NJ: Princeton UP, 1989), p. 44.

34 Marcel Hénaff, 'Naked Terror', *Substance*, vol. 27, number 2 (1998), p. 6.

35 Hénaff, p. 9.

36 Quoted in Paul Beik, ed., *The French Revolution* (New York: Harper and Row, 1970), p. 283.

37 Quoted in *The Times*, 11 September 1792, p. 1.

38 Quoted in Beik, p. 284.

39 David Jordan, 'The Robespierre problem', in Haydon and Doyle, pp. 29–30.

40 See Eli Sagan, *Citizens and Cannibals* (Lanham, MD: Rowman and Littlefield, 2001), p. 434.

41 Quoted in George Kelly, 'Conceptual sources of the Terror', in *Eighteenth-Century Studies*, vol. 14, number 1 (1980), p. 34.

42 Edmund Burke, *Writings and Speeches*, ed. Paul Langford (Oxford: Clarendon, 1981–2000), vol. 1, p. 238.

43 Burke, *Writings*, vol. 8, p. 319.

44 William Adams, *Sermons upon Several Subjects* (Shrewsbury, 1790), pp. 5, 315.

45 Quoted in Gatrell, *Hanging Tree*, pp. 202, 286. Paley also argued that it was desirable that death sentences should be frequent, but actual executions rare, so that 'few actually suffer death, whilst the dread and danger of it hang over many'. On public executions as a 'theatre of terror', see Foucault, chapter 2.

46 Quoted in Ian Bell, *Literature and Crime in Augustan England* (London: Routledge, 1991), p. 165. On contemporary theories of punishment in general, see Bell, chapter 4.

47 *General Evening Post*, 14 August 1792, p. 5. Moore is cited in Haywood, p. 116.

48 Quoted in Kelly, 'Conceptual sources', p. 21.

49 The Declaration was printed in almost every British newspaper. See, for example, *Morning Chronicle*, 4 September 1792.

50 *The Times*, 23 August 1793, p. 2.

51 *The Times*, 27 August 1793, p. 2.

52 Dan Edelstein, 'The law of 22 Prairal', *Telos*, number 141 (2007), p. 88.

53 Edelstein, 'The law of 22 Prairal', p. 87.

54 *The Times*, 23 November 1793, p. 3, see also Palmer, p. 194.

55 *The Times*, 23 April 1794, p. 3, *A Collection of State Papers, Relative to the War Against France* (London: 1794–1802), vol. 2, p. 138.

56 The full text of the law is reproduced in Edelstein, 'The law of 22 Prairal'.

57 *The Times*, 2 June 1794, p. 2, and 4 August 1794, p. 3.

58 See Andress, *Terror*, chapter 12.

59 Bronislaw Baczko, *Ending the Terror*, trans. Michel Petheram (Cambridge: Cambridge UP, 1994), pp. 49–52.

60 *The Times*, 22 September 1794, p. 2.

61 *The Times*, 6 October 1794, p. 3, 6 December 1794, p. 3, see also Baczko, p. 61.

62 *The Oracle*, 27 October 1795, p. 2.

63 Baczko, p. 13.

64 Andress, *Terror*, p. 358.

65 James Monroe, *A View of the Conduct of the Executive, in the Foreign Affairs of the United States* (Philadelphia, 1797), p. 172, Thomas Paine, *Dissertation on First Principles of Government* (London, 1795), p. 25.

66 Burke, *Writings*, vol. 9, p. 89.

67 Bernard Gainot, 'Aux origines du Directoire', *Annales Historiques de la Révolution française*, numéro 332 (2003), p. 141.

68 *True Briton*, 26 June 1795, p. 4, *Morning Chronicle*, 20 April 1796, p. 2.

69 On the post-Thermidorian emphasis on Robespierre alone as the creator of the Terror, see Marie-Hélène Huet, *Mourning Glory* (Philadelphia, PA: University of Pennsylania Press, 1997), p. 174, and Baczko, chapter 2.

70 *The Times*, 15 January 1795, p. 2, 11 May 1795, p. 2, 17 June 1795, p. 3, see also, for example, William Playfair, *The History of Jacobinism* (London, 1795), pp. 516, 701.

71 Thomas Bentley, *Considerations upon the State of Public Affairs* (London, 1796), p. 77, William Cobbett, *The Bloody Buoy* (London, 1796), p. 46, Jean Baptise Duvoisin, *Examination of the Principles of the French Revolution* (London, 1796), p. 93.

72 François Xavier Pagès, *Secret History of the French Revolution* (London, 1797), vol. 2, p. 328.

73 Pagès, vol. 2, p. 245.

74 Pagès, vol. 2, p. 319.

75 *New Annual Register for the Year 1799* (London, 1800), p. 476.

76 John Cartwright, *A Letter to the High Sheriff* (London, 1795), p. 32, Peter Pindar, *Works* (London, 1796), vol. 4, p. 133, Charles Burney, *Memoirs of the Life and Writing of the Abate Metastasio* (London, 1796), vol. 3, p. 377, *True Briton*, 30 July 1796, p. 3. On the description of Pitt's repressions as a 'reign of terror', see Clive Emesley, 'The impact of the French Revolution on British politics and society', in Ceri Crossley and Ian Small, eds., *The French Revolution and British Culture* (Oxford: Oxford UP, 1989), p. 54.

77 Robert Bisset, *Sketches of Democracy* (Dublin, 1798); Matthew Weld, *Constitutional Considerations* (Dublin, 1800), p. 77, Arthur O'Connor, *The Beauties of the Press* (London, 1800), p. 443, Herbert Marsh, *The History of the Politicks of Great Britain and France* (London, 1800), vol. 2, p. 69.

78 Mary Shelley, *The Last Man*, ed. Morton Paley (Oxford: Oxford UP, 1994), p. 258.

79 Baczko, p. 26. On the massacres of suspected Jacobins carried out in the prisons of the *Midi* after Thermidor, see Sutherland, *Murder*, pp. 6–7 and chapters 8 and 9.

80 On the 'counter-terror' of 1795–8, see Cobb, pp. 180–99, 271–8.

81 Howard Brown, *Ending the French Revolution* (Charlottesville, VA: University of Virginia Press, 2006), p. 47.

82   Norman Hampson, *The Terror in the French Revolution* (London: Historical
      Association, 1981), p. 31, Cobb, pp. 161–2, 236–7, 244–5.
83   On Robespierre's belief in the interchangeability of vice, crime, and anti-
      revolutionary subversion, see Norman Hampson, 'Robespierre and the Terror', in
      Haydon and Doyle, p. 170.
84   On the strength of the revolutionary army, see Hampson, *Terror*, p. 22.
85   Greer, pp. 28–9, 37.
86   Sutherland, *French Revolution*, 1st ed., pp. 229–39, see also Singer, pp. 158–9.
87   Figures drawn from William Scott, *Terror and Repression in Revolutionary
      Marseilles* (London: Macmillan, 1973), p. 336, see also Arasse, p. 108.
88   Palmer, pp. 66–7.
89   Quoted in Sutherland, *French Revolution*, 2nd ed., pp. 199, 211.
90   Palmer, p. 56. On the popularity of stories of plots and conspiracies among the
      French public during the revolutionary period, see Baczko, pp. 1–22. On the
      paranoia of the terrorists, see Sagan, p. 327.
91   Andress, *Terror*, p. 110.
92   On the obsession of the Revolution's leaders with the conspiracies they believed
      to be working against them, especially from 1792 onwards, see Timothy Tackett,
      'Conspiracy obsession in a time of revolution', *American Historical Review*, vol.
      105, number 3 (2000), pp. 691–713, and Thomas Kaiser, 'From the Austrian
      Committee to the Foreign Plot', *French Historical Studies*, vol. 26, number 4 (2003),
      pp. 587–8, 606–8. On Robespierre's belief in such conspiracies, see Geoffrey
      Cubitt, 'Robespierre and conspiracy theories', in Haydon and Doyle, pp. 75–91. For
      examples of the same fears among the French population at large, see Sutherland,
      Murder, pp. 98–106, and Cobb, pp. 20, 229–30.
93   Hampson, in Haydon and Doyle, p. 167.
94   Cited in *The Times*, 11 September 1792, p. 2.
95   'An English Lady', *Residence in France* (London, 1797), vol. 1, p. 172. On
      Revolutionary press culture, see J. Gilchrist and W.J. Murray, *The Press in the French
      Revolution* (London: Ginn, 1971), pp. 1–43.
96   On the increasingly abstract definitions of 'treason' used during the Terror, which
      came to include everything from wearing the wrong cockade in one's hat to making
      sub-standard shoes, see Carla Hesse, 'The law of the Terror', *MLN*, vol. 114, number
      4 (1999), pp. 716–17.
97   Jordan, in Haydon and Doyle, p. 27.
98   Sagan, p. 431, Singer, p. 163.
99   See Gregory Dart, *Rousseau, Robespierre and English Romanticism* (Cambridge:
      Cambridge UP, 1999), pp. 34, 46.
100   Sutherland, *French Revolution*, 2nd ed., p. 217, Hewson Clarke, *The History of
      the War* (London, 1816), vol. 3, p. 108. Collot's dramatic turn of phrase may have
      owed something to his background as an actor and playwright: it certainly sounds
      as though the mass executions are supposed to have an effect akin to that of
      some spectacular *coup de theatre*, involving flames, fireworks, and stage thunder,
      on a theatre audience. Marie-Hélène Huet has drawn attention to the persistent
      theatricality of the French Revolution, and Chantal Thomas to the theatrical
      character of the Terror in Lyons: see Huet, *Mourning Glory*, and Chantal Thomas,
      'Terror in Lyons', *SubStance*, vol. 27, number 2 (1998), p. 39.
101   See Martha Crenshaw, *Explaining Terrorism* (London: Routledge, 2011), p. 25.
      Summarising studies of genocide survivors and inhabitants of heavily bombed

cities during wartime, Crenshaw writes that 'the unpredictability of danger in such an environment is the most psychologically damaging factor'.

102   On Matthews, see Bindman, p. 12.

103   On the spectacular violence of public executions, see Foucault, chapter 2, especially pp. 48–50.

104   On the execution of Damiens, see Foucault, pp. 3–6, and Arasse, p. 13. On eighteenth-century campaigns against 'cruel or excessive punishments', see Gary Kelly, ed., *Newgate Narratives* (London: Pickering and Chatto, 2008), vol. 1, pp. xx–xxi.

105   Arasse, p. 13, Gatrell, *Hanging Tree*, pp. 7, 84, 286, 312–13, 317, 337–8.

106   On British law as a system of terror, see Douglas Hay, *Albion's Fatal Tree* (London: A.Lane, 1975), pp. 16–28, and Sue Chaplin, *Law, Sensibility, and the Sublime* (Aldershot: Ashgate, 2004), p. 30.

107   On Steadman's 'bloody vignettes', see Haywood, pp. 37–43.

108   Cobb, p. 142.

109   On the contemporary belief that the feelings of the lower orders were not just quantitatively but qualitatively different from those of their social superiors, see Leslie Mitchell, *The Whig World* (London: Hambledon and London, 2005), p. 31.

110   Hénaff, p. 6, Greer, p. 19.

111   Frank Ankersmit, *Sublime Historical Experience* (Stanford, CA: Stanford UP, 2005), pp. 352–3. On the cultural trauma of the Terror, see also Patrice Higonnet, 'Terror, trauma and the "young Marx" explanation of Jacobin politics', *Past and Present*, number 191 (2006).

112   *The Times*, 7 November 1791, p. 3. On the Avignon massacre, see Sutherland, *Murder*, p. 92.

113   *St James's Chronicle*, 18–21 August 1792, p. 4, *The World*, 21 August 1792, p. 3.

114   *The Star*, 18 August 1792, p. 3.

115   *Diary or Woodfall's Register, Public Advertiser*, and *The World*, all 1 September 1792, p. 2, 2, and 2, respectively.

116   *Evening Mail*, 3 September 1792, p. 2. This piece was written *before* news of the September Massacres had arrived in Britain.

117   See, among many others, *St James's Chronicle*, 8 September 1792, *The Times*, 10, 12, 14, and 20 September 1792, *Diary or Woodfall's Register*, 11 September 1792, and *Oracle*, 12 September 1792. Modern estimates of the numbers killed in the September Massacres range from 1,000 to 1,400: see Hampson, *Terror*, p. 8, Rudé, p. 110, and Singer, p. 157. In a sort of fearful symmetry, these ever-escalating estimates of the numbers killed in the September Massacres were mirrored, on the other side of the channel, by Robespierre's increasingly exaggerated estimates of the number killed by Lafayette's guardsmen in the Champ de Mars Massacre on 17 July 1791; the true figure was probably about a dozen, but by March 1793 Robespierre was claiming that 500 had been killed, and by March 1794 his estimate had risen to 2,000. See Hampson, in Haydon and Doyle, pp. 165, 171.

118   *Morning Penny Post*, 9 September 1751, p. 2.

119   *St James's Chronicle*, 8 September 1792, p. 4. Several of these stories also appeared in the *Oracle*, 11 September 1792, p. 2. Two of these, the stories of the Countess and the Swiss Gentleman, are also discussed in Haywood, p. 72.

120   See, for example, the eighteenth-century execution narratives collected together in Leigh Yetter, ed., *Public Execution in England* (London: Pickering and Chatto, 2009), vol. 4. Even so sensational a case as that of Elizabeth Brownrigg, executed

in 1767 for whipping and starving to death the parish girl entrusted to her care, was described by the narratives sold after her execution in a detached and clinical manner. See Yetter, vol. 4, pp. 287–97.

121	Anon., *The Malefactor's Register, or the Newgate and Tyburn Calendar* (London, 1779), vol. 1, pp. 29–32.

122	Anon., *Malefactor's Register*, vol. 1, p. 33.

123	See *The World*, 5 September 1792, p. 2, and *Oracle*, 12 September 1792, p. 2, and 13 September 1792, p. 2.

124	*Evening Mail*, 3 September 1792, p. 3, *Oracle*, 11 September 1792, p. 2, and *The World*, 10 September 1792, p. 3, and 11 September, p. 2.

125	Sasha Handley, *Visions of an Unseen World* (London: Pickering and Chatto, 2007), pp. 169–70.

126	John Locke, *Some Thoughts Concerning Education* (London, 1693), p. 159–60.

127	Burke, *Writings*, vol. 9, p. 58.

128	Grenby, p. 7.

129	*Evening Mail*, 3 September 1792, p. 2.

130	Bindman, pp. 22, 58. Frances Burney was similarly surprised by her visit to France in 1802, as she had imagined the French to have been 'all transformed into bloody monsters' by the Revolution. Quoted in Grenby, p. 44.

131	Miles, 'The 1790s', p. 42.

132	Dorothy Blakey, *The Minerva Press* (London: Oxford UP, 1939), pp. 273–80.

133	On Mackenzie, see James Foster, *History of the Pre-Romantic Novel in England* (New York: Modern Language Association of America, 1949), p. 219. For Smith's Gothic sonnets of 1794–5, see Charlotte Smith, *Poems*, ed. Stuart Curran (Oxford: Oxford UP, 1993), pp. 58–61.

134	On the very modern sentimentalism of Radcliffe's characters, see Elizabeth MacAndrew, *The Gothic Tradition in Fiction* (New York: Columbia UP, 1979), pp. 48–9.

135	Bertrand Evans, *Gothic Drama from Walpole to Shelley* (Berkeley, CA: University of California Press, 1947), pp. 8–9, see also J.M.S. Tompkins, *The Popular Novel in England, 1770–1800* (London: Methuen, 1962), p. 295, and Robert Utter and Gwendolyn Needham, *Pamela's Daughters* (London: Dickson, 1937), pp. 130–1.

136	To put Radcliffe's use of these words into context, Reeve's *Old English Baron* – which is roughly half the length of *The Romance of the Forest* – uses them only fifty-nine times, while Walpole's *Castle of Otranto* – which is about one-quarter of the *Romance*'s length – uses them on fifty-seven occasions. Radcliffe's frequency of usage, then, is about one-and-a-half times that of Walpole, and three times that of Reeve. Comparison of *The Romance of the Forest* with *The Italian* shows a slightly reduced rate of usage in the later novel – 386 instances in a work one-quarter again as long as the *Romance* – but still hugely above that of the earlier novels.

137	*The Recess* was unusual, but it was not unpopular; it reached a fourth edition by 1792, as well as two Dublin editions in 1786 and 1791. There is a tradition that Sophia Lee may have been Ann Radcliffe's schoolmistress at Bath, although Norton argues that this is improbable: see Rictor Norton, *Mistress of Udolpho* (London: Leicester UP, 1999), pp. 46–9. *The Recess* was also popular in Germany, where it may have provided Naubert with a model for her own historical fiction: see Hilary Brown, *Benedikte Naubert* (Leeds: Maney Publishing for the Modern Humanities Research Association and the Institute of Germanic Studies, 2005), pp. 67–70.

138 Alan Lloyd-Smith, 'Nineteenth century American Gothic', in David Punter, ed., *A Companion to the Gothic* (Oxford: Blackwell, 2000), p. 109.

139 Leslie Fiedler, *Love and Death in the American Novel*, revised edition (Harmondsworth: Penguin, 1984), p. 126, Maggie Kilgour, *The Rise of the Gothic Novel* (London: Routledge, 1995), p. 23.

140 Miles, 'The 1790s', p. 43.

141 Quoted in Norton, p. 103.

142 Emesley, in Crossley and Small, p. 54.

143 On the Pittite surveillance culture of 1790s Britain, see John Barrell, *The Spirit of Despotism* (Oxford: Oxford UP, 2006), *passim*.

144 On the persistent use of Gothic language by anti-Jacobin authors describing the Revolution, see Patrick Brantlinger, *The Reading Lesson* (Bloomington, IN: Indiana UP, 1998), pp. 51–5.

145 On the Committee's attempts to limit mass violence, see Sutherland, *Murder*, chapter 7. On Jourdan's execution, see p. 92.

146 On the theatricality of the revolutionary guillotine, see Foucault, p. 15.

147 Arasse, p. 89.

148 On the often-bloody rhetoric of revolutionary heroism and martyrdom, see A. Jourdan, 'Robespierre and revolutionary heroism', trans. William Doyle, in Haydon and Doyle, pp. 54–74, especially pp. 65–6.

149 Ann Radcliffe, *A Journey Made in the Summer of 1794, Through Holland and the Western Frontier of Germany* (New York: Olms, 1975), pp. 35, 179–83, 215, 231, 317.

150 Radcliffe, *Journey*, pp. 22–3.

151 On the figure of Milton's Satan in anti-revolutionary rhetoric, see Joseph Crawford, *Raising Milton's Ghost* (London: Bloomsbury Academic, 2011), chapter 3. For examples of the revolutionary imagined as a libertine seducer, see Edmund Burke, 'Letter to a Member of the National Assembly', in Burke, ed., *Writings*, vol. 8, p. 317, and Henry John Todd, 'Life of Milton', in John Milton, *Poetical Works* ed. Henry John Todd (London, 1801), vol. 1, p. cxlvii.

152 For a classic account of the development of the Radcliffean villain, see Edith Birkhead, *The Tale of Terror* (London: Constable and Company, 1921), p. 53.

153 Walter Scott, *Lives of the Novelists* (London: Dent, 1910), p. 216.

154 Eaton Stannard Barrett, *The Heroine* (London, 1813), vol. 1, p. 156.

155 Radcliffe, *The Romance of the Forest*, p. 87.

156 Ann Radcliffe, *The Italian* (Oxford: Oxford UP, 1968), pp. 34–5.

157 Clara McIntyre, 'Were the Gothic novels Gothic?' *PMLA*, vol. 36, number 36 (1921), pp. 646–9, and Varma, *Flame*, pp. 29, 117–20.

158 Kate Behr, *Representations of Men in the English Gothic Novel* (Lewiston: Edwin Mellen Press, 2002), p. 112. On the weakness of Gothic heroes in comparison with Gothic villains, see also William Watt, *Shilling Shockers* (New York: Russell and Russell, 1967), pp. 34–5, William Day, *In the Circles of Fear and Desire* (Chicago, IL: Chicago UP, 1985), p. 16, and Evans, *Drama*, pp. 56–60.

159 See, for example, Haywood, p. 61, and Brantlinger, *Reading Lesson*, p. 51.

160 Burke, *Writings*, vol. 8, pp. 121–2.

161 Burke, *Writings*, vol. 8, pp. 505, 512, vol. 9, pp. 70, 184, 190–91.

162 Clery, p. 172.

163 Haywood, p. 81.

164 Helen Maria Williams, *Letters from France* (New York: Scholar's Facsimiles and Reprints, 1975), vol. 1:1, p. 65.

165   Williams, *Letters*, vol. 2:1, p. 177, vol. 2:2, pp. 90, 66, 103.

166   Williams, *Letters*, vol. 2:2, p. 104.

167   Williams, *Letters*, vol. 2:2, p. 99.

168   Helen Maria Williams, *Poems*, ed. Jonathan Wordsworth (Oxford: Woodstock Books, 1994), p. 30.

169   Samuel Taylor Coleridge and Robert Southey, 'The Fall of Robsepierre', in Coleridge, *Complete Works* (Princeton, NJ: Princeton UP, 2001), vol. 16:3:1, p. 12. On depictions of the Revolution in anti-Jacobin novels, see Grenby, chapter 2.

170   Coleridge, 'Fall', p. 13.

171   Coleridge, 'Fall', p. 17.

172   Coleridge, 'Fall', p. 26.

173   Coleridge, 'Fall', p. 42.

174   Coleridge, 'Fall', p. 42.

175   On Robespierre's fall, see Ruth Scurr, *Fatal Purity* (London: Chatto and Windus, 2006), pp. 318–22.

176   Coleridge, 'Fall', p. 20. On Robespierre's use of 'the sentimental-melodramatic form' in his political rhetoric, see David Andress, 'Living the revolutionary melodrama', *Representations*, vol. 114, number 1 (2011), pp. 103–30.

177   David Punter, *Gothic Pathologies* (Basingstoke: Macmillan, 1998), pp. 82–5.

178   On Radcliffe's interpretation of Burke's aesthetics of terror, see her essay, 'On the supernatural in poetry', in Clery and Miles, pp. 163–172.

179   Cobbett, p. 126.

180   Cobbett, pp. 221–2.

181   Mary Wollstonecraft, review of Helen Maria Williams's *Letters from France* in the *Analytical Review*, December 1790, in Janet Todd and Marylin Butler, eds., *Works* (London: Pickering, 1989), vol. 7, p. 322. The very title of Wollstonecraft's own book on the subject, *An Historical and Moral View on the Origin and Progress of the French Revolution* (1795), demonstrates the sort of detached, objective perspective she considered desirable; and in her *Vindication of the Rights of Men* (1790) she attacked Burke's insistence on understanding the Revolution in Gothic terms instead.

182   On Carrier's trial, see Baczko, pp. 141–70. Exactly what happened in Nantes during the winter of 1793–4 is still disputed; there certainly seems to have been a very high number of deaths, but it is unclear how many were caused by Carrier's repression, and how many by the disease and famine which were then ravaging the region. Estimates of the number of people executed under Carrier vary immensely. See Baczko, pp. 148–9n.

183   Baczko, p. 150.

3

The Secret Masters Walk Among Us

I

Within the landscape of eighteenth-century British history, the years 1796–8 form a historical micro-climate of their own; and if the 1790s as a whole were a period of national crisis, then in 1796–8 that crisis was at its most acute. Freak weather and disrupted trade led to food shortages and brought the nation to the brink of famine, while economic collapse led the Bank of England, no longer able to pay its debts in gold, to issue paper currency for the first time in its century-long history. These were the years of the Irish Rebellion, the British navy mutinies at Spithead and the Nore, the Tranent Massacre, the attempted invasion of England by the French, and the disastrous British expedition to the West Indies to quell the Haitian revolution: an expedition which, by 1798, had been shattered by war and disease, its soldiers and sailors dying in their tens of thousands of yellow fever. Starving, bankrupt, and mutinous, threatened by invasion from without and rebellion from within, Britain seemed to be at risk of simply unravelling; while revolutionary France, which in truth had internal economic problems at least as severe as Britain's, appeared from the outside to be going from strength to strength, conquering much of Italy, striking deep into Germany, and finally crushing the revolt in the Vendée. If the Gothic rhetoric discussed in Chapter 2 arose in the years of anxiety, 1792–5, then it was in these years of crisis and disintegration that it took two new, distinctive forms: for it was these years which saw the appearance of both supernatural Gothic fiction and the rise of the genre of modern conspiracy theory. It is these forms which I shall examine in this chapter; first by exploring the influx of German conspiracy fiction and horror-poetry which made them possible, then by investigating first the conspiracy theory of the 1790s and then the supernatural Gothic fiction of the same years, and finally by discussing the connections between the two, and the ways in which they contributed to the developing mythology of revolutionary 'terrorism'.

The fear of malevolent hidden conspiracies, working secretly to undermine society, was not new in the 1790s. Fear of the secret anti-social activities of Jews, witches, and heretics reached far back into the Middle Ages and was particularly prominent during the social and religious upheaval of the sixteenth and seventeenth centuries, leading to witch-hunts and religious persecutions across much of Europe.[1] In late-seventeenth-century Britain there was much anxiety over the covert activities of the Jesuits, who were feared to be plotting a Catholic takeover of the country; and though the Popish Plot of 1678 was ultimately exposed as fantasy, concerns lingered for decades over what the Pope's agents might be planning behind closed doors.[2] As Freemasonry spread through eighteenth-century Europe, fearful rumours circulated regarding the organisation's true nature and purpose; one alarmed French writer of 1747 even asserted that the Freemasons were a secret society originally founded by Oliver Cromwell, with the ultimate purpose of overturning the institutions of property, religion, and government in all nations.[3] But as late as 1780, few informed observers believed that secret societies played any significant role in European politics. Various covert organisations were, of course, known to exist; governments maintained networks of spies and informers, banned religious groups met in secret, and the assorted esoteric offshoots of Freemasonry claimed to possess hidden arcana which were communicated to their initiates in clandestine ceremonies. But real political power was understood to belong to those who made no secret of possessing it: kings, generals, bishops, and ministers, and the highly public institutions of church, state, army, and government bureaucracy of which they were the heads.

Over the next twenty years, all this was to change. By 1800, many otherwise rational individuals professed to believe that real power in Europe lay in the hands, not of governments or churches, but of secret conspiracies, whose members had infiltrated every level of society and were capable of destroying entire nations if their secret masters instructed them to do so. Unlike the hunters of witches, Jews, and heretics in previous centuries, they did not generally assert that these organisations possessed actual supernatural powers – only a few eccentrics, such as Abbé Fiard, insisted that the conspiracies they described were actually in league with demonic forces – but the capabilities they ascribed to these conspirators were so extraordinary as to fall little short of sorcery.[4] In the more extreme versions of 1790s secret society mythology, it was asserted that these societies had existed for hundreds of years without detection, maintaining perfect discipline and secrecy throughout their entire history; that they commanded the total loyalty of all of their members, allowing the will of the secret masters to be communicated rapidly and perfectly throughout the entire organisation; that their initiates would break any law of God or man rather than disobey the orders of their superiors; and that, with superhuman patience, these societies had worked covertly towards their grand goals for centuries, waiting for the time to strike. With their elaborate hierarchies, superhuman abilities, and complete commitment to the cause of evil, these imaginary conspiracies bore less resemblance to fallible human organisations than to the baroque demonologies of earlier ages; and yet their existence was insisted upon by men and women who would have scoffed at tales of witchcraft, or at assertions that the demonic powers of Satan were to blame for all that was wrong in the world.

The groundwork for the secret society mythology of the 1790s was laid by the sensational exposure of the Bavarian Illuminati in the mid-1780s.[5] Late eighteenth-century Bavaria was a stronghold of counter-Enlightenment Catholicism: a nation where crowds had flocked to witness the spectacular public exorcisms carried out by Johann Joseph Gassner during the 1760s and 1770s, and whose courts had sentenced a woman to death for witchcraft as late as 1775. The Catholics of Bavaria and the pro-Enlightenment thinkers of northern Germany regarded one another with mutual incomprehension: travelling through Bavaria from Enlightened Berlin, Christoph Nicolai was astonished to find Catholic folk-magic still practised by his Bavarian hosts.[6] The Illuminati were a secret society founded at the University of Ingoldstadt in 1776 by the German academic Adam Weishaupt, who intended to use them as the vanguard of Enlightenment rationality in Bavaria, countering the influence of the Jesuits and covertly spreading progressive political and religious ideals. Under Weishaupt's direction, the Illuminati began to infiltrate Bavarian Freemasonry in 1779, becoming a secret society within a secret society; promising Freemasons were initiated into the Illuminati, with the aim of using them to steer the activities of their Masonic lodges in directions favourable to the pro-Enlightenment Illuminati project. Yet, in striking contrast to the perfect secrecy that was to be attributed to the imaginary conspiracies so much feared in the following decade, the Illuminati managed to remain secret for only a few years. Knowledge of their existence reached the public as early as 1784, and Weishaupt fled Bavaria, after a failed attempt to convince the authorities of his society's innocence and benevolence; the organisation was outlawed in 1785, and many of its papers were seized by the police in 1786 and published the following year.[7] The anti-clerical, pro-Enlightenment ideals of the Illuminati lived on as one ideological strand within European Freemasonry for decades to come; but, as an actual organisation, they survived for less than a decade, and their influence appears to have been negligible. The most significant effect of the entire Illuminati affair was to spread the idea, on the very eve of the French Revolution, that hidden forces with radical political agendas might be working in secret to engineer permanent social change, and that seemingly innocent organisations – such as mainstream Freemasonry – might unknowingly be serving as their pawns, unaware that their leadership structures had been infiltrated and corrupted by conspiracies with much more sinister and far-reaching agendas.

Unsurprisingly, such richly evocative material proved irresistible to German novelists, rapidly giving rise to a whole sub-genre of novels, the *Geheimbundroman*, whose plots revolved around the machinations of secret societies. The first and most influential of these was by Schiller, who had a long-standing interest in plots and conspiracies: in 1784 he had written a play, *Die Verschwörung des Fiesco*, on the 1547 Fieschi conspiracy in Genoa, and in 1786 he had planned to co-edit a projected series of historical studies entitled *Geschichte der merkwürdigsten Rebellionen und Verschwörungen* (*History of the most remarkable rebellions and conspiracies*).[8] His pioneering *Geheimbundroman*, *Der Geisterseher*, began to appear in instalments in 1787, and its final, unfinished version appeared in book form in 1789; it told the story of a German prince who falls under the influence first of a Cagliostro-like charlatan, and then of a mysterious man who is probably an agent of the Catholic Church, both of whom awe him with displays of apparently supernatural knowledge and power which are in fact achieved through carefully organised mundane means.[9] Next came Christiane Naubert's historical novel *Herman von Unna* (1788), which appeared while Schiller's novel was still being serialised; *Herman* was set in the fifteenth century, and its plot centred on the activities of the much-feared secret tribunal of medieval Westphalia, the Holy Vehm. Catejan Tschink's imitation of Schiller's novel, *Geschichte eines Geistersehers* (1790), gave the story a more revolutionary twist; in Tschink's version, the protagonist is a Portuguese aristocrat manipulated by a mysterious Irishman, who uses various elaborate stratagems to persuade his victim that he possesses supernatural powers and thereby win him over to the revolutionary cause he professes. Finally, and most significantly for subsequent conspiracy mythology, Karl Grosse's *Der Genius* (1791) told the supposedly autobiographical story of a German aristocrat who is first recruited by, and then persecuted by, an apparently all-powerful and omnipresent secret society dedicated to the overthrow of the social order. In writing their novels of revolutionary ferments stirred up by the activities of secret societies, Tschink and Grosse clearly drew upon the recent exposure of the Illuminati in Bavaria, but both men must also have been thinking of contemporary events in France; as early as 1790, pamphlets were circulating which claimed that the French Revolution was the result of a Masonic plot, re-asserting the legend that Freemasonry had been founded by Cromwell and secretly dedicated to the destruction of monarchy all along.[10]

This kind of paranoid myth-making did not, initially, gain much credence in Britain, where Freemasonry had long been regarded as a harmless and respectable institution, and the exposure of the Illuminati in 1784–7 seems to have aroused very little interest. Nor, initially, was much notice taken of the German *Geheimbundroman*. Eighteenth-century Britain was saturated with French literature and culture, but the literature of Germany was almost unknown, generally viewed as barbarous, primitive, and dull; when *The Speculator* published an article on German literature in April 1790, its author lamented that 'the polite literature of the Germans, has escaped the general spirit of enquiry, and by some fatality seems hitherto to have repressed learned curiosity, and damped the ardour of investigation'.[11] Very few German works seem to have been much read in Britain before 1790. There are some exceptions: Mary Collyer's 1761 translation of Gessner's *Death of Abel* was evidently extremely popular, several editions of Klopstock's *Messiah* appeared in the 1760s, and Britain was not exempt from the continent-wide popularity of Goethe's *Sorrows of Young Werther*, translations of which appeared frequently from 1779 onwards. But, aside from these, German literature was almost entirely neglected, and even authors such as Schiller and Lessing were virtually unknown.[12] It was only after 1790 that the growing interest in all things fearful and Gothic transformed Germany's reputation for primitive barbarity from a liability into a selling point: Germany was, after all, the original homeland of the Goths, whose superstitious mythology had been praised by Bishop Hurd as so much more terrifying than that of Greece and Rome.[13] The first German play ever performed in London, *The German Hotel*, was first staged in 1790, while novels 'from the German' started to appear in the catalogues of the Minerva Press from 1790 onwards, growing more numerous after 1793, when Britain found itself allied with Prussia and Austria in a major European war against revolutionary France; the first English translation of Schiller's *Robbers*, by Alexander Tytler, appeared in 1792, while in 1793 Eliza Parsons wrote *The Castle of Wolfenbach*, a German-themed Gothic novel in the Radcliffean mode, and in 1796 Bürger's ghost-ballad *Lenore* was first published in English translation, achieving almost immediate nationwide popularity and fame.[14] This influx of German literature had an electrifying effect on many British readers, especially among the young. In 1794 Coleridge read *The Robbers*, and wrote his famous letter to Southey: 'My God! Southey! Who is this Schiller? This Convulser of the Heart? [. . .] I tremble like an Aspen Leaf [. . .] Why have we ever called Milton sublime?'[15] In 1795, the teenage Hazlitt was similarly overwhelmed by Schiller's play, recalling many years later that '*The Robbers* [. . .] stunned me like a blow', while in 1796 Lamb was so struck by *Lenore* that he was lost for words, writing enthusiastically to Coleridge: 'Have you read the Balad [*sic*] called "Leonora" in the 2d No. of the "Monthly Magazine"?–. If you have –!!!!!!!!!!!!!!!'[16]

The translation of *The Robbers* was a particularly important milestone, as by 1792 the play had become infamous for its supposedly Jacobinical tendencies. Written by Schiller when he was just nineteen, and first published in 1781, its portrayal of a band of violent but heroic outlaws struggling against an unjust social order struck a chord with theatre audiences in revolutionary France; a French adaptation, *Robert, chef de brigands*, enjoyed popular success on the Parisian stage in 1792, and in the same year the National Assembly voted to make Schiller an honorary citizen of France.[17] Tytler's 1792 translation removed some of the most extreme material from Schiller's play, but what remained was more than enough to ensure it was refused an official licence for performance in Britain.[18] Its hero, Karl Moor, possessed the same combination of charisma, energy, rage, and violence which, over the next few years, would come to characterise the villains who appeared in the works of Lewis and the later novels of Radcliffe; but, unlike Lewis' Antonio or Radcliffe's Schedoni, Karl Moor was presented sympathetically, as a flawed but still basically heroic character. In the preface to his 1792 translation, Tytler described Moor as a grand and terrible figure, whom 'we admire, but it is with awe and horror'; he compares him to Milton's Satan, and in his translation he even has Moor, who is described as having 'an air of inexpressible majesty', paraphrase Satan by declaring: 'I am myself my heaven or my hell'.[19] Tytler also approvingly quoted Henry Mackenzie's description of Moor as a character who 'presents to the fancy a kind of preternatural personage, wrapped in all the gloomy grandeur of visionary beings'; this, too, was a trait which he would bequeath to his literary descendants, until it became a commonplace for Gothic villains or villain-heroes to be described as men so awesome in their aspect and fearful in their accomplishments that they seemed to be 'visionary' or 'preternatural' rather than mere flesh and blood.[20] Moor's combination of sympathetically presented political radicalism and near-superhuman ability and charisma was precisely what contemporary critics found so worrying about *The Robbers*; they feared the effect it might have upon British audiences at a time of such critical political tension, and took seriously the apocryphal story, sceptically retold by Tytler in his preface, that a group of German students had been so impressed by a performance of *The Robbers* that they decided to become outlaws themselves, forming a 'conspiracy' to which they 'had bound themselves by the most tremendous oaths'.[21] *The Robbers* was widely read: Tytler's translation reached a fourth London edition by 1800, despite competition from two American and three Irish editions, and two rival translations published in 1799. But such was the concern over its supposedly corrupting tendencies that *The Robbers* was not performed in Britain until 1799, in a massively rewritten adaptation which moved the action from Germany to Spain, transformed Schiller's band of lawless anti-clerical robbers into a troop of patriotic Christian crusaders, and added a dancing clown; and, even then, many critics were uncomfortable with the idea of a play which drew inspiration from such dangerous sources being permitted to appear on the British stage.[22]

II

It was this rising tide of interest in German literature, typified by the success of *The Robbers* and *Lenore*, which carried the German conspiracy novels to Britain: *Hermann of Unna* was translated in 1794, as was Karl Kahlert's 'Wundergeschichte' *Der Geisterbanner* (1792), which now appeared in English as *The Necromancer, or, the Tale of the Black Forest*. 1795 saw the translation of both Schiller's *Ghost-Seer* and Tschink's imitation of it, now given the politically suggestive title *The Victim of Magical Delusion, or the Mystery of the Revolution of P----L: A Magico-Political Tale, Founded on Historical Facts*, as well as an adaptation of *Hermann of Unna* for the London stage, entitled *The Secret Tribunal;* and in 1796 Tschink's translator, Peter Will, went on to translate Grosse's *Der Genius*, which was published in Britain as *Horrid Mysteries*.[23] It is important to note that both *The Victim of Magical Delusion* and *Horrid Mysteries* were presented to their British readers as being based on real events, a claim which may even have been believed by some of their readers; for in the same years in which they were translated, the supposedly non-fictional genre of revolutionary conspiracy theory was growing increasingly extreme and bizarre. 1796 saw the publication in Paris of Cadet-Gassicour's *Le Tombeau de Jacques Molay*, which asserted that the French Revolution was the result of a 500-year-old conspiracy initiated by the Knights Templar, who had plotted to take revenge for the persecution of their order by destroying the French monarchy and the Papacy; these secret Templars, the author claimed, covertly controlled the Freemasons, the Jesuits, the Swedenborgians, the British Whig party, and, of course, the Jacobins, using them all to accomplish their sinister objectives, while keeping most of them ignorant of the true purpose of their respective organisations.[24] Another French work of the same year, Montjoie's *Histoire de la Conjuration de Louis-Phillippe-Josèphe d'Orléans*, presented another variant on the Templar conspiracy; asserting that the Revolution had been organised by Orléans in his role as Grand Master of the Grand Orient of the French Freemasons, Montjoie claimed that Orléans had been initiated into the secret Masonic order of Kadosch, and had sworn to destroy the Bourbon monarchy in a ceremony held in the presence of the bones of Jacques de Molay, last Grand Master of the Knights Templar, who had been executed under King Phillip of France in 1314.[25] Such bizarre claims thrived in the extraordinarily heightened political atmosphere of post-Thermidorian France, in which a bewildered and traumatised population struggled to come to terms with the events of the previous seven years. These extreme versions of the Masonic plot theory never really took hold in Britain, but in the last years of the 1790s the basic assertion that the French Revolution was the result of an anti-Christian plot formed by a shadowy conspiracy was one that found increasingly wide acceptance, especially after the publication of two crucial works in 1797: the *Mémoires* of the Abbé Barruel, and John Robison's *Proofs of a Conspiracy Against all the Religions and Governments of Europe*.

Barruel was a French Jesuit, who emigrated to Britain after the September Massacres, and was living in London when he published the work that would make him famous. He had first come to the attention of the British reading public with his atrocity-filled *History of the Clergy During the French Revolution*, published in French in 1793; it was swiftly translated, and six English-language editions had appeared by 1795, providing ample material for anti-revolutionary propagandists such as Cobbett, who drew heavily on Barruel's *History* in *The Bloody Buoy*. This was followed in 1797 by his *Mémoires*, an immense, multi-volume work which explained the French Revolution as the work of a deep-rooted anti-Christian plot, of which the Jacobins, the Freemasons, the *Philosophes*, and the Illuminati were all component parts; according to Barruel, Swedenborg, Condorcet, Cagliostro, Necker, Lafayette, Orléans, Kant, Dr Guillotin, and the Comte de Sainte-Germain, among many others, had all been agents of this vast conspiracy.[26] In his preface, Barruel insisted on the reality of the plot that he described:

> We have seen men obstinately blind to the causes of the French Revolution: we have seen men who wished to persuade themselves that this conspiring and revolutionary sect had no existence anterior to the revolution. In their minds this long chain of miseries which has befallen France, to the terror of all Europe, was the mere offspring of that concourse of unforeseen events inseparable from the times; it is in vain, in their conceptions, to seek conspirators or conspiracies, vain to search for the hand that directs this horrid course...[27]

Barruel rejected, in other words, any account of the French Revolution which attributed its progress to mere historical contingency, 'that concourse of unforeseen events inseparable from the times'; in his view, whatever had happened in France must have been the result of 'one continued chain of deep-laid and premeditated villainy'.[28] Barruel's paranoid political fantasy seems to have grown in the making as he soaked up every anti-revolutionary rumour circulating through the French émigré community in London, which in 1796–8 was in a state of shocked despair, their last serious attempt to retake their homeland from the revolutionaries having ended in bloody disaster at the Battle of Quiberon Bay.[29] The first volume of Barruel's *Mémoires* asserted the existence of a conspiracy just a few decades old, an anti-Christian 'secret Academy' planned by Voltaire and founded in Paris by D'Alembert in order to spread subversive literature and pave the way for the French Revolution; but by the end of his second volume he was asserting that the conspiracy had existed for 1,500 years, manifesting successively as the Manichean heresy of late antiquity, the Cathar heresy of the Middle Ages, the Knights Templar, the Freemasons, and finally the Jacobin party, who, far from being a modern organisation, were in fact merely the latest mask of an anti-social conspiracy that pre-dated the fall of Rome.[30] By the time he came to write his fourth volume, Barruel had apparently convinced himself of the existence of a conspiracy so vast, ancient, all-powerful, and ubiquitous as to be responsible for almost all the political unrest in the world, from the French *Jacquerie* of 1358 to the Irish Rebellion four hundred and forty years later. This conspiracy, he claimed, had three million agents, lurking in every nation from Sweden to Egypt, America to India; there were five-hundred thousand of them in France alone.[31] The London Corresponding Society, the *Amis des Noirs*, the German Union of booksellers, the Freemasons, the French Economists, the Swedenborgian church, the Society for Constitutional Information, and the United Irishmen were all fronts for the conspiracy.[32] The conspirators had established a secret tribunal in Rome, which dispatched assassins to murder the monarchs of Europe: they had already executed Louis XVI, poisoned his son, murdered Gustavus III, deposed William V, and attempted to assassinate George III.[33] Every stage of the French Revolution had been carefully choreographed by these conspirators; even those events which seemed most spontaneous, such as the food shortages of 1789, the September Massacres, and the Flight to Varennes, had all, in fact, been planned out by them in advance.[34] The military successes of the French revolutionaries were all due to the conspiracy, which had infiltrated every army in Europe and sabotaged the efforts of the Revolution's enemies.[35] Barruel asserted, in short, that he lived in a world in which no political event was truly accidental, spontaneous, or contingent; everything that appeared to be so was, in fact, the work of this all-powerful conspiracy, whose 'legions of secret emissaries' had obtained 'that dominion of terror which forbids any sovereign within the astonished universe to say, Tomorrow I shall continue seated on my throne…'.[36]

Far-fetched and extraordinary though such claims were, they found a receptive audience in Britain. An English translation of the *Mémoires* was published in 1797, and a second edition issued the following year; a Dublin edition appeared in 1798, and an American edition in 1799. Barruel's translator, Robert Clifford, was so concerned by the material he was translating that in 1798 he published his own work of conspiracy theory, *An Application of Barruel's Memoirs of Jacobinism to the Secret Societies of Ireland and Great Britain*, in which he proved (at least to his own satisfaction) that every popular political society active in the British Isles was a front for the international Illuminati conspiracy. Clifford must have been a man of some courage, for the conspiracy he described was a brutal organisation which murdered those who crossed it as a matter of course:

> The reader will not be surprised to hear of the *Black List*, on which were inscribed the names of those who gave umbrage to the sect, and of the *Red List*, or *Blood List;* and when once a person was entered on that, it was, among the Order, held futile to flatter one's self with the hope of escaping the poisons or the assassins of the Sect.[37]

Barruel's work was welcomed by John Robison, whose own *Proofs of a Conspiracy Against All the Religions and Governments of Europe, Carried on in the Secret Meetings of Free Masons, Illuminati, and Reading Societies* appeared in 1797 (and was rapidly translated into French); according to Robison's *Postscript to the Second Edition*, the first edition of his book sold out within days of its initial publication, and by 1798 it had reached its fifth edition, with other editions appearing as far afield as Dublin, Philadelphia, and New York.[38] Robison's claims were substantially more modest than Barruel's, but his explanation of the French Revolution was still conspiratorial; he blamed the Revolution on the Illuminati, whom he believed had survived their initial exposure almost undamaged, taken control of French and German Freemasonry, recruited Mirabeau and Orléans, constructed the Jacobin party as a front for their nefarious activities, and now aimed at world domination through global revolution. It was these conspirators, Robison asserted, who were responsible for the atrocities of the Terror; they were powerful and dangerously unprincipled, and their agents were active not just in France and Germany, but also in London, leading Robison to conclude fearfully that 'The present is a season of anxiety'.[39] Barruel and Robison were learned, widely respected men: Robison, especially, was a pillar of the Scottish intelligentsia, Professor of Natural Philosophy at the University of Edinburgh, General Secretary of the Royal Society of Edinburgh, and a one-time colleague of James Watt, and in 1797 he was also engaged in contributing articles on science to the third edition of the *Encyclopaedia Britannica*, which he must have written alongside his *Proofs of a Conspiracy*.[40] Their theories at least appeared to be well supported by documentary evidence, and their works were taken seriously not just by fringe eccentrics, but by many respectable journalists, preachers, and other reputable commentators on current affairs. Thomas De Quincey, then a bookish child living in Bath, recalled decades later that 'I did not read [Barruel's *Mémoires*], but I heard it read and frequently discussed ... The Abbé, everybody said, was a good man; incapable of telling falsehoods'.[41] In an enthusiastic review of Robison's book in January 1798, the *London Review and Literary Journal* declared that his *Proofs of a Conspiracy* 'deserves every praise which can be bestowed upon it', and two months later the *British Critic* announced of Barruel's *Mémoires* that 'no book has appeared since the commencement of our labours, which was more necessary to be read, and weighed attentively by every person of property, whether hereditary or commercial; every person holding any rank in society; and every person who has within him a spark of zeal, either for the honour of God, or the welfare of mankind'; while, in New England, Jedidiah Morse, the 'father of American geography', was so persuaded by Robison's *Proofs* that he delivered a series of sermons in 1798, warning of the threat posed to the youthful American republic by the international Illuminati conspiracy.[42]

By 1798, then, when Jane Austen began to write the first draft of *Northanger Abbey* – in which Isabella Thorpe recommends that Catherine Morland should read half a dozen German and German-themed novels, including the conspiracy novels *The Necromancer* and *Horrid Mysteries*, on the grounds that they are 'all horrid' – Britain was awash with both fictional and supposedly non-fictional conspiracy literature.[43] The German conspiracy novels were presented to the British public in a fashion that deliberately blurred the line between fictional and non-fictional conspiracies; Grosse and Tschink's novels, as previously mentioned, were presented as being based upon real events, while the translator of *Hermann of Unna* prefaced the first British edition of the novel with an essay on the Westphalian Secret Tribunal – described as 'an institution which, though it could never be traced to its recesses, made monarchs tremble upon their thrones' – which depicted this historical organisation as an inescapable network of secret assassins, whose members were willing to kill 'their nearest relation, or their dearest friend' if the appropriate secret sign was given by a fellow conspirator, and explicitly compared it to the contemporary Freemasons and Illuminati.[44] In one famous scene in *Northanger Abbey*, Austen even draws attention to the near interchangeability of contemporary conspiracy fiction and conspiracy theory:

> The general pause which succeeded his short disquisition on the state of the nation, was put an end to by Catherine, who, in rather a solemn tone of voice, uttered these words, 'I have heard that something very shocking indeed, will soon come out in London.'
>
> Miss Tilney, to whom this was chiefly addressed, was startled, and hastily replied, 'Indeed! – and of what nature?'
>
> 'That I do not know, nor who is the author. I have only heard that it is to be more horrible than anything we have met with yet.'
>
> 'Good heaven! – Where could you hear of such a thing?'
>
> 'A particular friend of mine had an account of it in a letter from London yesterday. It is to be uncommonly dreadful. I shall expect murder and every thing of the kind.'
>
> 'You speak with astonishing composure! But I hope your friend's accounts have been exaggerated;– and if such a design is known beforehand, proper measures will undoubtedly be taken by government to prevent its coming to effect.'
>
> 'Government,' said Henry, endeavouring not to smile, 'neither desires nor dares to interfere in such matters. There must be murder; and government cares not how much.'[45]

The 'something very shocking' which Catherine is expecting to 'come out in London' is a Gothic novel, probably a work of German-style conspiracy fiction such as those recommended to her by Isabella Thorpe. But when Catherine speaks solemnly of something 'uncommonly dreadful', 'more horrible than anything we have met with yet', involving 'murder and everything of the kind', Eleanor Tilney assumes she is speaking of a real terrorist conspiracy, a 'design' which she hopes the government may yet prevent; and when Catherine says she does not know 'who is the author', Eleanor believes her to be explaining that the conspiratorial mastermind behind this monstrous plot is still unknown. Even Henry Tilney's mocking remark that 'Government... neither desires nor dares to interfere in such matters' is open to both readings; he means that the government refuses to censor 'terrorist' fiction, but his choice of words is reminiscent of the conspiracy theorists, who explained that even kings and emperors lived in fear of the Illuminati and their assassins. Through the circulation of such conspiracy literature, both fictional and non-fictional, organisations such as the Illuminati – previously utterly obscure in Britain – rapidly became well known and much discussed; and whereas previously British authors had explained the progress of the French Revolution without reference to such societies, some now asserted that their activities had been essential to its success. When the elderly Edinburgh clergyman John Erskine published the second volume of his *Sketches and Hints of Church History* in 1797, he translated extracts from the works of various German Protestant writers in order to illustrate the danger posed to German Protestantism by Roman Catholicism. The following year, an anonymous Catholic writer who signed himself 'AC' accused Erskine of 'countenancing the authors, and promoting the designs, of the infamous sect of the Illuminati', on the grounds that one of the authors he quoted – Christoph Nicolai, chiefly remembered today for his literary feud with Goethe – had been singled out by Robison and Barruel as one of that organisation's 'secret chiefs'. 'AC' explained:

> The Public are now no strangers to the existence of a Sect, which has of late made so much noise on the Continent under the name of *Illuminati*, or the *Enlightened*, and who, under the pretence of enlightening Mankind, and completing the Reformation of Religion and Government, have attempted, by the most deep-laid and diabolical arts, to accomplish the utter destruction of both. It has been asserted, and not without some appearance of foundation, that these daring Innovators have at least Abettors, if not Emissaries and Associates, in this Country...[46]

What is striking here is that 'AC' takes public awareness of the active existence of a 'diabolical' Illuminati conspiracy as given, when only a few years before the idea had been almost entirely unknown. The only evidence he feels required to give for this extraordinary claim is a single footnote, which reads '*Vide* Professor Robison and the Abbe Baruel [*sic*]', evidently assuming that Barruel and Robison's works are so widely known that not even their titles are required.[47] He concedes that 'all the readers of [Erskine's] sketches may not be readers of Professor Robison's proofs', although he clearly feels this to be a major failing on their part, as in his view the Illuminati are so poisonously dangerous that publishing any work by one of their members, even unintentionally, is little short of criminal.[48] The Illuminati, he explains, 'propagate their principles with astonishing success on every side', and it behoves Erskine as a clergyman to oppose 'a conspiracy that has "*Antichrist*" and "*Antichristian*" too conspicuously marked upon its banners to admit of any misapplication'.[49] The author of another anonymous 1798 pamphlet from Edinburgh, *The Advantages Resulting from the French Revolution*, explained that the Illuminati and other 'diabolical sets of men' had assisted the advance of French armies into Germany, and the same idea that secret cells of Illuminati conspirators were paving the way for French military success in Europe was evident in a satirical 'letter from Napoleon' printed in the same year in the *Anti-Jacobin* magazine, in which Napoleon proposes to donate the Temple of the Sun at Palmyra to the Bavarian Illuminati on the grounds that 'They may be of service in extending our future conquests'.[50] Also in 1798, in a footnote to the published edition of one of his sermons, the clergyman William Agutter explained that the entire revolutionary career of Orléans had been choreographed by the same conspiracy: 'I have no doubt but that on the same day that he combined himself with the *illuminati*, they sentenced him to infamy and the scaffold'.[51] That Orléans was a member of the Illuminati, as Barruel and Robison had asserted, is clearly viewed by Agutter as an established historical fact; all that remains for debate is the exact nature of their association. 'AC' may have been a crank (although he could as easily have been a respectable member of Edinburgh's literary world), but the *Anti-Jacobin* and the *London Review and Literary Journal* were widely read journals, and Agutter was a well-known and popular London preacher; nor, aside from this brief foray into conspiracy theory, does the anonymous *The Advantages Resulting from the French Revolution* differ much in its tone or content from most mainstream British accounts of the Revolution written in the late 1790s.[52]

By 1800, the Irish political writer Patrick Lattin could write of 'the learned Abbé Barruel, whose *History of Jacobinism* has met with such universal approbation'.[53] That such men were willing to assert the existence of a 'diabolical' international conspiracy of Illuminati, capable of toppling the French monarchy and threatening, as Robison's title had it, 'all the Religions and Governments of Europe', speaks volumes for the rapid spread of conspiracy theory in Britain in the last years of the eighteenth century.

It is hard to know to what extent these men really *believed* the conspiracy theories they propagated. In many ways, their actions suggest that they did not truly believe in the conspiracies they described, or did so only partially; aside from 'AC', they published their books under their own names, and continued to live public lives rather than going into hiding, which would hardly seem to be rational behaviour for men who actually believed they were exposing the existence of a powerful, amoral, omnipresent conspiracy which murdered its opponents as a matter of course. In 1797, Barruel had asserted that France was ruled by a sect of murderous monsters who aimed at world revolution; yet just five years later he returned to live there under Napoleon, even though the ancient conspiracy he described in his *Mémoires* could not possibly have been destroyed by so slight a setback as the Brumaire *coup d'état*, which did not even remove all the surviving revolutionaries from government.[54] Possibly, within the panic-stricken historical micro-climate of 1796–8, certain ideas may have seemed credible which no longer appeared persuasive when re-examined under calmer circumstances; all ghost stories seem more believable when one is alone in the dark. Barruel's belief in the Satanic omnipotence of revolutionary evil may have been sincere in the immediate aftermath of the Terror and the disaster at Quiberon Bay, but could have faded to much more manageable levels by the time he returned to France in the grubby dawn of 1802. As for the readers of Barruel and Robison, even men such as Morse and Agutter – who were evidently sufficiently convinced that they took it upon themselves to warn others of the Illuminist threat – may well not have given full credence to all of what they read, just as some of the readers of Grosse's supposedly autobiographical conspiracy novel may have believed it to be based on truth, while still suspecting much of it of being fiction. One could quite reasonably find Barruel's conspiratorial explanation for the success of the French Revolution highly persuasive without actually accepting his entire ancient Templar conspiracy theory as fact. Given the basically compensatory nature of all conspiracy theories, which replace threateningly chaotic events with comfortably comprehensible, human-scale narratives and shift all blame for the violence of history onto a hidden elite of deliberate villains, they may even have professed and propagated such beliefs because, on some level, they *hoped* they were true, rather than because they were fully convinced of their factual truth. As Tompkins remarks, 'in comparison with bearing blame oneself, it must have seemed almost tolerable to have been undone by so far-reaching, long prepared, diabolically ingenious a conspiracy'.[55]

One reason for the success of such conspiracy theories was that they professed to offer an explanation for the unprecedented, and for many people deeply worrying, spread of popular political organisations in Britain and Ireland during the 1790s. Political societies such as the Society for Constitutional Information had existed in Britain for decades, but they had been elite organisations, the preserve of lawyers, clergymen, and members of parliament. However, following the French Revolution and the popular success of Paine's *Rights of Man*, radicals such as Thomas Hardy had begun to organise genuinely popular political organisations, whose members were artisans rather than well-meaning gentry: the Sheffield Society for Constitutional Information was one of the first of these, founded in 1791, and followed in 1792 by the London Corresponding Society (which was soon in correspondence with regional societies in Norwich, Nottingham, Manchester, and other cities) and the Scottish Friends of the People, while in the same years the United Irishmen underwent a swift and radical metamorphosis, shifting from an elite political club to a popular society committed to democratic government.[56] 'AC', Robison, and other conservative Edinburgh literati must have been particularly alarmed when, in the last months of 1793, the Scottish Friends of the People invited representatives of the English corresponding societies and the United Irishmen to join them in Edinburgh and form a 'British Convention'; modelling themselves on the French Jacobins, the Convention's delegates called for immediate political reform, and for an end to the war with revolutionary France. The British Convention was broken up by the authorities, the leaders of the radical societies imprisoned or transported, and the societies themselves suppressed; but in the crisis years of 1797–8 the United Irishmen rose in armed rebellion against the British government, and many feared that other local insurrections, such as the naval mutinies at Spithead and the Nore and the anti-militia riots which led up to the Tranent Massacre in Scotland, might also have been instigated by popular radical societies: there were even rumours that the mutineers had taken their instructions from a mysterious 'gentleman in black', whose true identity no-one knew.[57] By 1799, the anxiety over popular national societies had grown so acute that even the annual Gorsedd of Iolo Morganwg's Order of Bards were shut down by the authorities, on the suspicion that they, too, might secretly be aiding the French and spreading sedition among the people of Wales.[58] For their supporters, the activities of groups such as the United Irishmen and the London Corresponding Society were exercises in legitimate political organisation, and risings such as those at Tranent, Spithead, and the Nore were natural and more or less spontaneous responses to intolerable conditions; but to men such as Robison and Barruel, used to thinking of politics as something orchestrated from above rather than arising from below, and committed to the idea that only ambitious villains could ever choose to oppose a government so obviously benevolent and legitimate as that of George III, it seemed impossible that such popular societies could ever arise except through the plotting of the powerful.[59] By such logic, if *Rights of Man* was being read everywhere, even by the very poor, it proved not that the people were actually hungry for political reform, but that sinister conspirators were seeking to spread political unrest; and if radical popular societies sprung up rapidly across the British isles in 1791–2, that demonstrated not the strength of genuine radical feeling among the populace, but the power and cunning of those who were manipulating them. Conspiracy theory allowed the popular clamour for reform to be reconciled with a belief in the obvious and self-evident rightness of existing systems of government, and provided a way for these new political movements to be conceptualised by people for whom 'mass politics' still seemed to be a contradiction in terms.

In a very similar way, these conspiracy theories were able to fill a crucial conceptual gap in their author's accounts of the French Revolution. As I have discussed, anti-revolutionary writers in the mid-1790s often struggled to explain the Revolution's continued survival and success; if the revolutionary republic was as irrational, chaotic, and bloodthirsty as they claimed, it was extremely unclear how it could have avoided disintegrating into ineffectual anarchy, let alone how it could vanquish half the armies of Europe. Conspiracy theory helped to connect the seemingly impossible events of the French Revolution into a more easily comprehensible narrative: whenever the historical record seemed to make no sense, as when Barruel had to explain how popular feeling had been aroused against the kings of France even though they had been good, wise, and much-loved monarchs under whom France had achieved unprecedented prosperity, it was a sign that the hidden hands of the conspirators had been at work.[60] Confronted by new forms of political mass-mobilisation, they attributed the unheard-of capabilities of the French revolutionary state to conspiratorial manipulation. As Roberts points out, such explanations seemed to make sense to people who were used to thinking of politics in terms of the manoeuvrings of factions and individuals in courts and parliaments, rather than in terms of popular mass movements.[61] Here, for example, is Robison's explanation of the French Revolution's progress:

> Hence too may be explained how the revolution took place almost in a moment in every part of France. The revolutionary societies were early formed, and were working in secret before the opening of the National Assembly, and the whole nation changed, and changed again, and again, as if by the beat of a drum. Those duly initiated into this mystery of iniquity were ready everywhere at a call.[62]

How else, Robison implicitly asks his readers, could the near-simultaneous rising of the French people in support of the Revolution possibly be explained, except as the result of a conspiracy? How could so much have changed so fast, unless it had all been carefully planned out in advance, and guided to fruition by the hidden hands of the Illuminati?

Such theories, ironically, were an exact mirror image of those which had been believed by Robespierre and his colleagues, who had attributed all the Revolution's failures to anti-revolutionary plots (and used the supposed existence of such plots, and the need to combat them, to justify their actions during the Terror), just as Barruel and his fellow conspiracy theorists now attributed all its successes to pro-revolutionary conspiracies. Barruel and Robespierre even shared the belief that the French food shortages of 1789 were the result of a 'famine plot', although they naturally had different opinions on who was responsible for it.[63] The crucial difference between the conspiracy theories believed in by Barruel and Robespierre was that Robespierre's account of the distribution of power in Europe remained traditional; the conspirators he believed to be plotting against him did their work covertly, but they ultimately answered to men who wielded their power overtly, such as Pitt the Younger or the Duke of Brunswick. As Cubitt puts it:

> The conspiracy theories of the Revolution were still, like those of the eighteenth century, largely theories of occult *intention*. The conspirators they denounced were not shadowy figures behind the scenes; they were known and often prominent public figures... What was hidden and had to be exposed was not their personal identity but their secret motivation.[64]

The conspiracy theories of Barruel and Robison, on the other hand, were what Cubitt terms 'theories of occult power', asserting the existence of conspirators who worked covertly for masters even more covert than they, and to believe in such theories was to believe that true power in Europe was hidden, and exercised in secret.

The belief that history was shaped, not by the overt actions of kings, popes, and ministers, but by invisible forces moving beneath the surface of events, was hardly unique to the 1790s; as Clery notes, 'The force of the myth of secret societies lay in its assimilation of theories of human agency to traditional theories of divine or infernal agency.'[65] Many medieval and early modern historians had interpreted historical events from a theological perspective, subscribing to what Hunter describes as 'the traditional Western view that human life was a manifestation of divine purpose, and history a record of the conflict between angelic and Satanic forces', while some nineteenth-century historians would go on to attribute almost all historical change to grand, impersonal, abstract forces such as economics, class struggle, evolution, 'progress', or racial destiny.[66] What was unique about the conspiracy theories of the late eighteenth and early nineteenth centuries was not their claim that invisible forces turned the wheels of history, but that they attributed such powers not to superhuman forces such as 'divine providence' or 'economic progress', but purely to the activities of cabals of wicked men.

To accept such theories, even partially, thus required one to believe in the existence of an extraordinary class of human beings: men of vast patience, great intellectual powers, and shocking amorality, capable of secretly organising and guiding immense conspiracies over many years. One had to believe, in short, that the kind of evil geniuses who appeared in German conspiracy fiction really existed, and exercised tremendous power over the fate of Europe. As the tools of the conspirators were universally agreed to be murder and massacre – the discovery of recipes for drugs and poisons among the seized papers of the Illuminati led conspiracy theorists to attribute every untimely or suspicious death among the Revolution's enemies to the work of Illuminati assassins – the figure of the conspirator blurred into the figure of the terrorist; not least because all the leading Jacobin *terroristes* of 1793–4 were held by Barruel and his followers to have been active agents of the conspiracy, which Barruel described as 'a sect whose empire is terror'.[67] The conspirator-terrorists imagined by these writers operated in a realm outside normal morality, unbound by all normal ties of society and religion, and capable of actions that any normal man would find doubly impossible; for anyone other than such a monster would be both intellectually incapable of successfully plotting an atrocity such as the September Massacres, and morally incapable of actually carrying it out. Being beyond normal human limitations, they were invoked to explain whatever these authors found most inexplicable: how could the French have been turned so quickly against their beloved and benevolent King? How could anyone have performed the sort of atrocities which were believed to have taken place during the Terror? Yet such 'explanations' did not dispel the mystery; they only deferred it. Even if one accepted this conspiratorial account of the Revolution, the mystery merely moved from the streets of Robespierre's Paris into the mind of Robespierre himself – or into the minds of those hypothetical Secret Masters whose expendable pawn

Robespierre might have been. Witness, for example, Robert Clifford's denunciation of Adam Weishaupt:

> This will be sufficient to pourtray the founder of the *Atheistical Illuminees*, who has, together with Zwack and the Baron Knigge, compiled so astonishing and progressive a code of rebellion, that one would be tempted to pronounce it supernatural. [. . .] Satan, when seeking vengeance against his Divine Creator, would have been proud to become the pupil of the modern Spartacus.[68]

The evil of Weishaupt, Zwack, and Knigge overflows the limits of the human, and carries them into the realms of the demonic: 'one would be tempted to pronounce it supernatural'. Traditional stories of witches and black magicians had always depicted them learning their evil arts from Satan; but Clifford, reversing the formula, suggests that these modern monsters are so evil that they would be qualified to instruct the Devil himself. This is not so much biography as demonology; and, in this sense, the respectable Abbé Barruel and the eccentric Abbé Fiard both effectively asked their readers to believe that the Revolution had been caused by demons and black magic. Fiard was simply more honest about it.

For over a century, the heirs of Locke and Addison had argued that evil was not grand or mysterious, just ugly and undesirable; but, faced with the inexplicable ongoing survival and success of the French Revolution, in the last years of the eighteenth century many of them seem to have given up the fight. The violence and wickedness of the Revolution appeared to them to be incommensurable with the rest of human history: either it could not be understood, or it could be comprehended only as the work of men so brilliant and monstrous that they might as well not be human at all. And it was against this backdrop that, for the first time in over a hundred years, literal demons – along with ghosts, witches, magicians, and the rest of the long-neglected machinery of 'Gothic superstition' – began to make their reappearance in the literature of Britain.

III

When the popularity of the supernatural Gothic fiction of the later 1790s is considered, it is worth recalling that it was a period when many people believed the world to be passing through a metaphysical crisis as well as a political one. Garrett has called attention to the proliferation of self-declared prophets and doomsday preachers around 1800 in both France and Britain, of whom the best-known today are Richard Brothers (who prophesied that he would be revealed as the true ruler of the world in 1795) and Joanna Southcott (who foretold that she would give birth to the Messiah in 1814).[69] In 1793, a book called *The Apocalyptical Key* was published in London: it reprinted an interpretation of the Book of Revelations written by the Presbyterian preacher Robert Fleming in 1701, in which he had predicted the downfall of the French monarchy in 1794 and the subsequent movement of the world towards the Second Coming of Christ.[70] In 1794, both Blake and Coleridge wrote poems speculating that the French

Revolution might usher in the Millennium.[71] Fiard's belief that France had been misled by magicians and demons has already been mentioned, but such supernatural and eschatological interpretations of the Revolution could also be found at a popular level: among those executed during the Terror in Arras was a gardener who predicted that 'a beast with seven horns' – presumably a confused recollection of the Beast with seven heads and ten horns described in Revelations 13:1 – 'will come to devour the patriots', while Brothers declared in 1794 that the war with France was, in fact, the Pale Horse of Death mentioned in Revelations 6:8.[72] Both Brothers and Southcott claimed to have encountered the Devil in person; and, even among the less mystically inclined, the need to combat the sceptical deism and rationalistic atheism associated with the Revolution led to a renewed emphasis on the supernatural elements of revealed religion.[73] With rationalist revolutionaries such as Fouché hanging signs over the cemeteries of Paris declaring that 'death is an eternal sleep', it became more important than ever for their opponents to insist on the literal reality of God and Satan, heaven and hell, and the immortality of the soul.[74]

Conspiracy theory, Gothic fiction, anti-revolutionary propaganda, and apocalyptic religious prophecies all circulated through the same cultural circles, appealing to the same appetites for stories of mysterious happenings, appalling revelations, and assurances of the ultimate inevitable triumph of righteousness. Joanna Southcott, who convinced many of the literal truth of her encounters with the supernatural powers of darkness, was also a reader of Gothic fiction; she even asserted that Radcliffe's *Romance of the Forest* was a prophetic and divinely inspired allegory of the progress of the French Revolution, in which de Montalt's murder of his brother stood for the execution of Louis XVI, which had not yet taken place when the novel was written in 1791.[75] At the other end of the social scale to Southcott, Hester Piozzi – the one-time companion of Dr Johnson – became increasingly convinced by the progress of the French Revolution that the end of the world was near; she saw parallels between contemporary events and the Book of Revelations, and believed from 1794 onwards in the imminent conversion of the Jews.[76] She was an avid reader of both Gothic novels and anti-revolutionary propaganda; she read *The Mysteries of Udolpho* in 1794, *The Monk* in 1796, and the conspiracy theories of Barruel and Robison in 1798, the latter of which persuaded her that Napoleon's military victories were being assisted by the work of the Illuminati.[77] Not everyone went as far as Southcott or Piozzi in absorbing the paranoid atmosphere of the age; but there was clearly a very widespread feeling that the tenor of the times was at best fantastical and unnatural, and at worst actually apocalyptic, and the result was a cultural climate more favourable to the writing of supernatural fiction than any since the later seventeenth century. 'The Taste in this Country is altered', Piozzi wrote to her daughter in 1796. 'People are tired of Figures in just proportion, some going to Court, some crying Fish, moving across a Camera Obscura in St James's Street; They want Gyants again, and Dragons...'[78]

Until 1795, British Gothic fiction made almost exclusive use of the explained supernatural. Prophetic dreams and low-key hauntings were as far as the novels of Reeve, Radcliffe, and their imitators wished to go in the direction of the fantastic; other events might appear to imply the existence of demons, magic, and so on, but all were explained as the result of human trickery by the end. The German conspiracy novels of the early 1790s likewise adopted a basically rationalistic approach to the apparently supernatural events that occur within them, although the scenes they attempted to explain away were often so extraordinary that the explanations offered were scarcely less remarkable than the events themselves. Only eccentric outsiders such as Walpole, Hutchinson, and Beckford had made heavy use of actual supernatural beings in their 'wonder tales', and their works had been critically controversial and little imitated. In 1796, however, a novel was published by another such eccentric, one that would create much more controversy than *Otranto* or *Vathek*. The man – or rather boy, as he was only nineteen at the time of its writing – was Matthew Gregory Lewis, and his infamous first novel was *The Monk*.[79]

Lewis had much in common with Walpole and Beckford: like them, he was wealthy, highly educated, politically well connected, and probably homosexual. Also like them, and in sharp contrast to Ann Radcliffe, he was international in outlook: his father was a diplomat, his family wealth came from sugar plantations in the West Indies, and by the time he wrote *The Monk* in 1794 he had already travelled in France, Germany, and the Netherlands.[80] It was his German connections which would prove most significant for Lewis' literary career, as his time in Weimar exposed him to a flourishing German literary culture which, as I have discussed, was then still almost unknown in Britain; he was thus well positioned to capitalise on the growing taste for Gothic and Germanic horrors in the mid-1790s. (In 1805–6, Lewis would go on to write English translations of popular German Gothic novels, and in 1816 he would read to Byron from his translation of Goethe's *Faust*.)[81] *The Monk*, although mostly set in Spain, made substantial use of German folklore and legend. In its pages appear the ghostly Bleeding Nun, the spiteful elemental Water-King, and the immortal Wandering Jew, all figures out of Northern European folklore; it includes a ghost-ballad modelled on Bürger's *Lenore*, and its central plot – in which a holy man of great ability is seduced to evil by making a deal with the Devil – inevitably recalls the most famous German legend of all, the story of Faust. Lewis was not the first British author to use German settings or legend-lore in a Gothic novel, but he was the first to present a fictional world in which these supernatural German legends were literally true, in the way that Walpole and Beckford had done for the mythology of medieval Europe and ancient Arabia, respectively. Where Lewis departed from Walpole and Beckford's template was in making no attempt to claim that his work was merely a translation of ancient material: in *The Monk*, a British author of the later eighteenth century presented a novel full of fantastical, impossible, and supernatural events to the reading public under his own name, openly admitting that it was his own original work. In this, too, Lewis may have followed German models; in Germany, unlike Britain, the fantastical chivalric romance had remained a popular literary genre throughout the eighteenth century, much to the dismay of German critics, and the success of Christian Speiss' *Das Petermännchen* (1791), a romance about a medieval knight torn between good and evil spirits, had initiated a vogue for overtly supernatural fiction which would have been in full swing during Lewis' time in Weimar.[82]

It was not only the supernaturalism of *The Monk* which made it controversial. The Radcliffean Gothic romance had always dealt with themes of oppression, violence, and socially illegitimate sexual desire, but had very seldom done so graphically; acts of rape, torture, and murder either took place off-stage, or were prevented at the last moment by fortuitous twists of the plot. In *The Monk*, however, this is not at all the case; the protagonist's lustful spying upon his naked sister, his murder of his mother, his incestuous rape and murder of his sister, the imprisonment of another character with the rotting corpse of her dead baby, and finally the gruesome deaths of the villains responsible for all this horror – one torn apart and left to die in agony by the Devil, the other beaten gradually to death by an angry mob – are all described in horrific and gloating detail, quite unlike anything in Radcliffe or the mainstream British Gothic fiction which followed her. Again, Continental influences are possible: Lewis may have read De Sade's *Justine* in Paris, or the anonymous German book of fictional medieval atrocities, *Schreckensscenen aus den Ritterzeiten* (1792), in Weimar.[83] But it is equally possible that Lewis came up with such ghoulish scenes without any such outside inspiration, drawing only upon the same perennial affinity between adolescent boys and imaginary horrors which, earlier in the century, had given rise to Warton's 'Pleasures of Melancholy', Schiller's *Die Räuber*, Wordsworth's 'Vale of Esthwaite', and Southey's 'To Horror'. Even when Lewis drew upon less ghastly sources, he generally ramped up the levels of horror involved. Among the German borrowings in *The Monk* is an inset ghost-ballad, 'Alonzo the Brave', which attained sufficient notoriety to be republished independently. Like Bürger's *Lenore*, it tells the story of a spectre bridegroom who returns from the dead to claim his bride, but whereas Bürger's knight becomes a skeleton when his spectral nature is revealed, Lewis' Alonzo is a much more hideous apparition:

> All present then uttered a terrified shout,
> All turn'd with disgust from the scene;
> The worms they crept in, and the worms they crept out,
> And sported his eyes and his temples about,
> While the spectre address'd IMOGENE:–[84]

Over the next few years, Lewis would continue to serve up scenes of violent supernatural horror in works such as *Osric the Lion! A Romance*, where a murder – which takes place, naturally enough, in a German castle by the Rhine – is interrupted by the vengeful ghost of one of the murderer's previous victims, Ulrilda, who arrives attended by a demonic host:

> and the demons their prey flock'd around
> They dash'd him with horrible yell on the ground
> And blood down his limbs trickl'd fast:
> His eyes from their sockets with fury they tore;
> They fed on his entrails, all reeking with gore,
> And his heart was Ulrilda's repast.[85]

Such scenes of extreme, graphic violence, reminiscent of the revenge tragedies and martyrologies of the early modern period, had for almost a century been almost entirely excluded from eighteenth-century English poetry and fiction – although, as I have discussed, not from notionally non-fictional works, such as abolitionist literature or the reporting on the September Massacres – and their inclusion in Lewis' works swiftly made him both highly popular and deeply controversial.

Shortly after the publication of *The Monk*, Lewis became a member of parliament for the Whig party. The first edition of his novel had been published anonymously; but when the second edition was published in October 1796, its title page announced that it was 'by M.G. Lewis, Esq., M.P.'[86] That a liberal member of parliament should be engaged in the circulation of such material was viewed by some as a cause for serious concern, at a time when, as I have discussed, anxieties were running high over the revolutionary forces which might be working to secretly undermine society, and Lewis was forced to expurgate the next edition of *The Monk*, which appeared in 1798.[87] 'The author of the Monk signs himself a LEGISLATOR!' Coleridge wrote, in his indignant review of the novel, published in the *Critical Review* in February 1797. 'We stare and tremble...'.[88] Cadet-Gassicour, it will be recalled, had claimed that the Whig party was a branch of the international revolutionary conspiracy, and Robison had asserted that the German book trade was under the complete control of the Illuminati; from such paranoid perspectives, the publication of an immoral and supernatural German-influenced novel by a Whig MP could easily be seen as part of the same assault on social order more blatantly carried on through the publication of political and philosophical works sympathetic to the ideals of the revolution. Germany's reputation as a playground for atheistic anarchist conspirators contributed to contemporary anxieties that the influx of German and German-themed Gothic fiction, poetry, and drama into Britain might be having a negative effect on British culture. Gamer points out that the success of German plays on the London stage led the *Dramatic Censor* to write in 1800 of 'an *actual conspiracy* against British genius' among the managers of London's theatres, while, as Watt notes, German novels were seen as inflaming pro-revolutionary sentiment among their readers:

> As a term of self-description for novels and romances, 'German' was much more current than 'Gothic' in the 1790s, but it increasingly carried a series of revolutionary associations which, by the end of the decade, led to the abuse of virtually every work claiming such a descent.[89]

Perhaps the best-known example of such abuse was that of William Wordsworth, who, in the preface to the 1800 edition of *Lyrical Ballads*, famously declaimed against the kind of German literature which had so impressed Coleridge six years earlier, and the genres of popular fiction, poetry, and drama to which it had since given rise:

> The invaluable works of our elder writers, I had almost said the works of Shakespear and Milton, are driven into neglect by frantic novels, sickly and stupid German Tragedies, and deluges of idle and extravagant stories in verse. – When I think upon this degrading thirst after outrageous stimulation I am almost ashamed to have spoken of the feeble effort with which I have endeavoured to counteract it; and reflecting upon the magnitude of the general evil, I should be oppressed with no dishonourable melancholy, had I not a deep impression of certain inherent and indestructible qualities of the human mind [...][90]

In Wordsworth's view, the popularity of such 'sickly and stupid' works was due to the temper of the times:

> For a multitude of causes unknown to former times are now acting with a combined force to blunt the discriminating powers of the mind, and unfitting it for all voluntary exertion to reduce it to a state of almost savage torpor. The most effective of these causes are the great national events which are daily taking place, and the encreasing accumulation of men in cities, where the uniformity of their occupations produces a craving for extraordinary incident which the rapid communication of intelligence hourly gratifies. To this tendency of life and manners the literature and theatrical exhibitions of the country have conformed themselves.[91]

The causal chain described by Wordsworth here is worth careful attention. Urbanisation and industrialisation have gathered men together in cities, creating large urban audiences whose boring, repetitive jobs predispose them to favour material rich in 'extraordinary incident'. This 'craving' is chiefly gratified, not by plays or novels, but by 'the rapid communication of intelligence' concerning 'the great national events which are daily taking place': by the daily newspapers, in other words, and their sensationalistic reporting on contemporary political events in Britain and France. The audience for 'frantic novels', then, is created by the kind of newspaper reportage discussed in Chapter 2; having grown used to getting daily doses of excitement and horror in the news, Wordsworth's imagined urban audience no longer has the patience for 'Shakespear and Milton', and seeks instead the 'outrageous stimulation' which German and German-themed plays and novels provide. Clery has remarked that, in the 1790s, 'the French Revolution was being written, and consumed by a paranoid British public, like a gripping romance translated from the German', but Wordsworth suggests the reverse: German romances were being read because they were the only genre capable of delivering the same kind of excitement and horror as the latest news from revolutionary France.[92]

In the mid-1790s, it was still possible to regard 'German novels' and 'Gothic romances' as two separate genres. Gothic romances were set in the feudal past, had despotic priests and aristocrats as their villains, featured uncanny events which often turned out to be the result of trickery, and were usually politically conservative; German novels were set in the present (or the very recent past), usually had secret societies as villains, featured extravagantly impossible events which were sometimes the result of elaborate conspiracies and sometimes of genuine supernatural forces, and had a (largely undeserved) reputation for being politically subversive. *The Monk*, however, combined the two genres, rewriting the Radcliffean Gothic romance in a German mode; and, in the wake of the controversy over its authorship and publication, two articles appeared which viewed both forms as being effectively interchangeable – both manifestations of a single tendency which they called 'the terrorist system novel writing', or simply 'terrorist fiction'.[93] In an article entitled 'Terrorist Novel Writing', one anonymous critic complained of 'the fashion to make *terror* the *order of the day*, by confining the heroes and heroines in old gloomy castles, full of spectres, apparitions, ghosts, and dead men's bones'; such a novel, the author warned, 'carries the young reader's imagination into such a confusion of terrors, as must be hurtful':

> It is to great purpose, indeed, that we have forbidden our servants from telling the children stories of ghosts and hobgoblins, if we cannot put a novel into their hands which is not filled with monsters of the imagination, more frightful than are to be found in Glanvil, the famous *bug-a-boo* of our fore fathers.[94]

Joseph Glanvill was a famous seventeenth-century author on witchcraft, whose compendium of legend-lore regarding ghosts and witches, *Saducimus Triumphatus*, was published in 1681, while the reference to forbidding servants to tell children 'stories of ghosts and hobgoblins' echoes Locke's well-known advice, in his *Thoughts Concerning Education* of 1693, to protect 'tender Mind[s]' from 'Impressions and Notions of *Sprites* and *Goblins* ... the usual Method of *Servants* to awe Children'.[95] 'Terrorist' novels, the author implies, are undoing the work of a century of enlightenment, returning their readers to the kind of superstitious fearfulness which Locke and his followers had tried to banish; a fearfulness which, as the reference to Glanvill implicitly reminds the reader, had led 'our fore fathers' to hang their neighbours as witches. Just as Locke had seen such superstitions as predisposing their believers to madness, so this author asserts that these 'terrorist' novels are psychologically 'hurtful' to their readers, and that their authors may actually be insane: 'A novel, if at all useful, ought to be a representation of human life and manners ... But what instruction is to be reaped from the distorted ideas of lunatics, I am at a loss to conceive ...'[96]

But what *were* these 'terrorist' novels? The editor of the *Spirit of the Public Journals*, in which this article appeared, asserted in a footnote that 'It is easy to see that the satire of this letter is particularly levelled at a literary lady of considerable talents', i.e. Ann Radcliffe, and goes on to mock Radcliffe for her lack of linguistic and historical knowledge. But many of the scenes and tropes which are mocked and criticised in this article do not sound much like Radcliffe at all; her novels did not feature 'spectres, apparitions, ghosts', or animated suits of armour, and while she did make use of skeletons hidden in chests, she never included such violent grotesquerie as 'the hideous visage of a *murdered* man, *uttering* piercing groans, and developing shocking mysteries' staring in through a window, or 'an old woman hanging by the neck, with her throat cut'.[97] These sound more like scenes from the plays and novels of Lewis, which did feature ghosts, walking armour, and extreme violence, or from German conspiracy fiction, which used gory murders and 'shocking mysteries' as its stock-in-trade. Yet the fact that the editor was able to make such a mistake, and to simply assume that Radcliffe's novels were essentially the same as such works – a view which the article's author may very well have shared – bears witness to the extent to which these widely divergent works were coming to be seen as part of a single genre, whose distinguishing mark was that, like the Jacobins, it made use of 'the *system of terror*'.[98]

The connections between Gothic novels and revolutionary politics, implicit in this article's use of politically loaded phrases such as 'terrorist' and '*system of terror*', were made more explicit in another satirical article, 'The Terrorist System of Novel-Writing', which appeared in John Aikin's *Monthly Magazine* in August 1797. Its author, who signed himself 'A JACOBIN NOVELIST', attributed the popularity of Gothic fiction – which he pointedly described as 'the wonderful revolution that has taken place in the *art* of novel-writing' – to the fascination of the British public with the events of the Terror:

> It has long, for example, been the fashion to advert to the horrible massacres which disgraced France during the tyranny of Robespierre; and, whatever a good and loyal subject happens to write, whether a history, a life, a sermon, or a posting bill, he thinks it his duty to introduce a due proportion of his abhorrence and indignation against all such bloody proceedings. Happy, sir, would it be, if we could contemplate barbarity without adopting it; if we could meditate upon cruelty without learning it; and if we could paint a man without a head, without supposing what would be the case if some of our friends were without their heads. But, alas! so prone are we to imitation, that we have exactly and faithfully copied the SYSTEM OF TERROR, if not in our streets, and in our fields, at least in our circulating libraries, and in our closets.[99]

In August 1797, Robespierre had been dead for three years; yet, as I have discussed, it was the events of his brief supremacy, rather than the entire chapters of bloody revolutionary history which had unfolded since his downfall, which continued to engross public attention, retaining their hold upon the collective imagination of the British reading public. The author implies that he views this fascination with the Terror as excessive, but his real objection is to the lessons which he views as having been learned from it:

> just at the time when we were threatened with a stagnation of fancy, arose Maximilian Robespierre, with his system of terror, and taught our novelists that *fear* is the only passion they ought to cultivate, that to frighten and to instruct were one and the same thing...[100]

In line with most mainstream eighteenth-century critics, 'A JACOBIN NOVELIST' takes for granted that the purpose of novels is to instruct their readers. Thus, in his view, the political terrorist and the terrorist novel writer are united in their dependence on fear in order to communicate the lessons they wish to teach; a method which, he implies, the novelists have learned from the terrorists. The tone of the article is light and satirical, and the author does not seem to believe, as Wordsworth would argue three years later, that 'terrorist' novels actually posed a serious threat to the mental health of their readers; if he did, he would hardly mention off-handedly that he lets his daughters read such novels, as they 'would read them whether I pleased or not'.[101] But he does suggest that the success of 'The Terrorist System of Novel-Writing' was symptomatic of the debased fascination with scenes of fear and blood which had taken root in Britain since the events of the Terror, and that the fictional vocabulary of the terrorist novel writers was very largely drawn from supposedly non-fictional accounts of those events. Such accounts, as I have discussed, proliferated in Britain during the years following Robespierre's fall, growing more rather than less frequent as the events themselves receded and the historical mythology of terrorism and the Terror began to take shape. Small wonder, then, that by 1797 they seemed to be everywhere, even in 'a history, a life, a sermon, or a posting bill...'.

If 'the terrorist system' was understood to be that form of revolutionary government which had prevailed in France during the Terror, a novel such as *The Monk* could be understood as being a work of 'terrorist fiction' in several senses. It was 'terrorist' insofar as it attempted to achieve its aesthetic objectives by inspiring terror in its readers, in a fashion which, these writers suggested, was analogous to the way in which the Jacobin 'terrorists' of 1793–4 had attempted to achieve their political goals by terrorising their enemies. It was 'terrorist' because it departed from the ordinary conventions governing the infliction of violence in fiction, just as the Jacobins had departed from such conventions in reality, the grotesque, incestuous rape-murders of *The Monk* being as far from normal literary depictions of violence and sentimentally suffering innocence as the events which were believed to have taken place during the September Massacres were from normal state executions. It was 'terrorist' because its politics and (lack of) morals were seen as being in sympathy with those of the Jacobin 'terrorists' themselves, as both were regarded as being contemptuous of ordinary religion and morality. Finally, in the eyes of Barruel and his ilk, it was 'terrorist' because both German-style fiction and Jacobin-style politics could be understood as emanations of the vast, shadowy, Franco-German Jacobin–Illuminati conspiracy whose existence they were so determined to demonstrate, ultimately orchestrated by monstrous terrorist masterminds willing to use everything from 'terrorist' novels to 'terrorist' massacres in order to hasten the unravelling of the social fabric and bring about their longed-for anti-Christian world revolution. But this choice of name for the genre points to another connection between the rhetoric of supernatural Gothic fiction and that of political terrorism: the former asserted explicitly, as the latter did implicitly, that some forms of evil and violence stand outside the natural order of things, and can be understood only as magical, numinous, or demonic, eruptions into human history of something beyond the normal limits of the natural and the possible. It was a viewpoint made explicit by Lewis' literary disciple, Charlotte Dacre, in her warning to the reader at the end of her second novel, *Zofloya*:

> The progress of vice is gradual and imperceptible, and the arch enemy ever waits to take advantage of the failings of mankind, whose destruction is his glory! That his seductions may prevail, we dare not doubt; for can we otherwise account for those crimes, dreadful and repugnant to nature, which human beings are sometimes tempted to commit? Either we must suppose that the love of evil is born with us (which would be an insult to the Deity), or we must attribute them (as appears more consonant with reason) to the suggestions of infernal influence.[102]

It is the existence of 'crimes, dreadful and repugnant to nature' which proves the reality of 'infernal influence', as Dacre argues that it would not be 'consonant with reason' to believe that humans, having been created by a benevolent God, could ever perform such crimes without the intervention of evil supernatural forces. Her logic seems questionable – it is unclear why it is 'more consonant with reason' to locate 'the love of evil' within fallen angels rather than fallen humans, given that both were presumably originally created by the same loving, well-intentioned God – but her basic point is clear: humans may be sinful, but we aren't *that* sinful, and while ordinary 'failings' can be attributed to normal human weakness, 'dreadful and repugnant' crimes can be explained only by the 'infernal influence' of 'the arch enemy', Satan. *Zofloya*, like *The Monk*, depicts such influence in action: its protagonist, Victoria, moves from simple selfishness, which is presented as the natural result of her spoiled education, to a string of atrocious murders and cruelties, the results of her seduction by the Devil. For Lewis and Dacre, as for Barruel and Robison, there is evil, and then there is *evil*. Normal historical or psychological causality and contingency can account for our ordinary moral failures and unkindnesses, but extreme wickedness can be explained only as the result of dark powers, demonic or conspiratorial, moving beneath the surface of things; and it was the deployment of such extreme, inhuman wickedness which was taken, in fiction as in reality, to be the hallmark of 'the terrorist system'.

The network of associations which, by the end of the decade, linked together 'terrorist' violence, revolutionary conspiracy, supernatural evil, and Gothic fiction into a single discourse can be seen with some clarity in Charles Lucas' comic anti-Jacobin novel, *The Infernal Quixote* (1801). Its villain, a renegade aristocrat named James Marauder, is inspired by his reading of 'Diabolist' Jacobin philosophy to model himself on Milton's Satan; viewing revolutionary politics as his best hope for personal advancement, he then becomes a member of the United Irishmen conspiracy, and helps to lead their violent uprising in 1798.[103] For Marauder – and for Lucas – conspiratorial politics, revolutionary ideology, Satanic wickedness, and violent, amoral criminality all form parts of a single whole, which Lucas calls 'DIABOLISM', but which his contemporaries were increasingly starting to refer to as 'terrorism'; and the literary templates for writing about the careers of diabolical revolutionary terrorists such as Marauder was provided, very largely, by Gothic fiction. As Butler notes:

> The nearest prototype for Lucas' infernal villain is probably Lewis's Ambrosio the Monk. The last-named exerts a powerful hold on the popular imagination from the year of his appearance, 1796; and incongruous though he may be in the would-be rational universe of the anti-Jacobins, it is really not surprising to find half-conscious fears of conspiracy, betrayal, the irrational itself taking on the features of the favourite bogey of the day.[104]

IV

In his 1797 review of *The Monk*, Coleridge objected to its plot on the grounds that, by making Ambrosio's tempter supernatural, Lewis had made his fall into sin all but inevitable:

> Human prudence can oppose no sufficient shield to the power and cunning of supernatural beings; and the privilege of being proud might be fairly conceded to him who could rise superior to all earthly temptations, and whom the strength of

the spiritual world alone would be adequate to overwhelm. So falling, he would fall with glory, and might reasonably welcome his defeat with the haughty emotions of a conqueror.[105]

Reasonable though it sounds, this is an extraordinary claim for any Christian writer to make. In Milton's day, it had been considered axiomatic that human faith, if not human prudence, *was* a 'sufficient shield' to defend the true believer from 'the power and cunning of supernatural beings': the entire plot of *Paradise Lost* revolves around the fact that Adam and Eve, while capable of being misled by Satan, are also capable of resisting him. Generations of Christians believed themselves to live in a state of perpetual demonic siege, like that described in Bunyan's *Holy War*, constantly tempted towards sin by evil spirits whose 'power and cunning' had to be resisted on a daily basis; yet, for Coleridge, such resistance is apparently virtually inconceivable. This belief in the invincibility of supernatural evil represents a further stage in the erosion of the traditional hero, which I have already discussed in connection with the novels of Radcliffe. The old literature of theological evil had always assumed that evil could be defeated, and that a brave and faithful Christian hero was equal to anything that Earth or Hell could muster against him. Radcliffe's novels had moved that struggle inwards; if the hero always loses, crushed by the villain's demonic strength, then the battle that counts is not the clash of external forces, but the internal battle against temptation and despair. But Coleridge suggests that this, too, may be a lost cause; a sufficiently potent villain is apparently enough to make the fall into temptation ineluctable. Such spiritual battles appear unwinnable because the powers of hell seem unopposed by the powers of heaven; Marlowe's Faustus had been competed for by good and evil angels, but *The Monk* and *Zofloya* are Faustian tales in which the good angel has vanished from the stage, leaving only the demons who first tempt their protagonist, and then mock and punish them for succumbing to temptation. Rather than depicting a traditional magical or theological understanding of the universe, these novels depict otherwise orderly, rational, recognisably late-Enlightenment fictional worlds onto which older demonologies have been incongruously grafted; and, as a result, their characters frequently seem bewildered by the cosmic unfairness of the worlds they live in, in which the demons and monsters can do whatever they like while everyone else has to play by the normal rules.

This world view, in which men and women are reduced to mere playthings of the powers of darkness, has obvious correspondences with that of contemporary conspiracy theory. Barruel, Robison, and the rest urged their readers to oppose the international Illuminist conspiracy; but the diabolical organisation they described was so vast and insidious that it is not clear how it could be effectively fought at all. According to Robison's account, the suppression of the Illuminati by the Bavarian government was completely ineffectual; the entire conspiracy simply reformed under the guise of reading societies and masonic lodges, and within a few years of its official suppression this supposedly disbanded society had managed to bring about the French Revolution.[106] Effective opposition was just as difficult in fiction. In *Horrid Mysteries*, the protagonists attempt to form a counter-conspiracy to oppose the revolutionary plots of the secret society they have encountered, but their efforts are entirely frustrated by the apparent omnipotence and omniscience of their invisible opponents: their letters are intercepted, their funds mysteriously vanish from their safe houses, and at last they disband their organisation in despair.[107] With its insistence upon the diabolic awfulness of the revolutionaries, anti-revolutionary propaganda such as Cobbett's tended to present a similarly lopsided picture of the apparent omnipotence of revolutionary evil: throughout *The Bloody Buoy* all power seems to rest in the hands of the Jacobin terrorists, whose victims can apparently do nothing but weep, scream, pray, and bleed as their monstrous persecutors rape, mutilate, and murder them at will.

Such a pessimistic and anxiety-ridden view of the power of evil, so antithetical to that of the previous generation of writers, flourished in Britain during the crisis years of 1796–8. Menaced by invasion, starvation, rebellion, and economic collapse, it is perhaps not surprising that many British readers were at least temporarily convinced by the accounts given by Cobbett, Robison, and Barruel of the virtual omnipotence of evil; nor, in a world grown increasingly threatening and strange, that they were more willing than they had been for generations to harken to tales of supernatural and demonic forces. As I have argued, both conspiracy literature and supernatural fiction appealed to a similar sense of disorientation and dread in their readers, and in the last years of the century the interpenetration of these two forms resulted in the rise of a new Gothic sub-genre: the 'Rosicrucian' novel, exemplified by Godwin's *St Leon* (1799). This sub-genre, which led ultimately to such later 'cursed immortal' novels as Shelley's *St Irvyne* (1810), Maturin's *Melmoth the Wanderer* (1820), and Bulwer-Lytton's *Zanoni* (1842), generally centred on a mysterious individual who appears to possess supernatural knowledge and power, as had most conspiracy novels from Schiller's *Geisterseher* onwards; but instead of being revealed as frauds who accomplished their seemingly magical feats through mundane means, as they always were in the German and German-influenced conspiracy fiction of the early- and mid-1790s, in the Rosicrucian novels these mystery men turn out to be genuine magicians. Schiller's inscrutable Armenian, like the historical Comte de Saint-Germain, cultivated rumours that he was ancient and immortal; his equivalents in the Rosicrucian novels usually really *are* immortal, often hundreds or thousands of years old, having attained eternal life through Rosicrucian alchemy.[108] The ease with which the figure of the conspiratorial mastermind thus merged into the figure of the Gothic necromancer demonstrates, once again, the basically magical and demonological attitudes which underpinned contemporary conspiracy literature, while Godwin's movement from the non-supernatural Gothicism of *Caleb Williams* in 1794 to the overt supernaturalism of *St Leon* in 1799 indicates the extent to which the supernatural had come to be taken for granted, even expected, in Gothic fiction and drama in the years following *The Monk*'s success. When Lewis followed up on the success of his notorious novel by writing a play, *The Castle Spectre*, the producers implored him to rewrite the scenes in which the eponymous ghost appeared onstage; generations of theatrical practice had insisted that such 'superstitious' scenes were inherently ridiculous.[109] Yet Lewis turned out to have a surer sense of contemporary taste than his colleagues: although sniffed at by critics, who thought the use of ghosts in modern drama 'contemptible', his play was an immediate commercial success, bringing in over fifteen thousand pounds in a single season.[110]

As Gamer has pointed out, it was in 1797 that the young Wordsworth and Coleridge began to write poetry on supernatural subjects: Wordsworth's 'Goody Blake and Harry Gill' and 'The Thorn', and Coleridge's 'Rime of the Ancient Mariner' and 'Christabel'. When Wordsworth and Coleridge criticised Matthew Lewis and the 'German' school, it may, as Gamer argues, have been less because they viewed a literature of fear and magic as inherently objectionable than because they were attempting to differentiate their own recent attempts at supernatural poetry from Lewis' more populist works.[111] The success of this new supernatural literature, typified by the popularity of *The Castle Spectre* and *The Monk*, was viewed with some alarm, as it was feared that the dissemination of such stories – especially among the young and the ignorant – might cause its readers and viewers to become fearful, superstitious, and even insane. It was a view that Lewis dismissed in his response to the critics of *The Castle Spectre*:

> Against my *Spectre* many objections have been urged: one of them I think rather curious. She ought not to appear, because the belief in ghosts no longer exists! In my opinion, this is the very reason why she *may* be produced without danger; for there is now no fear of increasing the influence of superstition, or strengthening the prejudices of the weak-minded. I confess I cannot see any reason why Apparitions may not be as well permitted to stalk in a tragedy, as Fairies be suffered to fly in a pantomime, or Heathen Gods and Goddesses to cut capers in a grand ballet; and I should rather imagine that *Oberon* and *Bacchus* now find as little credit to the full as the *Cock-Lane Ghost*, or the Spectre of *Mrs Veal*.[112]

The success of modern supernatural drama, Lewis argues, was not a sign that the public was increasingly superstitious, but that it was increasingly sceptical; modern audiences had so little dread of ghosts that they could regard them as light entertainment. His references to 'the Spectre of *Mrs Veal*' and 'the *Cock-Lane Ghost*', famous ghosts of the early- and mid-eighteenth century respectively, make clear his belief that modern audiences were not only less superstitious than their seventeenth-century ancestors – whom writers at the time, such as the anonymous author of 'Terrorist Novel Writing', generally regarded as having been almost pathologically credulous – but even less superstitious than the previous generation, who in the 1760s had flocked to hear 'scratching Fanny' at Cock Lane. With popular superstition at such an all-time low, Lewis implies, supernatural drama and fiction are rendered perfectly safe. His own dramatic practice in *The Castle Spectre* served to highlight the fact that its ghosts, murders, and fearful goings-on were not to be taken at all seriously, constantly intercutting serious events with scenes of comedy, and finally rounding the play off with a comic epilogue, spoken by the heroine directly to the audience:

> And all perforce, his crimes when I relate,
> Must own that Osmond well deserved his fate.
> He heeded not papa's pathetic pleading;
> He stabbed mama – which was extreme ill-breeding;
> And at his feet for mercy when *I* sued,
> The odious wretch, I vow, was downright rude.

Twice his bold hands my person dared to touch!
Twice in one day! – 'Twas really once too much!
And therefore justly filled with virtuous ire,
To save my honour, and protect my sire,
I drew my knife, and in his bosom stuck it;
He fell, you clapped – and then he kicked the bucket![113]

In this deflating speech, the audience is invited to consider the scenes of murder, haunting, and threatened rape which they have just watched as mere spectacle: exciting, enjoyable, but also rather absurd. As a leading purveyor of supernatural horror in his poetry, prose, and drama, Lewis held closely to this line in order to assert that his works would not, in fact, corrupt their audiences; that the reading and theatre-going public of the 1790s were less naïve than critics such as Coleridge supposed, sufficiently genre-savvy to know that works such as *The Monk, Osric the Lion!*, and *The Castle Spectre* were to be understood as light entertainment, rather than as serious invitations to rape their sisters, murder their nephews, believe in ghosts, and sell their souls to the Devil.

Lewis' defence of *The Castle Spectre* demonstrates, once again, that the craze for supernatural Gothic fiction was a distinctively *modern* phenomenon, rather than a resurgence of older cultural forms ploughed under by a century of Enlightenment. Lewis, like Radcliffe, certainly drew upon older sources, such as Shakespearean and Jacobean tragedies and (very heavily mediated) traditional European folklore; but his works remained firmly rooted in the 1790s, and their attitudes to their feudal, Catholic settings, and the violent and supernatural events which take place within them, are always recognisably those of late-eighteenth-century Britain. The traditional ghost-lore of northern Europe, such as that collected by Glanvill a century before, grew out of a cultural context in which violent death and apparently supernatural experiences were commonplace; but supernatural Gothic fiction emerged from an age in which, at least among the educated classes, the experience of violence was rare and the supernatural was assumed not to exist. As Lewis explained, it was precisely this distance and difference which made scenes of supernatural horror available and safe for use as dramatic and literary spectacles: just as Burke had theorised decades before, a literature of sublime terror was most aesthetically appealing and psychologically desirable for those audiences whose daily lives did *not* bring them into regular contact with awesome and fearful events. Thus, in Lewis' novels, poems, and plays, monstrous villains, supernatural beings, and acts of appalling violence tend to appear not as coherent elements of his fictional historical settings, but as mere effects, with causality and probability increasingly dropping away as he endeavours to cram in as much Gothic spectacle as possible. In 1800, the narrator of Charlotte Smith's *Letters of a Solitary Wanderer* anticipates complaints regarding:

the fashionable taste, which has filled all our modern books of entertainment with caverns and castles, peopled our theatres with spectres, and, instead of representing life as it is, has created a new school, where any thing rather than probability, or even possibility, is attended to.[114]

The narrator is clearly thinking of Lewis here, as the references to 'castles' and 'spectres' make clear. The 'thing rather than probability' which is 'attended to' in Lewis' works was spectacle, the more exciting, entertaining, and extraordinary the better; and his later stage dramas became famous for their special effects, paving the way for the lavishly produced stage melodramas of the early nineteenth century.[115]

It may have been the arbitrary and spectacular nature of this modern literary supernaturalism which gave it such resonance during the crisis of 1796–8, when the world itself seemed less and less like a place where 'probability, or even possibility, is attended to'. The accounts given by Cobbett or Barruel of the events of the French Revolution were as bizarre and horrible as any of Lewis' plots, full of monstrous villains who lurch suddenly onto the stage of history, construct impenetrable conspiracies, perpetrate unspeakable cruelties, and then die or vanish as swiftly as they arrived. With their superhuman capacities for organisation, violence, and deceit, Barruel and Cobbett's Jacobin terrorists often sound and behave more like supernatural beings than mortal men, and yet they hardly resemble the monsters and demons of traditional folk superstition, which generally occupied recognisable places within a broader spiritual status quo; they are much closer to the spirits imagined by Walpole, Beckford, and Lewis, enchanted beings viewed from the perspective of a disenchanted age, and thus seeming almost completely arbitrary in their abilities and operations. For terrorist conspirator and terrorist novelist alike, all that matters is *the plot*: anything, even the seemingly impossible, can be brought about if it is necessary to bring their (political or fictional) plot to fruition. Despite their attempts to distance themselves in other ways from Lewis and the 'terrorist' school, a similar sense of the basically illegible and incomprehensible nature of the supernatural pervades Wordsworth and Coleridge's poems of these years. In 'Christabel', it is clear that Geraldine is some kind of malevolent supernatural being, but exactly what she is, what she wants, and what she is capable of are left unclear; the poem even includes a version of Radcliffe's famous Black Veil scene, in which Christabel sees *something* fearful when Geraldine undresses, just as Emily sees *something* which makes her faint behind the Black Veil in *Udolpho*, but the reader is not told what it is. 'The Rime of the Ancient Mariner' and 'Kubla Khan' similarly depict worlds of bizarre and apparently random supernatural events, which hint at some underlying logic which the reader is not made privy to; the readers of these poems, like the audience at one of Étienne-Gaspard Robert's contemporary magic-lantern phantasmagoria, or the dupes and victims of the secret societies in German conspiracy fiction, or the horrified and uncomprehending observers of the progress of the French Revolution, are made witness to a series of strange, disturbing, spectacular, and apparently supernatural effects without ever fully understanding what, if anything, links them all together.[116] Even Wordsworth's 'The Thorn' refuses to finally explain its supernatural content. The narrator theorises that the bizarre events which take place around the 'little muddy pond' are due to its haunting by the ghost of an infant drowned there by its mother, but ultimately concludes that he cannot be sure: the seemingly supernatural happenings at the pool remain symptoms leading to no certain diagnosis.

It is this sense of something unknown, and perhaps unknowable, lurking within the scene of 'terrorism' which unites all these disparate texts, fictional and notionally non-fictional alike. Something bizarre and terrible appears to have happened, something that seems to make no rational sense: and either there is no explanation, as in 'Christabel' or the newspaper coverage of the September Massacres, or the explanations are as fantastical as the events they attempt to explain, as in *The Monk* (where a previously virtuous monk's decision to murder his mother and rape his sister is 'explained' as being due to his seduction by a shape-changing demon) or Barruel's *Mémoires* (where the decision of the French to murder the benevolent king under whom their nation had prospered is 'explained' as being the work of a fifteen-hundred-year-old, three-million-strong evil conspiracy). In novels such as *The Monk*, Capoferro remarks, 'the supernatural tends to be disconnected from the providential framework of orthodox religion, and does not have any intelligible moral purpose'.[117] The traditional demonology familiar to Milton and Bunyan had postulated demons which could be understood and combated, using the tools of revealed religion; but the modern demonology of the 'terrorist' novelists, like the rhetoric of the conspiracy theorists, postulated demons which were both incomprehensible and seemingly unstoppable. In this modern mythology of evil, the acts of the villain-as-terrorist are considered not as natural parts of a natural world (the Enlightenment perspective), nor as supernatural parts of a supernatural world (the pre-Enlightenment perspective), but as a supernatural part of a world which is otherwise governed by natural laws, and thus incommensurate with the rest of human action and human history, just as the giant ghost in *Otranto* is incommensurate with the modernised, disenchanted human characters whom it terrorises and destroys. It is this mythology – the mythology of terrorism – which the writers of the 1790s bequeathed to their successors.

Notes

1   On the persistent fear of secret anti-social conspiracies in medieval Europe, see Norman Cohn, *Europe's Inner Demons*, revised edition (London: Pimlico, 1993). On the witch-hunts of the Reformation era, see Hugh Trevor-Roper, *The European Witch-Craze of the Sixteenth and Seventeenth Centuries* (Harmondsworth: Penguin, 1969).

2   On the 'Popish Plot' conspiracy literature of the 1670s, see J. Paul Hunter, *Before Novels* (New York: W.W. Norton and Co., 1990), p. 181. On the survival of such fears into the nineteenth century, see Albert Pionke, *Plots of Opportunity* (Columbus, OH: Ohio State UP, 2004), chapter 3.

3   J.M. Roberts, *The Mythology of the Secret Societies* (London: Secker and Warburg, 1972), p. 87.

4   See Jean Baptiste Fiard, *La France Trompée Par Les Magiciens et Demonolatres* (Paris, 1803).

5   On the brief history of the Illuminati, see Roberts, *Mythology*, chapter 5.

6   See H.C. Midelfort, *Exorcism and Enlightenment* (New Haven: Yale UP, 2005), pp. 11, 20, 143.

7   Roberts, *Mythology*, pp. 128–9.

8   Florian Krobb, 'Friedrich Schiller: the first historiographer in Germany?', *Archivium Hibernicum*, vol. 59 (2005), p. 281.

9   On the publication history of *Der Geisterseher*, see Stefan Andriopoulos, 'Occult conspiracies: spirits and secret societies in Schiller's *Ghost Seer*', *New German Critique*, number 103 (2008), p. 65.

10 Roberts, *Mythology*, pp. 168–9. German conspiracy novels, full of revolutionary plots and secret tribunals, continued to appear throughout the 1790s; later examples included Durach's *Hellfried und Hulda* (1792), Wallenrodt's *Emma von Ruppin* (1794), Tieck's *William Lovell* (1795), and the anonymous *Die Schwarzen Brüder* (1794) and *Der Richterbund der Verborgenen* (1795). The genre came full circle and returned to its point of origin with Follenius' 1796 sequel to Schiller's unfinished *Der Geisterseher*, which revealed that all the events of Schiller's novel had been part of a plot by an evil secret society who were attempting to start a revolution. None of these, however, were translated into English. See Michael Hadley, *The Undiscovered Genre: The Search for the German Gothic Novel* (Berne: Lang, 1978), pp. 42, 86–9, 92, 101–2, 125.

11 Edward Ash, *The Speculator* (London, 1790), p. 53. On German literature in eighteenth-century Britain, see Hilary Brown, *Benedikte Naubert* (Leeds: Maney Publishing for the Modern Humanities Research Association and the Institute of Germanic Studies, University of London, 2005), pp. 8–10.

12 Norwich was something of an exception, due to its trading links with Hamburg. William Taylor of Norwich was an active early translator of German literature, and translated *Lenore* as early as 1790, although his translation circulated only in manuscript until 1796. See David Chandler, 'The Athens of England', *Eighteenth Century Studies*, vol. 43, number 2 (2010), p. 179.

13 Richard Hurd, *Letters on Chivalry and Romance*, ed. Edith Morley (London: Henry Frowde, 1911), p. 110.

14 On *The German Hotel*, see Bertrand Evans, *Gothic Drama from Walpole to Shelley* (Berkeley, CA: University of California Press, 1947), p. 90. On German-style Gothic fiction in Britain, see Jennifer Colosimo, 'Schiller and the Gothic', in Jeffrey High, ed., *Who Is This Schiller Now?* (Columbia, SC: Camden House, 2011), pp. 287–8. On *Wolfenbach*, see Angela Wright, 'Disturbing the female Gothic', in Diana Wallace and Andrew Smith, eds., *Female Gothic* (Basingstoke: Palgrave Macmillan, 2009), pp. 66–9. On *Lenore*, see Diane Hoeveler, *Gothic Riffs* (Columbus, OH: Ohio State UP, 2010), pp. 164–7. By the end of 1796, no less than nine English-language editions of *Lenore* had been printed in Britain: six in London, one in Norwich, one in Edinburgh, and one in Glasgow.

15 Letter to Southey, 3 November 1794, S.T. Coleridge, *Collected Letters*, ed. Earl Griggs (Oxford: Clarendon, 1956), vol. 1, p. 68.

16 William Hazlitt, 'Lectures on the dramatic literature of the age of Elizabeth', Lecture VIII, in *Selected Writings*, ed. Duncan Wu (London: Pickering and Chatto, 1998), vol. 5, p. 338, Charles Lamb, 'Letter to Coleridge, 5 July 1796', in Edwin Marrs, ed., *Letters of Charles and Mary Anne Lamb* (Ithaca, NY: Cornell UP, 1975), vol. 1, p. 41.

17 On Schiller's French popularity, see Peter Mortensen, 'Robbing *The Robbers*', *Literature and History*, 3rd series, vol. 11, number 1 (2002), pp. 43–4.

18 Mortensen, p. 43.

19 Friedrich Schiller, *The Robbers*, trans. Alexander Tytler, ed. Jonathan Wordsworth (Oxford: Woodstock Books, 1989), pp. xv–xvii, 163.

20 Schiller, p. x.

21 Schiller, pp. xiii–xiv.

22 On Schiller's early performance history in Britain, see Frederick Burwick, 'Schiller's plays on the British stage', in High, pp. 302–8. On Holman's 1799 rewrite of *The*

Robbers, The Red-Cross Knights, see Mortensen, pp. 52–6, 58, and Paul Ranger, *Terror and Pity Reign in Every Breast* (London: Society for Theatre Research, 1991), p. 16.

23   On the influx of translated German romances, see James Watt *Contesting the Gothic* (Cambridge: Cambridge UP, 1999), p. 72, and Robert Le Tellier, *Kindred Spirits* (Salzburg: Insitut für Anglistik und Amerikanistik, Universität Salzburg, 1982), pp. 58–60. On the reception of Naubert's novels, which in Britain were universally assumed to be the work of a man, see Brown, *Naubert*, chapter 5.

24   Roberts, *Mythology*, pp. 180–1.

25   Roberts, *Mythology*, pp. 183–4. The Knights of Kadosch, or Grades of Vengeance, were ranks within some variants of Templar Freemasonry, supposed to symbolise the warriors sent by King Solomon to take vengeance upon the murderers of Hiram, architect of the Temple and legendary founder of Freemasonry. They had a controversial place in the Freemasonry practised by the Grand Orient in the later eighteenth century and were specifically condemned as 'contrary to the principles of Freemasonry' by the Council of the Knights of the East in 1766, although they would later find a place within mainstream Freemasonry as the ninth, tenth, eleventh, and thirtieth degrees of the Ancient and Accepted Rite. See Roberts, *Mythology*, pp. 98–9, and A.C.F. Jackson, *Rose Croix* (London: Lewis Masonic, 1980), pp. 22, 38, 237, 247–8.

26   On Barruel, see Roberts, *Mythology*, pp. 188–99.

27   Augustin Barruel, *History of Jacobinism*, trans. Robert Clifford (London, 1797–8), vol. 1, p. xii.

28   Barruel, vol. 1, p. xiv.

29   On the Quiberon landings, see Maurice Hutt, *Chouannerie and Counter-Revolution* (Cambridge: Cambridge UP, 1983), chapter 8.

30   On the Secret Academy, see Barruel, vol. 1, p. 321. On the secret history of Jacobinism, see vol. 2, pp. 275, 385–402.

31   Barruel, vol. 2, p. 471, and vol. 4, pp. 113, 490–4.

32   Barruel, vol. 1, p. 257, vol. 2, p. 458, and vol. 4, pp. 113, 119, 545–6, chapter 10, and appendix.

33   Barruel, vol. 1, pp. 208–10, and vol. 4, pp. 487, 548.

34   Barruel, vol. 1, pp. 254–6, and vol. 4, pp. 411, 419–20.

35   Barruel, vol. 4, pp. 463–4, 479.

36   Barruel, vol. 4, pp. 2, 463.

37   Robert Clifford, *An Application of Barruel's Memoirs of Jacobinism to the Secret Societies of Ireland and Great Britain* (London, 1798), p. xviii.

38   John Robison, *Postscript to the Second Edition of Mr Robison's Proofs of a Conspiracy* (London, 1797), p. 3. For Robison's praise of Barruel, see John Robison, *Proofs of a Conspiracy Against all the Religions and Governments of Europe, Carried on in the Secret Meetings of Free Masons, Illuminati, and Reading Societies*, 5th ed. (Dublin, 1798), pp. 511, 519.

39   Robison, *Proofs*, pp. 468, 473, 478, 493.

40   H.C.G. Matthew and Brian Harrison, eds., *Oxford Dictionary of National Biography* (Oxford: Oxford UP, 2004), vol. 47, pp. 432–4.

41   Thomas De Quincey, *Works*, ed. Grevel Lindop (London: Pickering and Chatto, 2000–3), vol. 16, p. 147.

42   *The European Magazine and London Review* (London, 1798), vol. 33, p. 28, *The British Critic* (London, 1798), vol. 11, p. 293, James Morse, *Jedidiah Morse* (New York: Columbia UP, 1939), chapter 5. Conspiracy literature, fictional and

otherwise, has always flourished in America. Charles Brockden Brown's *Wieland* (1798), which is generally regarded as the first American Gothic novel, is a conspiracy novel in the tradition of Schiller; its fragmentary sequel, *Memoirs of Carwin the Biloquist* (1803–5) even describes how the novel's villain was originally recruited by a secret society which aimed for international social change. Another early American conspiracy novel, Sally Wood's *Julia and the Illuminated Baron* (1800), declared itself to be 'founded on recent facts, which have transpired in the course of the late revolution of moral principles in France'. See Charles Brockden Brown, *Wieland and Memoirs of Carwin the Biloquist*, ed. Jay Fliegelman (Harmondsworth: Penguin, 1991), pp. 299–316, and Sally Wood, *Julia* (Portsmouth, 1800), title page.

43   Jane Austen, *Northanger Abbey*, eds. Barbara Benedict and Deirdre Le Faye (Cambridge: Cambridge UP, 2006), pp. xxv, 33. On the general spread of conspiracy literature in this period, see E.J. Clery, *The Rise of Supernatural Fiction* (Cambridge: Cambridge UP, 1999), pp. 158, 163–4.

44   Benedikte Naubert, *Hermann of Unna* (London, 1794), pp. v, ix, xiii-xiv.

45   Austen, *Northanger Abbey*, p. 113–14.

46   AC, *A Letter to the Reverend John Erskine* (Edinburgh, 1798), title page, p. 3.

47   AC, p. 3. In a footnote to p. 5, AC does give the title of Robison's book.

48   AC, pp. 6–7.

49   AC, p. 13.

50   *The Anti-Jacobin or Weekly Examiner* (London, 1798), vol. 1, p. 263.

51   Anon, *The Advantages Resulting from the French Revolution* (Edinburgh, 1798), p. 13, William Agutter, *Deliverance from Enemies* (London, 1798), pp. 11–12. Agutter writes that Robison and Barruel's books deserve 'the serious attention of every Friend of Religion and Government'.

52   On Agutter, see Matthew and Harrison, eds., vol. 1, p. 468.

53   Patrick Lattin, *Observations on Dr. Duigenan's Fair Representation of the Present Political State of Ireland* (London, 1800), pp. 23–4.

54   Roberts, *Mythology*, p. 192.

55   J.M.S. Tompkins, *The Popular Novel in England, 1770–1800* (London: Methuen, 1962), p. 283.

56   On the formation of popular political societies in 1791–2, see E.P. Thompson, *The Making of the English Working Classes* (Harmondsworth: Penguin, 1968), chapter 5. On the metamorphosis of the United Irishmen, see Michael Duffy, 'War, revolution, and the crisis of the British Empire', in Mark Philp, ed., *The French Revolution and British Popular Politics* (Cambridge: Cambridge UP, 1991), p. 136. It was easy for hostile observers, such as Barruel and Clifford, to see the United Irishmen as Illuminist conspirators, not only because they actually planned an armed rebellion, but also because Freemasonry played a major role in the society's development, Masonic lodges being one of the few places in 1790s Ireland where Catholics and Protestants could meet as (at least notional) equals. See T.O. McLoughlin, *Contesting Ireland* (Dublin: Four Courts Press, 1999), p. 32 and chapter 9.

57   Thompson, *The Making of the English Working Classes*, pp. 136–8, 183–5.

58   The Order of Bards seems to have been apolitical, but Morganwg himself moved in radical circles, and as a result his organisation had been viewed as politically suspect ever since its foundation in 1792. See Prys Morgan, *Iolo Morganwg* (Cardiff: University of Wales Press, 1975), p. 13, and Marion Löffler, *The Literary and Historical Legacy of Iolo Morganwg* (Cardiff: University of Wales Press, 2007), p. 42.

59   In the nineteenth century, the same logic would be used to condemn trade unions as
     dangerous and criminal secret societies, which controlled their members through the
     use of '*insignia* of terror'. See Pionke, p. 23 and chapter 2.
60   Barruel, vol. 2, pp. 68–73.
61   Roberts, *Mythology*, pp. 355–7.
62   Robison, *Proofs*, p. 405.
63   See Barruel, vol. 1, pp. 254–6. On Robespierre's belief in the famine plot, see Geoffrey
     Cubitt, 'Robespierre and conspiracy theories', in Colin Haydon and William Doyle,
     eds., *Robespierre* (Cambridge: Cambridge UP, 1999), p. 78.
64   Cubitt, 'Robespierre and conspiracy theories', p. 78.
65   Clery, pp. 162–3.
66   Hunter, p. 229. Some writers continued to interpret these supposedly impersonal
     forces in conspiratorial terms, as in those explanations of international economics
     which claim that the entire world economy is secretly controlled by some shadowy
     elite; however, from the later nineteenth century onwards, such theories increasingly
     ceased to be intellectually respectable. See Jakob Tanner, 'The conspiracy of the
     invisible hand', *New German Critique*, number 103 (2008), pp. 51–64.
67   Barruel, vol. 4, p. 593. On the rumours which circulated in France after Robespierre's
     death, claiming that he had, among his various other secret crimes, claimed to be
     an Illuminate, see Bronislaw Baczko, *Ending the Terror*, trans. Michel Petheram
     (Cambridge: Cambridge UP, 1994), pp. 2–13.
68   Clifford, pp. viii–ix. 'Spartacus' was the code-name Weishaupt adopted among the
     Illuminati.
69   Clarke Garrett, *Respectable Folly* (Baltimore, MD: Johns Hopkins UP, 1975). Other
     important self-proclaimed prophets of this period include Suzette Labrousse and
     Catherine Théot in France, and Baroness von Krüdener in Russia.
70   Robert Fleming, *The Apocalyptical Key* (London, 1793), p. 53. A condensed edition
     of the *Key* also appeared in 1793, priced at sixpence, which suggests that there was a
     popular audience for such apocalyptic prophecies.
71   The idea that the French Revolution might represent the beginning of the end
     of history is found in both Blake's *Europe* and Coleridge's *Religious Musings*. See
     William Blake, *Complete Poetry and Prose*, ed. David Erdman (New Haven: Yale UP,
     1988), pp. 60–66, and S.T. Coleridge, *Poems*, ed. John Beer (London: Dent, 1993), pp.
     88–103.
72   Donald Greer, *Incidence of the Terror During the French Revolution* (Cambridge, MA:
     Harvard UP, 1935), p. 75, Morton Paley, *The Apocalyptic Sublime* (New Haven: Yale
     UP, 1986), p. 30.
73   For Brothers and Southcott's encounters with Satan, see Peter Schock, '*The Marriage
     of Heaven and Hell*: Blake's myth of Satan and its cultural matrix', *ELH*, vol. 60,
     number 2 (1993), p. 447, and Joanna Southcott, *A Dispute Between the Woman and
     the Powers of Darkness*, ed. Jonathan Wordsworth (Poole: Woodstock Books, 1995).
74   Jean Tulard, *Joseph Fouché* (Paris, 1998), pp. 46–7.
75   On Southcott's reading of Radcliffe, see Eugene Wright, 'A divine analysis of *The
     Romance of the Forest*', *Discourse*, vol. 13, number 3 (1970), pp. 379–87.
76   Hester Lynch Piozzi, *The Piozzi Letters*, ed. Edward Bloom and Lillian Bloom
     (Newark, NJ: University of Delaware Press, 1991), vol. 2, pp. 131, 157, 162–3,
     166–7.
77   Piozzi, vol. 2, pp. 189, 411, 480, 508.
78   Letter to Hester Maria Thrale, 25 October 1796, Piozzi, vol. 2, p. 391.

79   D.L. Macdonald, *Monk Lewis* (Toronto, ON: University of Toronto Press, 2000), p. xiii.

80   Macdonald, chapter 3, and pp. 100–6. On Lewis' sexuality, see Michael Gamer, *Romanticism and the Gothic* (Cambridge: Cambridge UP, 2000), p. 81, and Macdonald, chapter 4.

81   On Lewis' role in transmitting German culture to Britain, see Hadley, p. 22, and Le Tellier, pp. 58–9, 71–2. On *Faust*, see Bertrand Evans, 'Manfred's remorse', in *PMLA*, vol. 62, number 3 (1947), p. 752.

82   Hadley, pp. 24–30, 96–100. On the contemporary recognition of *The Monk*'s German sources, see Clery, p. 142.

83   Hadley, pp. 122–3, Le Tellier, p. 70.

84   Matthew Lewis, *Alonzo the Brave and Fair Imogene* (London, 1797), p. 4.

85   Matthew Lewis, *Osric the Lion!* (London, 1797), p. 7.

86   Gamer, pp. 73–4, 81, Macdonald, p. 129.

87   Jacqueline Howard, *Reading Gothic Fiction* (Oxford: Clarendon, 1994), p. 227.

88   Cited in Macdonald, p. 130.

89   Gamer, p. 149, James Watt, pp. 70, 78. On the popularity of foreign drama on the British stage, and the contemporary fear of its politically subversive potential, see Mortensen, pp. 42–3, and Jane Moody, *Illegitimate Theatre in London* (Cambridge: Cambridge UP, 2000), chapter 2.

90   William Wordsworth, *Lyrical Ballads*, ed. James Butler and Karen Green (Ithaca, NY: Cornell UP, 1992), pp. 746–7. As Gamer has pointed out, it was particularly important for Wordsworth and Coleridge to distance themselves from 'German' literature, as their own poetry had been accused of being 'German' (i.e. politically subversive, superstitious, extravagant, and incomprehensible) in its tendency. See Gamer, pp. 117–19.

91   Wordsworth, *Lyrical Ballads*, p. 746.

92   Clery, p. 172.

93   Clery, p. 148, and E.J. Clery and Robert Miles, eds., *Gothic Documents* (Manchester: Manchester UP, 2000), pp. 182–4. That the German conspiracy novel and the feudal Radcliffean romance did continue to be regarded as distinct sub-genres, however, is clear from Scott's 1814 introduction to *Waverley*. There Scott asserts that had he called his novel 'Waverley, a Tale of other Days', his readers would have expected 'a castle scarce less than that of Udolpho, of which the eastern wing had long been uninhabited', full of 'stories of blood and horror'; had he called it 'Waverley, a Romance from the German', on the other hand, then 'what head so obtuse as not to image forth a profligate abbot, an oppressive duke, a secret and mysterious association of Rosycrucians and Illuminati, with all their properties of black cowls, caverns, daggers, electrical machines, trap-doors and dark-lanterns?' See Walter Scott, *Waverley*, ed. Andrew Hook (Harmondsworth: Penguin, 1972), pp. 33–4.

94   Anon., 'Terrorist novel writing', in *Spirit of the Public Journals for 1797* (London, 1798), p. 224.

95   John Locke, *Some Thoughts Concerning Education* (London, 1693), pp. 159–60. On Glanvill, see Riccardo Capoferro, *Empirical Wonder* (Bern: Peter Lang, 2010), pp. 105–115.

96   Anon., 'Terrorist novel writing', p. 224.

97   Anon., 'Terrorist novel writing', p. 223n, 223–5.

98   Anon., 'Terrorist novel writing', p. 223n.

99   A Jacobin Novelist, 'The Terrorist system of novel-writing', in John Aikin, ed., *Monthly Magazine* (1797), vol. 4:21, pp. 102, 104.

100   A Jacobin Novelist, 'Terrorist system', p. 103.

101   A Jacobin Novelist, 'Terrorist system', p. 103.

102   Charlotte Dacre, *Zofloya*, ed. Devendra Varma (New York: Arno, 1974), vol. 3, pp. 235–6.

103   Charles Lucas, *The Infernal Quixote*, ed. M.O. Grenby (Peterborough, ON: Broadview Press, 2004), pp. 126, 174–5.

104   Marilyn Butler, *Jane Austen and the War of Ideas* (Oxford: Clarendon, 1987), p. 114.

105   S.T. Coleridge, *Complete Works* (Princeton, NJ: Princeton UP, 1995), vol. 11:1, p. 59.

106   Robison, *Proofs of a Conspiracy*, pp. 272, 355.

107   Carl Grosse, *Horrid Mysteries*, trans. Peter Will (London: Folio Press, 1968), pp. 172–3.

108   On Rosicrucian fiction, see Marie Roberts, *Gothic Immortals* (London: Routledge, 1990). Carol Davidson has also argued convincingly that this Rosicrucian conspiracy literature was essentially a re-packaging of traditional anti-Semitic mythology: with his cursed immortality and his ability to magically manufacture gold, the Rosicrucian alchemical conspirator blurs into both the figure of the Wandering Jew and the figure of the Jewish money-lender as Satanic economic manipulator. See Carol Davidson, *Anti-Semitism and British Gothic Fiction* (New York: Palgrave Macmillan, 2004), chapter 4.

109   On the controversy over stage ghosts, see Jeffrey Cox, ed., *Seven Gothic Dramas* (Athens, OH: Ohio UP, 1992), p. 36, and Hoeveler, *Gothic Riffs*, pp. 123–31. On the popularity of *The Castle Spectre*, and its controversial ghost, see James Allard, 'Spectres, spectators, spectacles', *Gothic Studies*, vol. 3, number 3 (2001), pp. 246–52.

110   Macdonald, pp. 136–7, Cox, p. 36. The script of the play also sold very well, going through eight official editions (and two Dublin editions) in a single year.

111   Gamer, pp. 98–102, 116–18.

112   Matthew Lewis, *The Castle Spectre*, 1st edition (London, 1798), p. 102.

113   Lewis, *The Castle Spectre*, p. vi.

114   Charlotte Smith, *Letters of a Solitary Wanderer*, ed. Jonathan Wordsworth (Oxford: Woodstock Books, 1995), p. 21.

115   On Lewis and the rise of melodrama, see Evans, *Drama*, pp. 145–73, and Maurice Disher, *Blood and Thunder* (London: Muller, 1949), pp. 80–2, 95–100.

116   On Robert, and the Gothic phantasmagoria shows of the 1790s, see Laurent Mannoni, *The Great Art of Light and Shadow*, trans. Richard Crangle (Exeter: University of Exeter Press, 2000), chapter 6. The use of magic lanterns to create moving images of ghosts and skeletons had a long history, stretching back to the 'Dance of Death' slides drawn by Huygens in 1659, but it was brought to perfection in revolutionary Paris, where such shows sometimes combined slides depicting ghosts and demons with others representing 'Rosicrucians', 'the *Illuminés* of Berlin', and the famous statesmen of the Revolution. Sometimes the categories overlapped: the showman Philidor depicted the Devil with the face of Robespierre, while Robert showed the dead Robespierre climbing out of his tomb, only to be struck down by lightning. See Mannoni, pp. 38–40, 141–6, 161.

117   Capoferro, p. 145.

4

Popular Gothic

I

In the 1790s, books were not cheap. Novels – including Gothic novels – were luxury items; and while virtually everyone among the educated elite may have been reading Radcliffe by the middle of the decade, the steep price of her romances would have placed them well out of the reach of the vast majority of the British population. The same price barrier excluded the general public – most of whom, by 1800, were at least semi-literate – from almost all the other texts discussed in the last three chapters: even if they wished to, the ordinary farm labourers, tradesmen, and artisans of Britain could not have afforded to furnish their shelves with the works of Lewis or Williams, Burke or Barruel, especially not amidst the economic crises and near famine of the later 1790s. Even the cheap Gothic romances of the Minerva Press, which sold for about three shillings and sixpence, would have been well out of the financial reach of many potential readers.[1] The rapid spread of circulating libraries throughout Britain in the later eighteenth century must have done something to widen the readership of such works, but, despite contemporary stereotypes of such libraries as being full of lower-class readers – especially women – borrowing trashy novels, recent scholarly research has demonstrated that their high fees guaranteed that most of their subscribers actually belonged to the respectable classes, and that their catalogues were dominated by non-fiction rather than novels and romances; as a result, the old assumption that popular Gothic fiction was able to reach a mass audience through the circulating libraries now looks increasingly shaky.[2] The literate poor did have some access to newspapers, which could be read in coffee shops or taverns even by people too poor to buy copies for themselves; but books, especially recent books, were largely out of their economic reach.[3] Many of the cultural trends I have been discussing were thus inherently elite phenomena, occurring in cultural circles to which most of the population had no access. Gothic culture *did* filter down to the 'lower orders' during this period; but it did so by different vectors to those which disseminated it among the cultural elite, and often assumed distinctive forms in the process. In this chapter, I aim to explore three of those vectors: popular theatre, chapbook literature, and the visual arts, all of which were accessible to those lower cultural strata which had little or no access to the kind of books which I have been discussing so far.

In the late eighteenth century, popular participation in literary culture took two main forms: attendance at the theatre, and the purchase of cheap literature such as chapbooks and broadside ballads. Theatre-going was popular with people of all classes, as the immense size of late-eighteenth-century theatres demonstrates. Covent Garden theatre was enlarged in 1792 to hold an audience of three thousand and thirteen, and when the new Drury Lane theatre opened in 1794, its interior designed to resemble a Gothic cathedral in deference to the tastes of the times, its auditorium was capable of holding over three and a half thousand people; so when a successful play such as Lewis' *The Castle Spectre* managed to fill such a theatre night after night, many of the tens of thousands of people who came to see it must have been ordinary working folk.[4] Chapbooks and broadsides were sold on the streets of cities, and carried by travelling pedlars into rural areas; cheaply produced, decorated with largely interchangeable woodcuts, and often printed with worn type on thin paper, they told the stories of famous crimes and executions, wonder-stories and fairy tales. From the early eighteenth century onwards, there had also been a market for chapbook novels: condensed, simplified versions of the most popular English novels, such as *Robinson Crusoe* and *Pilgrim's Progress*, reduced in length to a few pages and sold to a popular readership unable to afford the full versions, and perhaps with insufficient literacy to manage full-length novels.[5] From about 1800, the most popular Gothic novels of the 1780s and 1790s began to appear in chapbook form, alongside other, original Gothic chapbooks, inspired by such novels but not directly based upon them; and it is the emergence of this chapbook Gothic literature – ancestor of the 'Penny Blood' fiction of the mid-nineteenth century – which demonstrates the penetration of Gothic fiction into British culture as a whole, into cultural strata very distant from its original, elite audience.[6]

In this, as in so much else, Gothic literature was exceptional, as prior to its rise the changing literary fashions of the eighteenth century had, for the most part, extended little beyond the charmed circle of metropolitan literary culture; the most popular chapbook novels of the early eighteenth century, *Robinson Crusoe* and *Pilgrim's Progress*, were still the most popular chapbook novels at the century's end. The surviving chapbook literature from the period suggests that popular literary tastes, such as they were, seem to have been largely static, almost untouched by developments in English literature as a whole; even major bestsellers, such as Richardson's *Pamela* and *Clarissa* or MacKenzie's *The Man of Feeling*, do not seem to have found a genuinely popular mass readership like that of Bunyan or Defoe, while authors such as Frances Burney, popular enough by the standards of their day, remained entirely the cultural property of the elite.[7] But with Gothic, for the first time since *Robinson Crusoe*, an eighteenth-century literary fashion achieved a popular audience: a true mass readership extending down into the ranks of the poor and semi-literate who comprised the vast majority of the nation's population.

The reasons why Gothic fiction should have enjoyed greater mass popularity than earlier eighteenth-century literary fashions are not hard to grasp. As the eighteenth-century novel had developed, it had grown increasingly domestic, focusing more and more tightly on the lives and loves of young upper- and upper-middle-class characters in British settings rather than the widely roaming pirates, thieves, whores, and adventurers who had populated the earliest French and British novels. Defining themselves against the fabulous and improbable romances of the previous century, novels strove to establish their moral and educational credentials by limiting themselves strictly to portraying the same social world their readers were assumed to inhabit. Judging from the chapbook literature they purchased, however, popular audiences continued to enjoy dramatic stories of crime, shipwreck, and adventure throughout the century; nor did the taste for wonder tales ever die out among them, and stories of magic and miracles continued to circulate among the poor even at the very height of the Age of Reason. With the rise of Gothic fiction, however, literary tastes had finally returned to the kind of spectacular, action-packed stories which popular audiences had been reading all along, full of wonders, violence, adventure, exotic settings, and sudden reversals of fortune. Indeed, this kinship with popular fiction was one of the reasons why Gothic fiction was viewed with such suspicion in elite circles; tales of adventure were firmly associated with ill-educated readers, with servants and tradesmen whose tastes were too coarse for anything more subtle, and who were too dim-witted and ill educated to recognise the absurdities which such stories contained. From such a perspective, Gothic literature represented a return to primitive literary barbarism; and the popularity of Gothic fiction and plays with the lower orders only served to confirm their debased and debasing character.

In one sense, however, this return to a form of literary primitivism was entirely deliberate. As discussed in Chapter 1, early-eighteenth-century Britain had fought hard to escape from the shadow of the seventeenth century, with its persecutions and civil wars; but after the crisis of the mid-century, with the Jacobites defeated and an intercontinental empire successfully won and defended in the Seven Years War, Britain increasingly began to renegotiate its relationship with its own national past. Rather than seeing their history before 1688 as little more than an abyss of Gothic darkness, writers started to look to it for cultural resources which could be used to articulate and reinforce a new sense of British nationhood, to fit Britain's new military and imperial role on the world stage. The antiquarian revival of the 1750s and 1760s, with its reappraisal of the value of medieval chivalry and 'Gothic' literature, was one expression of this search; thus, in Hurd's *Dialogues*, Addison – the mouthpiece of Augustan critical orthodoxy – expresses his contempt for the old orders of knighthood and the romance literature which celebrated them, while Hurd's stand-in Arbuthnot argues instead for the cultural importance of both.[8] The loyalist Gothic romances of the 1780s, with their emphasis on a continuous tradition of British military heroism and aristocratic legitimacy stretching back into the medieval past, were one product of this revival; another was the growth of 'bardolatry', and the revival of literary and academic interest in the works of Shakespeare, now reclaimed as an exemplar of national genius rather than just an old-fashioned playwright whose works were written in a style now obsolete. The combination of this renewed fascination with Shakespearean drama and the contemporary passion for heroic medieval origins led to the rise of a whole genre of 'Gothic' dramas on the later eighteenth-century British stage: plays with medieval settings, depicting the wars and intrigues of aristocratic families, and usually drawing heavily upon Shakespeare's histories and tragedies. The first such play to attain wide popularity was Home's *Douglas* (1756), which continued to be performed regularly for decades; and its success inspired many others over the following years, including a dramatisation of Walpole's *The Castle of Otranto* – in a suitably modified, de-supernaturalised form – as *The Count of Narbonne* in 1781.[9] Nor was its influence limited to theatre; the popularity of plays such as *The Haunted Tower* (1789) and *Richard Coeur de Lion* (1786) on the London stage almost certainly influenced the Gothic romance writers of the 1780s, whose aristocratic characters and inheritance-based plots bore a strong resemblance to those of the popular medieval dramas of the day.

This new Gothic-antiquarian literature, with its interest in war, violence, and medieval superstition, was much closer in subject matter to the action-packed street literature of its day than, say, the contemporary fashion for sentimental novels. It flourished in the 1780s, but its years of greatest popularity came in the mid-1790s, when a series of spectacularly successful Gothic dramas dominated the London stage for several years. As I have discussed, it was Radcliffe's third and most terror-filled novel, *The Romance of the Forest*, which first won her a wide readership, at least among the cultural elite; and it was presumably due to this success that it was also the first of her novels to be adapted for the London stage, in 1794, by the journalist and novice playwright James Boaden. Years later, in his 1825 *Life of John Philip Kemble*, Boaden recalled his decision to adapt Radcliffe's *Romance*:

> MR. BOADEN had read the Romance of the Forest with great pleasure, and thought that he saw there the groundwork of a drama of more than usual effect. He admired, as every one else did, the singular address by which Mrs. Radcliffe contrived to impress the mind with all the terrors of the ideal world; and the sportive resolution of all that had excited terror into very common natural appearances; indebted for their false aspect to circumstances, and the overstrained feelings of the characters.
>
> But, even in romance, it may be doubtful, whether there be not something ungenerous in thus playing upon poor timid human nature, and agonizing it with false terrors. The disappointment is, I know, always resented, and the laboured explanation commonly deemed the flattest and most uninteresting part of the production. Perhaps, when the attention is once secured and the reason yielded, the passion for the marvellous had better remain unchecked; and an interest selected from the olden time be entirely subjected to its gothic machinery. However this may be in respect of romance, when the doubtful of the narrative is to be exhibited in the drama, the decision is a matter of necessity. While description only fixes the inconclusive dreams of the fancy, she may partake the dubious character of her inspirer; but the pen of the dramatic poet must turn every thing into shape, and bestow on these 'airy nothings a local habitation and a name'.[10]

Boaden's adaptation, *Fontainville Forest*, gave 'a local habitation' to more than just Radcliffe's 'inconclusive dreams'. It massively condensed her novel: whereas Radcliffe's Adeline travels across much of France and Italy, over many months, in search of safety, justice, and the truth of her ancestry, her counterpart in Boaden's drama achieves as much within a few days, within the confines of a single wood. The play placed a much greater emphasis on action and event, as opposed to Radcliffe's carefully orchestrated psychology of doubt and fear and depictions of subjectivity under strain: what Boaden calls 'the overstrained feelings of the characters' and 'the inconclusive dreams of the fancy', which he asserted could not be represented on the stage. Most controversially, Boaden broke both with Radcliffe's novel and with contemporary dramatic practice by introducing 'gothic machinery' into his play, in the form of an onstage ghost, entirely absent from the original:

> All that remained now was to dress the spirit; for which purpose I recommended a dark blue grey stuff, made in the shape of armour, and sitting close to the person; and when Follet (of course unknown) was thus drest, and faintly visible behind the gauze or crape spread before the scene, the whisper of the house, as he was about to enter, –the breathless silence, while he floated along like a shadow – proved to me, that I had achieved the great desideratum ; and the often-renewed plaudits, when the curtain fell, told me that the audience had enjoyed 'That sacred terror, that severe delight,' for which alone it is excusable to overpass the ordinary limits of nature.[11]

Boaden's ghost, creeping onstage in his 'dark blue grey stuff' behind a screen of gauze, embodied the condensing, localising, literalising tendency of his play: its movement from internal states to external situations, extended plots to rapid action, 'airy nothings' to 'local habitations', 'terrors of the ideal world' to 'gothic machinery', 'overstrained feelings' to actual apparitions. In Boaden's play, much more than in Radcliffe's novel, the Gothic romance began to resemble the fictional world of popular chapbook fictions, with their rapid piling up of adventures and incidents, casual use of the supernatural, and relative lack of interest in individual subjectivity; and it may have been this kinship with contemporary popular fiction which gave the play, and those which followed it, their mass appeal.

Boaden's claim that his ghost filled his audiences with 'sacred terror' and 'severe delight' seems almost comically optimistic in light of what followed, for neither the sacred nor the severe was much in evidence over the subsequent theatrical seasons in London; what attracted audiences was Gothic spectacle. *Fontainville Forest* paved the way for Boaden's subsequent adaptations – *The Secret Tribunal* (1795), based on Naubert's recently translated *Hermann of Unna*, *The Italian Monk* (1797), based on Radcliffe's *The Italian*, and *Aurelio and Miranda* (1798), based on Lewis' *The Monk* – and for a host of other Gothic plays in the same years, as well as laying the foundations for the dramatic career of Matthew Lewis, which began in 1797 with *The Castle Spectre* and continued through a whole run of increasingly spectacular Gothic dramas over the following fifteen years.[12] It was these popular plays – which, unlike many of the novels they were inspired by and adapted from, had large and socially varied audiences – which brought Gothic fiction to the British public at large.[13] Their version of Gothic was not the same as that of the novel-reading elite; it was more spectacular, more supernatural, and more exciting, filled with action and sudden reversals of fortune. There was much less emphasis on interior states: whereas characters in novels such as *The Italian* or *Caleb Williams* undergo agonies of anxiety and self-doubt, their equivalents in the plays based on them – *The Italian Monk* and *The Iron Chest*, respectively – have no such complexities, their inner lives reduced to a straightforward typology of guilt, remorse, anger, or fear. In this focus on action rather than interiority, they resembled the chapbook adaptations of eighteenth-century novels, which operated under similar constraints: the need to compress complex novelistic plots into the compass of a few pages or acts, while still remaining simple enough to be followed by a not necessarily overly attentive popular audience. Thus, as Toni Wein has shown, when the Gothic novels of the 1780s and 1790s were rewritten as chapbooks for popular readers in the first years of the nineteenth century, their redactors employed similar strategies to those used by the playwrights who adapted them for the stage, stripping out passages of description and psychological detail, simplifying and condensing complex plots, and foregrounding the most dramatic events within each story so that they come in rapid succession, rather than hundreds of pages apart.[14]

Although derived from Gothic novels, these Gothic melodramas were also capable of innovation, much of which fed back into the second wave of Gothic novels written from 1796 onwards. The supernaturalism of late-1790s Gothic literature was anticipated by Gothic drama, with onstage ghosts appearing as early as 1794, two years before *The Monk* brought the unexplained supernatural into the mainstream British Gothic novel. Similarly, the tormented hero-villains of the later Gothic novels were anticipated by their stage counterparts: villain roles in such plays tended to be written as vehicles for established star performers, and were thus often presented as more remorseful and sympathetic than their novelistic equivalents.[15] In this, too, Boaden's *Fontainville Forest* provided a prototype, as its villainous Marquis was a much more haunted and guilt-racked figure than his counterpart in *The Romance of the Forest*, his *Macbeth*-inspired soliloquies prefiguring the inner torments of later Radcliffean villains such as Schedoni. Given their popularity, it would be surprising if these dramas did not exercise at least some influence over the subsequent development of 1790s Gothic fiction, which, at least in these respects, appears to have followed its lead; indeed, much of the energy and urgency of Gothic writing in these years may have stemmed from these interactions between different fields of cultural production, made possible by the unprecedented appeal of Gothic fiction and drama to audiences of every social rank. For most of the eighteenth century, popular and elite literary culture had been kept strongly distinct: the rich read novels in the tradition established by Fielding, Richardson, and their successors, while the poor, when they read at all, preferred religious literature in the tradition of Bunyan, and stories about crime and adventure derived from popular folklore and the novels of Daniel Defoe. But with popular Gothic fiction and drama, these two worlds came together; and if they permitted elite fictions about the anxieties of young ladies to be communicated, in suitably simplified forms, down to the lower orders, they also allowed the popular taste for adventure stories and wonder tales to be transmitted, in suitably gentrified forms, up to the cultural elite. The exemplar of this cultural fusion was Matthew Lewis, whose combination of dramatic action, onstage spectacle, music, and song with sentimental scenes and sub-Shakespearean verse drama made him, for a decade and a half, one of the most reliably popular playwrights in Britain with audiences of all social classes.[16]

The emergence of this vibrant popular Gothic culture is particularly striking given that, in the fraught political climate of the 1790s, all forms of popular literature and drama were regarded with acute suspicion by the authorities. Hanoverian Britain was a nation in which print culture was still primarily the property of the cultural elite, and it had been relatively slow to adapt to the idea that sedition might spread through the medium of print, rather than the traditional verbal channels of popular discontent, preaching, oratory, and rumour; press censorship was extremely limited, and official action against popular protest movements had generally concentrated on breaking up organisations and imprisoning leading agitators rather than suppressing publications. However, following the success of Paine's influential *Common Sense* in revolutionary America and the enormously wide readership achieved by his *Rights of Man* in 1791–2, this tolerance had rapidly vanished; the distribution of cheap, seditious literature among the British working poor came to be viewed as a major ideological threat, regarded fearfully as a means of spreading discontent among the people and laying the groundwork for a pro-French revolution in Britain. Paine was prosecuted, fled the country, and was tried *in absentia* for seditious libel in 1792; the first of a whole series of such trials that took place over the course of the decade.[17]

It was widely held that the popularity of Paine's works, and others like them, among the populace at large was due not to the actual desire of the working poor to read about such matters, but to the machinations of London radicals, who distributed such works at below cost price – or even for free – in order to poison the minds of the people against their rightful government; the conspiracy theorists of 1797 even identified the distribution of such literature as one of the tactics used by the pro-revolutionary Illuminati conspiracy to subvert the nations they intended to destroy, with Barruel asserting that Voltaire's Secret Academy had been covertly engaged in such subsidised distribution of printed pro-revolutionary propaganda among the poor for decades.[18] Furthermore, it soon became well-known in Britain that the French revolutionaries used the Parisian theatres as a way of communicating pro-revolutionary messages to the people, staging plays such as *Le jugement dernier des rois* and *Les victimes cloîtrées* in order to persuade the theatre-going public of the wickedness of the old monarchy and the church.[19] The idea of such seditious dramas being staged in Britain was particularly worrying because the theatre itself was potentially a politically dangerous space, as it brought people from opposite extremes of the social hierarchy together in a single auditorium; it was in Drury Lane theatre that James Hadfield attempted to assassinate George III in May 1800, firing his pistol up from his seat in the stalls towards the royal box above.[20] In this new 'season of anxiety', as Robison called it, popular Gothic fiction and drama were thus, naturally, a target for suspicion; after all, their villains tended to be clergymen and aristocrats, who were ultimately depicted as being cast down or destroyed as the consequences of their crimes caught up with them. As early as 1789, plays in London depicting the fall of the Bastille were rapidly censored and forced to close; the 1792 translation of Schiller's *Robbers* was refused a licence for performance in Britain, and when Lewis published the printed edition of his first play, *The Castle Spectre*, in 1798, he included notes to rebut the accusations of disloyalty and sedition which had been levelled against it while it was in performance.[21]

Was popular Gothic a political, or at least politicised, form of writing? David Worrall has argued that it was; that plays such as *The Secret Tribunal* were crypto-radical productions, with strong links to the radical artisan press, and reflected contemporary concerns about government oppression.[22] Backscheider, in contrast, argues that it was in fact strongly *de*-politicised; that such Gothic plays, precisely because they *were* popular, tended to be much more politically cautious and conservative than the novels on which they were based, containing rather than emphasising the subversive energies their plots invoked.[23] These claims are not necessarily incompatible; it is entirely possible that at least some of these plays, although outwardly shorn of their radical trappings in order to appease the censors, were still intended to communicate a pro-revolutionary message to their audiences, or indeed that they might have communicated such a message to some of their viewers whether their producers intended them to or not. But, overall, Backscheider's perspective seems closer to the truth: far from being radical plays struggling with official censorship, they seem for the most part to instead be apolitical plays struggling with their own potential radicalism. Both *Fontainville Forest* and *The Secret Tribunal* deal with what was potentially highly politically charged subject matter – the downfall of an evil French aristocrat, and the proceedings of an arbitrary court, respectively – and both attempt to defuse the potentially threatening resonances of their topics by opening with strongly patriotic, anti-revolutionary Prologues. Here is part of the prologue from *Fontainville Forest*:

> Our Author chuses to prepare the way,
> With lines at least suggested by his play.
> Caught from the Gothic treasures of Romance,
> He frames his work, and lays the scene in France.
> The word, I see, alarms – it vibrates here,
> And Feeling marks its impulse with a tear.
> It brings to thought, a people once refin'd,
> Who led supreme the manners of mankind;
> Deprav'd by cruelty, by pride inflam'd,
> By traitors madden'd, and by sophists sham'd,
> Crushing that freedom, which, with gentle sway,
> Courted their revolution's infant day,
> 'Ere giant Vanity, with impious hand,
> Assail'd the sacred Temples of the Land.
> Fall'n is that Land beneath oppression's flood;
> Its purest sun has set, alas, in blood![24]

These lines position *Fontainville Forest* squarely within mainstream British responses to the Revolution in 1794, describing it as a movement which at its outset was politically promising, France's 'purest sun', but which rapidly degenerated into cruelty, pride, vanity, madness, and shame. The play's villain, the Marquis, cannot avoid representing the corruptions of the *ancien regime*, swept away by the 'infant day' of the Revolution. But the audience is also encouraged to view him as representing the excesses of the Revolution itself, as when, in the play's final scene, one of his adversaries declaims:

> What, is it thus in France? that a foul murderer,
> Harden'd in crimes himself, and stain'd with blood,
> Shall deal his sentence out on virtuous men,
> And write his ruffian vengeance in their hearts!
> O soil accurs'd! I know thee then no more.[25]

The Marquis may be a criminal, but he is hardly a 'ruffian'; he is an aristocrat, whose murders are carried out by his henchmen, not with his own hands. Nor does he articulate his violent deeds in terms of a legal 'sentence' on his victims; he simply takes what he desires because he can, although he is happy to use and abuse the legal system when it suits his purposes to do so. This rhetoric of 'ruffian vengeance' wielding judicial authority over 'virtuous men' on the 'soil accurs'd' of France is grounded not in the events of the play, to which it is inapplicable, but in British writing about the Reign of Terror, which often dwelt with appalled fascination on the idea of the revolutionary tribunals as courts in which guilty, lower-class, 'ruffian' criminals sat in judgement over the virtuous, aristocratic innocents who, in a properly ordered society, would be the ones passing judgement on *them*; another example of the Revolution as a world turned upside down.[26] (Helen Maria Williams, for example, writes of 'Robespierre and his jury of assassins' in her *Letters from France*.[27]) This speech, like the prologue, emphasises that *Fontainville Forest* is not to be understood as a pro-revolutionary play, and that, despite his title, the villainous Marquis is as much the spiritual kinsman of the revolutionary 'traitors' as of the *ancien regime* tyrants they have supplanted, while the speaker's disowning of France's 'soil accurs'd' aligns the play's heroes with the French émigrés who were then arriving in Britain, fleeing the 'ruffian vengeance' of the Revolution.

A similarly patriotic gesture can be seen in the prologue to Boaden's second play, *The Secret Tribunal*, which was first performed in 1795, just a year after the extremely high-profile trials of the radicals Thomas Hardy, John Thelwall, and John Horne Tooke for high treason.[28] In such a politically fraught context, when criticism of courts or tribunals could easily be interpreted as attacks on the British government and legal system, the play's prologue insists that it has nothing but praise for Britain's courts:

> BRITAIN! Rejoice! – The envied pow'r is THINE
> To punish malice, and to thwart design;
> Open as day *our* courts judicial move,
> And RICH or POOR their *equal* influence prove;
> REJOICE! Your UPRIGHT JURIES make you *free*,
> Bulwarks of FAME, of LIFE and LIBERTY.[29]

These lines are not necessarily anti-radical, as it was thanks to their juries that Hardy, Thelwall, and Horne Tooke were acquitted; but they do assert that the play's villainous Secret Tribunal is not intended as an attack on Britain's legal system. Instead, it is introduced as a distinctly revolutionary-sounding institution, whose judges are so 'unconfin'd and *free*' that 'even MONARCHS TREMBLED ON THEIR THRONES': lines which, in 1795, would surely have evoked the trial and execution of Louis XVI rather than the recent trials of British radicals. The play's anti-revolutionary credentials are reinforced by the fact that its villain, Ratibor, speaks in revolutionary, 'levelling' language, urging the heroine to 'disregard the difference of rank', claiming that it is only 'prejudice' which opposes his fratricidal ambitions, and insisting that his followers must be willing to murder their own families on the tribunal's orders – a common theme of anti-revolutionary propaganda – while its hero, Herman, looks forward instead to the day when his homeland shall 'emulate the "Isle of Glory"', Britain.[30] The play's epilogue even contains a dig at opposition politicians such as Fox, insisting that they only praise the Revolution because they 'want a PLACE' in government themselves.[31] Like *Fontainville Forest*, *The Secret Tribunal* is not immune to radical readings, but its text works hard to forestall them; its ideals are those of mainstream patriotic constitutionalism, and it was thus unlikely to offend any but a tiny fraction of the popular audience to which it aspired. An even more striking example is offered by *The Iron Chest*, Colman's adaptation of Godwin's radical Gothic novel *Caleb Williams* for the popular stage: aware of the book's controversial reputation, he explained in his 'Advertisement to the Reader' that in his adaptation he had 'cautiously avoided all tendency to that which [. . .] is called Politicks', because 'the stage has, now, no business with Politicks: and, should a Dramatick Author endeavour to dabble in them, it is the Lord Chamberlain's office to check his attempts'.[32] Accordingly, Colman moved the action of the play from 1790s Britain to the mid-seventeenth century, thus projecting it safely back into the primitive past and removing all force from Godwin's bitter alternate title for his novel: *Things as They Are.*

As Wein has pointed out, the Gothic chapbooks of the 1800s and 1810s tended to be similarly apolitical; they sometimes placed a greater emphasis on the courage and heroism of servants and other lower-class characters than the Gothic novels upon which they were based, but usually they ultimately affirmed the validity of the social hierarchy, with loyal servants rewarded by benevolent masters, rather than questioning the social structures of which they were a part.[33] In some respects, they were substantially less subversive than the novels upon which they were based: Wein notes that Gothic chapbooks were often much more anti-feminist than Gothic novels, insisting strictly on female obedience, a point which Backscheider also makes about the stage adaptations of the same texts.[34] It may have been for these reasons that those writers who were most directly engaged with the British radical movement, such as Thomas Paine, Charles Pigott, Richard 'Citizen' Lee, and Thomas Spence, made very little use of Gothic in their own writings: committed to a Paineite aesthetic of straightforward clarity, as opposed to the deliberate obfuscation they saw as characteristic of the reactionary forces of church and state which they opposed, their preferred forms were reasoned arguments, lectures, political songs, and allegorical satires and fables, all of which plainly and clearly communicated their ideological claims.[35] They did not shun violent, Gothicised language: like their anti-Jacobin opponents, plebeian radical propagandists were swift to condemn their political enemies as 'ruffians', 'anthropophagi', 'outrageous cannibals', 'BLOODY HELL HOUNDS!', 'INSATIATE MONSTERS', and 'Hell's grand Agents', the perpetrators of 'abominable barbarities', who 'wear Robes dyed in BLOOD'.[36] But Gothic fiction, with its fantastical trappings and obsession with aristocratic feudalism, appears to have held little interest for such writers, whose urgent priority was to present their arguments as directly as possible to the widest audience they could reach; and insofar as there was a literature of popular radicalism in the 1790s, it seems to have had very little crossover with popular Gothic literature. Radical publishers such as Daniel Isaac Eaton and James Ridgway did not generally publish popular Gothic fiction or drama, though Ridgway did publish other dramatic works, such as the plays of Kotzebue; nor did publishers of popular Gothic chapbooks, such as S. Fisher or T. Hurst, generally publish political works, radical or otherwise. (The Minerva Press, whose popular Gothic romances were aimed at a wealthier and more respectable audience than Hurst's sixpenny chapbooks, did publish political works, but its politics were staunchly loyalist and patriotic.)[37] Elite authors with radical sympathies, such as Mary Wollstonecraft and William Godwin, did write Gothic novels with radical messages; but these works appear to have found no real popular audience. The authorities permitted the publication of Godwin's political magnum opus, *Political Justice*, because it was believed that its price was high enough to keep it out of the hands of the lower orders, among whom it was thought capable of doing the most harm; yet the radical corresponding societies clubbed together to raise money, and bought themselves copies anyway.[38] Tellingly, they do not seem to have gone to the same lengths to procure copies of Godwin's radical Gothic novel, *Caleb Williams*.

Thus, despite the anxieties of those who worried that the spread of 'terrorist novel writing' might lead to the admiration or imitation of actual revolutionary terrorism, the success of popular Gothic fiction and drama does not seem to have been directly connected to the growth of popular political radicalism. Indeed, the chronology of its rise suggests the opposite. Popular radicalism in Britain was at its height in the first half of the 1790s, dying away at the decade's end under the impact of government repression from above and a resurgent, militaristic patriotism from below; the new Gothic drama only really became popular in 1794, and reached its height in the first decade of the nineteenth century – the same decade which witnessed the publication of most of the Gothic chapbooks – by which point popular loyalism was at its height, and the British radical movement was in a state of demoralised disarray.[39] Popular Gothic, then, was the mass entertainment of choice during the long years of war with France, during which the revolutionary hopes of 1789–92 came to seem an increasingly distant dream. By 1807, when Lewis – now a seasoned veteran of the London stage – lamented the public's seemingly insatiable taste for the kind of Gothic spectacle upon which he had built his career, Britain had been at war with France for fourteen out of the last fifteen years, and an entire generation had grown up who barely remembered the years of peace. These were the years which witnessed the greatest set-piece battles Europe had seen since the days of the Caesars: and it is perhaps not surprising that a generation which grew up amidst news of burning cities, falling empires, and tens of thousands slain on the battlefield in a single day should have hungered, as Wordsworth suggested, for spectacle and excitement in their fiction and drama, as well.

II

So far, I have discussed popular Gothic as a primarily literary phenomenon. In the 1790s, however, literacy was still far from universal in Britain; estimates of literacy rates vary, but all agree that, at the end of the eighteenth century, a substantial portion of the British population was still illiterate, and many more may have had only very limited ability to read and write.[40] Much of late-eighteenth-century popular culture was thus visual and oral rather than written, communicated through songs, pictures, dances, speeches, and performances, and the most genuinely popular forms were those which could be enjoyed by both the literate and illiterate: plays, which required no literacy to watch and enjoy, broadside ballads, which could be sung and learned by heart even by those unable to read them, and chapbook fiction, short enough for even the semi-literate to read, and sufficiently brief and action-packed to be read aloud to an audience. Forms which required complete literacy, such as full-length novels and poetry, were simply inaccessible to a large section of the population.

Songs, plays, and storytelling all had long histories in British popular culture, stretching back to the Middle Ages and beyond. But starting in the seventeenth century, and accelerating rapidly in the eighteenth century, a new form began to appear: the popular print. Until the rise of printing, high-quality visual images had been the exclusive preserve of the cultural elite, who were able to afford the services of skilled professionals such as painters and engravers: the illiterate poor might be able to appreciate those paintings, carvings, and sculptures they had the opportunity to see, but they could never aspire to own them. But with the steady improvement of printing technologies, printed images became more and more common, and consequently cheaper. By the end of the century, books – even chapbooks – often included printed illustrations, and a thriving market in second-hand prints gave the urban poor, for the first time, access to affordable images with which they could decorate the walls of their homes.[41] Satirical prints on topical subjects and recent events were produced regularly, and pasted up on the windows of print shops, where they could be seen even by those unable to read their captions: according to Thackeray, even in the 1820s it was common to see the poor gather in the street outside such shops to look at the latest prints, with those among them who possessed some literacy reading out their captions, and explaining the scenes being depicted to the rest.[42] The potential of such prints to communicate ideas to the illiterate and semi-literate poor was clearly recognised at the time; as Dickinson writes, 'when the middle classes feared revolution they pasted prints on the walls of taverns, shops and workshops in an effort to influence the lower orders', and political organisations such as Reeve's Association sometimes subsidised the distribution of cheap prints favourable to their ideological positions.[43] Thus, while changing fashions in the visual arts a century before might have gone largely unnoticed by the population at large (which, aside from works displayed in public spaces such as churches, had almost no access to such art anyway), by the late eighteenth century the direct and indirect audiences for popular prints were large enough that any changes to their style and content may have attracted very general attention, at least among the urban population.

In fact, in the 1790s such a change *did* take place, for the visual arts were no more immune than any other art form to the tremendous energies and anxieties that were then sweeping through British society. The satirical print tradition flourished, for amidst the decade's often-frantic political shifts there was much to satirise; and Burke, Fox, Pitt, George III, and other public figures were caricatured and mocked in popular prints much as their predecessors had been before them. But from 1792 onwards, a new note of horror began to creep into popular prints. The beginning of this shift is perhaps marked by Gillray's famous print, *Un Petit Souper a la Parisienne*; engraved in response to the news of the September Massacres and published on 20 September 1792, it depicts in nightmarish detail a family of monstrously fanged cannibal *sans-culottes* feasting on human flesh, seated on stripped and mutilated corpses, while a row of severed heads hang outside their doorway and a grotesque crone bastes a skewered baby with human blood as it roasts before the fire. Above their heads hang severed arms and legs, evidently stored up for later cannibal meals, while, on the floor, a trio of *sans-culotte* infants feast from a bucket of human offal. This print was the visual equivalent to the hysterical reports of the massacres which were then appearing in British newspapers, and, like them, it represented a break from earlier practices; eighteenth-century political prints had traditionally dealt with violent events such as wars, battles, and rebellions in symbolic terms.[44] But it was a sign of things to come; for, over the next three decades, British printmakers were to record the events of the Revolution and the wars which followed it in popular prints of surreal and shocking ghastliness, which stand out sharply from the popular print traditions which came both before and after them. They made frequent use of violent scenes, depicting murders, decapitations, and other acts of blood; but they also employed symbolic figures, such as Death, Satan, and the Four Horsemen of the Apocalypse. Both the violence and the supernatural figures employed in these prints harked back to the popular print culture of the seventeenth century, in which such grotesque, violent, and supernatural imagery had frequently been employed.[45] In the political prints of the eighteenth century, however, as in eighteenth-century literature, such material had largely fallen out of use – until given a new significance by the events of the Revolution.[46]

As with the rise of popular Gothic melodrama and street literature, the gruesomeness and supernaturalism of popular visual culture in the 1790s was prefigured by earlier developments in elite circles. The Gothic revival of the 1760s had led to a taste for paintings of dark, wild, and fearful scenes, often with exotic or historical settings, such as Joseph Wright of Derby's *The Alchemist in Search of the Philosopher's Stone* (1771) and *Vesuvius in Eruption* (1776); and in the 1780s this interest in dark and extravagant compositions was heightened by the career of the Swiss painter Henry Fuseli, whose dream-painting *The Night Mare* was sensationally exhibited at the Royal Academy in 1782.[47] In subsequent paintings such as *The Weird Sisters* (1783), *Percival Delivering Belisane from the Enchantment of Urma* (1783), and *Thor Battering the Midguard Serpent* (1790), Fuseli introduced the British gallery-going public to a visual world of gods, monsters, knights, and witches – all rendered more dream-like by being depicted against vaguely rendered backdrops of rock, mist, and shadow, as Fuseli famously hated painting landscapes.[48] Fuseli was a friend of James Gillray, who, as the most famous and perhaps the most prolific engraver of his day, was excellently placed to adapt his style to a more popular context; and in the 1790s Gillray drew explicitly upon Fuseli's compositions in several of his satirical prints.[49] But, despite his obvious interest in scenes of violence and cruelty, Fuseli's paintings never ventured into the terrain of grotesque bodily dismemberment which Gillray explored with such glee. As Fuseli wrote in 1792, 'horror and loathsomeness in all its branches are equally banished from the painter's and the poet's province. Terror, as the chief ingredient of the Sublime, composes in all instances, and in the utmost extent of the word, fit material for both.'[50] The Burkean aesthetic of sublime terror legitimated Fuseli's paintings of witches and monsters; but no composition based on Gillray's *Petit Souper* could ever have been exhibited at the Royal Academy.

Gillray, like Fuseli, was clearly fascinated by monstrosity and pornographic violence well before the bloodiest days of the French Revolution. In 1790, when a string of violent attacks against young women were carried out by a man whom the press dubbed 'The London Monster', Gillray's print was much the most extreme of those produced on the subject; it showed an immense, ogre-like Monster holding a woman in the air, her skirts fallen to expose her bare legs and buttocks, into which he was about to thrust a gigantic fork.[51] But it was in illustrating the revolutionary horror stories of the 1790s that his gruesome talents were to be given full scope, as the visual arts shifted to reflect the mood of the times. Over the course of the decade the taste for dark and supernatural scenes intensified, a taste exemplified by the acclaim with which Benjamin West's apocalyptic painting of the Four Horsemen of the Apocalypse, *The Opening of the Four Seals*, was greeted in both London and Paris.[52] But even painters such as West and Fuseli kept their depictions of violence within conventional boundaries; they painted writhing, falling bodies, but never actual mutilation or bloodshed. It was only prints such as Gillray's which mirrored back the violence reported in contemporary newspapers and propaganda: in horrific designs such as his *Apotheosis of Hoche* (1798), in which the general is welcomed into a revolutionary heaven by armies of decapitated corpses and flying, bleeding severed heads, while beneath him his soldiers continue to murder and mutilate their way across the Vendée, or *Nightly Visitors* (1798), in which Charles James Fox wakes to find a bloody ghost standing at the foot of his bed and three headless corpses kneeling beside it with halters around their bleeding necks, while snake-haired imps fly overhead brandishing the documents which prove his responsibility for their shameful deaths. These were elaborate, high-quality works, and would certainly not have been bought by the poor except, perhaps, at second hand; but unlike West and Fuseli's paintings, hanging safely in galleries from which the lower orders were excluded, they may well have been *seen* by the poor. In *The Anti-Jacobin Novel*, Grenby quotes Moore's novel *Mordaunt* (1800) as declaring that 'The very chimney-sweeps in London have become aristocrats, from their hatred to their brethren the blackguards and sans-culottes of Paris', and comments:

> How these chimney-sweeps gained their putative knowledge of the Revolution is a matter of some interest to the historian. Presumably, unlike the protagonists of Pye and Moore they, as with most Britons, had not had the opportunity to travel through France and observe the Revolution at first hand. Like most Britons, the chimney-sweeps relied, in other words, on representations of revolution, perhaps of [*sic*] the representations of novelists every bit as much as journalists or returning travellers.[53]

Now, in 1800 a London chimney-sweep would have been very unlikely to be a reader of novels; even if they were lucky enough to be sufficiently literate to read such works, they could never have afforded their prices. Nor were the published 'representations' of 'returning travellers' such as Arthur Young any more available to them. Those who could read might have had some access to newspapers, and thus might have learned their 'hatred' from contemporary journalism on the Revolution. But anyone, even a chimney-sweep, could loiter outside a print-shop window, and Gillray's nightmare scenes could be understood and appreciated even by those with no literacy at all; once one was able to recognise a few basic visual signs, such as the guillotine and the revolutionary cockade, one could often grasp the gist of such scenes even without the help of a literate or semi-literate friend to read out the captions and explain exactly what was being depicted. To the extent that the urban poor had a knowledge of the French Revolution, it was probably derived mostly from rumour rather than from written accounts; but their mental picture of it may also have been heavily shaped by popular print culture, which for many of them would have been virtually the only form of visual culture to which they had any real access.

The picture of the Revolution drawn by these prints was essentially derived from contemporary journalism and propaganda; but it also had a certain kinship with contemporary Gothic melodrama and fiction. Such prints depicted the Revolution as one long massacre, and often showed the revolutionaries as monsters, engaged in acts of frightful carnage: rape, cannibalism, mutilation, and, above all, decapitation. The Revolution, they made clear, was a scene of unnatural (and probably supernatural) evil; their designs are full of ghosts, demons, and furies, and are haunted by the figures of Satan and King Death, establishing a Gothicised visual vocabulary noticeably distinct from that which had predominated in such prints earlier in the century. It was a style which would give rise to such subsequent works as Thomas Rowlandson's *Two Kings of Terror* (1813), which depicts Death and Napoleon sitting together while, behind them, French armies are driven by their enemies into a vast abyss, and *The English Dance of Death* (1814–6), Rowlandson's modern version of a famous sixteenth- and seventeenth-century theme, in which a whole series of domestic scenes – hunts, honeymoons, drinking bouts, trips to the apothecary – are interrupted by the arrival of the grim trickster, Death, depicted as a walking skeleton strikingly at odds with the homely, contemporary scenes into which he intrudes. This Gothic-grotesque engraving style reached its peak in the prints produced by George Cruikshank in response to the Peterloo Massacre, such as *The Radical's Arms* (1819), in which a bloody guillotine is manned by a monstrous radical, one with an impossibly stretched neck which suggests that he has already suffered death by hanging; *Death or Liberty!* (1819), in which a masked skeleton – pretending to be Liberty, but actually Death – prepares to rape Britannia to death with the arrow that hangs between its thighs, while monsters, including a man made of chains, follow in its wake; and *Social Reform* (1819), in which a monstrous living guillotine pursues the rich, breathing fire, cascading blood, and roaring: 'I'm a coming! I'm a coming! I shall have you!'[54] While demons and devils had never entirely ceased to appear in British popular prints during the eighteenth century, these works by Gillray, Rowlandson, and Cruikshank collectively represented a resurgence in British popular visual culture of an older visual vocabulary of evil and violence, paralleled by the increasing use of such Gothic visual and verbal rhetoric in contemporary fiction, drama, propaganda, and journalism.[55] They established a powerful popular iconography in which the figures of 'demon' and 'revolutionary' were virtually interchangeable; and, as late as the Reform Act controversy of 1831, the threatening figure of the Jacobin demon was still appearing in political prints, continuing to embody the threat of political radicalism even though the Jacobin party itself had been defunct for decades.[56]

This Gothicised visual culture had strong links to the popular Gothic drama which flourished in the same years, for the stage spectaculars of Lewis and his contemporaries made very heavy use of visual iconography: costumes, painted backdrops, and special effects. For those seated at the back of a hall built to seat almost four thousand people, the audibility of the onstage actors must often have been hit-and-miss; it was thus important for popular plays to have strong-enough visual elements that their plots could be followed even by those who couldn't necessarily hear all the speeches, just as the illustrations in Gothic chapbooks must have assisted those who, due to low levels of literacy or the poor quality of the print, had difficulty reading all the words. Thus, in January 1798, the enormous new Drury Lane theatre followed up on the success of *The Castle Spectre* the month before with a new melodrama, *Blue-Beard*, by George Colman. The play turned out to be another major hit for the theatre, its success due largely to its unprecedented use of stage spectacle much more extravagant than Lewis or Boaden's stage ghosts.[57] Here are the stage directions for the scene in which the interior of the Blue Chamber, where the villain's secrets are hidden, is first revealed:

> SHACABAC *puts the Key into the Lock; the Door instantly sinks, with a tremendous crash: and the* Blue Chamber *appears streaked with vivid streams of Blood. The figures in the Picture, over the door, change their position, and* ABOMELIQUE *is represented in the action of beheading the Beauty he was, before, supplicating. – The Pictures, and Devices, of Love, change to subjects of Horror and Death. The* interior apartment *(which the sinking of the door discovers,) exhibits various Tombs, in a sepulchral building; – in the midst of which ghastly and supernatural forms are seen; some in motion, some fix'd – In the centre, is a large Skeleton seated on a tomb, (with a Dart in his hand) and, over his head, in characters of Blood, is written* 'THE PUNISHMENT OF CURIOSITY.'
>
> [. . .]
>
> SHACABAC *lays the Dagger at the foot of the Skeleton. – It Thunders and Lightens violently. The inscription, over the Skeleton's head, changes to the following –*
>
> 'THIS SEPULCHRE SHALL INCLOSE HER WHO MAY ENDANGER THE LIFE OF ABOMELIQUE'
>
> *The Skeleton raises his arm which holds the Dart; then lets his arm fall again.* SHACABAC *staggers from the sepulchre, into the Blue Chamber, and falls on his face; when the Door, instantly rising, closes the interior building.*[58]

And here is the no-less spectacular moment when Abomelique meets his end:

> SELIM *and* ABOMELIQUE *fight with Scymetars – During the Combat, Enter* IRENE *and* SHACABAC. *– After a hard contest,* SELIM *overthrows* ABOMELIQUE *at the foot of the Skeleton. – The Skeleton instantly plunges the Dart, which he had held suspended,*

into the breast of ABOMELIQUE, *and sinks with him beneath the earth. (A volume of flame arises, and the earth closes.)*[59]

Colman himself was under no illusions about the qualities which had made *Blue-Beard* a success. In the preface to the printed edition of the play, Colman declared that he was pleased with it not because it had allowed him to display his literary abilities, but because of the opportunity it had offered to showcase the talents of his three collaborators: Kelly the composer, Greenwood the scene-painter, and Johnstone the 'machinist' (i.e. the technician responsible for the play's special effects). 'I have made the Dialogue and Songs (such as they are) subservient to the above-mention'd Artists', Colman wrote, 'and, no men, surely, ever made better use of a vehicle.'[60]

I have cited these stage directions at some length, not just in order to emphasise their extravagance, but because they demonstrate the extent to which the same Gothicised visual vocabulary which was then appearing in popular prints was also being employed by the scene-painters and machinists who worked on the most popular and successful stage melodramas of the day. Animated skeletons, bloody messages, 'ghastly and supernatural forms', and 'Pictures, and Devices, of Love' changing into 'subjects of Horror and Death' were just the sort of images which were then being used to illustrate the progress of the French Revolution; and, indeed, as a villainous serial decapitator of young gentlewomen, Colman's Bluebeard, Abomelique, is himself a somewhat Jacobinical figure, especially as revolutionary violence was sometimes compared to the proverbial cruelty of Bluebeard in the political writings of the day.[61] *Blue-Beard* is not an obviously political play, although, as with most Gothic melodrama, politicised readings are certainly possible; but it does demonstrate the ways in which popular melodrama could provide a channel through which the Gothicised artistic culture of the later 1790s was able to reach a mass audience beyond any that Radcliffe or Fuseli could have aspired to.

The vogue for supernatural spectacle established by Boaden and Lewis no doubt contributed to the popular success of Colman's 'dramatic romance'. But some of its popularity may also have been due to the fact that, while Boaden and Lewis had drawn upon recent developments in elite literary culture to furnish their melodramas with spectacular incident, Colman drew instead upon the resources of popular folklore: Bluebeard's story had been regularly reprinted throughout the century among the fairy-tale collections favoured by the very poor, and the mass appeal of his play may have been enhanced by the fact that the Bluebeard legend was known among the general population in a way that, say, Radcliffe's *Romance of the Forest* could never hope to be. However, the folkloric Bluebeard is a very different figure to Colman's Abomelique, with his ranting, grandstanding speeches and his spectacular use of black magic; the only magical element in the traditional Bluebeard story is the key which, once stained with blood, can never be wiped clean. What Colman's play accomplishes is the assimilation of this folklore villain to the conventions of contemporary Gothic fiction and drama; its popularity and success demonstrate the new connections between elite and popular literary culture which the rise of Gothic had made possible, while its dependence upon spectacle – music, scene-painting, machinery, sword-fights, and pantomime – emphasises the fact that, while Gothic was primarily a literary phenomenon among the cultural elite, popular Gothic relied upon media other than the printed word in order to reach a mass audience which still possessed only variable literacy and extremely limited access to books.

In the mid-eighteenth century, one chapbook retelling of what it called 'The Story of a Man with a Blue Beard' reassured its readers that the story was set long ago, in lines translated from Perrault's 1697 version of the tale, *La Barbe bleue*:

> A very little share of common sense
> And knowledge of the world will soon evince
> That this a story is of long time past;
> No husband now such pannic terrors cast[62]

This, broadly, was how violent fairy tales such as 'Bluebeard' had tended to be viewed in the eighteenth century; as remnants of 'long time past'. But in the 1790s, with 'pannic terrors' the order of the day in both politics and art, 'low' and old-fashioned cultural resources such as folklore and fairy tales took on a new relevance, and the result was the creation of a culture of popular Gothic fiction, art, and drama in which elite material (such as Radcliffe's stories) and popular material (such as the story of Bluebeard) were able to appear side by side. The very inclusivity of popular Gothic was precisely what many cultural commentators found so worrying about it; it seemed to threaten confusion, jumbling up high and low, modern and old-fashioned, British and foreign material. But such inclusivity also gave it an unusual vigour, allowing it to draw upon an extraordinarily wide range of cultural resources, and this range may, in turn, have contributed to the surprising longevity of popular Gothic. Literary Gothic faded away after 1820; but, fifty years after Colman's *Blue-Beard*, Gothic melodramas and 'penny bloods' – the descendants of the 'dramatic romances' and Gothic chapbooks of Colman's day – were, to the persistent despair of the self-appointed guardians of culture, still the literary and theatrical entertainments of choice among the British poor.

Notes

1   The average Minerva romance sold for three shillings in 1790, rising to three-and-a-half shillings over the course of the decade under the impact of wartime inflation. See Dorothy Blakey, *The Minerva Press* (London: Oxford UP, 1939), pp. 276–80.

2   On circulating libraries, see Jacqueline Pearson, *Women's Reading in Britain, 1750–1832* (Cambridge: Cambridge UP, 1999), pp. 162–9, and Franz Potter, *The History of Gothic Publishing, 1800–1835* (Basingstoke: Palgrave Macmillan, 2005), chapter 2.

3   On the cost of books in the 1790s, see Pearson, p. 163. On newspapers, see J. Paul Hunter, *Before Novels* (New York: W.W. Norton and Co., 1990), p. 174.

4   Michael Gamer, *Romanticism and the Gothic* (Cambridge: Cambridge UP, 2000), p. 135; Paula Backscheider, *Spectacular Politics* (Baltimore, MD: Johns Hopkins UP, 1993), p. 153. Cox states that the new Drury Lane theatre's true capacity may have been closer to 3,900: see Jeffrey Cox, ed., *Seven Gothic Dramas* (Athens, OH: Ohio UP, 1992), pp. 8–10. This gigantic theatre burned down in 1809, and was subsequently rebuilt on a smaller scale.

5   On chapbooks, see Pat Rogers, 'Chapbooks and classics', in Isobel Rivers, ed., *Books and Their Readers in Eighteenth-Century England* (Leicester: Leicester UP, 1982), p. 27; Diane Hoeveler, *Gothic Riffs* (Columbus, OH: Ohio State UP, 2010), chapter 6, and Robert Collison, *The Story of Street Literature* (London: Dent, 1973). At the end of the eighteenth century the standard price for a chapbook novel, or a collection of short fiction such as *Gothic Stories* (London, 1800), was sixpence; one could thus purchase seven such volumes for the same price as a Minerva romance, and a small library of fifty for the price of a single new copy of Radcliffe's *Mysteries of Udolpho*. See David Punter, *The Literature of Terror* (London: Longman, 1980), p. 24.

6   Gothic novels redacted into chapbook form for popular audiences included *The Recess, The Old Manor House, A Sicilian Romance*, and *The Italian*. See Gary Kelly, ed., *Varieties of Female Gothic volume 2: Street Gothic* (London, 2002), p. xiv. See also William Watt, *Shilling Shockers* (New York: Russell and Russell, 1967), and Potter, chapter 3. Potter argues that these Gothic 'bluebooks' – so called because of their thin blue covers – were distinct from chapbook street literature, as they were not primarily sold by street hawkers, and probably had a substantial middle-class readership; but as their low prices placed them, like street literature, within the reach of the working poor, I have followed Kelly and Hoeveler in grouping both together as forms of popular Gothic literature. See Potter, pp. 43–4, 70–6.

7   Rogers, pp. 28–39.

8   Richard Hurd, *Letters on Chivalry and Romance*, ed. Edith Morley (London: Henry Frowde, 1911), pp. 51–65.

9   Bertrand Evans, *Gothic Drama from Walpole to Shelley* (Berkeley, CA: University of California Press, 1947), pp. 19, 43–71.

10 James Boaden, *Memoirs of the Life of John Philip Kemble* (London, 1825), pp. 313–14.

11 Boaden, *Memoirs of the Life*, p. 326.

12 On Boaden's early plays, see Backscheider, pp. 154, 178–80.

13 On the popularity of Gothic drama, see Backscheider, pp. 218–33.

14 Toni Wein, *British Identities, Heroic Nationalisms, and the Gothic Novel* (Basingstoke: Palgrave Macmillan, 2002), pp. 160–1.

15 On Gothic villain roles as star vehicles, see Evans, *Drama*, pp. 87–8.

16 On Lewis' commercial success, see H.C.G. Matthew and Brian Harrison, eds., *Oxford Dictionary of National Biography* (Oxford: Oxford UP, 2004), vol. 33, pp. 637–9, and D.L. Macdonald, *Monk Lewis* (Toronto, ON: University of Toronto Press, 2000), pp. 136–77.

17 George Woodcock, 'The meaning of revolution in Britain, 1770–1800', in Ceri Crossley and Ian Small, eds., *The French Revolution and British Culture* (Oxford: Oxford UP, 1989), p. 26.

18 Augustin Barruel, *History of Jacobinism*, trans. Robert Clifford (London, 1797–8), vol. 1, pp. 140–4, 315–18. Barruel's translator, Robert Clifford, went much further, asserting that the Illuminati conspiracy had turned every form of popular culture to its own seditious purposes:

> The attempt to accomplish this End has appeared in the shape even of play-bills and songs; seditious toasts, and a studied selection of the tunes which have been most in use in France since the Revolution, have been applied to the same purpose, of endeavouring to render deliberate incitements to every species of treason familiar to the minds of the people. (Clifford, p. 29)

19   Cox, 'English Gothic Theatre', in Hogle, ed., *Companion* p. 129.
20   Matthew and Harrison, eds., *Dictionary of National Biography*, vol. 24, p. 422.
21   Cox, 'English Gothic theatre', pp. 130, 134; Maurice Disher, *Blood and Thunder* (London: Muller, 1949), pp. 49–51.
22   David Worrall, 'The political culture of Gothic drama', in David Punter, ed., *A Companion to the Gothic* (Oxford: Blackwell, 2000), pp. 96–7.
23   Backscheider, pp. 232–3.
24   James Boaden, *Fontainville Forest* (London, 1794), Prologue.
25   Boaden, *Fontainville Forest*, p. 64.
26   On depictions of Revolutionary Tribunals in contemporary fiction, see M.O. Grenby, *The Anti-Jacobin Novel* (Cambridge: Cambridge UP, 2001), pp. 39–42.
27   Helen Maria Williams, *Letters from France* (New York: Scholar's Facsimiles and Reprints, 1975), vol. 2:2, p. 103.
28   On *The Secret Tribunal*, see Evans, *Drama*, pp. 124–5.
29   James Boaden, *The Secret Tribunal* (London, 1795), Prologue.
30   Boaden, *Secret Tribunal*, pp. 7, 9, 27, 41–2. For stories of Jacobins executing their own families in the name of the Revolution, see William Cobbett, *The Bloody Buoy* (London, 1796), pp. 29–30, 42–3, 127.
31   Boaden, *Secret Tribunal*, Epilogue.
32   George Colman, *The Iron Chest* (London, 1796), Advertisement.
33   Wein, pp. 172–3. Potter also notes the strongly moralistic character of cheap Gothic literature: see Potter, pp. 56–70.
34   Wein, pp. 178–80, and Backscheider, pp. 204–5.
35   On the politics of clarity, see Ronald Paulson, *Representations of Revolution* (New Haven: Yale UP, 1983), p. 47.
36   Daniel Isaac Eaton, *Politics for the People* (London, 1794), pp. 76–7, 137; 'Citizen' Bailey, *The White Devils Un-Cased* (London, 1795), pp. 7, 9, 16–17.
37   On the loyalist politics of William Lane, founder of the Minerva Press, see Blakey, p. 20. For examples of the political works published by it in the 1790s, see pp. 168–9.
38   George Woodcock, 'The meaning of revolution in Britain, 1770–1800', in Ceri Crossley and Ian Small, eds., p. 24.
39   On the rise of loyalism, see Robert Dozier, *For King, Constitution, and Country* (Lexington, KY: UP of Kentucky, 1983), chapter 3, and H.T. Dickinson, *The Politics of the People in Eighteenth-Century Britain* (Basingstoke: Macmillan, 1995), pp. 272–3. On the production of chapbook Gothic, see Potter, p. 47.
40   For late-eighteenth-century literacy rates, see Alan Richardson, *Literature, Education, and Romanticism* (Cambridge: Cambridge UP, 1994), p. 45, and Hunter, pp. 62–85.
41   William Blake, for example, the son of a London tradesman, had been able to buy cheap, discounted prints from print shops as a boy. See G.E. Bentley, Jr, *The Stranger From Paradise* (New Haven: Yale UP, 2001), p. 24. On chapbook illustrations, see Kelly, *Varieties*, vol. 2, p. xii.
42   On print shops as 'the people's real picture galleries', see Vic Gatrell, *City of Laughter* (London: Atlantic, 2006), pp. 210–12. A picture of such a shop from 1801, with pictures on the windows and people gathered outside to examine them, is reproduced on p. 211. Dickinson argues that, as there were only ten such shops in central London, the number of people able to see such prints must still have been fairly low; I would suggest, however, that in comparison to previous generations, even this must have represented a substantial increase in the availability of printed

images. See H.T. Dickinson, ed., *Caricatures and the Constitution* (Cambridge: Cambridge UP, 1986), pp. 13–15.

43 Dickinson, *Caricatures*, pp. 15–17.

44 Gillray's print is reproduced in Gatrell, *City*, p. 263. For examples of the symbolic treatment of wars, such as the War of Jenkins' Ear and the Jacobite rising of 1745, in earlier eighteenth-century prints, see Herbert Atherton, *Political Prints in the Age of Hogarth* (Oxford: Clarendon, 1974), plates 25–6, 58–9, 61.

45 On the popular print culture of the seventeenth century, see Andrew Cunningham and Ole Peter Grell, *The Four Horseman of the Apocalypse* (Cambridge: Cambridge UP, 2000), chapter 2. Particularly spectacular examples of such prints are reproduced on pp. 29, 46 143, 153–5, 217.

46 One place in which extremely violent printed images did continue to appear was in martyrologies. Eight illustrated editions of Foxe's *Book of Martyrs* appeared over the course of the eighteenth century, and the violent illustrations of such works were clearly a selling point: a mid-century *Select History of the Lives and Sufferings of the Principal English Protestant Martyrs* (London, 1746), which declared itself to be 'designed as a Cheap and Useful book for *Protestant* Families of all Denominations', announced on its title-page that it was 'Adorned with COPPER-PLATES, shewing the different Kinds of Cruelties that were exercised upon them'. (In fact, the book contains only five illustrations, none of them very explicit.) This 'Cheap and Useful book' was a 324-page octavo, while illustrated editions of Foxe could run to over 1,000 folio pages, so popular access to such texts must have been limited. Some editions of Foxe were, however, broken up into cheap instalments, so a poor but pious household might have owned a few chapters of the *Book of Martyrs* – complete with one or two gory illustrations – even if they could never aspire to own the entire work. See Linda Colley, *Britons*, new edition (London: Pimlico, 2003), pp. 25–8.

47 Gatrell, *City*, p. 276. On the development of Romantic painting in Britain, see Raymond Lister, *British Romantic Painting* (Cambridge: Cambridge UP, 1989).

48 On Fuseli's career, see Martin Myrone, ed., *Gothic Nightmares* (London: Tate Publishing, 2006). On Fuseli's dislike of natural landscapes, see Lister, p. 12.

49 At his busiest, Gillray sometimes completed as many as two satirical engravings a week. See Gatrell, *City*, pp. 266, 278.

50 Christopher Frayling, 'Fuseli's *The Nightmare*', in Myrone, p. 13.

51 For prints of the Monster, see Jan Bondeson, *The London Monster* (Stroud: Tempus, 2003), pp. 60–1.

52 Paley, pp. 19–31.

53 Grenby, p. 35.

54 *Death or Liberty!* and *Social Reform* are reproduced in Dickinson, *Caricatures*, pp. 259–61.

55 For examples of demonic figures in earlier political prints, see Dickinson, *Caricatures*, pp. 45, 51, 68, 82.

56 Dickinson, *Caricatures*, pp. 311, 321.

57 Backscheider, pp. 153–4, 185–6.

58 George Colman, *Blue Beard* (London, 1798), pp. 17–19.

59 Colman, *Blue Beard*, p. 52.

60 Colman, *Blue Beard*, pp. iv–vi.

61 See, for example, 'Citizen Bluebeard' in 'Jack Cade', *The Quartern Loaf for Eight-Pence* (London, 1795), p. x; Louis Sébastien Mercier, *New Picture of Paris* (London, 1800), vol. 2, p. 192.

62 Anon., *The Master Cat* (London, no date), p. 24.

The Gothic Legacy

I

In 1815, after twenty-three years of war in Europe, Napoleon faced his opponents in battle one last time on the field of Waterloo. Looking back many years later, De Quincey wrote of that pivotal battle:

> [De Quincey's brother William] often thrilled our young hearts by supposing the case (not at all unlikely, he affirmed), that a federation, a solemn league and conspiracy, might take place among the infinite generations of ghosts against the single generation of men at any one time composing the garrison of earth. [. . .] My brother, dying in his sixteenth year, was far enough from seeing or foreseeing Waterloo; else he might have illustrated this dreadful duel of the living human race with its ghostly predecessors, by the awful apparition which at three o'clock in the afternoon, on the 18th of June, 1815, the mighty contest at Waterloo must have assumed to eyes that watched over the trembling interests of man.[1]

For De Quincey, Waterloo was the battle of the living against the undead: the last stand of European civilisation against Old Boney, the King of Terrors, and his army of revolutionary phantoms. Yet the allies won the day, and by the time De Quincey wrote these lines Old Boney had been safely buried on St Helena, beneath an unmarked tomb.[2] The Revolution and all its terrors were over, vanquished, and laid to rest. Kings once more sat firmly and securely upon their thrones.

Gothic literature, which had first become popular during the revolutionary panic of the early 1790s, had followed a similar historical arc. Miles estimates Gothic fiction to have enjoyed its greatest popularity between 1795 (the year in which it commanded the greatest market share of novel production, at 38 per cent of all novels) and 1800 (the year in which the single greatest number of Gothic novels were published in Britain); thereafter its market share dwindled, and by 1821 – the year of Napoleon's death – it had sunk to less than 10 per cent.[3] Surveying Gothic fiction in the *Ladies Magazine*, Mayo came to much the same conclusions: first appearing in 1791, Gothic short stories accounted for over three-quarters of all fiction published in the magazine by 1805, only to fall away rapidly thereafter and vanish almost entirely after 1814.[4] Byron's *Manfred* (1817) and *Cain* (1821), Shelley's *Frankenstein* (1818), Scott's *The Monastery* (1820),

Polidori's *The Vampyre* (1819), and Maturin's *Melmoth the Wanderer* (1820) are usually taken to represent the end of the romantic-era tradition of literary Gothic poetry and prose fiction; in the 1820s and 1830s it lived on largely in the form of stage melodramas and short stories in magazines.[5] Major late works such as James Hogg's *Memoirs and Confessions of a Justified Sinner* (1824), being born out of their time, were little read, largely ignored by a public which now considered the entire fad passé.

Yet, as De Quincey's use of hyperbolically Gothic rhetoric indicates, the Gothic did not simply vanish after 1821; and if the British novelists and poets of the 1820s and 1830s no longer wrote reflexively about haunted castles, necromantic Rosicrucians, and sinister conspiracies meeting in secret chambers, their works were still strongly marked by the Gothic enthusiasms of the previous three decades. Gothic props were increasingly laid aside; but Gothic rhetoric and figures of speech lived on. In his *Defence of Poetry*, written in 1821, Shelley famously wrote:

> [The language of poets] is vitally metaphorical; that is, it marks the before unapprehended relations of things and perpetuates their apprehension, until the words which represent them, become, through time, signs for portions or classes of thoughts instead of pictures of integral thoughts.[6]

Something very similar to the process Shelley describes, by which metaphors which were once striking and original are, through repetition, naturalised into 'signs for portions or classes of thoughts', was taking hold of the rhetoric of Gothic fiction in the 1820s and 1830s; for, after thirty years of popular Gothic, its imaginative and rhetorical vocabulary had become so pervasive that they were now deployed routinely and reflexively even by writers who would never dream of actually writing anything so low status and unfashionable as a Gothic romance. The Gothic fiction which flourished between 1790 and 1820 bequeathed to the nineteenth century a whole new rhetorical idiom for writing about evil and violence, fear and madness, grief and death, an idiom quite distinct from that which had dominated eighteenth-century writing on these matters. This rhetorical language of ghosts and hauntings, monsters and demons, ancestral curses and family secrets, first developed by the Gothic novelists of the 1790s, would go on to be used by many of the most popular and significant British novelists of the nineteenth century, precisely as 'signs for portions or classes of thoughts', even in novels whose ostensible subject matter was entirely modern and realistic. Nor was such rhetoric popular only, or even primarily, among writers of fiction; for, as the quotation from De Quincey indicates, such an idiom was also deployed by writers on non-fictional subjects, such as politics and current affairs, history, geography, and crime.

The steady absorption of Gothic tropes into mainstream British culture over the first decades of the nineteenth century was facilitated by the literary careers of Lord Byron and Walter Scott, who, at their heights, were respectively the most popular writers of poetry and prose in Britain, and who jointly dominated the British literary landscape of the 1820s, despite Byron's early death in 1824. Scott had begun his literary career in the 1790s, as a translator of German horror-poems and an author of German-style poetry in the same style, some of which had appeared in Matthew Lewis' collection of horror poems, *Tales of Wonder* (1801).[7] He first achieved literary fame with his narrative poems, *The Lay of the Last Minstrel* (1805), *Marmion* (1808), and *The Lady of the Lake* (1810), all of which demonstrate his clear debts to the Gothic poetry, drama, and fiction popular at the time: all three have medieval settings and feature supernatural events and themes, while their plots – each of which revolves around a virtuous knight, a beautiful maiden, and their long and difficult road to love and happiness together, against a backdrop of violence and war – are strongly reminiscent of the Gothic romances of the 1790s. These Gothic motifs are most obvious in *The Lay of the Last Minstrel*, which contains scenes of necromantic magic and opened graves strongly reminiscent of the kind of German-influenced Gothic literature Scott had been writing a few years earlier, and while these Gothic elements grew less pronounced in his subsequent poems, they did not disappear: *Marmion* involves a maiden walled up alive in an isolated nunnery, and *The Lady of the Lake* features the bizarre figure of Brian the Hermit, whose magical and prophetic powers apparently result from having been fathered by a ghost or spirit at midnight in 'a dreary glen/Where scattered lay the bones of men'.[8] As Scott recalled in 1829, at the outset of his career he had intended to write Gothic fiction, too:

> I had nourished the ambitious desire of composing a tale of chivalry, which was to be in the style of the Castle of Otranto, with plenty of Border characters and supernatural incident. [. . .] Those who complain, not unreasonably, of the profusion of the Tales which have followed Waverley, may bless their stars at the narrow escape they have made, by the commencement of the inundation which had nearly taken place in the first year of the century, being postponed for fifteen years later.[9]

The novel Scott planned to write was to have been a supernatural romance entitled 'Thomas the Rhymer', set in medieval Scotland and revolving around the magic sword which, according to Scottish folklore, hung in the enchanted hall of Thomas of Hersildoune. Had the 'inundation' of his fiction begun in 1800 with 'Thomas the Rhymer', rather than in 1814 with *Waverley*, Scott would have been straightforwardly classed alongside Lewis as an author of Gothic romance, and probably remembered today as one of the major Gothic novelists of the Romantic period; but the popularity of Gothic fiction had waned in the intervening years, and Scott's enthusiasm for the genre had evidently waned with it. Years later, he reflected that it was probably fortunate that 'Thomas the Rhymer' was never finished:

> Although admitting of much poetical ornament, it is clear that the legend would have formed but an unhappy foundation for a prose story, and must have degenerated into a mere fairy tale.[10]

As James Kerr has argued, 'Scott defined his position as a novelist within and against the Gothic mode', using his biographical essays on Walpole, Reeve, and Radcliffe to distinguish his own novels, with their serious and carefully researched use of history, from the sort of ahistorical Gothic fiction in which 'ghosts, knights-errant, and damsels gent, are all equipped in hired dresses from the same warehouse in Tavistock Street'.[11]

Yet his historical novels did not so much break away from this Gothic tradition as evolve out of it: they fore-grounded precise period detail and processes of historical change, and de-emphasised (without ever entirely abandoning) scenes of violence and the supernatural, but they always retained features inherited from the Gothic romances, such as melodramatic, coincidence-driven plotting, a preference for sublime settings such as mountains, castles, and abbeys, and a fascination with fearsome aristocratic warriors and outlaw bands – 'my Gothic Borderers', as Scott referred to them.[12] It was this literary balancing act which allowed the author of *The Bride of Lammermoor* – rich in feudal lords, ruined castles, madness, violence, and the fulfilment of dark prophecies, but conspicuously lacking the overt and spectacular supernaturalism of Scott's earliest works – to become the most celebrated novelist of his age, while the author of 'Thomas the Rhymer' could only have been a teller of 'mere fairy tale[s]'.

In the poems and novels he wrote after *Waverley*, Scott continued this step-by-step retreat from the overtly Gothic material which had characterised his earliest writings, with *The Monastery* (1820) – a tale of fanatical monks, robber barons, and ancestral spirit-guardians – being perhaps the last of his works which could be straightforwardly classed as belonging to the same Gothic tradition as the novels of Radcliffe and Lewis. As his fame grew, Scott supplanted Radcliffe as the most popular novelist of the day, and his novels – masculine, educational, and founded on historical fact – attained a degree of respectability which had always been denied to Radcliffe's romances, and which would probably have been denied to 'Thomas the Rhymer', too.[13] In one sense, the triumph of Scott was the downfall of Gothic; certainly it coincided with, and probably contributed to, the final waning of the Gothic romance as a genre, and the story Scott obsessively retold in his novels – of an old, enchanted world giving way to a newer, more rational order of things – was enacted through his writings in the domain of contemporary English literature.[14] But, at the same time, Scott's poems and novels – which, like the Gothic romances of the 1790s, were very widely adapted for the stage – acted as crucial conduits, through which a wide range of Gothic tropes escaped from the ghetto of genre fiction and were diffused into British literature at large. Thus, by 1864, Le Fanu could defend *Uncle Silas* – a novel so self-consciously Gothic that its heroine reads Gothic literature even while being subjected to actual Gothic persecution, and explicitly compares her situation to that of Adeline in Radcliffe's *Romance of the Forest* – against the charge that it was a mere 'sensation novel' by citing the example of Scott's 'unapproachable *Waverley Novels*'; it was true, Le Fanu argued, that his novel made abundant use of Gothic props and situations, but so too did 'those grand romances of *Ivanhoe, Old Mortality*, and *Kenilworth*, with their terrible intricacies of crime and bloodshed, constructed with so fine a mastery of the art of exciting suspense and horror', and no-one could deny their status as legitimate literature, even though 'in that marvellous series [i.e. the Waverley novels] there is not a single tale in which death, crime, and, in some form, mystery, have not a place'.[15] Thanks to the success of Scott's fiction, 'death', 'crime', 'mystery', 'suspense', 'horror', and 'bloodshed' were no longer the province of Gothic romance alone; even the supernatural was no longer entirely forbidden to the serious novelist, for Scott's continuing use of supernatural material in otherwise entirely historical novels such as *A Legend of Montrose* (1819), while not uncontentious with contemporary reviewers, had helped to break down the hard division between the Gothic romance, which could employ supernatural themes, and the realist novel, which could not, thus paving the way for the much more fluid use of supernatural elements such as ghosts, prophecies, visions, and predictive dreams in otherwise realistic fiction by subsequent novelists such as Dickens and the Brontës.[16] Perhaps most significant of all was the militarism of Scott's works, and although Watt has drawn attention to Scott's scepticism regarding the value of chivalric violence, Bainbridge points out that it is with Scott's poetry that 'the eighteenth-century emphasis on war's horrors gives way to the nineteenth century stress on its glory'; a shift that would come to be taken for granted in much Victorian fiction and propaganda.[17] Before Scott's rise to literary fame, the language of knighthood, crusade, and chivalry was found only in Gothic fiction; but, afterwards, such militaristic medievalism entered into the general cultural vocabulary of the age, such that Victorian military men could be found articulating their imperial and colonial ambitions as though they were medieval knights marching on Palestine.[18]

Scott was one such conduit for Gothic tropes; Byron was another. Like Scott, Byron was an associate of Lewis, and was heavily influenced by Radcliffe and the Gothic novelists of the 1790s; and, again like Scott, his fame was primarily established by his earliest and most Gothic works, such as *Childe Harold's Pilgrimage* (1812–18) and his 'oriental tales' *The Giaour, The Bride of Abydos, Lara*, and *The Corsair* (1813–14).[19] (To this list should perhaps be added Polidori's novel *The Vampyre*, which was widely believed to have been written by Byron when it was first published in 1819, and which led to the staging of popular vampire-themed melodramas in both London and Paris.[20]) The immense influence and popularity of Byron's poetry bequeathed to the nineteenth century a fascination with 'Byronic heroes': dark and tortured hero-villains, all more or less modelled on the villains of Gothic romance, but now released into more mainstream poetry and fiction.[21] The Byronic hero-villain, like the hero-villains of Gothic melodrama and romance, is emphatically not a man like other men, but something else entirely, as Manfred, perhaps the greatest of them all, scornfully declares when he is advised to be patient:

> Patience and patience! Hence – that word was made
> For brutes of burthen, not for birds of prey;
> Preach it to mortals of a dust like thine,–
> I am not of thine order.[22]

As he later tells the Witch of the Alps, 'From my youth upwards/My spirit walk'd not with the souls of men/Nor look'd upon the earth with human eyes'.[23] His soul-deep otherness manifests not only in his possession of magical powers which are literally unearthly, originating on another planet, 'a star condemn'd,/The burning wreck of a demolish'd world,/A wandering hell in the eternal space', but also in his psychological capabilities, which allow him to endure experiences so dreadful that, he claims, even dreaming about them would be enough to kill an ordinary man:

> No, friend! I would not wrong thee, nor exchange
> My lot with living being: I can bear –

However wretchedly, 'tis still to bear –
In life what others could not brook to dream,
But perish in their slumber.[24]

Manfred's sublime otherness, superhuman power, and total mental and spiritual superiority over other men place him in a line of literary descent that runs from Radcliffe's Montoni and Schedoni in the 1790s, down to Polidori's Lord Ruthven, Shelley's St Irvyne, and Maturin's Bertram and Melmoth the Wanderer in Byron's own day. The same otherness and superiority is attributed, in less hyperbolic forms, to the heroes of Byron's other early narrative poems, such as Lara and Childe Harold; they may not literally possess magic powers from other planets, as Manfred does, but they tend to behave as though they did, holding themselves contemptuously aloof from ordinary life, commanding awe and fear from those around them, and effortlessly demonstrating their superiority when they deign to exert themselves at all. As with Scott's historical tales, Byron's innovation was not so much in content – for such sublime misanthropes had been appearing in Gothic romances and plays for decades – as in repositioning Gothic material in new, more respectable literary contexts. Gothic had always been a low-status genre, critically marginalised even during its years of commercial dominance: it had been associated with women, eccentrics, political radicals, and Germans, and its target audience assumed to be young, ignorant, semi-literate, lower-class, and probably female. But Scott and Byron were well-connected, high-status writers – Byron a baron, Scott a baronet – who wrote in high-status genres, and their fame and reputation were such that their works were praised and imitated by writers who would never have shown such kindness to the sort of Gothic romances and horror-poetry upon which they drew. Thus, even as Gothic dwindled as a genre, its tropes – sublime hero-villains, exotic and historical settings, melodramatic plots, and supernatural themes – came to be more generally employed than ever before.

If Scott's engagement with Gothic took the form of a long, slow retreat, played out over decades, Byron's was little more than a phase; and if *Childe Harold*'s first cantos, published in 1812, marked its beginning, then the last cantos, published in 1818, came virtually at its end. In later works such as 'Beppo' and *Don Juan*, Byron returned to the older, pre-Gothic poetic resources of Augustan satire; and, with it, to the world view of Swift, Pope, and Dryden, whom he had praised at the very outset of his literary career in *English Bards and Scotch Reviewers*. These poets had been men with little interest and no confidence in what Johnson had called 'men splendidly wicked', and Byron himself increasingly appeared to share their scepticism of the sort of grand posturing which had initially made him famous.[25] In *Don Juan*, he demonstrated the ease with which the epic feats of such overblown figures as Manfred and Lara could be undercut and rendered absurd, even contemptible:

'Fierce loves and faithless wars' – I am not sure
If this be the right reading – 'tis no matter;
The fact's about the same, I am secure;
I sing them both, and am about to batter
A town which did a famous siege endure,

And was beleaguer'd both by land and water
By Suvaroff, or anglicè Suwarrow,
Who loved blood as an Alderman loves marrow.[26]

In *Don Juan*, 'heroes' of the Manfred type are repeatedly shown up as ridiculous, their claims of uniqueness dismissed as so much rhetorical bluster designed to conceal the truth that their wars are not glorious but 'faithless', and that, as the comparison of Suvorov to an alderman indicates, their 'epic' deeds are in fact driven by very ordinary motives of vanity, cruelty, and pettiness. The enormous audience Byron had won with his earlier poetry were understandably taken aback by this sudden shift; but the question of whether he might ultimately win them back, and persuade them of the validity of this new perspective, was rendered moot by his death in Greece at the age of thirty-six, leaving *Don Juan* forever unfinished. It was thus the Gothicised Byron of *Childe Harold*, rather than the neo-Augustan satirist of his last years, who came to be remembered, and whose works cast such long shadows over subsequent nineteenth-century literature; and if Gothic fiction gave to Victorian literature, via Scott, its obsessions with medievalism and the supernatural, then via Byron it gave the figure of the larger-than-life villain, with his apparently supernatural capabilities and his amoral, aristocratic contempt for other men, a figure which would ultimately attain a kind of cultural apotheosis in the form of Bram Stoker's Count Dracula.[27] Through Byron's influence, the scornful sneers of second-hand Schedonis continued to adorn the villains – and sometimes heroes – of Victorian poetry and fiction long after Radcliffe's romances themselves had ceased to be widely read.

II

As I have discussed in previous chapters, the Gothic rhetoric of evil – a rhetoric developed in the political and fictional writings of the 1790s, and popularised in the mass-market melodramas and chapbooks of the 1800s – was markedly different from the earlier discourse on the same subject generated by the British Enlightenment. Like the early modern discourse familiar in Milton's day, it depicted extreme evil as something basically unnatural, something which pointed to or derived from a source outside that normal, human order of things in which the thinkers and writers of the Enlightenment had attempted to locate the causes of all acts of wickedness, however great. But, unlike the demonology of the seventeenth century, this Gothic discourse generally did not locate such unnatural evil within a broader theological framework; instead, it remained ultimately inexplicable and unassimilable, radically 'other', a wound in the fabric of the world. The Gothic monster, like the revolutionary terrorist, is a walking paradox: a being defined by its ability to perform those actions which are understood to be impossible and incomprehensible. Over the course of the nineteenth century, this rhetoric of Gothic monstrosity was deployed, both in fiction and non-fiction, in order to demonise a whole range of cultural 'others': criminals, foreigners, political radicals, the indigenous inhabitants of other continents, homosexuals, and the urban poor. Within this Gothicised discourse, the wickedness and otherness of such groups appeared not as relative and situational – the result of a different perspective on the world, generated by different circumstances – but as innate and essential, the result of a basic, ineffable monstrousness that could be erased only by extermination. At the end of the nineteenth century, this Gothic discourse of innate evil found its fullest expression in the ideology of eugenics and scientific racism, which articulated all of human history and human life as a Gothic nightmare in which the white races of northern Europe struggled endlessly, both against contamination or conquest by the monstrous sub-humans of other regions without, and against the invisible ancestral curse of tainted blood within.[28] In the writings of late-nineteenth-century theorists such as the criminologists Cesare Lombroso and Enrico Ferri, reality often seems to have been completely overwritten by Gothic narratives of lurking monsters and ancestral secrets:

> No doubt the idea of a born criminal is a direct challenge to the traditional belief that the conduct of every man is the outcome of his free will, or at most of his lack of education rather than of his original physio-psychical constitution. But, in the first place, even public opinion, when not prejudiced in favour of the so-called consequences of irresponsibility, recognises in many familiar and everyday cases that there are criminals who, without being mad, are still not as ordinary men; and the reporters call them 'human tigers', 'brutes', and the like. And in the second place, the scientific proofs of these hereditary tendencies to crime, even apart from the clinical forms of mental alienations, are now so numerous that it is useless to insist upon them further.[29]

Although ostensibly writing about matters of scientific fact, Ferri describes a nightmarish world in which, moving among us, are creatures which look human but are 'not as ordinary men'. (In fact, his rhetoric is similar to that of De Quincey's ghost-obsessed brother William, who warned his siblings that 'sham men' – beings who appear to be human, but were actually the ghosts of 'people who had been dead for centuries' – were 'distributed extensively among the human race, and meditating treason against us all'.[30]) These mock-human monsters are apparently 'born criminal', driven instinctively to acts of violence and crime, and yet, Ferri insists, they perform such actions 'without being mad': their criminal compulsions arise not from the derangement of brains which, though malfunctioning, are basically similar to those of ordinary people, still less from outward circumstances such as 'lack of education', but as natural outgrowths of their completely alien 'physio-psychical constitution'. To these moral mutants, criminal violence presumably comes as naturally as sociability and affection do to the true humans upon whom they prey; yet their mask of humanity is sufficiently convincing that they can mingle among us and even interbreed with us, spawning new generations of 'brutes' whose 'hereditary tendencies to crime' will continue to spread chaos and mayhem through society for years to come. A whole history of Gothic fiction, with its doppelgängers, monstrous and motiveless villains, inherited curses, and demons in human form, lies behind Ferri's rhetoric; and so too, perhaps, does the memory of those original 'human tigers', the revolutionary terrorists of 1792–4, the description of whom as 'tigers' or 'tygers' was so commonplace that it was employed by writers as diverse as Blake, Burke, Cobbett, Wordsworth, Dickens, and the journalists of *The Times*. It is thus hardly surprising that the proto-Fascist eugenicist imperialism of the late nineteenth century, although notionally scientific, was so readily and so frequently combined with psychical research, spiritualism, and the race-based mysticism of the theosophists; for eugenicists and occultists alike essentially understood the world in terms of Gothic fantasy, filled with monsters and magical thinking.[31]

This is a relatively extreme example; but the same general tendency to describe the world in Gothic terms can be seen in the works of many nineteenth-century writers. As might be expected, such rhetoric was employed when writing on literally infernal subjects: thus Victorian teachings on hell were often much more Gothic and grotesque than those of the eighteenth century, dwelling upon the tortures inflicted upon the damned in sadistic detail not dissimilar to that used by Lewis and his successors in fiction.[32] But such language was also extensively used to describe secular subjects. Thus, Josephine McDonagh has drawn attention to the extraordinarily Gothic language in which the early-nineteenth-century debate over population, infanticide, and child mortality was conducted; one editorial of 1838 described factories as 'the dungeon of the remorseless Devil King', manned by 'a squalid race of living skeletons' who inhabited 'dens of misery', while in *The Political Preacher* (1839) Joseph Stephens referred to the new children's cemeteries as 'the garden of the ghosts of our little ones scientifically slaughtered by the high priests of Moloch, the blood-thirsty monster, whom they would impiously install in the holy seat of the eternal'.[33] Gary Kelly has demonstrated that a similarly Gothic rhetoric was employed in the same decades by writers on crime, prisons, and the popular press, and the writings he quotes, like those cited by McDonagh, are littered with tropes and clichés derived from Gothic romance: the 'gloomy strength and dark intricacy' of a prison, the 'trembling horror' of an execution, and radical authors who are described as 'the demons of hell', to be fought not with 'prosecutions and dungeons', but 'the sword of truth'.[34] Wheeler has pointed out that the comparison of industrial cities to hell was a nineteenth-century commonplace, and in *London Labour and the London Poor* Henry Mayhew provided his readers with a taxonomy of the contemporary criminal classes which amounted to a virtual bestiary or demonology, warning them of the 'Dead Lurkers', 'Skinners', 'Sawney Hunters', and other tribes of modern monsters who hid among them; the Sawney Hunters probably deriving their name from Sawney Beane, the legendary cannibalistic serial killer whose exploits appeared in contemporary Penny Blood fiction.[35] In *Images of Fear*, Martin Tropp argues that Victorian authors wrote about their world in such Gothic terms because no other language could adequately convey its cruelty and darkness:

> By the middle of the nineteenth century, a growing number of writers tried to throw light upon the dark corners of the contemporary world. And the language of realism was simply inadequate to describe what those explorers saw. Meaning came by reading the world with the tools of the tale of terror. In the Gothic universe already existed places and creatures, mythologies and emotions, equal to the task. Given a new focus, that apparatus made the Victorian tale of terror immediate and inescapable.[36]

Tropp's explanation, however, raises further questions. Were these intrepid Victorians, attempting to 'throw light upon the dark corners of the contemporary world', the first generation to discover things lurking in those corners which 'the language of realism' was 'simply inadequate to describe'? The stories Tropp recounts, of men eaten alive by rats, feral hogs living in the sewers under Highgate, London's soil filled to bursting with half-buried human corpses, and prisons modelled on Gothic castles and filled with mad, silent inmates forced to wear masks or veils, paint a picture of Victorian Britain as a kind of Gothic hell-scape; and, if we may judge by the way in which the period tends to be depicted in film and television, it is as such a hell-scape that it has generally come to be remembered in the popular imagination.[37] As Killeen remarks, 'the Victorian Age itself is, to the general public, a Gothic one'.[38] But were the slums, sewers, prisons, and factories of the nineteenth century truly so much more dreadful than those of the century before? By about 1850, mainland Britain was much richer and better-organised than it had been in Paine's day, let alone in Pope's; crime and murder rates had fallen, famine was unknown, and the working poor could afford small luxuries such as tea and sugar, whereas in the eighteenth century they had subsisted almost entirely on coarse bread and small beer.[39] Why, then, should the writers of the nineteenth century, unlike those of the eighteenth, have found 'the language of realism' to be 'simply inadequate' to describe their world? In some cases, the horrors with which they were confronted may have been genuinely worse, or at least more disturbing, than anything before them: one might debate whether the 'separate system' and 'silent system' used in Victorian prisons were better or worse than the chaotic squalor of eighteenth-century gaols, where prisoners simply languished in filth, but their silent, masked inmates must certainly have seemed more uncanny than the raucous prison mobs of old Newgate.[40] The Gothic revival architecture which flourished in Victorian Britain must also have encouraged writers to draw parallels between Gothic fiction and the contemporary realities of life in nineteenth-century cities and institutions, built as they were in extravagantly neo-Gothic styles, like so many Victorian Otrantos.[41] Fundamentally, however, I believe that Tropp's account mistakes cause for effect. Victorian Britain was not written about in Gothic terms because it was a nest of unprecedented Gothic horrors; rather, it has come to be remembered as such a nest of horrors because it was written about, at the time, in Gothic terms. Just as it had done when applied to the French Revolution, such rhetoric served to inflate and heighten its subjects, and did so with such powerful and lasting effectiveness that Victorian Britain, like revolutionary France, has tended to be remembered, imagined, and depicted ever since as a landscape out of Gothic romance, full of demonic evil, inhuman cruelty, and suffering, persecuted innocence.[42]

As I have discussed, by about 1830 the Gothic rhetoric developed in the 1790s had been naturalised, absorbed into the language to such an extent that it had become one of the standard way of writing in English about evil, violence, and fear. The establishment of this new rhetoric can be seen clearly in the 'Newgate novels' of the 1830s, with their focus on violence and crime, of which the most notable were Bulwer-Lytton's *Paul Clifford* (1830) and *Eugene Aram* (1832), Ainsworth's *Rookwood* (1834) and *Jack Sheppard* (1839), and Dickens's *Oliver Twist* (1838). These novels were in many ways the successors of the Gothic romances of the previous generation, and the continuities between the two genres are not hard to trace. Ainsworth, who began his career as an author of Gothic magazine fiction, stated explicitly that he planned *Rookwood* as 'a story in the bygone style of Mrs Radcliffe', while after the success of his early crime novels Bulwer-Lytton went on to write more traditionally Gothic works such as *The Last Days of Pompeii* (1834) and *Zanoni* (1842), full of historical settings, immortal Rosicrucians, sinister conspirators, and hidden catacombs.[43] Like the Gothic romances upon which they drew, these 'Newgate novels' gave rise to a derivative street literature of chapbook crime stories and melodramas aimed at popular audiences; and this street literature, like the cheap Gothic literature which had preceded it, gave rise in turn to a moral panic over its supposedly 'depraved character', and its potentially corrupting effects upon the minds of the lower orders.[44] The problem with the Newgate novels, according to their critics, was that they presented crime in too exiting, interesting, and sympathetic a fashion, so that their readers were encouraged to emulate rather than shun the criminal behaviour of their protagonists: thus, in its review of *Jack Sheppard*, the *Athenaeum* complained that in Ainsworth's novel 'an attempt is made to invest Sheppard with good qualities, which are incompatible with his character and position'.[45] In 1839, Thackeray singled out Ainsworth and Dickens for criticism on this score, unfavourably contrasting the Newgate novels with the works of Fielding, Hogarth, and Gay, whom he felt had depicted crime without romanticising its perpetrators. As he declared, 'our thieves are nothing more than thieves'; to depict them as anything more was to risk corrupting one's readership.[46]

Thackeray's comparison of Dickens and Ainsworth with Fielding, Gay, and Hogarth – a comparison also made by John Forster in *The Examiner* – is worth some consideration, as it foregrounds the cultural shift which had taken place between these two literatures of crime.[47] In the early eighteenth century, when the men he cites had written and drawn, it had been generally agreed that crime was to be combated through deflating satire, by showing it up as the cruel, mean, selfish, and ultimately self-destructive activity they believed it to be. Rather than a figure to be admired or pitied, the criminal was to be mocked for their folly and wickedness in choosing so dangerous and anti-social a career: as Forster put it, in emphatic italics, *'The vulgarity of vice was the object at which they drove, and not its false pretensions to heroism or its vile cravings for sympathy.'*[48] Gay's Macheath and Peachum, Fielding's Jonathan Wild, and Hogarth's Tom Idle and Tom Nero may be amusing, but they are hardly glamorous, still less heroic; they are, as Thackeray put it, 'nothing more than thieves', and certainly do not possess the 'good qualities, incompatible with [their] character and position', of which the *Athenaeum* complained.[49] 'In the dreadful satire of *Jonathan Wild*', Thackeray wrote, 'no reader is so dull as to make the mistake of admiring, and can overlook the grand and hearty contempt of the author for the character he has described'.[50] But in the century that separated them from Dickens and Ainsworth, the rise of Gothic fiction and drama had led to the creation of a new and very different fictional idiom for writing about violence and crime.

Hogarth and Gay actually appear as characters in Ainsworth's *Jack Sheppard*, in which they visit the hero in prison. In Ainsworth's novel, Sheppard provides Gay and Hogarth with the inspiration for Macheath and Tom Idle, respectively; but he seems scarcely to resemble either Gay's highwayman, with his comic songs and romantic difficulties, or Hogarth's idle apprentice, who drifts into crime simply because it is the path of least resistance. Quite unlike these merry, thoughtless criminals, Ainsworth's Sheppard is a haunted, driven figure, more reminiscent of Radcliffe's heroines, Godwin's Caleb Williams, or Shelley's Victor Frankenstein than of Tom Idle or Macheath; like them, he is constantly persecuted, hunted, and imprisoned by implacable enemies, and repeatedly escapes only to find himself hunted once again. We see almost nothing of his criminal career, which vanishes into the gap in the text between 'Epoch the Second' (which ends with Sheppard becoming a thief) and 'Epoch the Third' (which begins on the day of his last 'professional' robbery), so neither the dangers nor the fruits of his crimes actually appear in the novel; only the interminable nightmare of his pursuit by Jonathan Wild. For, as Ainsworth's Sheppard shrinks down into a Gothic victim, his Jonathan Wild dilates into a Gothic demon, complete with a fortified stronghold in the middle of London packed with corpses, dungeons, hidden rooms, and instruments of torture; at one point, he even casually fishes a severed human head out of the Thames, remarking that 'it'll do for my collection'.[51] A century earlier, Henry Fielding – who attended the execution of the historical Jonathan Wild in 1725 – wrote his novel *Jonathan Wild* to mock the idea that any amount of criminality could make someone a 'Great Man', insisting instead that Wild was prodigious only in his impudence, selfishness, and moral imbecility.[52] But Ainsworth's Wild truly *is* a great man:

> Jonathan Wild, at this time, was on the high-road to the greatness which he subsequently, and not long afterwards, obtained. He was fast rising to an eminence that no one of his nefarious profession ever reached before him, nor it is to be hoped, will ever reach again. He was the Napoleon of knavery, and established an uncontrolled empire over all the practitioners of crime. This was no light conquest; nor was it a government easily maintained. Resolution, severity, subtlety, were required for it; and these were qualities which Jonathan possessed in an extraordinary degree. The danger or difficulty of an exploit never appalled him. What his head conceived his hand executed. [. . .] No wonder that Trenchard, as he gazed at this fearful being, should have some misgivings cross him.[53]

Ainsworth's Jonathan Wild, the 'Napoleon of knavery', prefigures Conan Doyle's 'Napoleon of crime', Professor Moriarty, in assimilating the attributes of the Gothic hero-villain to the figure of the urban criminal mastermind.[54] (Midway between the two, in *The Mystery of Edwin Drood*, Dickens too would write of 'the criminal intellect' as 'a horrible wonder apart', one that is impossible to 'reconcile' with 'the average intellect of average men'.[55]) Like the villains and monsters of Gothic romance – and strikingly *unlike* Fielding's Jonathan Wild, who is remarkable only for his low cunning and lack of scruples – Ainsworth's Wild possesses 'extraordinary' mental and physical abilities, which at times seem to verge on the supernatural. 'This fearful being' is nocturnal, never sleeps, appears inhumanly huge when glimpsed by twilight, and seems to bear a charmed life, which he attributes to the fact that 'the devil never deserts me'; of the three guns fired at his head at point-blank range over the course of the novel, one misses and two misfire, and even having his throat slit doesn't slow him down for long.[56] Small wonder, then, that Sheppard's unhinged mother concludes that 'it *is* the fiend!' when Wild seizes her with 'the roar of a demon', that other characters call him 'fiend' and 'monster', and that even the narrative voice of the novel ultimately refers to him as 'the demon'.[57]

As I have mentioned, several reviewers compared Ainsworth's novel unfavourably with Fielding's, but the difference between them which they chiefly deplored was Ainsworth's obvious sympathy with his criminal protagonists, the thief Jack Sheppard and the murderer Blueskin, rather than the relative degrees of 'greatness' with which they invest their respective Jonathan Wilds.[58] Reynolds protested at Ainsworth making Wild 'a downright assassin', when there was no historical evidence that he ever killed anyone with his own hands, and objected to him 'swelling into fits of passion', which did not coincide with Reynolds' own, purely mercenary, interpretation of Wild's character; Forster, picking up on the novel's supernatural language, noted that Wild was 'meant to be the very demon of shrewd penetration', and mocked the ease with which this supposed prodigy was taken in during the novel by some of Jack Sheppard's tricks.[59] Wild's Gothicised 'greatness', however, seems to have gone largely unremarked, although Thackeray's approving mention of Fielding's 'grand and hearty contempt' for his Wild might be read as implying that he felt Ainsworth had not made him nearly contemptible enough.[60] (Did the reviewer who complained that *Jack Sheppard* was 'calculated to ... serve as the cut-throat's manual, or the midnight assassin's *vade mecum*' remember that *The Midnight Assassin* had been the title of a popular Gothic chapbook a generation before?[61]) This lack of comment on Ainsworth's depiction of Wild, even among his most hostile reviewers, demonstrates the extent to which, by 1839, this had simply become the way in which villains were written about: by stressing their evil, their power, and their 'extraordinary' qualities. The rhetoric of Gothic fiction had been so thoroughly assimilated by mainstream literary culture that the demonic charisma of evildoers, so fiercely contested by Fielding, Johnson, and their contemporaries a century before, had come to be taken for granted.

This contrast between pre- and post-Gothic modes of writing about evil can be seen even more strikingly in *Oliver Twist*, the final chapters of which appeared alongside the first chapters of *Jack Sheppard* in the 1839 issues of *Bentley's Miscellany*.[62] In the defensive preface he wrote for the novel's third edition, Dickens explicitly invoked Hogarth and Fielding as his models, and the tone of *Oliver Twist's* early chapters are, indeed, strongly reminiscent of the satirists of the early eighteenth century:[63]

> Everybody knows the story of another experimental philosopher, who had a great theory about a horse being able to live without eating, and who demonstrated it so well, that he got his own horse down to a straw a day, and would most unquestionably have rendered him a very spirited and rampacious animal upon nothing at all, if he had not died, just four-and-twenty hours before he was to have had his first comfortable bait of air. Unfortunately for the experimental philosophy of the female to whose protecting care Oliver Twist was delivered over, a similar result usually attended the operation of *her* system; for at the very moment when a child had contrived to exist upon the smallest possible portion of the weakest possible food, it did perversely happen in eight and a half cases out of ten, either that it sickened from want and cold, or fell into the fire from neglect, or got half-smothered by accident; in any one of which cases, the miserable little being was

usually summoned into another world, and there gathered to the fathers which it had never known in this.

Occasionally, when there was some more than usually interesting inquest upon a parish child who had been overlooked in turning up a bedstead, or inadvertently scalded to death when there happened to be a washing, (though the latter accident was very scarce, – anything approaching to a washing being of rare occurrence in the farm,) the jury would take it into their heads to ask troublesome questions, or the parishioners would rebelliously affix their signatures to a remonstrance: but these impertinences were speedily checked by the evidence of the surgeon, and the testimony of the beadle; the former of whom had always opened the body, and found nothing inside (which was very probable indeed), and the latter of whom invariably swore whatever the parish wanted, which was very self-devotional. Besides, the board made periodical pilgrimages to the farm, and always sent the beadle the day before, to say they were going. The children were neat and clean to behold, when *they* went; and what more would the people have?[64]

This is bleak and bitter satire, reminiscent of Hogarth or Fielding – and still more strongly of Swift, whose *Modest Proposal*, with its mock-philosophical arguments and agricultural metaphors, surely hovers behind this scene of murderous human 'farming' justified by 'experimental philosophy'. Of the batch of 'twenty or thirty' infants handed over to Mrs Mann, Oliver is, according to Dickens's figures, likely to be one of only three or four survivors; the rest will be starved, frozen, burnt, scalded, or smothered to death, in a continual slow-motion massacre of the innocents carried on with the wilful connivance of the parish authorities. Yet the evil and cruelty of Mann's baby farm is evoked in an understated, matter-of-fact manner, with none of the hyperbolic rhetoric which was the hallmark of the Gothic tradition; indeed, Mrs Mann is pointedly *not* a Gothic witch, ogress, or similar embodiment of ineffable evil, merely a grasping old woman who values her profit margin more than the lives of the children under her care. No prodigy of wickedness is needed to instigate or maintain this parish murder machine, in the way that Jonathan Wild instigates and maintains virtually all the evil in *Jack Sheppard*; the indifference of a handful of parish officials is quite enough. But as the novel moves towards its conclusion, the newer, Gothic notes sound more and more loudly and frequently, reaching an extraordinary crescendo with the murder of Nancy and the death of Sikes. On her way to her fatal meeting on London Bridge – on what is, naturally, 'a very dark night' – Nancy sinks into Gothic delirium, her mind filled with 'horrible thoughts of death, and shrouds with blood upon them, and a fear that made me burn':

'Imagination', said the gentleman, soothing her.

'No imagination', replied the girl in a hoarse voice. 'I'll swear I saw the word "coffin" written in every page of the book in large black letters, – aye, and they carried one close to me, in the streets to-night.'

'There is nothing unusual in that', said the gentleman. 'They have passed me often.'

'*Real ones*', rejoined the girl. 'This was not.'

There was something so uncommon in her manner, that the flesh of the concealed listener crept as he heard the girl utter these words, and the blood chilled within him.[65]

If Oliver in the baby farm is a scene of Swiftean satire, Nancy on London Bridge is a scene from Gothic melodrama, full of portents and terrors. The visionary coffin she has seen carried close to her is, of course, her own, for within a few pages she will be murdered by Sikes, dying in a Gothic tableau of martyred innocence: on her knees, her hands raised in prayer, holding Rose Maylie's handkerchief up towards Heaven as Sikes beats her to death with a club. The special, even unique, awfulness of the murder is emphasised by the narrator:

Of all bad deeds that, under cover of the darkness, had been committed within wide London's bounds since night hung over it, that was the worst. Of all the horrors that rose with an ill scent upon the morning air, that was the foulest and most cruel.[66]

Maddened by the horror of his deed, Sikes is driven to his own destruction, in a pattern made familiar by innumerable Gothic melodramas and romances. He is 'haunted' by Nancy's 'ghastly figure following at his heels':

He could trace its shadow in the gloom, supply the smallest item of the outline, and note how stiff and solemn it seemed to stalk along. He could hear its garments rustling in the leaves, and every breath of wind came laden with that last low cry. If he stopped, it did the same. If he ran, it followed – not running too, that would have been a relief, but like a corpse endowed with the mere machinery of life, and borne upon one slow melancholy wind that never rose or fell.

At times he turned with desperate determination, resolved to beat this phantom off, though it should look him dead; but the hair rose on his head, and his blood stood still; for it had turned with him, and was behind him then. He had kept it before him that morning, but it was behind him now – always. He leant his back against a bank, and felt that it stood above him, visibly out against the cold night-sky. He threw himself upon the road – on his back upon the road. At his head it stood, silent, erect, and still – a living grave-stone, with its epitaph in blood.

Let no man talk of murderers escaping justice, and hint that Providence must sleep. There were twenty score of violent deaths in one long minute of that agony of fear.[67]

We are very far from Fielding and Hogarth, here, in this Gothic dreamscape of vengeful Providence, shadows and spectres, living grave-stones, walking corpses, and messages written in blood. Like Wringham, Falkland, and many other Gothic murderers before him, Sikes has become the victim of a mental persecution even more terrible and relentless than the physical persecution he inflicted upon his victim. Pursued by this inescapable phantom, just as Nancy had been pursued by her own coffin, Sikes is drawn back to London, where he is effectively executed by Nancy's vengeful ghost:

> At that very instant the murderer, looking behind himself on the roof, threw his arms above his head, and uttered a yell of terror.
> 'The eyes again!' he cried, in an unearthly screech.
> Staggering as if struck by lightning, he lost his balance and tumbled over the parapet. The noose was at his neck. It ran up with his weight, tight as a bow-string, and swift as the arrow it speeds. He fell for five-and-thirty feet. There was a sudden jerk, a terrific convulsion of the limbs, and there he hung, with the open knife clenched in his stiffening hand.[68]

It is not just Sikes' screech which is 'unearthly' here, and if he staggers 'as if struck by lightning' it is because that is effectively what has happened; he has been struck down by Heaven for his crimes. Just as he is about to escape justice, the murderer is providentially hanged by the intervention of a ghost; even the phrase 'the noose was at his neck' (as a dog might be at your throat?) suggests a rope somehow instinct with supernatural life. Nancy's ghost, with its terrible eyes, is seen only by the half-mad Sikes, so the scene can just about be claimed as a non-supernatural one, but its structure is the stuff of pure Gothic melodrama; indeed, it is not dissimilar to the finale of *The Castle Spectre*, where the villain's moment of triumph is transformed into his moment of destruction due to the providential intervention of his victim's ghost.

What I wish to draw attention to here is the contrast between these two episodes. Mann and Bumble take the routine, deliberate, industrial-scale starvation of the parish children in their stride, without a twinge of pity or remorse; but when Sikes kills Nancy, his world falls apart. Theirs had been the kind of banal evil satirised by Swift, Hogarth, and Fielding; his is the transcendental evil of Gothic fiction, an act utterly incommensurate with the rest of human life. Nancy's murder is not just another wicked act in a world already filled with wickedness; instead, it is 'of all bad deeds... the worst', and 'of all the horrors... the foulest and most cruel', and as such it calls down the vengeance of Providence and exposes him to the persecution of supernatural powers. 'Let no man talk of murderers evading justice', the narrator declares of Sikes; but while in the extremity of his terror he suffers 'twenty score of violent deaths in one long minute', no such Gothic 'agony of fear' appears to trouble Mann or Bumble, as they complacently arrange the deaths of children by the dozen. In them still survives the older, Enlightenment-era view of evil as something so common and ordinary that it may often go unnoticed, even by its perpetrators, unless our attention is drawn to it by satire; but in Sikes and Nancy, as in *Jack Sheppard*, can be seen the triumph of the newer Gothic rhetoric, in which acts of evil have such metaphysical weight that they transform both victim and perpetrator utterly. For Dickens, as for nineteenth-century literary culture in general, it was this Gothic rhetoric which would come to dominate almost all depictions of human evil and misery, until by the time of *Bleak House* (1853) it no longer seemed strange to describe old men as vampires, detectives as ghosts, curtains as banshees, money-lenders as changelings, or court regalia as demons, even in a novel set in almost-contemporary London and notionally lacking any supernatural content.[69] When a slum in Fleet Ditch, supposed to have contained many secret passages connecting one building to another for criminal purposes, was demolished in 1855, the *Quarterly Review* described its mysteries as 'surpassing those of Udolpho'.[70] The Gothic perspective had become habitual.

III

Gothic is an aesthetic, and, as such, it inevitably aestheticises its subject matter. It turns violence into performance, as Dickens did when he performed Nancy's death-scene as the highlight of his readings from his own works; and, in so doing, it invites its audience to view the act of violence as a work of performance art.[71] It was a tendency within early-nineteenth-century culture to which De Quincey was particularly alert, and on which he wrote at length in his three essays 'On Murder Considered as One of the Fine Arts':

> People begin to see that something more goes to the composition of a fine murder than two blockheads to kill and be killed – a knife – a purse – and a dark lane. Design, gentlemen, grouping, light and shade, poetry, sentiment, are now deemed indispensable to attempts of this nature.[72]

What De Quincey simultaneously enacts and satirises in 'On Murder' is the process through which a real act of violence – such as his chief subject, the Ratcliffe Highway murders of 1811 – is transformed into an artistic 'composition', to be 'treated aesthetically'.[73] His criteria of 'design, [. . .] grouping, light and shade, poetry, [and] sentiment' are derived principally from the visual arts, but were also applicable to contemporary fiction and drama; novels such as *Oliver Twist*, which were written with both illustration and subsequent stage adaptation in mind, included set-piece scenes such as Nancy's murder whose 'composition' made them suitable subjects for pictures in the illustrated editions, and for dramatic tableaux in the stage adaptations. Tellingly, the death of Nancy is littered with details which read like stage directions, or instructions to the illustrator: 'raising herself with difficulty on her knees, [she] drew from her bosom a white handkerchief – Rose Maylie's own – and holding it up in her folded hands as high towards Heaven as her feeble strength would let her, breathed one prayer for mercy to her Maker'.[74] In Nancy's dying gesture can be seen 'design', 'poetry', and 'sentiment', while 'grouping', and 'light and shade' are provided by her juxtaposition with the brutish Sikes, who at this moment is 'staggering backward to the wall, and shutting out the sight with his hand' – more stage directions, surely – allowing the scene to fulfil all De Quincey's criteria for successful 'composition' in murder. This is murder most theatrical; and when the scene was staged in melodrama adaptations, the audience went wild.[75]

This kind of artistic 'composition' was intended to have a moral effect upon its audience, heightening the emotional impact of the scene in order to emphasise the evil and horror of the murder it depicts. However, while the audiences who read, saw, or watched Nancy's death may have been shocked, horrified, or disturbed by it, they must also have found it exciting, stimulating, even enjoyable; if they had not, it is hard to imagine them flocking back to watch Sikes murder Nancy on-stage, night after night. What De Quincey points out in 'On Murder' is the ease with which such scenes can come to be regarded as mere entertainment, appreciated purely for the aesthetic pleasure they generate, without any regard for their intended moral significance:

> Everything in this world has two handles. Murder, for instance, may be laid hold of by its moral handle, (as it generally is in the pulpit, and at the Old Bailey;) and *that*, I confess, is its weak side; or it may also be treated *aesthetically*, as the Germans call it, that is, in relation to good taste.[76]

In the third of his 'On Murder' essays, De Quincey gives a virtuoso demonstration of what murder might look like when 'treated aesthetically', in a long narrative description of three historical cases of multiple murder. In each case, as in the 'Newgate novels' of Dickens and Ainsworth or the famously violent 'penny blood' street literature of the 1840s, the narrator dwells with breathless excitement upon the tense unfolding of each horrible scene, and the hair's-breadth escapes of those who witness them and live to tell the tale; but in De Quincey's narratives no moral lesson is drawn, and we are instead invited to enjoy these scenes as 'compositions', examples of 'murder considered as one of the fine arts'. De Quincey is a skilled storyteller and expertly handles the build-up of narrative tension in each story in order to maximise the excitement and enjoyment of the reader; with the result that, by the essay's end, the reader is in the position of having gained aesthetic pleasure from reading a series of factual accounts of violent death. The essays thus demonstrate the ease with which a real scene of horror, such as the violent murder of the Marr and Williamson families by blade and hammer in December 1811, could be transformed into a source of entertainment, in which aggravating factors such as the youth and innocence of the victims become mere aesthetic adornments:

> A philosophic friend, well-known for his philanthropy and general benignity, suggests that the subject chosen [i.e. the murder victim] ought also to have a family of young children wholly dependent on his exertions, by way of deepening the pathos. And, undoubtedly, this is a judicious caution. Yet I would not insist too keenly on this condition. Severe good taste unquestionably demands it; but still, where the man was otherwise unobjectionable in point of morals and health, I would not look with too curious a jealousy to a restriction which might have the effect of narrowing the artist's sphere.[77]

This, as De Quincey makes clear, is the potential problem with the death of Nancy, and all similarly Gothicised scenes of suffering innocence. Motivated by 'philanthropy and general benignity', one may wish to make a murder scene as heinous as possible, in order to emphasise the wickedness of violent crime; one may thus choose a victim who is young, healthy, innocent, and good, or else one with 'a family of young children wholly dependent on his exertions', in the hope of thus 'deepening the pathos'. But, by doing so, youth, innocence, and human suffering can become trivialised into mere effects, rhetorical embellishments to heighten the contrast of 'light and shade' and improve the 'poetry' and 'sentiment' of the scene. The victim's innocence thus ceases to matter in and of itself, becoming significant only insofar as it improves the aesthetic effect of their violent death; ultimately, the humanity of the victims themselves is erased by such narratives, which transform them into mere elements in a 'composition'. The historical Marr and Williamson families had lives of their own; but in De Quincey's retelling of their deaths they exist only as a string of picturesque victims, each stepping into the narrative only so that they can be thrillingly brutalised by their murderer. As De Quincey's device of an imaginary 'Society of Connoisseurs in Murder' makes clear, it was not necessarily in the author's power to prevent such readings of their work, no matter how much at variance it may have been from their original intentions; such rhetorically heightened scenes of violence were always in danger of being read as a form of sadistic, semi-pornographic spectacle for its own sake by audiences more interested in gory entertainment than the moral messages such scenes were intended to convey. (It may be worth noting in this context that pornography, like popular fiction, appears to have become increasingly violent and sadistic during this period.[78]) Edward Lloyd, who in the 1830s and 1840s was the leading publisher of serial 'penny blood' fiction, insisted that the violent stories he published were meant to teach their readers that 'wild turbulence of vice will bring nothing but evil fruits and deep vexation of spirits', but his critics were not convinced; in their view, the buyers of 'penny bloods' read them only because they contained exciting scenes of combat, torture, murder, and rape, and paid scant heed to the moral lessons which were intended to justify all these sanguinary proceedings.[79]

As I have discussed, Gothic rhetoric serves to magnify its villains, by articulating acts of human evil and criminality in terms of the supernatural and the superhuman. De Quincey's essays, however, draw attention to another potential effect of such rhetoric: the aesthetic appeal it can bestow upon the evildoer. Within any 'composition' of violent death, the murderer must be the chief and most active element; and thus, in De Quincey's retelling of the Ratcliffe Highway murders, the murderer Williams is not just 'the most aristocratic and fastidious of artists', explicitly compared to Aeschylus, Milton, Michelangelo, Wordsworth, Titian, Rubens, and Van Dyke, he is himself a work of art, who goes out 'for a grand compound massacre' wearing 'a long blue frock [coat], of the very finest cloth, and richly lined with silk' and 'black silk stockings and pumps', his hair dyed bright yellow, his teeth tended by 'the first of dentists'.[80] This psychopathic dandy, a portrait of the artist as a young murderer, is marked out by his 'aristocratic' manner and dress as a cultural descendant of the high-born villains of eighteenth-century Gothic, and a forerunner of later gentleman-murderers such as Dracula and Dorian Grey, his 'fastidious' attention to his appearance demonstrating his awareness that he, like the actor portraying the villain in a tragedy, is to form part of a 'composition', a work of performance art. Furthermore, as De Quincey makes clear, Williams is an artist of a very specific kind: he is a composer of tragedies, whose favoured aesthetic is that of the Burkean sublime of terror. Traditionally, fine art and violent crime had been viewed as existing at opposite ends of the spectrum of human activity: art is beautiful while crime is ugly, art exults while crime debases, the artist seeks higher and deeper meanings in the world while the criminal is sunk in mere materialism and brutish appetite, valuing material goods and physical pleasure more than morality or human life. But for Williams, De Quincey's essay insists, violent crime *is* fine art, and what makes his murders artistic is the extent of their horror; it is this that gives them their 'sublimity'. De Quincey writes:

> I could mention some people (I name no names) who have been murdered by other people in a dark lane; and so far all seemed correct enough; but, on looking further into the matter, the public have become aware that the murdered party was himself, at the moment, planning to rob his murderer, at the least, and possibly to murder him, if he had been strong enough. Whenever that is the case, or may be thought to be the case, farewell to all the genuine effects of the art. For the final purpose of murder, considered as a fine art, is precisely the same as that of Tragedy, in Aristotle's account of it, viz. 'to cleanse the heart by means of pity and terror'. Now, terror there may be, but how can there be any pity for one tiger destroyed by another tiger?[81]

Williams makes no such artistic errors in his acts of mass-murder, and if he is a 'tiger', his victims are lambs and sheep. It is his willingness to murder the harmless and innocent which raise his crimes to the level of 'fine art', for they propel him and his actions into the realm of the Gothic sublime, just as the ghastliness of their crimes grant to Dickens's Sikes and Ainsworth's Wild an aura of Gothic horror which, in both novels, is denied to lesser criminals. As De Qunicey makes clear, those ordinary acts of violence which consist only of 'two blockheads to kill and be killed' have no aesthetic appeal. The point of Fielding's *Jonathan Wild* had been that if the common criminal is brutish and base, the 'great' criminal is even more so. De Quincey's essays, however, reverse this proposition: the common criminal is a brute, but the great criminal – the Gothic villain, the terrorist – is an artist, and he and his crimes are (terribly) sublime. The essays aim to satirise such a position, but the murder narratives they contain also demonstrate its rhetorical power, a power which made it increasingly attractive to nineteenth-century writers on evil and crime; for, through the adoption of such rhetoric, even the most squalid acts of cruelty and violence could be charged with the borrowed grandeur of the Burkean sublime of terror. It was a rhetoric which Gothic had made possible; but, by the 1850s, it was increasingly used in fields of writing far beyond the boundaries of the Gothic romance.

IV

De Quincey's 'On Murder' essays were published at wide intervals in time: the first appeared in 1827, the second in 1839, and the third in 1854. It was in the period between the Ratcliffe Highway murders themselves, in 1811, and De Quincey's final account of them, in 1854, that the aesthetic fascination with evil and violence, which De Quincey identified and satirised in these essays, took root in British literary culture; and it was in these same decades, during which the men and women who remembered the events of the 1790s were gradually dying off, that Britain began to renegotiate its relationship with the legacy of the French Revolution. As the revolutionary decade faded into history, known increasingly from books rather than personal experience, literary representations of the period – whether in works of history or works of fiction – became ever-more significant factors in determining how the Revolution was remembered and interpreted, especially by the new generations of readers born after the Bastille's fall. As I have discussed, during the 1790s the meaning of the French Revolution had been hotly contested; but, as the nineteenth century progressed, it was the Gothicised accounts of the Revolution which increasingly won out, as Burgess notes:

> By the time Parliament passed its Reform Act in 1832, the New Whig account of the French Revolution – Burke's account – had triumphed, at least within the field of letters. This version of the story, popularised by Williams, Scott, William Wordsworth, Thomas Carlyle, and Charles Dickens, among others, is heavily weighted toward gothic, with a corresponding alliance between Britain and sentiment.[82]

Several factors contributed to this Gothic 'weighting' of the Revolution in British writing and cultural memory. Most obvious was the patriotic desire to magnify Britain's achievement in winning its generation-long war with France; the more wicked the French were shown to have been, the more glory was due to their conquerors. Furthermore, even when historical writers aimed to be scrupulously fair and accurate, the sources upon which they drew were not necessarily reliable. As Hedva Ben-Israel makes clear in her study of nineteenth-century British histories of the French Revolution, the first generation of post-Waterloo historians were eager to seek out surviving figures from the Revolutionary epoch, and record their memories before they died; and, as a result, they were often led astray by the partial and self-exculpatory accounts these survivors offered, which tended to emphasise the crimes of the defeated revolutionary regime, while throwing the blame for the Revolution's failure onto men who were already safely dead.[83] Robespierre was a favourite scapegoat, as he was already primed for demonisation by decades of anti-Jacobin propaganda in both Britain and France, with the result that, as Ben-Israel remarks, 'The early historians of the Revolution, agreeing on little else, were united in presenting an inhumanly monstrous picture of Robespierre': a picture which won widespread assent and approval in the reactionary political climate of the 1820s and 1830s.[84] Troubled by ongoing political and civil unrest in Britain – the Luddite frame-breakers and Swing rioters in England, the Rebecca riots in Wales, the Ribbonmen in Ireland, the Radical War in Scotland, and ultimately the rise of Chartism – and by the July Revolution in France, the British elite drew comfort from such reassurances that the French Revolution had been a disaster whose only real effect had been to channel power into the hands of bloodthirsty monsters such as Robespierre, and that they were thus entirely right to suppress any movement so disastrously wrong-headed as to attempt to revive any of the revolutionary principles of the 1790s.[85]

As I have argued, this 'inhumanly monstrous picture' of Robespierre and his brief supremacy was not new, having first arisen in the anti-revolutionary literature of the 1790s. But by the 1820s this perspective had ceased to be mere contemporary opinion, appearing in works of polemic or propaganda; it had hardened into accepted historical 'fact', included in serious and scholarly historical works. Thus, stories which had begun as semi-fictional propaganda or quasi-pornographic fantasy, such as the grotesque fate of Princess Lamballe, slid into the historical record, often to rest there unchallenged for generations to come. The same consolidation of this Gothic interpretation of the French Revolution also occurred in contemporary fiction; indeed, in fiction it was much more extreme, for novelists, unlike historians, were under no obligation to tell anything like the whole story of the Revolution's rise and fall, and were free to focus almost exclusively on its most bloody and spectacular incidents. As Grenby comments, by the end of the Napoleonic Wars the fictional iconography of the Revolution had become almost completely fixed, established by decades of anti-revolutionary novelists:

> By the time we reach the next generation of novels describing the early Revolution, Louisa Sydney Stanhope's *The Nun of Santa Maria de Tindaro* of 1818 say, the process is complete. The Revolution is only blood and death, blood and rapine, blood and savagery, something absolutely requiring execration, but never explanation.[86]

In reality, the period of Jacobin supremacy had been only one phase in the Revolution's long and complex history, the policy of terror had been only one of several policies the Jacobins had pursued during their brief period in power, and Robespierre had been only one leading Jacobin politician among many, and not even the most ideologically extreme of them, at that. But as the story of the Revolution was told and retold, it increasingly acquired a kind of mythic simplicity. The Revolution as a whole was identified with the period of Jacobin dominance; that period was identified with its most infamous policy, to the extent that it was simply referred to as 'the Terror'; the Terror was identified with Robespierre, as though he had borne almost sole responsibility for its excesses; and Robespierre was identified with that demonic, inhuman wickedness which, since the 1790s, had been the defining mark of the terrorist. The entire Revolution could thus be condensed into a Gothic fable, complete with a suitably monstrous Gothic villain meting out quantities of extravagant and ultimately inexplicable violence upon his innocent victims, and thus, as Grenby puts it, 'requiring execration, but never explanation'.

When Marie Tussaud opened her famous waxwork exhibition on Baker Street in 1835, its chief attraction, then as now, was its 'Chamber of Horrors'; and, in the Chamber, gory waxwork models of the Terrorists and their victims were given pride of place. (In her 1838 autobiography, Tussaud tells the grisly story of how, as a young woman in revolutionary Paris, she had honed her skills by making wax death-masks of the decapitated heads of famous men and women guillotined during the Terror, on the orders of the revolutionary government.)[87] In its arrangement of exhibits, Tussaud's exhibition functioned as a sort of diagram of the contemporary British cultural psyche. As I have argued, scenes of Gothicised horror were objects of increasing fascination for the writers and artists of the 1830s and 1840s, and at the very heart of this cultural chamber of horrors lay the increasingly distorted memory of the French revolutionary Terror, the original scene of 'terrorism', stripped of its original meanings and complexities and recalled only as what it became in Tussaud's museum: a series of grotesque set-piece spectacles, a Gothic melodrama all the more thrilling because it was understood to have actually happened in real life.

Perhaps the greatest literary monument to the age's fascination with the Terror was Carlyle's epic history, *The French Revolution* (1837). Despite its great length, Carlyle's work did not give anything like universal coverage of the revolutionary period: of the twenty 'books' into which it is divided, thirteen deal with the events of the early Revolution, six with the period from the September Massacres to the death of Robespierre, and only one brief book – little more than an epilogue – to the events which followed the end of the Terror. For Carlyle, as for his contemporaries more generally, the period from 1789 to 1794 *was* the Revolution, with the Terror as its climax – or its 'consummating', as Carlyle put it – and Thermidor as its conclusion; the rest, more or less, was silence.[88] By the time Carlyle came to write his history the Gothic interpretation of the events of 1792–4 was already well established, a fact which he noted and deplored in his discussion of the September Massacres:

> It is unfortunate, though very natural, that the history of this Period has so generally been written in hysterics. Exaggeration abounds, execration, wailing; and, on the whole, darkness. But thus too, when foul old Rome had to be swept from the Earth, and those Northmen, and other horrid sons of Nature, came in, 'swallowing formulas' as the French now do, foul old Rome screamed execratively her loudest; so that the true shape of many things is lost for us. Attila's Huns had arms of such length that they could lift a stone without stooping. Into the body of the poor Tatars execrative Roman History intercalated an alphabetic letter; and so they continue Tartars, of fell Tartarean nature, to this day. Here, in like manner, search as we will in these multiform innumerable French Records, darkness too frequently covers, or sheer distraction bewilders. One finds it difficult to imagine that the Sun shone in this September month, as he does in others. Nevertheless it is an indisputable fact that the Sun did shine...[89]

In this passage Carlyle picks up on the fact that, in the immediate aftermath of the September Massacres, the revolutionaries had been compared in the British press to the 'Goths and Vandals' who sacked Rome.[90] Carlyle suggests here that the revolutionaries may resemble these ancient barbarians not only because they were violent and destructive, but also because, like the Goths, Vandals, Huns, and Tartars, they have been slandered and misrepresented by histories written by defenders of the 'foul old' civilisations which they swept away. As a result, 'the true shape of many things is lost for us': just as the original Gothic invaders of Rome are known only through the distorting representations of Roman writers, which made 'Gothic' a byword for violent barbarism, so too these new Goths, the French revolutionaries, can be seen only through the distortions of anti-revolutionary history, and they have thus, like the Huns and Tartars of the ancient world, come to be remembered more as monsters than as men. Carlyle's remark that 'One finds it difficult to imagine that the Sun shone in this September month' neatly articulates the way in which the September Massacres, like other scenes of revolutionary 'terrorism', were frequently described as interruptions of the normal order of nature and history, as disturbing and as radically unnatural as a month of continuous night. This presentation of revolutionary violence as merely a series of inexplicable aberrations was of little help when it came to actually understanding such events, as Carlyle complained when he described the way in which the Terror had hitherto been written about by historians:

> History, however, in dealing with this Reign of Terror, has had her own difficulties. While the Phenomenon continued in its primary state, as mere 'Horrors of the French Revolution', there was an abundance to be said and shrieked. With and also without profit. Heaven knows, there were terrors and horrors enough: yet that was not all the Phenomenon; nay, more properly, that was not the Phenomenon at all, but rather was the *shadow* of it, the negative part of it.[91]

The problem with earlier histories of the Terror, Carlyle argues, was that they had been content to remain mere horror-shows, obsessed with gory anecdotes but uninterested in the meanings of such violence, except as so many proofs of the self-evident wickedness of the revolutionary project. The result is mere 'shrieked... terrors and horrors', a catalogue of bloody death that seems to lack any meaning, explanation, or purpose; historians have even, he complains, overlooked the essential fact that the Terror was carried out in order to defend France from its enemies, rather than from the simple love of slaughter.[92] Carlyle's response to such 'hysterics' was to draw attention to the wider historical picture, emphasising that while there was much in the bloody history of the French Revolution that was evil, there was also much that was good, much that was unpleasant but necessary, and much that was simply inevitable, given the history of France up to that point: the Revolution as a whole was a 'death-birth', 'streaked with rays as of heaven on one side; girt on the other as with hell-fire!'[93] The Terror was not just an explosion of pointless brutality; it was part of a larger history, in which good and evil, right and wrong, were not so easily disentangled.

As his language in these passages indicates, however, Carlyle's deliberate width of vision and even-handedness of judgement was articulated in his customary ultra-heightened prose style, with the result that his retelling of the revolutionary story, far from being anti-Gothic, was, if anything, even more Gothic and melodramatic than those of many previous historians.[94] Gothic rhetoric is never far away in *The French Revolution;* and, despite his stated scepticism of the 'execration, wailing, and [. . .] darkness' school of revolutionary history, Carlyle is fond of horror stories. He retells the legends of Princess Lamballe, unspeakably mutilated in the streets of Paris, and Mademoiselle de Sombreuil, forced to drink human blood in order to save her father's life; he tells the story of the tannery at Meudon, where the corpses of the guillotined were supposedly skinned and scalped, their skins tanned for leather and their hair used to make wigs; he reports the rumour that, just before his death, Robespierre – whom Carlyle describes as 'a seagreen ghost' – gave orders for 'new Catacombs' to be dug beneath Paris, in preparation for an immense, final massacre of all his remaining rivals.[95] His estimates of the numbers killed in various revolutionary atrocities are low and cautious, deliberately avoiding the exaggerated figures of some anti-revolutionary writers, but he articulates the events themselves in astonishingly Gothic terms. Of the September Massacres, he writes:

> What phantasms, squalid-horrid, shaking their dirk and muff, may dance through the brain of a Marat, in this dizzy pealing of tocsin-miserere and universal frenzy, seek not to guess, O Reader! Nor what the cruel Billaud 'in his short brown coat' was thinking; nor Sergent, nor yet *Agate*-Sergent; nor Panis the confidant of Danton; – nor, in a word, how gloomy Orcus does breed in her gloomy womb, and fashion her monsters and prodigies of Events, which thou seest her visibly bear! Terror is on these streets of Paris; terror and rage, tears and frenzy [. . .] In such tocsin-miserere, and murky bewilderment of Frenzy, are not Murder, Até, and all Furies near at hand? On slight hint – who knows on how slight – may not Murder come, and with *her* snaky-sparkling head, illuminate this murk![96]

Later, he attempts to sum up and define the Revolution as a whole:

> What then is this Thing, called *La Révolution*, which, like an Angel of Death, hangs over France, noyading, fusilading, fighting, gun-boring, tanning human skins? [. . .] It is the Madness that dwells in the hearts of men. In this man it is, and in that man; as a rage or as a terror, it is in all men. Invisible, impalpable; and yet no black Azrael, with wings spread over half a continent, with sword sweeping from sea to sea, could be a truer Reality.[97]

Unlike the anti-revolutionary historians of whom he complains, Carlyle did not view the Revolution's violence as meaningless and purposeless, but he did describe it in terms of supernaturalism, demonism, and insanity, reinforcing the sense of the Revolution and its 'Horrors' as something utterly distinct from the ordinary business of life and history; there is something in it which remains fundamentally inaccessible, something at which we must 'seek not to guess'. The early readers of Carlyle's *French Revolution*, such as Charles Dickens, may have risen from it with a new sense of the Revolution's world-historical significance; but they must surely also have carried away the sense that it had been very largely carried out by monsters, demons, spirits, ghosts, and madmen, rather than by relatively ordinary men and women such as themselves.

To depict the Revolution, as Carlyle does, as a Greek tragedy or a Gothic melodrama, packed with phantasms, monsters, terror, madness, and invisible demons, was inevitably to prioritise the grand drama of the Terror over the rest of the Revolution's history; for if the Revolution was simply 'the Madness that dwells in the hearts of men', then the years 1795–1800 – years which, in France, were not notable for their madness, despite their huge political significance and their appalling harvest of human misery – could hardly form part of the Revolution proper. There was nothing strange or new about Carlyle's emphasis on the Terror, or his use of Gothic tropes in order to describe its horrors; but what is striking about Carlyle's *French Revolution* is the prominence of such a Gothicised account of the Terror in a work whose attitude to the Revolution was not, on the whole, a hostile one by the standards of its day. During the original debates over the French Revolution, its defenders had insisted that the revolutionaries were *not* Gothic monsters, recognising that such rhetoric served to deny any validity to their political claims: if they were madmen or demons, then their demands for justice could be dismissed as mere wickedness or insanity. In *The French Revolution*, however, Carlyle views many of the claims of the revolutionaries as being basically valid – and yet describes them as demons and madmen anyway. It is as though, by the late 1830s, this Gothic, Terror-obsessed reading of the Revolution had become virtually the only possible historical perspective on the 1790s, almost regardless of one's degree of sympathy for the revolutionaries or scepticism regarding the existing historiography of the Revolution.

Carlyle's *French Revolution* was an influential and widely read work in its day, and doubtless contributed to the ongoing consolidation of the Gothic mythology of the French Revolution, a consolidation to which the mid-nineteenth-century vogue for fiction set during the Reign of Terror also contributed: works such as Washington Irving's 'The Adventure of the German Student' (1824), Georg Büchner's *Danton's Death* (1835), and Alexandre Dumas' 'The Slap of Charlotte Corday' (1849) and 'The Woman with the Velvet Necklace' (1851). In Britain, however, this mythology was given its final, definitive shape not by Carlyle's history but by a later work which was, in some degree, derived from it: Charles Dickens' *A Tale of Two Cities* (1859). Carlyle's *French Revolution* was Dickens' major historical source for the novel, and its influence is visible throughout the *Tale*, especially in Dickens' basic understanding of the Revolution as ghastly but probably inevitable.[98] But the readership it attained dwarfed that of Carlyle's history; indeed, as the bestselling novel written by the century's bestselling novelist, the *Tale* probably did more to shape the memory of the French Revolution in the English-speaking world than the works of any historian, or indeed of all historians put together, for generations to come.[99] (That Dickens' most popular novel, and the one that he hoped would be 'the best story I have written', should be a story of the Reign of Terror is another sign of the central place which the memory of 1792–4 continued to hold in the British cultural psyche.[100]) It was thus a matter of some significance that Dickens, following Carlyle and many earlier writers, chose to depict the French revolutionaries as demonic, nightmarish figures, escapees from some Gothic horror-poem of the Romantic period:

> There could not be fewer than five hundred people, and they were dancing like five thousand demons. [. . .] At first, they were a mere storm of coarse red caps and coarse woollen rags; but, as they filled the place, and stopped to dance around Lucie, some ghastly apparition of a dance-figure gone raving mad arose among them. [. . .] No fight could have been half so terrible as this dance. It was so emphatically a fallen sport – a something, once innocent, delivered over to all devilry – a healthy pastime changed into a means of angering the blood, bewildering the senses, and steeling the heart. Such grace as was visible in it, made it the uglier, showing how warped and perverted all things good by nature were become. The maidenly bosom bared to this, the pretty almost-child's head thus distracted, the delicate foot mincing in this slough of blood and dirt, were types of the disjointed time.[101]

Here are demons indeed; for, like demons, they are 'fallen' and 'terrible', and having been themselves 'warped and perverted' they now devote themselves to warping and perverting the 'innocent' through their 'devilry'. They, like their dance, are 'ghastly apparition[s]...gone raving mad': insane spirits who, at first, do not even seem human – just a mass of revolutionary emblems, 'a mere storm of coarse red caps and coarse woollen rags', apparently thrown into animation more by angry ghosts than by human bodies. The bodies they do have seem, like the time, to have been 'disjointed', for they appear as mere fragments: here a 'maidenly bosom', there a 'delicate foot', all scattered amidst a 'slough of blood' like body parts after a massacre in one of Gillray's horrific revolution-era prints. An entire Gothic plot of innocence seduced to sin by wicked and subversive demons is embedded in the rhetoric of these lines, in which are crystallised seventy years of Gothic revolutionary mythology: the Revolution's madness, its supernatural demonism, and its terrifying and 'bewildering' effect upon those who are compelled to witness it.

Other passages in the *Tale* reinforce the basic message of such rhetoric: that revolutionary France is Hell, and the revolutionaries are devils. Thus a disassembled guillotine is described as 'a toy-puzzle for a young Devil', and the guillotine itself becomes a sort of anti-Christian Mark of the Beast:

> It superseded the Cross. Models of it were worn on breasts from which the Cross was discarded, and it was bowed down to and believed in where the Cross was denied.[102]

Under the Satanic dispensation of this revolutionary Antichrist, something strange seems to happen to time. Perhaps with Carlyle's remark that the sun still shone during the September Massacres in mind, Dickens writes that, during the Terror, 'Though days and nights circled as regularly as when time was young [. . .] other count of time there was none. Hold of it was lost in the raging fever of a nation'. We are told that 'it seemed almost in the same breath' that Louis XVI and Marie Antoinette were executed, even though 'eight weary months of imprisoned widowhood' divided her death from his; that 'the time was long, while it flamed by so fast'; that mass executions and the Law of Suspects 'became the established order and nature of appointed things, and seemed to be ancient usage before they were many weeks old':

> Yet the current of time swept by, so strong and deep, and carried the time away so fiercely, that Charles had lain in prison one year and three months when the Doctor was thus steady and confident. So much more wicked and distracted had the Revolution grown in that December month, that the rivers of the South were encumbered with the bodies of the violently drowned by night, and prisoners were shot in lines and squares under the southern wintry sun. Still, the Doctor walked among the terrors...[103]

Something curious is happening, here. Why should the eight months between the deaths of Louis XVI and his queen have seemed to pass 'almost in the same breath'? Surely these seasons of war and unrest must have seemed long to those who actually lived through them. On the other hand, why should the Law of Suspects – which was in force for less than a year – ever have 'seemed to be ancient usage'? In what sense was 'count of time' lost under the highly bureaucratic Jacobin government, which was so preoccupied with time-keeping that it introduced a new calendar in October 1793, and won its wars largely through the superior organisational and administrative abilities of men such as Lazare Carnot?[104] These oddities draw attention to the fact that what is being described here is not the Terror as it actually was, but the Terror as it was represented in early-nineteenth-century novels and histories: as one huge jumble of horror-stories, in which the executions of Louis XVI and Marie Antoinette, the shootings at Lyons, the drownings at Nantes, and the guillotinings carried out by the Revolutionary Tribunals all seem to occur 'almost in the same breath', part of a single paroxysm of violence, 'the raging fever of a nation'. Yet, because of the tendency to write about the Terror as though it *was* the French Revolution, this single moment of violence is paradoxically extended across years, so that it seems at once longer and briefer than the historical Terror: everything happens at once, while simultaneously going on and on and on. As a result, the reader is left with an impression of continual slaughter, as though the September Massacres continued without ceasing all the way to Thermidor.

This vision of the Revolution, as a kind of nightmarish Black Mass celebrated for years on end by a race of demons drunk on human blood, appears most clearly in the scene in which Lucie watches a group of revolutionaries sharpening the weapons of the mob during the September Massacres. They are described as 'wildest savages', 'barbarous', 'horrible and cruel', 'beastly', 'hideous', and 'devilish':

> As these ruffians turned and turned, their matted locks now flung forward over their eyes, now flung backward over their necks, some women held wine to their mouths that they might drink; and what with dropping blood, and what with dropping wine, and what with the stream of sparks struck out of the stone, all their wicked atmosphere seemed gore and fire. The eye could not detect one creature in the group free from the smear of blood.

These revolutionary monsters are not even human, just blood-soaked 'creatures' so addicted to violence that, it is implied, blood and wine have for them become almost interchangeable beverages. They seem to radiate horror and corruption, so that the very 'atmosphere' around them becomes 'wicked': where they go, the world warps into a hell of 'gore and fire'. They have blood on their bodies, their clothes, their weapons, and their 'spoils'; even the 'ligatures' which tie their weapons to their arms are soaked in blood, a horrible detail which implies that their slaughters have left them almost elbow-deep in human gore. Above all, they have blood in their 'frenzied' eyes: 'eyes which', we are told, 'any unbrutalised beholder would have given twenty years of life, to petrify with a well-directed gun'.[105]

This last rhetorical move, which concludes a long paragraph of horror and execration, is of crucial significance, for it recapitulates in miniature the entire drift of such Gothicised anti-revolutionary rhetoric: first the revolutionary is demonised and dehumanised, and then the reader is invited to desire his violent destruction. The claim being made here is not just that we may have to destroy such 'creatures', as their mad blood-lust means we must either kill or be killed if they come upon us; it is that we should *want* to destroy them, that the desire to exterminate such 'ruffians' is a healthy and virtuous urge, natural to any 'unbrutalised beholder'. The measure of the beholder's humanity, the proof that he is not as brutal or 'beastly' as these revolutionary 'savages', is not the extent to which he is able, unlike them, to *refrain* from violence, but the extent to which he is driven to acts of retributive violence against them. In these lines, the reader is invited to indulge in fantasies of revenge against these revolutionary devils, just as Carlyle invites his readers to fantasise about defending Princess Lamballe with 'some Sword Balmung or Thor's Hammer' in *The French Revolution*.[106] It was, of course, the 'well-directed gun[s]' of Britain and her allies which would ultimately bring down the French revolutionary state established in 1792 by 'ruffians' like these; but the incongruously medieval weaponry imagined by Carlyle, like the popularity of Walter Scott's war-poetry among soldiers serving under Wellington, points to the ways in which this counter-revolutionary war was persistently articulated, both at the time and subsequently, in terms of Gothic romance, as a chivalric crusade against the forces of evil. What better weapon than a magic sword to take into battle against an army of demons?

For this was the legacy of all anti-revolutionary Gothicism, and of the invention of terrorism: the creation of a political rhetoric which permitted the dehumanisation of one's enemies, and thus the legitimation of violence against them as natural, desirable, heroic, and glorious. The writers of the Enlightenment had been immensely sceptical about the value of war and violence; but this Gothic rhetoric reached back to the early modern period, drawing upon the language of chivalry, demonology, and holy war which Addison and his contemporaries had tried so hard to suppress a century before. For Swift, the idea of a good or just war had been laughable; but Dickens and his contemporaries, like the men who fought in the religious wars of the seventeenth century, had been persuaded by the experience of the French Revolution and its aftermath that there were some evils so great as to make their extermination a matter of moral necessity.

As Brantlinger notes, Dickens wrote *A Tale of Two Cities* at a time when Britain was much preoccupied with a more recent revolution: the Indian Rebellion of 1857. When rebellion forces under Nana Sahib massacred the British inhabitants of Cawnpore, popular opinion in Britain demanded retribution, a demand that would ultimately result in the deaths of tens of thousands of Indians in the indiscriminate reprisals carried out by British forces during the rebellion and its aftermath.[107] Brantlinger points out that the Cawnpore massacre was persistently compared in the British press to the September Massacres, and suggests that the *Tale* may, at least to some extent, have been an 'Indian Mutiny' novel.[108] It is certainly true that Dickens' fantasy of murderous revenge against the revolutionaries echoes the extraordinarily violent language with which he, like many others, called for vengeance against the Indian rebels after news of the Cawnpore massacre reached Britain:

I wish I were Commander in Chief in India, The first thing I would do to strike that Oriental race with amazement (not in the least regarding them as if they lived in the Strand, London, or at Camden Town), should be to proclaim to them, in their language, that I considered my holding that appointment by the leave of God, to mean that I should do my utmost to exterminate the Race upon whom the stain of the late cruelties rested; and that I begged them to do me the favour to observe that I was there for that purpose and no other, and was now proceeding, with all convenient dispatch and merciful swiftness of execution, to blot it out of mankind and raze it off the face of the earth.[109]

As both Brantlinger and Druce note, the Indian Rebellion, like the French Revolution before it, was a popular subject for novels and melodramas, which almost invariably described it in highly Gothic, quasi-pornographic terms; the fate of British women captured by the Indians was a subject of particular interest for these writers, just as the anti-revolutionary propaganda of the 1790s had dwelt upon the fate of noblewomen who fell into the hands of the plebeian revolutionaries. Like the Revolution, the Rebellion was widely explained as the result of an evil conspiracy among the Indians, rather than as the expression of any kind of legitimate political grievance; and just as the whole history of the Revolution was assimilated to the most spectacular events of the Terror, so the whole history of the Rebellion was assimilated to the massacres at Cawnpore, which – like the September Massacres to which it was compared – were asserted to be acts of evil so great as to be unspeakable: what De Quincey called 'inexpressible terrors', 'things not utterable in human language or to human ears'.[110] In all of these respects, the French Revolution – or rather, that Gothicised narrative which, by the 1850s, had become the standard historical account of the French Revolution – provided the template through which the events of the Rebellion could be understood, or rather *not* understood; for if the rebellion was simply rape and massacre orchestrated by utterly wicked cabals of conspirators, a string of atrocities that could not even be spoken, let alone comprehended, then the proper response was not to attempt to understand the rebels, but merely 'to exterminate the Race' like the demonic monsters they so evidently were. The scale of British reprisals in India dwarfed that of the Cawnpore massacre they were intended to avenge; indeed, they probably claimed more victims than the entire French revolutionary Terror of 1792–4.[111] Yet, in Britain, the war was overwhelmingly viewed as just and glorious; and the aged De Quincey, who decades earlier had celebrated the defeat of Napoleon and his army of ghosts, now praised Britain's triumph over this latest race of Gothic monsters.[112]

Throughout this chapter, I have attempted to demonstrate the pervasiveness of Gothic rhetoric in nineteenth-century British culture; the ways in which this rhetoric of evil, initially developed as a response to the French revolutionary Terror, subsequently provided a model for writing about violence and wickedness in a variety of forms, from urban criminality to colonial rebellion. The use of this Gothic rhetoric, and the conceptual vocabulary which went with it, became so widespread and habitual that it has come to colour the era itself, at least in popular historical memory; and if the Victorian age is now frequently depicted as an age of Gothic darkness, it is largely because its writers wrote about their world so frequently in such Gothic terms. As I have indicated throughout, I believe that the use of this Gothic idiom has had serious political and historical consequences. The writers of the Enlightenment discouraged belief in monsters, magic, and inexplicable, seemingly supernatural wickedness, not just because they viewed such beliefs as being factually incorrect, but because they saw them as freighted with negative consequences for society: believers in Gothic superstition, they argued, were fatally easy to manipulate into the kind of unlimited, ideologically motivated violence which had blighted the seventeenth century. The nineteenth century did not witness a resurgence of a literal belief in witches; but it *did* see the return of basically supernatural modes of understanding and articulating human evil, and those modes *were* frequently used in order to legitimate the political repression or physical destruction of those to whom they were applied.

Clearly, the naturalisation of Gothic rhetoric had other consequences as well, many of them much less morally problematic. As the radical Gothic novels of the 1790s demonstrated, this rhetoric was adopted by both parties; and if it provided a rhetorical methodology for the demonisation of social others and outsiders, it also provided those same outsiders with a language through which to articulate their experiences of a world which insisted on treating them like monsters. But the fact remains that, compared to the resolutely un-Gothic century which preceded it, the Victorian era was notable for the rhetorical intensity with which it expressed its fear and hatred of those who defied its norms: criminals, social 'deviants', 'fallen women', and non-whites who refused to allow themselves to be colonised and controlled. Eighteenth-century writers were often contemptuous of disobedient women and non-whites; but, if their rhetoric is anything to go by, many nineteenth-century writers appear to have actually *hated* them, and longed for their violent obliteration. It is very hard to imagine Fielding, Richardson, or Defoe writing about the enemies of England, or indeed about anyone at all, in terms like those used by Dickens about the Indian Rebellion.

Obviously, Gothic fiction did not make the British army butcher the inhabitants of Delhi in 1858, any more than it made them slaughter the people of Wexford sixty years before. But I would argue that the habits of mind inculcated by such fictions, and especially by their application to real political events, made such massacres *easier;* easier to propose, easier to approve of, perhaps even easier to actually carry out. Just as the mass violence of the seventeenth century was facilitated by the identification of its targets with the literal demons of Christian tradition, so the mass violence of the nineteenth century was facilitated by their identification with the metaphorical demons of Gothic fiction. I have argued that Gothic terror fiction arose initially as a way of writing about those forms of evil and violence which seemed to defy all comprehension. But when Gothic ceases to be the language of the violated, attempting to articulate what has happened to them, and becomes instead the language of the violent, articulating what they're going to do about it, then its insistence on the incomprehensibility of violence can all too easily become an excuse for further bouts of bloodshed, just as the supposedly unspeakable nature of the massacre at Cawnpore was used to legitimate the mass reprisals at Delhi and elsewhere. If evil cannot be comprehended, there is no point in trying to understand it: we just need to kill it. Such rhetoric makes for good horror fiction; but the ugly and bloody history of the Indian Rebellion, and many similar police and military actions carried out over the course of the nineteenth century, demonstrates how dangerous it could become when applied to real life.

Notes

1   Thomas De Quincey, *Works*, ed. Grevel Lindop (London: Pickering and Chatto, 2000–3), vol. 19, p. 27.

2   J.M. Thompson, *Napoleon Bonaparte* (Oxford: Basil Blackwell, 1988), p. 403. Napoleon's body was returned to France for a state funeral in 1840.

3   Robert Miles, 'The 1790s: The effulgence of the Gothic', in Hogle, ed., *Companion*, and Leslie Fiedler, *Love and Death in the American Novel*, revised edition (Harmondsworth: Penguin, 1984), p. 42. See also Franco Moretti, *Graphs, Maps, Trees* (London: Verso, 2005), p. 15.

4   Robert Mayo, 'How long was Gothic fiction in vogue?', *Modern Language Notes*, vol. 58, number 1 (1943).

5   On magazine fiction, see Robert Morrison and Chris Baldick, eds., *Tales of Terror from Blackwoods Magazine* (Oxford: Oxford UP, 1995). On the popular Gothic melodramas of the 1820s and 1830s, and the career of T.P. Cooke, who played Frankenstein's monster, Ruthven the vampire, and the demon Zamiel on the 1820s London stage, see Maurice Disher, *Blood and Thunder* (London: Muller, 1949), pp. 91–100, and Jane Moody, *Illegitimate Theatre in London* (Cambridge: Cambridge UP, 2000), pp. 93–5, 133–4. The migration of Gothic fiction from novels to magazines after 1820 is vividly tabulated in Potter, p. 96.

6   Percy Shelley, *Defence of Poetry*, in John Shawcross, ed., *Literary and Philosophical Criticism* (London: Humphrey Milford, 1909), p. 123.

7   Coleman Parsons, *Witchcraft and Demonology in Scott's Fiction* (Edinburgh: Oliver and Boyd, 1964), pp. 44–57; James Watt, *Contesting the Gothic* (Cambridge: Cambridge UP, 1999), pp. 132–4.

8   Walter Scott, *Selected Poems*, ed. Thomas Crawford (Oxford: Clarendon, 1972), p. 188.

9   Walter Scott, 'General Preface to the 1829 Edition', in Andrew Hook, ed., *Waverley* (Harmondsworth: Penguin, 1972), p. 522.

10 Scott, *Waverley*, p. 540.

11 James Kerr, *Fiction Against History* (Cambridge: Cambridge UP, 1989), p. 5, Walter Scott, *Lives of the Novelists* (London: Dent, 1910), p. 198. See also Scott, *Waverley*, pp. 33–6, for Scott's own account of the differences between his form of historical fiction and the Gothic romance tradition.

12 Michael Gamer, *Romanticism and the Gothic* (Cambridge: Cambridge UP, 2000), pp. 165–72; Simon Bainbridge, *British Poetry and the Revolutionary and Napoleonic Wars* (Oxford: Oxford UP, 2003), p. 127.

13 Ian Duncan, *Modern Romance and Transformations of the Novel* (Cambridge: Cambridge UP, 1992), p. 13; James Watt, pp. 153–4. On Scott's role in bringing 'a new masculinity' to the novel, preventing it from 'becoming the preserve of the woman writer and the woman reader', see Andrew Hook, 'Introduction', in Scott, *Waverley*, p. 10.

14 On Scott's endless retelling of this story, see Duncan, p. 135. On Scott's supplanting of the Gothic, see Mayo, p. 64, and Moretti, p. 15.

15 Sheridan Le Fanu, *Uncle Silas* (London: Cresset Press, 1947), pp. 236, 401, 27. On *Uncle Silas* as a Radcliffean Gothic novel, see Alison Milbank, *Daughters of the House* (Basingstoke: Macmillan, 1992), chapter 8.

16 James Watt, p. 151.

17 James Watt, pp. 144–5; Bainbridge, p. 139.

18 On British imperialism and the rhetoric of chivalry, see Mark Girouard, *The Return to Camelot* (New Haven: Yale UP, 1981), chapter 14.

19 On Byron and Gothic, see Paul Douglas, 'Byron's life and his biographers', in Drummond Bone, ed., *Cambridge Companion to Byron* (Cambridge: Cambridge UP, 2004), pp. 7–8.

20 Douglas, p. 15, Erik Butler, *Metamorphoses of the Vampire* (New York: Camden House, 2010), pp. 94–5.

21 See Peter Thorslev, *The Byronic Hero* (Minneapolis, MN: University of Minnesota Press, 1962). On Byron's nineteenth-century fame, see Frances Wilson, ed., *Byromania* (Basingstoke: Macmillan, 2000), introduction and chapter 2.

22 George Gordon, Lord Byron, '*Manfred*, Act II, Scene 1', in Jerome McGann, ed., *Complete Poetical Works* (Oxford: Clarendon, 1980–93), vol. 4, p. 68.

23 *Manfred*, Act II, Scene 2, p. 72.

24 *Manfred*, Act I, Scene 1, p. 54; Act II, Scene 1, p. 69.

25 Johnson, *The Rambler*, number 4, in *Major Works*, p. 177..

26 *Don Juan* is in Lord Byron, *Complete Poetical Works*, ed. Jerome McGann, 7 volumes (Oxford: Clarendon, 1980–93),vol. 5, p. 339.

27 On Byron's influence on subsequent vampire fiction, see Tom Holland, 'Undead Byron', in Wilson, chapter 8.

28 On the Gothicism of nineteenth-century racism, see H.L. Malchow, *Gothic Images of Race in Nineteenth-Century Britain* (Stanford, CA: Stanford UP, 1996), and Cannon Schmitt, *Alien Nation* (Philadelphia, PA: University of Pennsylvania Press, 1997).

29 Enrico Ferri, *Criminal Sociology* (1895), cited in Peter Hutchings, *The Criminal Spectre* (London: Routledge, 2001), pp. 184–5.

30 De Quincey, *Works*, vol. 19, pp. 27–8.

31 The theosophist mythology propounded by Blavatsky, which divided history into different epochs ruled over by different races, was particularly influential in this respect. On the crossover between imperialist and occult thought in the 1890s, see Patrick Brantlinger, *Rule of Darkness* (Ithaca, NY: Cornell UP, 1988), pp. 228–30. On late nineteenth-century occultism in general, see James Webb, *The Flight from Reason* (London: Macdonald and Co., 1971).

32 See, for example, Michael Wheeler, *Heaven, Hell, and the Victorians* (Cambridge: Cambridge UP, 1994), pp. 181–2. Compare Philip Almond, *Heaven and Hell in Enlightenment England* (Cambridge: Cambridge UP, 1994), for eighteenth-century views on the same subject.

33 Josephine McDonagh, *Child Murder and British Culture, 1720–1900* (Cambridge: Cambridge UP, 2003), pp. 117–18.

34 Gary Kelly, ed., *Newgate Narratives*, 5 volumes (London: Pickering and Chatto, 2008), pp. xlix–liii, lxvi.

35 Wheeler, pp. 197–203; see also Roy Porter, *London* (London: Hamish Hamilton, 1994), pp. 257–8. The monstrousness of the Dead Lurkers and the rest was enhanced by the fact that Mayhew, like many at the time, asserted that such 'vagabonds' constituted a distinct 'race', one whose brains developed differently from those of ordinary people. See Patrick Brantlinger, *The Reading Lesson* (Bloomington, IN: Indiana UP, 1998), pp. 84–6, and Simon Joyce, *Capital Offences* (Charlottesville, VA: UP of Virginia, 2003), pp. 126–7. On Sawney Beane, see Peter Haining, *The Penny Dreadful* (London: Gollancz, 1975), pp. 25–9.

36 Martin Tropp, *Images of Fear* (Jefferson, MO: McFarland and Co., 1990), p. 82.

37 Tropp, pp, 76–82.

38 Jarlath Killeen, *Gothic Literature 1825–1914* (Cardiff: University of Wales Press, 2009), p. 4.

39   On rising living standards, see Boyd Hilton, *A Mad, Bad, and Dangerous People?*
     (Oxford: Clarendon, 2006), p. 573. On falling crime rates, see Porter, p. 242. On urban
     death rates – which rose between the 1810s and 1840s, but fell both before and after
     this period – see George Rosen, 'Disease, debility, and death', in H.J. Dyos and Michael
     Wolff, eds., *The Victorian City* (London: Routledge and Kegan Paul, 1973), vol. 2,
     pp. 625–67. On famine and food supply in 1790s Britain, see Roger Wells, *Wretched
     Faces* (Gloucester: Sutton, 1988). Ireland, of course, was quite another matter, and
     continued to experience food security crises until the later nineteenth century.

40   On conditions in Newgate during the eighteenth century, see Kelly, *Newgate
     Narratives*, pp. xxxiv–xxxvii. On the 'separate system' and 'silent system', which
     started to be introduced into British prisons in the 1830s, see pp. xxix–xxx, xl–xlix.
     For an example of the extremely matter-of-fact way in which Newgate's horrors were
     written about in the eighteenth century, see Batty Langley, 'An *Accurate* Description
     of Newgate', in Kelly, *Newgate Narratives*, pp. 3–9.

41   On Gothic architecture in Victorian cities, see Nicholas Taylor, 'The awful sublimity
     of the Victorian city', in Dyos and Wolff, eds., vol. 2, pp. 432–4.

42   On Gothic representations of Victorian Britain in contemporary culture, see Killeen,
     pp. 3–6. That Victorian London continues to be regarded as an essentially Gothic
     locale is evident from the titles of recent books on the city such as Lynda Nead's,
     Victorian Babylon (New Haven: Yale UP, 2000), and Francis Sheppard's, *London
     1808-1870: The Infernal Wen* (London: Secker and Warburg, 1971), titles whose
     Gothic tones echo those of such nineteenth-century non-fiction works as James'
     Greenwood's, *The Seven Curses of London* (1869), and W.T. Stead's, 'The Maiden
     Tribute of Modern Babylon' (1885).

43   Keith Hollingsworth, *The Newgate Novel* (Detroit, MI: Wayne State UP, 1963),
     pp. 88–9, 98.

44   On the panic over popular Newgate literature, see Kelly, *Newgate Narratives*,
     pp. lxi–lxxi, Hollingsworth, pp. 14–16, and Joyce, pp. 63–95.

45   *Anthenaeum* 626; cited in William Ainsworth, *Jack Sheppard*, ed. Edward Jacobs and
     Manuela Mourão (Peterborough, ON: Broadview Editions, 2007), p. 504. See also
     Hollingsworth, pp. 106–7.

46   Cited in Joyce, pp. 67–8.

47   *The Examiner*, number 1657; cited in Ainsworth, p. 511.

48   Cited in Ainsworth, p. 511.

49   In his own day, however, Gay was criticised for making a life of crime seem too
     attractive. See Hollingsworth, pp. 9–10.

50   Cited in Hollingsworth, p. 159.

51   Ainsworth, pp. 236–40, 248, 466–7.

52   See, for example, book 3, chapter 5, which is entitled 'More and more GREATNESS,
     unparalleled in history or romance', but describes only a series of low deceptions and
     an attempt by Wild to persuade an innocent man to commit murder. Henry Fielding,
     Jonathan Wild (London: Hamish Hamilton, 1947), pp. 114–19. On Fielding's presence at
     Wild's execution, see Martin Battestin, *Henry Fielding* (London: Routledge, 1989), p. 46.

53   Ainsworth, p. 240.

54   On the Gothic figure of the 'criminal genius' in nineteenth-century literature, see
     Hutchings, chapter 6, and John Cawelti, *Adventure, Mystery, and Romance* (Chicago,
     IL: Chicago UP, 1976), pp. 94–5.

55   Charles Dickens, *The Mystery of Edwin Drood*, ed. David Paroissien (London:
     Penguin, 2003), p. 220. In his note on this passage, Paroissien states that 'in his fiction

and journalism, [Dickens] repeats his belief in a species of criminal who have "no heart" ': a singularly supernatural characteristic. On Dickens' fascination with evil and criminality, see John Beer, *Post-Romantic Consciousness* (Basingstoke: Palgrave Macmillan, 2003), p. 40.

56 Ainsworth, pp. 157, 235–6, 356, 385, 390, 455.

57 Ainsworth, pp. 358–9, 465.

58 Comparisons of the two in contemporary reviews are cited in Ainsworth pp. 500, 505–6, 511, 517, 521.

59 Cited in Ainsworth, pp. 514–15, 520–1.

60 Cited in Hollingsworth, p. 159.

61 Brantlinger, *Reading Lesson*, p. 72. *The Midnight Assassin* is reprinted in Gary Kelly, *Varieties of Female Gothic Volume 2: Street Gothic* (London: Pickering and Chatto, 2002).

62 Introduction, in Charles Dickens, *Oliver Twist*, ed. Kathleen Tillotson (Oxford: Clarendon, 1966), p. xxv.

63 Dickens, *Oliver*, pp. lxi–lxiv.

64 Dickens, *Oliver*, pp. 4–5.

65 Dickens, *Oliver*, p. 312.

66 Dickens, *Oliver*, p. 323.

67 Dickens, *Oliver*, p. 327.

68 Dickens, *Oliver*, p. 347.

69 On the Gothicism of *Bleak House*, see Christopher Hebert, 'The occult in *Bleak House*', in Harold Bloom, ed., *Charles Dickens's Bleak House* (New York: Chelsea House Publishers, 1987), pp. 121–38, Allan Prichard, 'The urban Gothic of *Bleak House*', *Nineteenth-Century Literature*, vol. 45, number 4 (1991), pp. 432–52, Milbank, chapter 3, and Killeen, pp. 16–19.

70 Joyce, p. 102.

71 Philip Collins, *Dickens and Crime*, 3rd ed. (Basingstoke: Macmillan, 1994), pp. 265–72.

72 Thomas De Quincey, *On Murder*, ed. Robert Morrison (Oxford: Oxford UP 2006), p. 10.

73 On De Quincey's aesthetics of violence, see Joel Black, *The Aesthetics of Murder* (Baltimore, MD: Johns Hopkins UP, 1991), chapters 1–3.

74 Dickens, *Oliver*, pp. 322–3.

75 Michael Booth, ed., *Hiss the Villain* (London: Eyre and Spottiswoode, 1964), p. 20.

76 De Quincey, *On Murder*, p. 11.

77 De Quincey, *On Murder*, p. 33.

78 Hilton, p. 626.

79 On Lloyd, see Haining, pp. 30–2, 37, 264–6.

80 De Quincey, *On Murder*, pp. 10, 100, 102.

81 De Quincey, *On Murder*, pp. 31–2.

82 Miranda Burgess, *British Fiction and the Production of Social Order* (Cambridge: Cambridge UP, 2000), p. 135.

83 Hedva Ben-Israel, *English Historians on the French Revolution* (London: Cambridge UP, 1968), pp. 64–5.

84 Ben-Israel, p. 165.

85 Conservative historians may have been even keener to demonise Robespierre due to his adoption as a hero by some contemporary Chartist writers, such as O'Brien. See Gwynne Lewis, 'Robespierre through the Chartist looking-glass', in Colin Haydon and William Doyle, eds., *Robespierre* (Cambridge: Cambridge UP, 1999), pp. 194–211.

86   M.O. Grenby, *The Anti-Jacobin Novel* (Cambridge: Cambridge UP, 2001), p. 43.

87   On Tussaud's significance in perpetuating the memory and iconography of the Terror in Britain, see David Bindman, *The Shadow of the Guillotine* (London: British Museum Publications, 1989), pp. 40–2, 75–6, 147, 212–14.

88   Thomas Carlyle, *The French Revolution*, ed. K.J. Fielding and David Sorensen (Oxford: Oxford UP, 1989), p. 333.

89   Carlyle, vol. 3, pp. 124–5.

90   *The Times*, 10 September 1792, p. 1. See also *Gentleman's Magazine* 43, quoted in Mary Poovey, *The Proper Lady and the Woman Writer* (Chicago, IL: Chicago UP, 1984), p. 16.

91   Carlyle, vol. 3, p. 332.

92   Carlyle, vol. 3, p. 360.

93   Carlyle, vol. 3, p. 124.

94   On the Gothicism of *The French Revolution*, see Chris Baldick, *Frankenstein's Shadow* (Oxford: Clarendon, 1990), chapter 5.

95   Carlyle, vol. 3, pp. 152–3, 376, 405. On Carlyle's depiction of Robespierre, see Mark Cumming, 'Carlyle's seagreen Robespierre', in Haydon and Doyle, pp. 177–93.

96   Carlyle, vol. 3, p. 147.

97   Carlyle, vol. 3, p. 377.

98   Charles Dickens, *A Tale of Two Cities*, ed. Andrew Sanders (Oxford: Oxford UP, 1988), p. viii and Preface.

99   On the *Tale's* popularity, see Paul Schlicke, ed., *Oxford Reader's Companion to Dickens* (Oxford: Oxford UP, 1999), pp. 549, 553–4, and Colin Jones, Josephine McDonagh, and Jon Mee, eds., *Charles Dickens, A Tale of Two Cities and the French Revolution* (Basingstoke: Palgrave Macmillan, 2009), p. 2.

100 Letter to François Régnier, 15 October 1859. Charles Dickens, *Letters*, ed. Graham Storey (Oxford: Clarendon, 1997), vol. 9, p. 132.

101 Dickens, *Tale*, pp. 342–3. On the *Tale's* use of Gothic tropes, despite Dickens's insistence on its realism, see Barton Friedman, *Fabricating History* (Princeton, NJ: Princeton UP, 1988), pp. 158–9, 161–3.

102 Dickens, *Tale*, p. 336.

103 Dickens, *Tale*, pp. 335–7.

104 On Carnot, the 'organiser of victory', see Jean Dhombres and Nicole Dhombres, *Lazare Carnot* (Paris: Fayard, 1997).

105 Dickens, *Tale*, pp. 321–2.

106 Carlyle, vol. 3, p. 152.

107 Brantlinger, *Rule*, p. 208; Schmitt, pp. 76–82.

108 Brantlinger, *Rule*, p. 203.

109 Letter to Miss Burdett Coutts, 4 October 1857. Dickens, *Letters*, ed. Graham Storey and Kathleen Tillotson (Oxford: Clarendon, 1995), vol. 8, p. 459 and n. Storey and Tillotson note that this genocidal fantasy was 'less horrific than those expressed by many British commanders in the field as well as by sectors of the press'.

110 Brantlinger, *Rule*, pp. 205–10; Robert Druce, 'An excursion into porno-Gothic', in Tinkler-Villani, ed., *Exhibited by Candlelight* (Amsterdam: Rodopi, 1995), pp. 238–9; De Quincey, *Works*, vol. 18, pp. 162, 171. On conspiratorial explanations for the rebellion, see Pionke, chapter 4.

111 On British reprisals, see Rosie Llewellyn-Jones, *The Great Uprising in India* (Woodbridge, VA: Boydell Press, 2007), chapter 5.

112 De Quincey, *Works*, vol. 18, pp. 170–1.

Epilogue: The Wars on Terror

On 20 September 2001, in a televised address, President George W. Bush declared to the world: 'Our war on terror begins with al Qaeda, but it does not end there.'[1] The ensuing war certainly did *not* end with al Qaeda, as the people of Iraq have since learned to their cost; but, then, it did not really begin with them, either, for the West has been struggling against one 'terrorist' movement or another ever since the 1790s. The original 'terrorists' were the French Jacobins and their international supporters and sympathisers, but in the nineteenth century the 'terrorist' label was applied to nihilists, anarchists, and nationalists, in the twentieth to Communists and religious fundamentalists, and, in the twenty-first, to Islamists such as al Qaeda.[2] D.C. Rapoport has divided the history of modern terrorism, from the 1860s to the present, into four forty-year 'waves' dominated by anarchist, nationalist, Marxist, and religious terrorism, respectively; but, through all these metamorphoses, the mythology of terrorism has remained remarkably consistent.[3] In every case, it has been asserted that a hidden network of conspirators have concealed themselves within the body of society; that they meet and plan in secret; that, inspired by some radical ideology, they aim for total social transformation; and that their primary tool for achieving it is the sudden deployment of spectacular violence in those times and places where it is least expected. As they possess limited firepower by military standards, these groups cannot change society by direct physical force, so instead they rely on psychological shock to maximise the impact of their attacks. The sudden, violent destruction of a single bus, train, or office block may not inflict meaningful damage on the infrastructure of a developed nation, but it can create a very widespread sense of fear among those who work in office blocks, or travel by bus or train; the fear that such ordinary, routine spaces can suddenly become radically unsafe. Through the multiplication of such actions, such terror networks aim to place their targets under so much pressure that they are ultimately compelled to capitulate to their demands.

I have referred to this as a 'mythology', because in practice it bears only a slight resemblance to the actual history of terrorist violence in Europe and America over the last two hundred years. Despite intense and recurrent fears over the supposed existence of extensive, highly organised terrorist conspiracies, such terrorist violence has so far almost always consisted of fitful, disconnected actions, carried out by either alienated individuals or small, fragmentary groups on the fringes of society.[4] In our own times, 'al Qaeda' has proven almost as phantasmal as the international anarchist conspiracy in Chesterton's *The Man Who Was Thursday*; as Carol Winkler puts it, with some understatement, 'The characterisation [by the Bush administration] of a united global terrorist effort with designs to destroy all free nations exaggerated the conclusions available from US intelligence.'[5] Rather than a global organisation run on quasi-military lines, complete with formal chains of command, since 2002 'al Qaeda' has been little more than a convenient name under which a shifting constellation of different Islamist groups, united by nothing more than a broad ideological sympathy with one another's goals – and sometimes not even that – have been able to operate.[6] As Benjamin Friedman writes:

> Al Quaeda was never a global conspiratorial organisation strategically dispatching well-trained operatives. Even in its late 1990s heyday, al Quaeda was instead a small, vicious group, based in Afghanistan, vying for control of a larger and far-flung collection of jihadist groups and cliques of varying competence and aims [. . .] In its ability to do harm, al Quaeda is more like the anarchist movement in its heyday, transnational troublemakers, than the Nazis.[7]

Lacking such large-scale 'conspiratorial organisation', these clandestine terrorist networks have never posed any serious threat to the ordinary functioning of Western society. As Friedman notes, 'Mass violence has historically been the product of bureaucratic, hierarchical organisations that belong to states or insurgencies that approximate them'; however, 'terrorist groups usually lack these attributes', and they have consequently been historically ineffectual at seriously damaging the states they choose to target.[8] Modern irregular warfare is often described as 'terrorism' by those against whom it is directed, and, when carried out by full-scale guerilla insurgencies backed by sufficient popular support, such warfare is quite capable of bringing down governments and crippling the military forces sent to suppress it. But the more closely any given terrorist group resembles the clandestine, conspiratorial 'enemy within' of terrorist mythology, as opposed to the sort of irregular armies which are sometimes labelled 'terrorists' by their enemies, the less likely they are to pose any kind of credible military or political threat; compared to the violence inflicted in wars, or even by violent crime, the total damage that such terrorist groups have been able to inflict on Western nations over the last two centuries is virtually negligible. Even the most spectacular terrorist successes, such as the assassination of Tsar Alexander II in 1881 or the destruction of the World Trade Centre in 2001, have seldom caused more than localised political and economic disruption; as Maeller points out, their most lasting legacies have usually been the enormous backlashes which they have triggered against those groups and ideologies seen as responsible.[9]

Given the extremely limited scope and effectiveness of such terrorism, why has the myth of the terrorist conspiracy exercised such a continuing hold over our cultural imagination? One obvious answer is that the cultural imagination is precisely what the terrorist seeks to target; the whole point of terrorist violence is its symbolic resonance, and it is thus hardly surprising that the murder of, say, ten people in some symbolic fashion should echo in the memory much more than a hundred victims of ordinary violent crime or wartime 'collateral damage'. Like other forms of deliberately symbolic violence, such as ritual sacrifice and public execution, terrorist violence is, by its very nature, a form of theatre, a spectacular act of public performance art in which none of the blood is fake.[10] But I believe that this persistent tendency to over-rate the capacities of terrorist networks also has a deeper historical source. Ever since the revolutionary panic of the 1790s, the West has been haunted by the fear of a secret 'terrorist' conspiracy hidden among us, and this fear has proven far more durable than any of the actual organisations or ideological movements which have been associated with it. It is emphatically *not* the case that the West has been menaced by a succession of highly organised terrorist conspiracies – Jacobin, anarchist, nihilist, nationalist, communist, Islamist – and survived each in turn; rather, the myth of such a conspiracy has been successively applied to each of these movements, even though the terrorist activities carried out in the name of each have in fact been highly fragmentary and enjoyed extremely limited operational success, only to be reapplied to a new threat each time the previous one fades away.[11] The specific target changes from generation to generation; but the belief that *something* is out there, fanatically devoted to some reprehensible ideology and tirelessly plotting our destruction, has so far proven ineradicable.

Over the course of this book, I have sought to demonstrate that the events of the 1790s – and especially the unprecedented symbolic violence inflicted by the Jacobins on their enemies in 1792–4 – led to new ways of thinking and writing about evil, violence, and fear, among whose symptoms were the rise of popular Gothic fiction and drama, and the discourses of terrorism and conspiracy theory. These genres, all of which were heavily interlinked and at least semi-fictional, gave rise to a whole constellation of narrative tropes: the superhuman villain, the omniscient criminal or conspiratorial mastermind, the incomprehensibility and inexplicability of acts of extreme wickedness, and the existence of concealed worlds of secret evil existing in parallel with our own. In the nineteenth century, these tropes became one of the default ways of thinking and writing about evil, applied not only to world-historical events such as the Terror but also as a way of understanding and articulating criminal and colonial violence; thus the criminal and the rebellious colonial subject, like the Jacobin revolutionary before them, came to be understood as Gothic terrorists, figures at once more and less than human. In the twentieth century these tropes have been deployed still more widely in both fiction and non-fiction media, generating entire new pantheons of modern monsters, from the gangsters and 'Yellow Peril' villains of the 1920s and 1930s to the serial killers and international terrorists of the present day. This modern mythology of evil, which has now pervaded both fictional and non-fictional writings on the subject for over two hundred years, imbues the figure of the villain with a quasi-religious significance which marks it out as what it is: a displaced demon, haunting a supposedly demythologised age. Thus our constant invention of modern demonologies: our persistent over-estimation of the capacities of terrorist networks, intelligence agencies, secret societies, and organised crime, and the consequent investiture of terrorists, spies, conspirators and Mafiosi with an aura of demonic glamour and importance which is seldom warranted by their historical effectiveness.[12] These modern fears are cultural descendants of the actual demonologies of the early modern period, in which Protestants and Catholics viewed Jesuit or heretic conspiracies, respectively, as the literal emissaries of Antichrist; but since the 1790s they have come loose from their moorings, leading to essentially magical or theological interpretations of the nature of evil being reflexively applied to individuals and organisations which are not believed to be literally supernatural in nature. Indeed, such demonologies are often articulated by individuals who profess not to believe in the supernatural at all.

As I have argued, such tendencies result from the naturalisation of Gothic rhetoric: the tropes of Gothic fiction have become so pervasive that real events, such as violent crimes and terrorist attacks, are assimilated almost automatically to plots and tropes derived from Gothic fiction. The huge popular literature on serial killers, for example, like the modern crime fiction in which they play so large a role, almost always depicts these usually confused and damaged individuals as Gothic monsters: it emphasises their extraordinary feats and abilities, and the incomprehensible evil of their crimes, rather than the sad and sordid stories of physical and sexual abuse in childhood leading to compulsive and opportunistic sexual violence in adulthood which generally lie behind such cases in reality.[13] In much contemporary serial killer fiction, such as *Dexter* or *The Silence of the Lambs*, the serial killer is even explicitly framed as superhuman, with capabilities far beyond those of ordinary mortal men. The paradigmatic example of this process of mythologisation is the most famous serial murderer of all, Jack the Ripper, who essentially has no existence *except* as a Gothic modern myth. The historical record tells us only that several gruesome unsolved murders of women took place in 1888, in the always violent slum area of Whitechapel; that they were the work of a single individual, 'Jack the Ripper', remains no more than a plausible hypothesis. Yet an immense amount has been confidently written on this hypothetical late-Victorian monster, including a steady flow of material which has interpreted his crimes in occult or supernatural terms.[14] The serial killer, like the terrorist, is a modern demon, resulting from the interpretation of actual violence in Gothic terms; and it is telling that earlier societies, which generally believed in the literal reality of demons, had no terms for either 'serial murder' or 'terrorism', despite existing in worlds which contained no lack of ideologically motivated violence or murderous insanity.

Nor is this persistence of Gothic rhetoric limited only to discourses concerned with violence and crime: Marxist thought, for example, is shot through with Gothic metaphors of monstrosity, haunting, vampirism, ancestral curses, and relentless persecution. This Gothicism was largely deliberate, for Marx, like Godwin and Wollstonecraft before him, understood society in essentially Gothic terms, as a system which turned men into monsters; a Gothic castle built on fraud and violence, and doomed ultimately to fall, Otranto-like, into ruins once its dreadful origins were brought to light.[15] A similar Gothicism has tended to pervade popular interpretations of Darwinism. Darwin himself, the heir of one of the great intellectual dynasties of the British Enlightenment, viewed evolution by natural selection in basically positive terms, as a progressive force which enriched the world; but the popular understanding of Darwinism, from the heyday of eugenics onwards, has always been of evolution as a brutal monster factory, with each species forever at risk of climbing up or slipping down the evolutionary ladder into a state of Gothic monstrosity.[16] To these two names one might perhaps add that of Freud, who, like Marx, was open about the extent to which his theories drew upon Gothic tropes and fictions; in his case, especially the short stories of Hoffman.[17] In Freudian thought the human mind is understood as a kind of Gothic ruin, beset by ancestral sins and curses, and haunted by emanations of the unspeakable forces lurking in the hidden and imperfectly sealed-off catacombs below. Marx, as I have indicated, used similar metaphors to describe human society; for both, in a narrative cliché beloved of Gothic novelists, the status quo was built upon a concealed act of violent or sexual crime, the proof of which had been thrust down somewhere into the depths of our history or psychology, but which continued to haunt the present in the form of the contradictions, incoherences, and insanities generated by the ongoing consequences of its hidden existence. The great success with which Freudian and Marxist thought have been used in the analysis of Gothic fiction is, perhaps, largely due to the fact that both Freud and Marx consciously wrote within the larger Gothic literary tradition. Just as, in the eighteenth century, the works of Adam Smith, John Locke, Isaac Newton, and Jean-Jacques Rousseau were assimilated to the sentimental novel tradition in order to 'prove' that the natural state of human life was basically orderly, benevolent, and harmonious, so in the nineteenth and twentieth centuries the works of Darwin, Marx, and Freud have been assimilated to the Gothic tradition in order to 'prove' that humanity is inherently haunted, fearful, demon-driven, and forever at risk of lapsing into monstrosity or chaos.

This essentially Gothic understanding of the world has gained ground even as our material circumstances have shifted away from the kind of violence and instability which would seem to provide the most obvious encouragement for such beliefs. The developed nations of the contemporary West constitute what is, by a considerable margin, the most secure, peaceful, orderly, and prosperous civilisation the world has ever seen; yet stories of horror and terror, both fictional and notionally non-fictional, continue to proliferate among us. As Edmundson noted in 1999, news media coverage of high-profile violent crimes tends to be characterised by implicit but powerful Gothic narratives, a tendency which seems if anything to have grown more marked as actual crime and violence have fallen from their mid-century highs: and modern Western fiction is preoccupied with violence, horror, and crime to a far greater extent than the media of most nations in the developing world, despite the exponentially greater exposure of such nations to actual violence and criminality.[18] Indeed, it may well be the case that the lack of such exposure is a basic precondition for the flourishing of such fictions; that, as Burke hypothesised, violence and chaos are mythologised only in those cultural contexts where they have ceased to be routine. Should this be true, then our ongoing cultural entanglement with Gothic fiction may, counter-intuitively, be an index of our cultural progress; but, even if this should be so, it remains a potentially distorting influence. As actual crime has fallen, the fear of crime has risen steadily, with each generation seemingly more convinced than the last that violence and disorder is on the rise; and our distorted sense of the power and significance of terrorists and criminals, which I have argued to be rooted in our Gothicised interpretations of human evil, can have serious legal and political consequences, as the events of the 'war of terror' have made copiously clear.

As Richard Devetak noted some years ago, the 'war on terror' has been an exemplary instance of the application of Gothic narratives to international relations.[19] A number of writers on contemporary terrorism have drawn attention to the way in which the supporters of the 'war on terror' have persistently framed it as a battle against absolute evil, in which the terrorists are depicted as entirely monstrous, their aims and tactics utterly distinct from those of rational political actors.[20] George W. Bush has described

Islamist terrorists as 'an enemy that knows no values', who 'hate freedom' and are opposed to 'all law, all liberty, all morality, all religion', and declared:

> We're not facing a set of grievances that can be soothed and addressed. We're facing a radical ideology with inalterable objectives: to enslave whole nations and intimidate the world. No act of ours invited the rage of the killers – and no concession, bribe, or act of appeasement would change or limit their plans for murder.[21]

The 'killers' described here are utterly outside the normal political domain. We cannot persuade them to pursue a different path, because they have 'inalterable objectives', but those objectives cannot be political in the ordinary sense of the word: if they were, there would be some imaginable 'concession, bribe, or act of appeasement' which would fulfil them, yet we are told instead that their 'rage' cannot be 'soothed', or even 'addressed'. There is literally nothing we can offer these people which will 'change' or 'limit' their desire for 'murder' and destruction: a desire not triggered by any 'act of ours', but apparently arising spontaneously within their monstrous minds. We cannot negotiate with them by offering or threatening things they value, because they 'know no values'. We cannot appease them by passing laws in their favour, because they hate 'all law' and 'all morality'; and, yet, if we were to repeal 'all law' and allow everyone to do as they wish, these madmen would still try to kill us, because they 'hate freedom' as well. Clearly there is no possibility of reasoning, bargaining, or compromising with such monsters, who seem to combine the 'inalterable' obsessions of monomaniacs with the irrationality of schizophrenics and the murderous 'rage' of psychopaths. All we can do is try to destroy them before they destroy us.

Devetak, who describes Bush as a 'gothic storyteller' in the tradition of Edgar Allen Poe, points out that both the battle against al Qaeda and the invasion of Iraq were persistently framed by Bush and his supporters in Gothic terms: as a struggle against monsters, with Saddam Hussein as an evil aristocrat whose nation was figured as a Gothic mansion with basements full of corpses, and Osama bin Laden as a malevolent ghost, unseen and untouchable, haunting unholy caverns in distant lands while magically broadcasting terror and destruction across the world. Such a Gothicised perspective, in which America and its allies march onward as Christian soldiers against an array of foreign devils, has obvious sympathies with the Manichean world view of Bush's own much-publicised evangelical Christianity; yet the 'war on terror' has been very widely described and discussed in similar rhetorical terms, even by individuals who might not be expected to sympathise with such overtly supernaturalist readings of current affairs.[22] Days before the tenth anniversary of the 11 September terrorist attacks, *The Guardian* published an article by the famous atheist polemicist Christopher Hitchens, in which he looked back over the events of the previous decade. On the rise of Islamist terrorism, he wrote:

> Especially over the course of the last 10 years, the word 'martyr' has been utterly degraded by the wolfish image of Mohammed Atta: a cold and loveless zombie – a suicide murderer – who took as many innocents with him as he could manage.

The organisations that find and train men like Atta have since been responsible for unutterable crimes in many countries and societies, from England to Iraq, in their attempt to create a system where the cold and loveless zombie would be the norm, and culture would be dead. They claim that they will win because they love death more than life, and because life-lovers are feeble and corrupt degenerates. Practically every word I have written, since 2001, has been explicitly or implicitly directed at refuting and defeating those hateful, nihilistic propositions, as well as those among us who try to explain them away.

[...]

'Barbarism', wrote Alain Finkielkraut not long ago, 'is not the inheritance of our pre-history. It is the companion that dogs our every step.' In writing, quite a lot, about the examples and lessons of past totalitarianisms, I try not to banish the spectre too much. And how easy it is to recognise the revenant shapes which the old unchanging enemies – racism, leader-worship, superstition – assume when they reappear among us (often bodyguarded by their new apologists).[23]

Hitchens wrote and spoke on many occasions about what he believed to be the mentally and morally degrading effects of belief in supernatural forces; yet his rhetoric, here, is drenched with Gothic supernaturalism. The terrorist is a 'zombie', who, like the infectious zombies in *Night of the Living Dead*, attempts to create a world of zombies, 'where the cold and loveless zombie would be the norm'. Barbarism – which, for Hitchens, is embodied in the figure of the Islamist terrorist – is a 'spectre', which comes to us, like a ghost or vampire, in 'revenant shapes'. The reason he reaches for such language, despite his own well-publicised contempt for supernatural beliefs, is perhaps implicit in what he has to say about terrorist organisations themselves. Their crimes are 'unutterable', beyond language or comprehension: indeed, he is scornful of those 'apologists' who 'try to explain them away', refusing to recognise the 'nihilistic' blankness which, for Hitchens, characterises terrorist violence. Terrorism, it seems, cannot and should not be understood, or even spoken; it is not part of the normal, human order of things, and can thus be articulated only in supernatural terms, as the work of 'zombies' or 'spectres' animated by the 'revenant shape' of 'superstition'. As I have endeavoured to demonstrate, it is not an accident that such discussions of terrorism are so often filled with Gothic rhetoric; it has always been so, ever since the word 'terrorist' first entered the language in 1795. Terrorism and Gothicism created one another, and they have gone hand in hand ever since.

There is a strange appropriateness in the fact that, after his conquest of the Kingdom of Naples, Napoleon awarded the title 'Duke of Otranto' to Joseph Fouché, his formidable Minister of Police.[24] A Jacobin extremist in his day, Fouché had been one of the original 'terrorists' of 1793–4, who had proudly reported that 'salutary terror is now the order of the day here' after carrying out the mass-executions which made him infamous across Europe as 'the Executioner of Lyons'; yet such was his mastery of conspiracy and counter-plot that he weathered every shift of revolutionary and Napoleonic politics, falling from power only in 1816.[25] Literary histories of Gothic fiction have generally viewed it as beginning with a fictional Duke of Otranto, Walpole's Manfred; but it has been my contention that the historical Duke of Otranto, Fouché, and his fellow

Jacobin 'terrorists' were at least as significant a point of origin for the genre, giving to Gothic a new relevance which transformed it from a minor sub-genre of historical fiction to a mass-market literature of terror. If any one man embodied all the different fears of the revolutionary epoch – its fears of secret conspiracy, social disintegration, and unlimited revolutionary violence – then it was surely the revolutionary atheist, Jacobin terrorist, mass-murderer, and Napoleonic spymaster, Joseph Fouché, First Duke of Otranto; and it was in order to articulate the anxieties created by men such as Fouché and his contemporaries that both the genre of Gothic 'terror fiction' and the discourse of political 'terrorism' first came into being. Fouché's biological descendants still hold the title to the Duchy of Otranto; and his historical descendants, the radicals, revolutionaries, spies, conspirators, and ideological extremists who have troubled the history of the last two hundred years, continue to be frequently spoken, written, and thought about in Gothic terms even today. It is my hope that the death of Osama bin Laden – who, with his aristocratic background, love of conspiracy, and commitment to terrorist violence, has truly been a Duke of Otranto for our times – and the apparent waning of the war on terror may mark a turning point away from such Gothicised interpretations of current affairs, at least for now; but Gothic is one of the most repetitive of genres, and its monsters are notorious for never staying dead. Conspiratorial masterminds fake their own demises; evil aristocrats return as ghosts or vampires from beyond the grave. If the evidence of the last two centuries is anything to go by, our wait for a new monster is unlikely to be a long one.

Notes

1   *The Washington Post*, 20 September 2001. Available online at http://www.washingtonpost.com/wp-srv/nation/specials/attacked/transcripts/bushaddress_092001.html, accessed 6 December 2012.

2   On the terrorist scares of the nineteenth century, see Adrian Wisnicki, *Conspiracy, Revolution, and Terrorism* (New York: Routledge, 2008).

3   On Rapoport's model, see Karen Rasler and William Thompson, 'Looking for waves of terrorism', in Jean Rosenfeld, ed., *Terrorism, Identity, and Legitimacy* (London: Routledge, 2011), chapter 1. This Epilogue focuses on Rapoport's 'fourth wave', the religious terrorism of the late twentieth and early twenty-first centuries; but much of what I argue here would also pertain to the first three 'waves', the perpetrators of which were also frequently described, in their day, using the language of Gothic monstrosity.

4   On the decentralised nature of nineteenth-century terrorism, see Alexander Spencer, *The Tabloid Terrorist* (Basingstoke: Palgrave Macmillan, 2010), p. 25.

5   Carol Winkler, *In the Name of Terrorism* (Albany, NY: State University of New York Press, 2006), p. 170.

6   See Peter Taylor, *Talking to Terrorists* (London: HarperPress, 2011), chapter 10.

7   Benjamin Friedman, 'Managing fear', in Benjamin Friedman, Jim Harper, and Christopher Preble, eds., *Terrorizing Ourselves* (Washington, DC: Cato Institute, 2010), pp. 188, 190.

8   Friedman, 'Managing fear', p. 189.

9   See John Maeller, 'Action, reaction, and overreaction', in Rosenfeld, ed., chapter 8.

10   On terrorism as theatre or spectacle, see Spencer, p. 11, Winkler, p. 189, and O'Hair et al., *Terrorism: Communication and Rhetorical Perspectives* (Cresskill, NJ: Hampton Press, 2008), pp. 50–1, and chapter 2.

11   According to one estimate, 90 per cent of terrorist groups last less than one year, and only 5 per cent achieve their stated aims. See Audrey Cronin, 'Defeating Al Quaeda', in Friedman, Harper, and Preble, eds., p. 16.

12   On the modern demonology of organised crime – which frequently employs the rhetoric of conspiracy theory – and its contrast with reality, see John Cawelti, *Adventure, Mystery, and Romance* (Chicago, IL: University of Chicago Press, 1976), pp. 62–5. On the continuity of modern conspiracy theories with those of the eighteenth and nineteenth centuries, see Jovan Byford, *Conspiracy Theories* (Houndmills: Palgrave Macmillan, 2011), chapters 3 and 5.

13   On the mythology of serial murder, and its contrast with reality, see Eric Hickley, *Serial Murderers and Their Victims*, 5th ed. (Belmont, CA: Wadsworth, 2010), pp. 1–7. On the frequency with which serial killers turn out to have been abused as children, see pp. 67–71, 90–1.

14   On nineteenth-century beliefs that the Ripper murders were carried out by an individual with supernatural powers, see Martin Tropp, *Images of Fear* (Jefferson, MO: McFarland and Co., 1990), p. 114. For a modern, fictional interpretation of the 'occult Ripper' hypothesis, which also includes a summary of twentieth-century 'Ripperology' in its appendices, see Alan Moore, *From Hell* (London: Knockabout Comics, 2000).

15   On Marx's Gothicism, see Peter Hutchings, *The Criminal Spectre* (London: Routledge, 2001), pp. 6–8, and Chris Baldick, *Frankenstein's Shadow* (Oxford: Clarendon, 1990), chapter 6. The most famous discussion of Marx's use of ghostly language is Derrida's *Spectres of Marx*, especially chapter 5, 'Apparitions of the inapparent': see Jacques Derrida, *Spectres of Marx*, trans. Peggy Kamuf (New York: Routledge, 2006).

16   On the deployment of Darwinian ideas in popular Gothic fiction, see Lisa Hopkins, *Giants of the Past* (Lewisburg, PA: Bucknell UP, 2004).

17   On Gothic as 'an intellectual tradition which makes Freud possible in the first place', see Andrew Smith, *Gothic Radicalism* (Basingstoke: Macmillan, 2000), p. 7, and Dale Townshend, *Orders of Gothic* (New York: AMS Press, 2007), pp. 17, 32. On the Freudian case-history as a sub-genre of Gothic detective fiction, see Cawelti, pp. 95–6.

18   Mark Edmundson, *Nightmare on Main Street* (Cambridge MA: Harvard UP, 1997), p. 32.

19   Richard Devetak, 'The Gothic scene of international relations', *Review of International Studies*, vol. 31, number 4 (2005), pp. 634–43.

20   On the framing of the 'war on terror' in absolute or religious terms, see Marc Redfield, *The Rhetoric of Terror* (New York: Fordham UP, 2009), p. 45, Winkler, p. 175, O'Hair et al., pp. 83–6, Spencer, pp. 49, 103, 126–7. On the contrast between the popular conceptions of terrorists as 'crazed fanatics', and the reality that men who engage in terrorist violence actually tend to be more psychologically stable than other violent criminals, see John Horgan, 'The search for the terrorist personality', and Andrew Silke, 'Becoming a terrorist', in Andrew Silke ed., *Terrorists, Victims, and Society* (Chicester: Wiley, 2003), pp. 17, 29–33. Peter Knight points out that the architects of the 'war on terror', like the conspiracy theorists who reject their explanations of the 9/11 attacks, share 'a similar demonological structure of explanation that usually apportions all responsibility to an evil enemy', one which

drew upon the earlier conspiracy theories of the Cold War era. See Peter Knight, 'Outrageous conspiracy theories', *New German Critique*, number 103 (2008), pp. 166, 178–80.

21 Quoted in O'Hair et al., p. 84, Winkler, p. 169, Martha Crenshaw, *Explaining Terrorism* (London: Routledge, 2011), p. 55.

22 On the prominence of absolutist 'sacred rhetoric' in contemporary Republican political rhetoric, see Morgan Marietta, *The Politics of Sacred Rhetoric* (Waco, TX: Baylor UP, 2012), chapters 6–8.

23 Christopher Hitchins, 'From 9/11 to the Arab Spring', *Guardian*, 9 September 2011. Available online at http://www.guardian.co.uk/books/2011/sep/09/christopher-hitchens-911-arab-spring, accessed 6 December 2012.

24 Jean Tulard, *Joseph Fouché* (Paris: Fayard, 1998), pp. 239–40.

25 Alan Schom, *Napoleon Bonaparte* (New York: HarperCollins, 1998), pp. 253–5. On Fouché's career, see Tulard's biography.

Bibliography

NB: Place and date of publication are listed for all texts. Names of publishers are listed for all books published after 1850. 'University Press' has been abbreviated to 'UP' throughout.

Newspapers and Journals

The Anti-Jacobin or Weekly Examiner (London, 1799–1821).
The British Critic (London, 1793–1825).
Diary or Woodfall's Register (London, 1789–93).
The European Magazine and London Review (London, 1782–1826).
Evening Mail (London, 1789–1868).
General Evening Post (London, 1733–1822).
The Guardian (Manchester and London, 1821–2011).
Morning Chronicle (London, 1769–1865).
Morning Penny Post (London, 1744–51).
The Oracle (London, 1791–4).
Public Advertiser (London, 1752–93).
The Star (London, 1792–1828).
St James's Chronicle (London, 1761–1822).
The Times (London, 1785–2011).
True Briton (London, 1793–1804).
The Washington Post (Washington, DC, 1877–2011).
The World (London, 1787–94).

Primary Sources

'AC', *A Letter to the Reverend John Erskine* (Edinburgh, 1798).
Adams, William, *Sermons upon Several Subjects* (Shrewsbury, 1790).
Addison, Joseph and Steele, Richard, *The Spectator*, ed. Donald Bond, 5 volumes (Oxford: Clarendon, 1965).
Agutter, William, *Deliverance from Enemies* (London, 1798).
Ainsworth, William, *Jack Sheppard*, ed. Edward Jacobs and Manuela Mourão (Peterborough, ON: Broadview Editions, 2007).
Anon., *Advantages Resulting from the French Revolution* (Edinburgh, 1798).
———, *The Malefactor's Register, or the Newgate and Tyburn Calendar*, 5 volumes (London, 1779).
———, *The Master Cat* (London, no date).

——, *Select History of the Lives and Sufferings of the Principal English Protestant Martyrs* (London, 1746).

——, 'Terrorist novel writing', *Spirit of the Public Journals for 1797* (London, 1798).

Ash, Edward, *The Speculator* (London, 1790).

Austen, Jane, *Northanger Abbey*, ed. Barbara Benedict and Deirdre Le Faye (Cambridge: Cambridge UP, 2006).

Bailey, 'Citizen', *The White Devils Un-Cased* (London, 1795).

Barrett, Eaton Stannard, *The Heroine*, 3 volumes (London, 1813).

Barruel, Augustin, *History of Jacobinism*, trans. Robert Clifford, 4 volumes (London, 1797–8).

Bentley, Thomas, *Considerations upon the State of Public Affairs* (London, 1796).

Bisset, Robert, *Sketches of Democracy* (Dublin, 1798).

Blair, Robert, *The Grave* (London: Methuen, 1903).

Blake, William, *Complete Poetry and Prose*, ed. David Erdman (New Haven: Yale UP, 1988).

Boaden, James, *Fontainville Forest* (London, 1794).

——, *Memoirs of the Life of John Philip Kemble* (London, 1825).

——, *The Secret Tribunal* (London, 1795).

Booth, Michael, ed., *Hiss the Villain: Six English and American Melodramas* (London: Eyre and Spottiswoode, 1964).

Boswell, James, *Life of Johnson*, ed. R.W. Chapman (London: Oxford UP, 1970).

Brockden Brown, Charles, *Wieland and Memoirs of Carwin the Biloquist*, ed. Jay Fliegelman (Harmondsworth: Penguin, 1991).

Burke, Edmund, *A Philosophical Enquiry into the Origins of our Ideas of the Sublime and Beautiful*, ed. James Boulton (Notre Dame, IN: University of Notre Dame Press, 1968).

——, *Writings and Speeches*, ed. Paul Langford, 9 volumes (Oxford: Clarendon, 1981–2000).

Burney, Charles, *Memoirs of the Life and Writing of the Abate Metastasio*, 3 volumes (London, 1796).

Carlyle, Thomas, *The French Revolution*, ed. K.J. Fielding and David Sorensen (Oxford: Oxford UP, 1989).

Cartwright, John, *A Letter to the High Sheriff* (London, 1795).

Clarke, Hewson, *The History of the War*, 3 volumes (London, 1816).

Clery, E.J. and Miles, Robert, eds, *Gothic Documents* (Manchester: Manchester UP, 2000).

Clifford, Robert, *An Application of Barruel's Memoirs of Jacobinism to the Secret Societies of Ireland and Great Britain* (London, 1798).

Cobbett, William, *The Bloody Buoy* (London, 1796).

Coleridge, Samuel Taylor, *Collected Letters*, ed. Earl Griggs, 6 volumes (Oxford: Clarendon, 1956–71).

——, *Complete Works*, ed. Kathleen Coburn, 16 volumes (Princeton, NJ: Princeton UP, 1969–2001).

——, *Poems*, ed. John Beer (London: Dent, 1993).

A Collection of State Papers, Relative to the War Against France, 11 volumes (London, 1794–1802).

Collins, William, *Works*, ed. Richard Wendorf and Charles Ryskamp (Oxford: Clarendon, 1979).

Colman, George, *Blue Beard* (London, 1798).

——, *The Iron Chest* (London, 1796).

Cooper, Elizabeth, *The Muses Library* (London, 1741).

Cox, Jeffrey, ed., *Seven Gothic Dramas* (Athens, OH: Ohio UP, 1992).

Dacre, Charlotte, *Zofloya*, ed. Devendra Varma, 3 volumes (New York: Arno Press, 1974).

Dennis, John, *The Grounds of Criticism in Poetry* (London, 1704).

De Quincey, Thomas, *On Murder*, ed. Robert Morrison (Oxford: Oxford UP, 2006).

——, *Works*, ed. Grevel Lindop, 21 volumes (London: Pickering and Chatto, 2000–3).

Dickens, Charles, *Letters*, ed. Madeline House, Graham Storey, and Kathleen Tillotson, 12 volumes (Oxford: Clarendon, 1965–2002).

——, *The Mystery of Edwin Drood*, ed. David Paroissien (London: Penguin, 2003).

——, *Oliver Twist*, ed. Kathleen Tillotson (Oxford: Clarendon, 1966).

——, *A Tale of Two Cities*, ed. Andrew Sanders (Oxford: Oxford UP, 1988).

Dodsley, Robert, *Melpomene* (London, 1757).

Dryden, John, *Of Dramatic Poesy and Other Critical Essays*, ed. George Watson (London: Dent, 1962).

Dunlop, John, *The History of Fiction*, 3 volumes (Edinburgh, 1814).

Duvoisin, Jean Baptise, *Examination of the Principles of the French Revolution* (London, 1796).

Eaton, Daniel Isaac, *Politics for the People* (London, 1794).

'An English Lady', *Residence in France*, 2 volumes (London, 1797).

Fiard, Jean Baptiste, *La France Trompée Par Les Magiciens et Demonolatres* (Paris, 1803).

Fielding, Henry, *Jonathan Wild* (London: Hamish Hamilton, 1947).

——, *Tom Jones*, ed. John Bender and Simon Stern (Oxford: Oxford UP, 1996).

Fleming, Robert, *The Apocalyptical Key* (London, 1793).

George Gordon, Lord Byron, *Complete Poetical Works*, ed. Jerome McGann, 7 volumes (Oxford: Clarendon, 1980–93).

Grosse, Carl, *Horrid Mysteries*, trans. Peter Will (London: Folio Press, 1968).

Hazlitt, William, *Selected Writings*, ed. Duncan Wu, 9 volumes (London: Pickering and Chatto, 1998).

Hume, David, *Four Dissertations* (London, 1757).

Hurd, Richard, *Letters on Chivalry and Romance*, ed. Edith Morley (London: Henry Frowde, 1911).

Hutchinson, William, *The Hermitage* (York, 1772).

——, *The Spirit of Masonry* (London, 1775).

'Jack Cade', *The Quartern Loaf for Eight-Pence* (London, 1795).

'A Jacobin Novelist', 'The Terrorist system of novel-writing', in *Monthly Magazine*, ed. John Aikin, volumes 4:21 (London, 1797).

Johnson, Samuel, *Major Works*, ed. Donald Greene (Oxford: Oxford UP, 2000).

Kelly, Gary, ed., *Newgate Narratives*, 5 volumes (London: Pickering and Chatto, 2008).

——, *Varieties of Female Gothic Volume 2: Street Gothic* (London: Pickering and Chatto, 2002).

Lamb, Charles and Mary, *Letters of Charles and Mary Anne Lamb*, ed. Edwin Marrs, 3 volumes (Ithaca, NY: Cornell UP, 1975).

Lattin, Patrick, *Observations on Dr. Duigenan's Fair Representation of the Present Political State of Ireland* (London, 1800).

Le Fanu, Sheridan, *Uncle Silas* (London: Cresset Press, 1947).

Lewis, Matthew, *Alonzo the Brave and Fair Imogene* (London, 1797).

——, *The Castle Spectre*, 1st edition (London, 1798).

——, *Osric the Lion!* (London, 1797).

Locke, John, *Some Thoughts Concerning Education* (London, 1693).

Lucas, Charles, *The Infernal Quixote*, ed. M.O. Grenby (Peterborough, ON: Broadview Press, 2004).

MacPherson, James, *The Poems of Ossian*, ed. Howard Gaskill (Edinburgh: Edinburgh UP, 1996).

Marsh, Herbet, *The History of the Politicks of Great Britain and France*, 2 volumes (London, 1800).

Mercier, Louis Sébastien, *New Picture of Paris* (London, 1800).

Milton, John, *Complete Poems*, ed. John Leonard (London: Penguin, 1998).

——, *Poetical Works*, ed. Henry John Todd, 6 volumes (London, 1801).

Monroe, James, *A View of the Conduct of the Executive, in the Foreign Affairs of the United States* (Philadelphia, PA, 1797).

Montesquieu, Baron de, *The Spirit of the Laws*, trans. Thomas Nugent (New York: Hafner, 1949).

Moore, Alan, *From Hell* (London: Knockabout Comics, 2000).

Morrison, Robert and Baldick, Chris, eds, *Tales of Terror from Blackwoods Magazine* (Oxford: Oxford UP, 1995).

Naubert, Benedikte, *Hermann of Unna* (London, 1794).

New Annual Register for the Year 1799 (London, 1800).

O'Connor, Arthur, *The Beauties of the Press* (London, 1800).

Pagès, François Xavier, *Secret History of the French Revolution*, 2 volumes (London, 1797).

Paine, Thomas, *Dissertation on First Principles of Government* (London, 1795).

Parnell, Thomas, *Collected Poems*, ed. Claude Rawson and F.P. Lock (Newark, NJ: University of Delaware Press, 1989).

Pindar, Peter, *Works*, 4 volumes (London, 1796).

Piozzi, Hester Lynch, *The Piozzi Letters*, ed. Edward Bloom and Lillian Bloom, 6 volumes (Newark, NJ: University of Delaware Press, 1991).

Playfair, William, *The History of Jacobinism* (London, 1795).

Radcliffe, Ann, *The Italian* (Oxford: Oxford UP, 1968).

——, *A Journey Made in the Summer of 1794, Through Holland and the Western Frontier of Germany* (New York: Olms, 1975).

——, *The Romance of the Forest*, ed. Chloe Chard (Oxford: Oxford UP, 1986).

Reeve, Clara, *The Old English Baron* (London, 1788).

Richardson, Samuel, *Clarissa*, ed. Angus Ross (London: Penguin, 1985).

——, *Sir Charles Grandison*, ed. Jocelyn Harris (Oxford: Oxford UP, 1986).

Robison, John, *Postscript to the Second Edition of Mr Robison's Proofs of a Conspiracy* (London, 1797).

——, *Proofs of a Conspiracy Against all the Religions and Governments of Europe, Carried on in the Secret Meetings of Free Masons, Illuminati, and Reading Societies*, 5th edition (Dublin, 1798).

Schiller, Friedrich, *The Robbers*, trans. Alexander Tytler, ed. Jonathan Wordsworth (Oxford: Woodstock Books, 1989).

Scott, Walter, *Lives of the Novelists* (London: Dent, 1910).

——, *Selected Poems*, ed. Thomas Crawford (Oxford: Clarendon, 1972).

——, *Waverley*, ed. Andrew Hook (Harmondsworth: Penguin, 1972).

Shakespeare, William, *Hamlet*, ed. Harold Jenkins (London: Methuen, 1982).

Shelley, Mary, *The Last Man*, ed. Morton Paley (Oxford: Oxford UP, 1994).

Shelley, Percy, *Literary and Philosophical Criticism*, ed. John Shawcross (London: Humphrey Milford, 1909).

Smith, Adam, *The Theory of Moral Sentiments* (London, 1759).

Smith, Charlotte, *Elegiac Sonnets*, ed. Jonathan Wordsworth (Oxford: Woodstock Books, 1992).

———, *Letters of a Solitary Wanderer*, ed. Jonathan Wordsworth (Oxford: Woodstock Books, 1995).

———, *Poems*, ed. Stuart Curran (Oxford: Oxford UP, 1993).

Smollett, Tobias, *The Adventures of Ferdinand Count Fathom*, ed. Paul-Gabriel Boucé (London: Penguin, 1990).

Southcott, Joanna, *A Dispute Between the Woman and the Powers of Darkness*, ed. Jonathan Wordsworth (Poole: Woodstock Books, 1995).

The Statutes, 3rd revised edition, 33 volumes (London: HMSO, 1950).

Voltaire, *Commentaires sur Corneille*, ed. David Williams (Oxford: Voltaire Foundation, 1974).

Walpole, Horace, *The Castle of Otranto*, ed. W.S. Lewis (Oxford: Oxford UP, 1996).

———, *Correspondence*, ed. W.S. Lewis *et al.*, 48 volumes (London: Oxford UP, 1937–83).

Warton, Thomas, *The History of English Poetry*, 4 volumes (London, 1774).

———, *Poetical Works*, 2 volumes (Farnborough: Gregg International Publishers, 1969).

Weld, Matthew, *Constitutional Considerations* (Dublin, 1800).

Williams, Helen Maria, *Letters from France*, 2 volumes (New York: Scholar's Facsimiles and Reprints, 1975).

———, *Poems*, ed. Jonathan Wordsworth (Oxford: Woodstock Books, 1994).

Wollstonecraft, Mary, *Works*, ed. Janet Todd and Marylin Butler, 7 volumes (London: Pickering, 1989).

Wood, Sally, *Julia* (Portsmouth, NH, 1800).

Wordsworth, William, *Early Poems and Fragments*, ed. Carol Landon and Jared Curtis (Ithaca, NY: Cornell UP, 1997).

———, *Lyrical Ballads*, ed. James Butler and Karen Green (Ithaca, NY: Cornell UP, 1992).

———, *Poems*, ed. John Hayden (Harmondsworth: Penguin, 1977).

Critical and Historical Works

Aers, David, ed., *Romanticism and Ideology* (London: Routledge and Kegan Paul, 1981).

Allard, James, 'Spectres, spectators, spectacles', *Gothic Studies*, vol. 3, number 3 (2001), pp. 246–61.

Almond, Philip, *Heaven and Hell in Enlightenment England* (Cambridge: Cambridge UP, 1994).

Andress, David, 'Living the revolutionary melodrama', *Representations*, number 114 (2011), pp. 103–128.

———, *The Terror* (London: Little, Brown, 2005).

Andriopoulos, Stefan, 'Occult conspiracies: Spirits and secret societies in Schiller's *Ghost Seer*', *New German Critique*, number 103 (2008), pp. 65–81.

Ankersmit, Frank, *Sublime Historical Experience* (Stanford, CA: Stanford UP, 2005).

Arasse, Daniel, *The Guillotine and the Terror*, trans. Christopher Miller (London: Lane, 1989).

Atherton, Herbert, *Political Prints in the Age of Hogarth* (Oxford: Clarendon, 1974).

Backscheider, Paula, *Spectacular Politics* (Baltimore, MD: Johns Hopkins UP, 1993).

Baczko, Bronislaw, *Ending the Terror*, trans. Michel Petheram (Cambridge: Cambridge UP, 1994).

Bainbridge, Simon, *British Poetry and the Revolutionary and Napoleonic Wars* (Oxford: Oxford UP, 2003).

Baldick, Chris, *Frankenstein's Shadow* (Oxford: Clarendon, 1990).

Barnett, Brooke and Reynolds, Amy, *Terrorism and the Press* (New York: Peter Lang, 2009).

Barrell, John, *The Spirit of Despotism* (Oxford: Oxford UP, 2006).

Battestin, Martin, *Henry Fielding* (London: Routledge, 1989).

Beer, John, *Post-Romantic Consciousness* (Basingstoke: Palgrave Macmillan, 2003).

Behr, Kate, *Representations of Men in the English Gothic Novel* (Lewiston: Edwin Mellen Press, 2002).

Beik, Paul, ed., *The French Revolution* (New York: Harper and Row, 1970).

Bell, Ian, *Literature and Crime in Augustan England* (London: Routledge, 1991).

Ben-Israel, Hedva, *English Historians on the French Revolution* (London: Cambridge UP, 1968).

Bentley, Jr, G.E., *The Stranger from Paradise* (New Haven: Yale UP, 2001).

Bindman, David, *The Shadow of the Guillotine* (London: British Museum Publications, 1989).

Birkhead, Edith, *The Tale of Terror* (London: Constable and Company, 1921).

Black, Jeremy, *Eighteenth-Century Europe* (Basingstoke: Macmillan, 1999).

——, *European Warfare, 1660–1815* (London: UCL Press, 1994).

Black, Joel, *The Aesthetics of Murder* (Baltimore, MD: Johns Hopkins University, 1991).

Blakey, Dorothy, *The Minerva Press* (London: Oxford UP, 1939).

Bloom, Harold, ed., *Charles Dickens's Bleak House* (New York: Chelsea House Publishers, 1987).

Bondeson, Jan, *The London Monster* (Stroud: Tempus, 2003).

Bone, Drummond, ed., *Cambridge Companion to Byron* (Cambridge: Cambridge UP, 2004).

Brantlinger, Patrick, *The Reading Lesson* (Bloomington, IN: Indiana UP, 1998).

——, *Rule of Darkness* (Ithaca, NY: Cornell UP, 1988).

Briggs, Julia, *Night Visitors* (London: Faber, 1977).

Brown, Hilary, *Benedikte Naubert* (Leeds: Maney Publishing for the Modern Humanities Research Association and the Institute of Germanic Studies, University of London, 2005).

Brown, Howard, *Ending the French Revolution* (Charlottesville, VA: University of Virginia Press, 2006).

Burgess, Miranda, *British Fiction and the Production of Social Order* (Cambridge: Cambridge UP, 2000).

Butler, Erik, *Metamorphoses of the Vampire* (New York: Camden House, 2010).

Butler, Marilyn, *Jane Austen and the War of Ideas* (Oxford: Clarendon, 1987).

Byford, Jovan, *Conspiracy Theories* (Houndmills: Palgrave Macmillan, 2011).

Capoferro, Riccardo, *Empirical Wonder* (Bern: Peter Lang, 2010).

Castle, Terry, *The Female Thermometer* (Oxford: Oxford UP, 1995).

Cawelti, John, *Adventure, Mystery, and Romance* (Chicago, IL: University of Chicago Press, 1976).

Chandler, David, 'The Athens of England', *Eighteenth Century Studies*, vol. 43, number 2 (2010), pp. 171–92.

Chaplin, Sue, *Law, Sensibility, and the Sublime* (Aldershot: Ashgate, 2004).

Clark, Stuart, *Thinking with Demons* (Oxford: Clarendon, 1997).

Clery, E.J., *The Rise of Supernatural Fiction* (Cambridge: Cambridge UP, 1999).

Cobb, Richard, *The French and Their Revolution*, ed. David Gilmour (London: John Murray, 1998).

Cohn, Norman, *Europe's Inner Demons*, revised edition (London: Pimlico, 1993).

Colley, Linda, *Britons*, new edition (London: Pimlico, 2003).

Collins, Philip, *Dickens and Crime*, 3rd edition (Basingstoke: Macmillan, 1994).

Collison, Robert, *The Story of Street Literature* (London: Dent, 1973).

Connell, Philip, 'Death and the author', *Eighteenth Century Studies*, vol. 38, number 4 (2005), pp. 557–85.

Cook, Malcolm, 'Politics in the fiction of the French Revolution, 1789–1794', *Studies on Voltaire and the Eighteenth Century*, number 201 (Oxford: Voltaire Foundation, 1982), pp. 233–335.

Crawford, Joseph, *Raising Milton's Ghost* (London: Bloomsbury Academic, 2011).

Crenshaw, Martha, *Explaining Terrorism* (London: Routledge, 2011).

Crossley, Ceri and Small, Ian, eds, *The French Revolution and British Culture* (Oxford: Oxford UP, 1989).

Cunningham, Andrew and Grell, Ole Peter, *The Four Horsemen of the Apocalypse* (Cambridge: Cambridge UP, 2000).

Danziger, Marlies, 'Heroic villains', *Comparative Literature*, number 11 (1959), pp. 35–46.

Dart, Gregory, *Rousseau, Robespierre and English Romanticism* (Cambridge: Cambridge UP, 1999).

Davidson, Carol, *Anti-Semitism and British Gothic Fiction* (New York: Palgrave Macmillan, 2004).

Davies, Owen, ed., *Ghosts: A Social History*, 5 volumes (London: Pickering and Chatto, 2010).

Day, William, *In the Circles of Fear and Desire* (Chicago, IL: Chicago UP, 1985).

De Bruyn, Frans, 'Hooking the Leviathan', *The Eighteenth Century*, vol. 28, number 3 (1987), pp. 195–215.

Derrida, Jacques, *Spectres of Marx*, trans. Peggy Kamuf (New York: Routledge, 2006).

Devetak, Richard, 'The Gothic scene of international relations', *Review of International Studies*, vol. 31, number 4 (2005), pp. 621–43.

Dhombres, Jean and Dhombres, Nicole, *Lazare Carnot* (Paris: Fayard, 1997).

Dickinson, H.T., ed., *Caricatures and the Constitution* (Cambridge: Chadwyck-Healey, 1986).

——, *The Politics of the People in Eighteenth-Century Britain* (Basingstoke: Macmillan, 1995).

Disher, Maurice, *Blood and Thunder* (London: Muller, 1949).

Dozier, Robert, *For King, Constitution, and Country* (Lexington, KY: UP of Kentucky, 1983).

Duncan, Ian, *Modern Romance and Transformations of the Novel* (Cambridge: Cambridge UP, 1992).

Dyos, H.J. and Wolff, Michael, eds, *The Victorian City*, 2 volumes (London: Routledge and Kegan Paul, 1973).

Edelstein, Dan, 'The law of 22 Prairal', *Telos*, number 141 (2007), pp. 82–100.

——, *The Terror of Natural Right* (Chicago, IL: University of Chicago Press, 2009).

Edmundson, Mark, *Nightmare on Main Street* (Cambridge, MA: Harvard UP, 1997).

Eisner, Manuel, 'Long-term historical trends in violent crime', *Crime and Justice: a Review of Research*, vol. 30 (2003), pp. 83–142.

Elton, G.R., ed., *The Reformation*, 2nd edition (Cambridge: Cambridge UP, 1990).

Evans, Bertrand, *Gothic Drama from Walpole to Shelley* (Berkeley, CA: University of California Press, 1947).

——, 'Manfred's remorse', *PMLA*, vol. 62, number 3 (1947), pp. 752–73.

Evans, Chris, *Debating the Revolution: Britain in the 1790s* (London: I.B. Tauris, 2006).

Favret, Mary, *War at a Distance* (Princeton, NJ: Princeton UP, 2010).

Fehér, Ference, ed., *The French Revolution and the Birth of Modernity* (Berkeley, CA: University of California Press, 1990).

Fiedler, Leslie, *Love and Death in the American Novel*, revised edition (Harmondsworth: Penguin, 1984).

Foster, James, *History of the Pre-Romantic Novel in England* (New York: Modern Language Association of America, 1949).

Foucault, Michel, *Discipline and Punish*, trans. Alan Sheridan (Harmondsworth: Penguin, 1991).

Friedman, Barton, *Fabricating History* (Princeton, NJ: Princeton UP, 1988).

Friedman, Benjamin, Harper, Jim, and Preble, Christopher, eds, *Terrorizing Ourselves* (Washington, DC: Cato Institute, 2010).

Fry, Carol, *Charlotte Smith* (New York: Arno Press, 1980).

Gainot, Bernard, 'Aux origines du Directoire' *Annales Historiques de la Révolution française*, numéro 332 (2003), pp. 129–45.

Gamer, Michael, *Romanticism and the Gothic* (Cambridge: Cambridge UP, 2000).

Garrett, Clarke, *Respectable Folly* (Baltimore, MD: Johns Hopkins UP, 1975).

Gatrell, V.A.C., *The Hanging Tree* (Oxford: Oxford UP, 1994).

Gatrell, Vic, *City of Laughter* (London: Atlantic, 2006).

Gay, Peter, *The Enlightenment*, 2 volumes (London: Wildwood House, 1973).

Gilchrist, J. and Murray, W.J., *The Press in the French Revolution* (London: Ginn, 1971).

Girouard, Mark, *The Return to Camelot* (New Haven: Yale UP, 1981).

Graham, Kenneth, ed., *Gothic Fictions* (New York: AMS Press, 1989).

Grant, Douglas, *The Cock Lane Ghost* (New York: St Martin's Press, 1965).

Green, Clarence, *Neo-Classic Theory of Tragedy in England* (Cambridge, MA: Harvard UP, 1934).

Greer, Donald, *Incidence of the Terror During the French Revolution* (Cambridge, MA: Harvard UP, 1935).

Grenby, M.O., *The Anti-Jacobin Novel* (Cambridge: Cambridge UP, 2001).

Hadley, Michael, *The Undiscovered Genre: The Search for the German Gothic Novel* (Berne: Lang, 1978).

Haining, Peter, *The Penny Dreadful* (London: Gollancz, 1975).

Hallie, Phillip, *Cruelty*, revised edition (Middletown, CT: Wesleyan UP, 1982).

Hampson, Norman, *The Terror in the French Revolution* (London: Historical Association, 1981).

Handley, Sasha, *Visions of an Unseen World* (London: Pickering and Chatto, 2007).

Hay, Douglas, *Albion's Fatal Tree* (London: A. Lane, 1975).

Haydon, Colin and Doyle, William, eds, *Robespierre* (Cambridge: Cambridge UP, 1999).

Haywood, Ian, *Bloody Romanticism* (Basingstoke: Palgrave Macmillan, 2006).

Hénaff, Marcel, 'Naked Terror', *Substance*, vol. 27, number 2 (1998), pp. 5–32.

Hesse, Carla, 'The law of the Terror', *MLN*, vol. 114, number 4 (1999), pp. 702–18.

Hickley, Eric, *Serial Murderers and Their Victims*, 5th edition (Belmont, CA: Wadsworth, 2010).

High, Jeffrey, ed., *Who Is This Schiller Now?* (Columbia, SC: Camden House, 2011).

Higonnet, Patrice, 'Terror, trauma and the "young Marx" explanation of Jacobin politics', *Past and Present*, number 191 (2006), pp. 121–64.

Hilton, Boyd, *A Mad, Bad, and Dangerous People?* (Oxford: Clarendon, 2006).

Hoeveler, Diane, *Gothic Feminism* (Liverpool: Liverpool UP, 1998).

———, *Gothic Riffs* (Columbus, OH: Ohio State UP, 2010).

Hogle, Jerrold, ed., *Cambridge Companion to Gothic Fiction* (Cambridge: Cambridge UP, 2002).

Hollingsworth, Keith, *The Newgate Novel* (Detroit, MI: Wayne State UP, 1963).

Hopkins, Lisa, *Giants of the Past* (Lewisburg, PA: Bucknell UP, 2004).

Howard, Jacqueline, *Reading Gothic Fiction* (Oxford: Clarendon, 1994).

Huet, Marie-Hélène, *Mourning Glory* (Philadelphia, PA: University of Pennsylvania Press, 1997).

Hunter, J. Paul, *Before Novels* (New York: W.W. Norton and Co., 1990).

Hutchings, Peter, *The Criminal Spectre* (London: Routledge, 2001).

Hutt, Maurice, *Chouannerie and Counter-Revolution* (Cambridge: Cambridge UP, 1983).

Jackson, A.C.F., *Rose Croix* (London: Lewis Masonic, 1980).

Jacob, Margaret, *The Radical Enlightenment* (London: Allen and Unwin, 1981).

Johnson, Eric, *Nazi Terror* (New York: Basic Books, 2000).

Jones, Colin, McDonagh, Josephine, and Mee, Jon, eds, *Charles Dickens, A Tale of Two Cities and the French Revolution* (Basingstoke: Palgrave Macmillan, 2009).

Joyce, Simon, *Capital Offences* (Charlottesville, VA: UP of Virginia, 2003).

Kaiser, Thomas, 'From the Austrian Committee to the Foreign Plot', *French Historical Studies*, vol. 26, number 4 (2003), pp. 579–617.

Keener, Frederick, *English Dialogues of the Dead* (New York: Columbia UP, 1973).

Kelly, George, 'Conceptual sources of the Terror', *Eighteenth Century Studies*, vol. 14, number 1 (1980), pp. 292–312.

Kerr, James, *Fiction Against History* (Cambridge: Cambridge UP, 1989).

Kilgour, Maggie, *The Rise of the Gothic Novel* (London: Routledge, 1995).

Killeen, Jarlath, *Gothic Literature 1825–1914* (Cardiff: University of Wales Press, 2009).

Knight, Peter, 'Outrageous conspiracy theories', *New German Critique*, number 103 (2008), pp. 165–93.

Krobb, Florian, 'Friedrich Schiller: The first historiographer in Germany?', *Archivium Hibernicum*, vol. 59 (2005), pp. 277–89.

Lefebvre, Georges, *The Great Fear of 1789* (London: NLB, 1973).

Le Tellier, Robert, *Kindred Spirits* (Salzburg: Insitut für Anglistik und Amerikanistik, Universität Salzburg, 1982).

Lindsay, J.O., ed., *The Old Regime* (Cambridge: Cambridge UP, 1957).

Lister, Raymond, *British Romantic Painting* (Cambridge: Cambridge UP, 1989).

Llewellyn-Jones, Rosie, *The Great Uprising in India* (Woodbridge, VA: Boydell Press, 2007).

Löffler, Marion, *The Literary and Historical Legacy of Iolo Morganwg* (Cardiff: University of Wales Press, 2007).

Loomis, Stanley, *Paris in the Terror* (Harmondsworth: Penguin, 1970).

MacAndrew, Elizabeth, *The Gothic Tradition in Fiction* (New York: Columbia UP, 1979).

Macdonald, D.L., *Monk Lewis* (Toronto, ON: University of Toronto Press, 2000).

Malchow, H.L., *Gothic Images of Race in Nineteenth Century Britain* (Stanford, CA: Stanford UP, 1996).

Mannoni, Laurent, *The Great Art of Light and Shadow*, trans. Richard Crangle (Exeter: University of Exeter Press, 2000).

Manuel, Frank, *The Eighteenth Century Confronts the Gods* (Cambridge, MA: Harvard UP, 1959).

Marietta, Morgan, *The Politics of Sacred Rhetoric* (Waco, TX: Baylor UP, 2012).

Matthew, H.C.G. and Harrison, Brian, eds, *Oxford Dictionary of National Biography*, 60 volumes (Oxford: Oxford UP, 2004).

Mayo, Robert, 'How long was Gothic fiction in vogue?', *Modern Language Notes*, vol. 58, number 1 (1943), pp. 58–64.

McDonagh, Josephine, *Child Murder and British Culture, 1720–1900* (Cambridge: Cambridge UP, 2003).

McIntyre, Clara, 'Were the Gothic novels Gothic?' *PMLA*, vol. 36, number 4 (1921), pp. 644–67.

McLoughlin Barry and McDermott, Kevin, eds, *Stalin's Terror* (Basingstoke: Palgrave Macmillan, 2003).

McLoughlin, T.O., *Contesting Ireland* (Dublin: Four Courts Press, 1999).

Midelfort, H.C., *Exorcism and Enlightenment* (New Haven: Yale UP, 2005).

Milbank, Alison, *Daughters of the House* (Basingstoke: Macmillan, 1992).

Mitchell, Leslie, *The Whig World* (London: Hambledon and London, 2005).

Moody, Jane, *Illegitimate Theatre in London* (Cambridge: Cambridge UP, 2000).

Moretti, Franco, *Graphs, Maps, Trees* (London: Verso, 2005).

Morgan, Prys, *Iolo Morganwg* (Cardiff: University of Wales Press, 1975).

Morse, Donald, *The Fantastic in World Literature* (Westport: Greenwood, 1987).

Morse, James, *Jedidiah Morse* (New York: Columbia UP, 1939).

Mortensen, Peter, 'Robbing *The Robbers*', *Literature and History*, 3rd series, vol. 11, number 1 (2002), pp. 41–61.

Mowl, Timothy, *Horace Walpole: The Great Outsider* (London: John Murray, 1996).

Myrone, Martin, ed., *Gothic Nightmares* (London: Tate Publishing, 2006).

Nead, Lynda, *Victorian Babylon* (New Haven: Yale UP, 2000).

Newman, Gerald, *The Rise of English Nationalism* (London: Weidenfeld and Nicolson, 1987).

Norton, Rictor, *Mistress of Udolpho* (London: Leicester UP, 1999).

O'Hair, Dan, *et al.*, *Terrorism: Communication and Rhetorical Perspectives* (Cresskill, NJ: Hampton Press, 2008).

Outram, Dorinda, *The Body and the French Revolution* (London: Yale UP, 1989).

Paley, Morton, *The Apocalyptic Sublime* (New Haven: Yale UP, 1986).

Palmer, Robert, *Twelve Who Ruled* (Princeton, NJ: Princeton UP, 1989).

Parker, Geoffrey, *The Thirty Years War* (London: Routledge and Kegan Paul, 1984).

Parsons, Coleman, *Witchcraft and Demonology in Scott's Fiction* (Edinburgh: Oliver and Boyd, 1964).

Patey, Douglas, *Probability and Literary Form* (Cambridge: Cambridge UP, 1984).

Paulson, Ronald, *Representations of Revolution* (New Haven: Yale UP, 1983).

Pearson, Jacqueline, *Women's Reading in Britain, 1750–1832* (Cambridge: Cambridge UP, 1999).

Philp, Mark, ed., *The French Revolution and British Popular Politics* (Cambridge: Cambridge UP, 1991).

Pionke, Albert, *Plots of Opportunity* (Columbus, OH: Ohio State UP, 2004).

Poovey, Mary, *The Proper Lady and the Woman Writer* (Chicago, IL: University of Chicago Press, 1984).

Porter, Roy, *London* (London: Hamish Hamilton, 1994).

Potter, Franz, *The History of Gothic Publishing, 1800–1835* (Basingstoke: Palgrave Macmillan, 2005).

Prichard, Allan, 'The urban Gothic of *Bleak House*', *Nineteenth Century Literature*, vol. 45, number 4 (1991), pp. 432–52.

Punter, David, ed., *A Companion to the Gothic* (Oxford: Blackwell, 2000).

——, *Gothic Pathologies* (Basingstoke: Macmillan, 1998).

——, *The Literature of Terror* (London: Longman, 1980).

Purkiss, Diane, *The English Civil War* (London: Harper Perennial, 2006).

Ranger, Paul, *Terror and Pity Reign in Every Breast* (London: Society for Theatre Research, 1991).

Reddin, Chitra, *Forms of Evil in the Gothic Novel* (New York: Ayer, 1980).

Redfield, Marc, *The Rhetoric of Terror* (New York: Fordham UP, 2009).

Richardson, Alan, *Literature, Education, and Romanticism* (Cambridge: Cambridge UP, 1994).

Rivers, Isobel, ed., *Books and Their Readers in Eighteenth-Century England* (Leicester: Leicester UP, 1982).

Roberts, J.M., *The Mythology of the Secret Societies* (London: Secker and Warburg, 1972).

Roberts, Marie, *Gothic Immortals* (London: Routledge, 1990).

Rosenfeld, Jean, ed., *Terrorism, Identity, and Legitimacy* (London: Routledge, 2011).

Rudé, George, *The Crowd in the French Revolution* (Oxford: Clarendon, 1959).

Sagan, Eli, *Citizens and Cannibals* (Lanham: Rowman and Littlefield, 2001).

Schechter, Ronald, 'Gothic Thermidor', *Representations*, number 61 (1998), pp. 78–94.

Schlicke, Paul, ed., *Oxford Reader's Companion to Dickens* (Oxford: Oxford UP, 1999).

Schmitt, Cannon, *Alien Nation* (Philadelphia, PA: University of Pennsylvania Press, 1997).

Schock, Peter, '*The Marriage of Heaven and Hell*: Blake's myth of Satan and its cultural matrix', *ELH*, vol. 60, number 2 (1993), pp. 441–70.

Schom, Alan, *Napoleon Bonaparte* (New York: HarperCollins, 1998).

Scott, William, *Terror and Repression in Revolutionary Marseilles* (London: Macmillan, 1973).

Scurr, Ruth, *Fatal Purity* (London: Chatto and Windus, 2006).

Sheppard, Francis, *London 1808-1870: The Infernal Wen* (London: Secker and Warburg, 1971).

Shoemaker, Robert, *The London Mob* (London: Hambledon and London, 2004).

Silke, Andrew, ed., *Terrorists, Victims, and Society* (Chicester: Wiley, 2003).

Smith, Alan Lloyd and Sage, Victor, eds, *Gothick Origins* (Amsterdam: Rodopi, 1994).

Smith, Andrew, *Gothic Radicalism* (Basingstoke: Macmillan, 2000).

Spacks, Patricia, *The Insistence of Horror* (Cambridge, MA: Harvard UP, 1962).

Spencer, Alexander, *The Tabloid Terrorist* (Basingstoke: Palgrave Macmillan, 2010).

Stevens, Anne, *British Historical Fiction Before Scott* (Basingstoke: Palgrave Macmillan, 2010).

Summers, Montague, *The Gothic Quest* (London: Fortune, 1938).

Sutherland, Donald, *The French Revolution and Empire* (Oxford: Blackwell, 2003).

——, *Murder in Aubagne* (Cambridge: Cambridge UP, 2009).

Tackett, Timothy, 'Conspiracy obsession in a time of revolution', *American Historical Review*, vol. 105, number 3 (2000), pp. 691–713.

Tanner, Jakob, 'The conspiracy of the invisible hand', *New German Critique*, number 103 (2008), pp. 51–64.

Taylor, Peter, *Talking to Terrorists* (London: HarperPress, 2011).

Thomas, Chantal, 'Terror in Lyon', *SubStance*, vol. 27, number 2 (1998), pp. 33–42.

Thompson, E.P., *The Making of the English Working Classes* (Harmondsworth: Penguin, 1968).

Thompson, J.M., *Napoleon Bonaparte* (Oxford: Basil Blackwell, 1988).

Thorslev, Peter, *The Byronic Hero* (Minneapolis, MN: University of Minnesota Press, 1962).

Tinkler-Villani, Valeria, ed., *Exhibited by Candlelight* (Amsterdam: Rodopi, 1995).

Tompkins, J.M.S., *The Popular Novel in England, 1770–1800* (London: Methuen, 1962).

Townshend, Dale, *Orders of Gothic* (New York: AMS Press, 2007).

Trevor-Roper, Hugh, *The European Witch-Craze of the Sixteenth and Seventeenth Centuries* (Harmondsworth: Penguin, 1969).

Tropp, Martin, *Images of Fear* (Jefferson, MO: McFarland and Co., 1990).

Tucker, Herbert, *Epic* (Oxford: Oxford UP, 2008).

Tulard, Jean, *Joseph Fouché* (Paris: Fayard, 1998).

Utter, Robert and Needham, Gwendolyn, *Pamela's Daughters* (London: Dickson, 1937).

Varma, Devendra, *The Gothic Flame* (New York: Russell and Russell, 1966).

Wallace, Diana and Smith, Andrew, eds, *Female Gothic* (Basingstoke: Palgrave Macmillan, 2009).

Watt, Ian, *The Rise of the Novel* (London: Chatto and Windus, 1957).

Watt, James, *Contesting the Gothic* (Cambridge: Cambridge UP, 1999).

Watt, William, *Shilling Shockers* (New York: Russell and Russell, 1967).

Webb, James, *The Flight from Reason* (London: Macdonald and Co., 1971).

Wein, Toni, *British Identities, Heroic Nationalisms, and the Gothic Novel* (Basingstoke: Palgrave Macmillan, 2002).

Weisser, Susan, *A 'Craving Vacancy'* (New York: New York UP, 1997).

Wells, Roger, *Wretched Faces* (Gloucester: Sutton, 1988).

Wheeler, Michael, *Heaven, Hell, and the Victorians* (Cambridge: Cambridge UP, 1994).

Wilson, Frances, ed., *Byromania* (Basingstoke: Macmillan, 2000).

Winkler, Carol, *In the Name of Terrorism* (Albany, NY: State University of New York Press, 2006).

Wisnicki, Adrian, *Conspiracy, Revolution, and Terrorism* (New York: Routledge, 2008).

Wood, Marcus, *Slavery, Empathy, and Pornography* (Oxford: Oxford UP, 2002).

Wright, Eugene, 'A divine analysis of *The Romance of the Forest*', *Discourse*, number 13 (1970), pp. 379–87.

Wright-Neville, David, *Dictionary of Terrorism* (Cambridge: Polity Press, 2010).

Yetter, Leigh, *Public Execution in England, 1573–1868*, 8 volumes (London: Pickering and Chatto, 2009–10).

Index

9/11 attacks xiii, 190, 194
Abolitionism 45–6
Adams, William 50, 51
Addison, Joseph 2–3, 5–10, 12, 20, 26–7, 133, 181
Aeschylus 14–15, 19
Agutter, William 103, 104
Ainsworth, William
    Jack Sheppard 162–6, 168, 170, 172
Al Qaeda vii, 189–90, 194
American War of Independence 25, 26, 40
Amis des Noirs 100
Antiquarianism 2, 19–28, 133
Antoinette, Marie 77, 179, 180
Aristotle 10–11
Austen, Jane
    Northanger Abbey 101–2

Barère, Bertrand 51, 52
Barrett, Eaton Stannard
    The Heroine 75
Barruel, Augustin
    Mémoires 98–109, 117, 118–19, 122–3, 131, 137
Bastille 37, 39, 40, 41, 46, 137
Bavarian Illuminati, *see* Illuminati, the
Beane, Sawney 161
Beckford, William
    Vathek 23–6, 30, 110, 122
Bentley, Thomas 54
Bin Laden, Osama xiii, 194, 196
Blair, Robert 12
Blake, William 108–9, 161
Blenheim, battle of 3
Boaden, James 134–40, 147
    Fontainville Forest 134–40
    The Secret Tribunal 135, 138–40
Book trade 131–3
Boswell, James 50
Boyd, William 19
Boydell, John 26

British Convention 105
Brothers, Richard 108–9
Browne, Thomas 6
Büchner, Georg 178
Bulwer-Lytton, Edward 119, 162–3
Bunyan, John 28–9, 118, 123, 132, 136
Bürger, Gottfried
    Lenore 96, 98, 110–11
Burke, Edmund viii, 13, 17–23, 40, 49–51, 53, 68, 77, 81, 121, 131, 142, 144, 161, 171–2, 193
    A Philosophical Enquiry into the Origin of Our Ideas of the Sublime and Beautiful viii, 13, 17–19, 21, 40, 49–50
    Letter to a Member of the National Assembly 50
    Letters on a Regicide Peace 53, 77
    Reflections on the Revolution in France 77
Burney, Charles 55
Burney, Frances 132
Bush, George W. vii, 189, 193–4
Byron, George Gordon, Lord 110, 153–4, 157–9

Cadet-Gassicour, Charles Louis
    Le Tombeau de Jacques Molay 98, 112
Cagliostro, Alessandro 99
Carlyle, Thomas
    The French Revolution 173, 175–9, 181
Carnot, Lazare 180
Carrier, Jean-Baptiste 83–4
Cartwright, John 55
Cathar heresy 99
Champ de Mars Massacre 89
Chapbooks 131–3, 136, 140–2, 148, 149, 163, 165
Chatterton, Thomas 22
Chénier, Marie-Joseph 54
Chesterton, G.K. 189

Circulating libraries 131
Clifford, Robert 100, 108
Cobbett, William
    The Bloody Buoy 54, 69, 72, 79, 82, 99,
        119, 122, 161
Cock Lane Ghost 7–8, 120
Coleridge, Samuel Taylor 79–81, 96–7,
        108–9, 117–18, 120–3
    The Fall of Robespierre 79–81
    millennialism 108–9
    response to *The Robbers* 96–7
    review of *The Monk* 117–18
    supernatural poetry 120–3
Collins, William 13–21, 43–4, 71
    'Ode to Fear' 13–16, 21, 44
Colman, George 135–6, 140, 146–8
    Blue-Beard 146–8
    The Iron Chest 135–6, 140
Committee for the Abolition of the Slave
        Trade 45
Committee of Public Safety 38, 46, 47, 52,
        57, 72–3
Conan-Doyle, Arthur 164
Conspiracy theory x, 59, 84, 93–109,
        116–23, 127, 137, 149, 191, 197–8
Condorcet, Marie Jean Antoine Nicolas de
        Caritat, marquis de 99
Cooke, T.P. 184
Cooper, Elizabeth 22
Corday, Charlotte 46
Covent Garden theatre 132
Craik, Helen 79
Cromwell, Oliver 94, 96
Cruikshank, George 145

Dacre, Charlotte
    Zofloya 116–17, 118
Damiens, Robert-François 60
Danton, Georges 43, 73
Dartmouth Massacre of 1751 64–6
Darwin, Charles 192–3
D'Alembert, Jean-Baptiste le Rond 99
Day of Daggers 59
Declaration of the Princes of the Blood 50
Defoe, Daniel 2–3, 7, 132, 136, 183
Dennis, John 11, 17–18
De Sade, Donatien Alphonse François 40,
        66, 111
Desmoulins, Camille 73

De Quincey, Thomas 101, 153–4, 160,
        169–72, 182
    'On Murder Considered as One of the
        Fine Arts' 169–72
D'Herbois, Collot 60, 61, 88
Diamond Necklace Affair 59
Dickens, Charles 157, 161, 162–72, 173,
        177, 178–83
    Bleak House 168–9
    Oliver Twist 161, 162–70
    reactions to the Indian Rebellion of
        1857 181–3
    A Tale of Two Cities 178–81
Directory 56
Dodsley, Robert 21–22
Doulcet, Louis Gustave le 54
Drury Lane theatre 132, 137, 146, 148
Dryden, John 6, 11, 158
Dumas, Alexandre 178
Dunlop, John
    History of Fiction 1
Duvoisin, Jean Baptise 54

English Civil War, *see* War of Three
        Kingdoms
Enlightenment viii, xiii, 1, 5–8, 18, 94–5,
        123, 159, 181–3
Erskine, John 102–3
Eugenics 160–1
Execution 13, 19, 24, 42, 50, 56, 60–1, 73,
        81, 86, 161, 190

Ferri, Enrico 160
Fiard, Jean Baptiste
    *La France Trompée Par Les Magiciens
        et Demonolatres* 94, 108, 109
Fielding, Henry 3–5, 8–11, 16, 26, 163–8,
        172, 183
    Tom Jones 4–5, 9, 16
    Jonathan Wild 4, 8, 82, 163–5
Fletcher, Robert
    The Apocalyptical Key 108
Flight to Varennes 37–8, 100
Fouché, Joseph 109, 195–6
Fox, Charles James 37, 142, 144
Freemasonry 34–5, 94–6, 98–101, 118, 126
French Revolution ix–xiii, 23, 30, 37–41,
        45–68, 71–4, 77–84, 96–109, 113–19,
        122–3, 137–9, 143–7, 172–82

in British fiction 174, 178–82
British history writing on 172–8
British newspaper reporting on 46,
    50–3, 55, 62–69, 113, 123, 143–5
described in Gothic terms 72, 77–83,
    172–82
French Wars of Religion 5
Freud, Sigmund 192–3
Fuseli, Henry 26, 143–4, 147

Garrick, David 16–17
Gassner, Johann Joseph 94
Gay, John 4, 163
Geheimbundroman 95, 98, 101, 107,
    109–10, 119, 122, 124
George III 100, 137, 142
German literature in Britain 96–8, 110–13
Gessner, Salomon
    Der Tod Abels 96
Ghosts 1–2, 7–8, 9–10, 12–13, 15–17,
    20–2, 25–7, 30, 32–5, 39, 43–4, 68,
    79, 96, 108, 110–14, 119–23, 135–6,
    144–6, 153, 157, 168
    in art 26, 144–5
    in fiction 9–10, 25, 30, 39, 108, 110–14,
        123, 157, 168
    in poetry 12–13, 15, 20–1, 43–4, 79, 96,
        111, 122
    in political rhetoric 46
    on stage 16–17, 119–21, 135–6, 146
Gillray, James 69, 143–5, 179
Girondins 46, 59
Glanville, Joseph
    Saducimus Triumphatus 114
Godwin, William 71, 72, 83, 119, 135–6,
    140–1, 164, 192
    Caleb Williams 72, 83, 119, 135–6, 141,
        164
    The Iron Chest, stage adaptation of
        Caleb Williams 135–6, 140
    Political Justice 141
    St Leon 119
Goethe, Johann Wolfgang 96, 103, 110
Gorsas, Antoine 59
Gothic fiction vii–xiii, 1–4, 8–9, 11, 22–30,
    38–44, 69–84, 93, 95–8, 102, 109–23,
    131–41, 146–8, 153–69, 171, 183,
    191, 195–6
    conspiracy fiction, *see Geheimbundroman*

decline of 153–7
Gothic drama 42–3, 97–8, 119–21,
    132–40, 146–8, 169–70, 184
loyalist Gothic 25, 39–40, 133
popular Gothic 131–41, 146–8, 191
Radcliffean Gothic 70–84, 109–14
Rosicrucian fiction 119, 129
supernatural Gothic 109–23
'Terrorist fiction' 113–17, 122–3, 141
Victorian Gothic vii, xi–xii, 156–9,
    162–9, 171
Gothic rhetoric viii–xii, 46, 72, 77–83,
    153–4, 159–63, 169–83, 192–6
    applied to Napoleon 145, 153, 182
    applied to the French Revolution 72,
        77–83, 172–82
    in the nineteenth century 153–4,
        159–63, 169–83
    in the twentieth and twenty-first
        centuries 192–6
Graveyard poetry 11–13
Gray, Thomas 19, 21, 22, 43–4
Great Fear, The 37–8, 58
Great Northern War 2–3
Grosse, Karl
    Der Genius 96, 98, 101, 104, 118–19
Guillotin, Joseph-Ignace 99
Guillotine, execution by 41–2, 52, 56, 73, 179

Hadfield, James 137
Haitian Revolution 93
Hardy, Thomas 105, 139
Hazlitt, William 97
Hébert, Jacques 57, 73
Hitchens, Christopher 194–5
Hogarth, William 3, 5, 163, 166–8
Hogg, James 154
Home, John
    Douglas 21, 22, 27, 133–4
Homer 9, 27
Hurd, Richard
    Letters on Chivalry and Romance 22,
        96, 133
Hussein, Saddam 194
Hutchinson
    The Hermitage ix, 24–5, 34–5, 110

Illuminati, the 94–6, 100–9, 112, 116, 118,
    137, 149

Indian Rebellion of 1857 xii, 181–3
Irving, Washington 178

Jack the Ripper 192
Jacobins xi, 52–6, 59–60, 74, 78–9, 83,
    98–9, 105, 116, 119, 122, 145–6,
    174–81, 189, 191, 195–6
    demonisation of 74, 78–9, 83, 174, 174–81
Jacobite Rising of 1715 3
Jacobite Rising of 1745 3, 13, 19, 24
James I
    Daemonologie 19
Jesuits 94, 95, 98, 99, 191
Johnson, Samuel 3, 7–11, 16–17, 20, 22,
    50, 109, 165
Jourdan, Mathieu 73, 83

Kadosch, knights of 98, 125
Kahlert, Karl
    Der Geisterbanner 98, 101
Kant, Immanuel 99
Klopstock, Friedrich
    Messias 96

Lafayette, Marie-Joseph Paul Yves Roch
    Gilbert du Motier, Marquis de 59,
    89, 99
La Glacière, Massacre of 62
Lamb, Charles 97
Lamballe, Princess, Maria Teresa Luisa 42,
    174, 176
Lane, William 25
Lattin, Patrick 104
Law of 22 Prairal 52, 58
Law of Suspects 58, 179
Le Fanu, Sheridan
    Uncle Silas 156
Lee, Sophia
    The Recess ix, 71, 90
Lepilletier, Louis-Michel 59
Lessing, Gotthold 96
Lewis, Matthew viii, 71, 97, 109, 110–13,
    116–23, 131–2, 135–7, 141, 146–7,
    155, 157, 168
    The Castle Spectre 119–22, 132, 135,
    137, 146, 168
    The Monk viii, 97, 109, 110–113,
    116–23, 135–6

Osric The Lion! 111, 121
    Tales of Wonder 154
Lloyd, Edward 171
Locke, John 5–6, 9–12, 26–7, 68, 82, 114,
    193
    Some Thoughts Concerning Education
    6, 68, 114
Lombroso, Cesare 160
London Corresponding Society 100, 105
London Monster, the 144
Louis XVI 37–8, 46, 68, 100, 109, 140, 179,
    180
Lucas, Charles
    The Infernal Quixote 117
Lyons, civil war and Jacobin repression in
    51, 52, 57, 60, 180, 195

Mackenzie, Anna Maria, 70
Mackenzie, Henry 97, 132
Macpherson, James
    Ossian 22, 27, 44
Manichean heresy 99
Marat, Jean-Paul 46, 59, 177
Marlowe, Christopher 11, 29, 67, 118
Marx, Karl 192–3
Mason, William 19, 22, 43
Matthews, James Tilley 60
Maturin, Charles
    Melmoth the Wanderer 119, 153–4, 158
Mayhew, Henry
    London Labour and the London Poor
    161, 185
Milton, John
    Paradise Lost 19, 20, 28–9, 74, 76, 97,
    112–13, 118, 123
Minerva Press 25, 69–70, 71, 96, 131, 141,
    148
Mirabeau, Honoré Gabriel Riqueti 101
Mischianza tournament 26
Montesquieu, Charles-Louis de
    Secondat, Baron de La Brède et de
    Montesquieu 8, 48–9, 51, 53
Monroe, James 53
Montjoie, Galart de
    *Histoire de la Conjuration de Louis-
    Phillippe-Josèphe d'Orléans* 98
Montmorin, Armand Marc, comte de
    Montmorin 50
Moore, Sir John 50

Morganwg, Iolo 105, 126
Morse, Jedidiah 101, 104

Nantes, civil war and Jacobin repression in
51, 52, 83–4, 92, 180
Napoleon 43, 103, 109, 145, 153, 182, 195
Napoleonic Wars 56, 141, 153, 174
National Assembly 97
National Convention vii, 47–54, 72, 80, 83
Naubert, Christian
Herman von Unna 95, 98, 101, 135,
138–40
The Secret Tribunal, stage adaptation of
Herman 135, 138–40
Necker, Jacques 99
Newgate Calendar 66–7
Newgate novels 162–70
Nicolai, Christoph 95, 103

Order of Bards 105, 126
Orléans, Louis-Philippe, Duc de 98, 99,
101, 103

Pagès, François Xavier
Secret History of the French Revolution
54–5
Paine, Thomas 53, 105, 137, 140
Parnell, Thomas 12
Parsons, Eliza
The Castle of Wolfenbach 96
Paley, William 50
Percy, Thomas
Reliques of Ancient English Poetry 22
Perrault, Charles 148
Pétion, Jérôme 63
Pindar, Peter (John Wolcot) 55
Piozzi, Hester 109
Pitt, William, the Younger 55, 72, 106, 142
Polidori, John
The Vampyre 153–4, 157–8
Popish Plot 93–4
Prévost, Antoine François 25
Prisons 161–2

Quiberon Bay, battle of 99

Radcliffe, Ann viii–ix, 39, 70–84, 97, 109,
110, 114, 118, 131, 134–40, 147,
155–9, 163–4

The Castles of Athlin and Dunbayne
39
Fontainville Forest, stage adaptation
of *The Romance of the Forest*
134–40
influence on nineteenth-century
literature 155–9, 163–4
The Italian 71, 74–6, 81–2, 135–6
The Mysteries of Udolpho viii, 71, 72,
74, 81–2, 109
The Romance of the Forest 39, 71, 72,
74–6, 81–2, 109, 147, 156
A Sicilian Romance 39
Radical politics in Britain 72, 79, 104–5,
137–41, 145–6, 161, 173
Ratcliffe Highway Murders 61, 169–72
Reeve's Association 142
Reeve, Clara
The Old English Baron ix, 24–6, 30, 34,
39, 70, 155
Reign of Terror, *see* Terror, the
Revolutionary Tribunals 47, 51, 52, 56,
57–8, 72–3, 81, 83, 180
Richardson, Samuel 2–4, 8, 10, 12, 25, 26,
29, 132, 183
Clarissa 4, 8, 10, 29, 82, 132
Pamela 4, 132
Sir Charles Grandison 29
Robert, Étienne-Gaspard 122, 129
Robespierre, Maximilian xi, 43, 46–9,
51–60, 73, 78–83, 89, 106, 107–8,
115, 139, 173–6
blamed for the Terror 54, 173–4
described in Gothic terms 78–82,
107–8, 173–4, 176
paranoia of, and belief in conspiracy
theories 58–60, 89, 106
rhetoric of terror 47–9, 51–4
Robison, John
*Proofs of a Conspiracy Against all the
Religions and Governments of Europe*
98, 100–7, 109, 117, 118–19, 137
Roland, Jean-Marie 48
Rowlandson, Thomas 145
Royal Academy 143–4

Sainte-Germain, Comte de 99, 119
Saint-Just, Louis de 53, 61, 73
Satirical prints 142–5

Schiller, Friedrich 95–8, 111, 119, 137
  Der Geisterseher 95, 98, 119
  Die Raüber 96–8, 111, 137
Scott, Walter 74, 128, 153–8, 173
Scottish Friends of the People 105
Secret Academy, the 99, 137
Sentimental fiction 25–6, 39, 66, 70
September Massacres 38, 41–2, 57, 59,
    63–9, 72, 81, 89, 99, 100, 107, 116,
    123, 143, 175, 177, 180, 182
  described in Gothic terms 41–2, 63–9,
    72, 81, 123, 180
  explained through conspiracy theory
    100, 107
  in British fiction and drama 180
  in British history-writing 175, 177
  in British newspapers 63–9, 72,
    81, 123
Serial murder 192
Seven Years War 2–3, 133
Shakespeare, William 11, 15–17, 20, 27,
    28–9, 71, 76, 112–13, 121, 133
Shelley, Mary 56, 71, 153–4, 164
Shelley, Percy 119, 154, 158
Sheffield Society for Constitutional
    Information 105
Slave trade 3, 44–6, 61
Smith, Adam 18, 193
Smith, Charlotte 26, 39, 70, 121–2
Smollett, Tobias
  Ferdinand, Count Fathom 3–4, 8, 82
Society for Constitutional Information
    104
Sophocles 11, 15–16
Southcott, Joanna 108–9
Southey, Robert 44–6, 79–81, 96–7, 111
  To Horror 44–6, 111
  The Fall of Robespierre 79–81
Speiss, Christian
  Das Petermännchen 110
Spithead and Nore Mutinies 93, 105
St Bartholomew's Day Massacre 67
Steadman, John Gabriel 61
Stoker, Bram viii
  Dracula viii
Sublime of terror viii, 17–19, 40, 81–2,
    121, 143–4, 171–2
Swedenborgianism 98–100
Swift, Jonathan 2, 158, 166–8, 181

Tallien, Jean-Lambert 54
Templars 98, 99
Terror, the vii, ix–xi, 38–9, 42, 47–62, 69,
    72–4, 78–84, 106–7, 109, 115–16,
    139, 174–80, 182, 191, 195–6
  described in Gothic terms 78–82,
    115–16, 174–80
  explained through conspiracy theory
    106–7
  in British fiction and drama 73, 79–81,
    115–16, 174, 178–80
  in British history-writing 174–8
  in British newspapers 53, 62, 69, 72,
    81–2
  mass imprisonment during 57
  mass violence in 51–2, 56–8, 72–3,
    83–4, 195
  spectacular violence in 60–2, 73,
    83–4
  psychological effects of 58, 60–2, 69,
    78–9
Terrorism ix–xiii, 38–9, 47–9, 53–6, 73, 77,
    93, 122–3, 174–6, 189–98
  origins of the word 47, 53–6
  relationship to Gothic fiction and
    conspiracy theory 122–3
  since the French Revolution 189–98
Thackeray, William 142, 163
Thermidor 42, 47, 52, 54–6, 80–1, 83, 98,
    175, 180
Theosophy 185
Thibaudeau, Antoine Claire 58
Thirty Years War 5
Tragedy 10–11, 14–18, 21, 73, 76, 121
Tranent Massacre 93, 105
Treason trials of 1794 69, 139–40
Tschink, Catejan
  Geschichte eines Geistersehers 95–6, 98,
    101
Tuileries, storming of 62–3
Tussaud, Marie 174–5
Two Acts of 1795 69
Tytler, Alexander 96–7

United Irishmen 105, 117, 126

Valmy, battle of 68
Vendée, civil war in the 42, 46, 51, 56, 57,
    73, 85, 93, 144

Visual culture 26, 142–7, 150–1
Voltaire, François-Marie d'Arouet 16, 99, 137

Walpole, Horace
    The Castle of Otranto viii–ix, 1–2, 11,
      19, 22–30, 34, 40, 71, 110, 122–3,
      134, 155, 195
War of the Austrian Succession 2–3, 13
War of the Spanish Succession 2–3
War of Three Kingdoms 5
War on Terror vii, xii–xiii, 189, 193–4
Warton, Thomas 19–21, 43–4, 71, 79, 111
Waterloo, battle of 153
Weishaupt, Adam 95, 108
West, Benjamin 144
Wexford Rebellion of 1798 xii, 50, 93, 99,
    105, 117, 183

Whig party 98, 112
Wild, Jonathan 3, 163–6
Will, Peter 98
Williams, Helen Maria 59, 69, 77–9, 81,
    131, 139, 173
Williams, John 61, 171–2
Witchcraft 5–6, 9, 19, 26–7, 31, 36, 93,
    183
Witchcraft Act 9, 19, 31
Wollstonecraft, Mary 82–3, 141, 192
Wordsworth, William 43–6, 79, 111,
    112–13, 115, 120, 122, 141, 161, 173
    Preface to *Lyrical Ballads* 112–13
    Supernatural poetry 120, 122
    'The Vale of Esthwaite' 43–6, 79, 111
Wright, Joseph, of Derby 143